Flight
OF THE
Hummingbird

Tenochtitlán

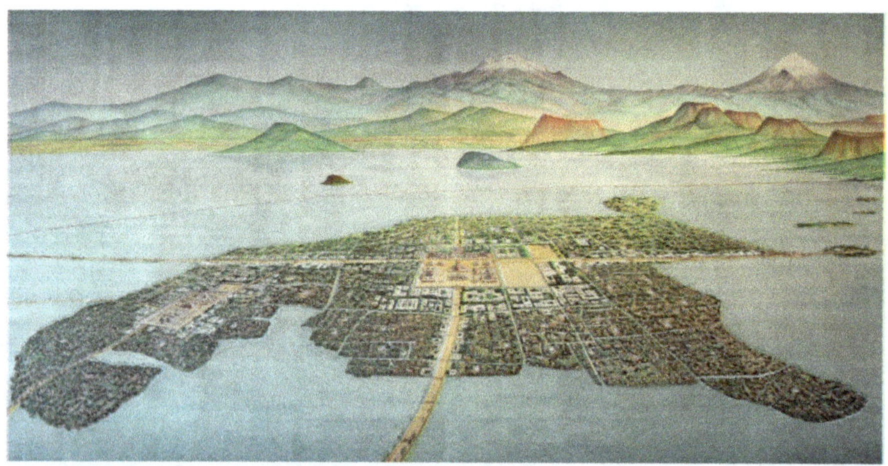

Painting of Tenochtitlán-Tlatelolco on Lake Texcoco, by Luis Covarrubias, National Museum of Anthropology, Mexico City; photo by Sean Sprague/Mexicolore.co.uk

Before the story begins, the world must be seen.
Here lies Tenochtitlán, born of prophecy,
cradled by water, watched by mountains.
This is the mirror that smokes,
where gods whisper and ancestors watch.
From these sacred causeways,
Huitzilin, the hummingbird, will rise.

Flight
OF THE
Hummingbird

*An Aztec Tale of Fire and Rain
and the End of the Fifth Sun*

By Salomón Quintero, Esq. (Ret.)
San Carlos, California

ISBN: 979-8-9937954-4-7

Printed in the United States of America

Cover art by Tim Byrne, Bristol, UK
Design and layout by Nigel French, Lewes, UK
Editor: Kristen Bakis, New York, NY, USA

Special thanks to Mexicolore.co.uk and Wikimedia Foundation.

May, 2026

DEDICATION

To my father – born fatherless, raised penniless in Douglas, Arizona – who flourished in Los Angeles during the Great Depression, who fought the Japanese Imperial Army in the Philippines, a war that never left him.

To my mother – whose father left before she was born, a teacher in Culiacán, Sinaloa, who followed the ideals of the Mexican Revolution, and who created a loving home where our family could thrive.

To my wife, who wrapped my life with loving support for over 50 years, who holds me steady, who keeps my path with high ideals.

To my children and grandchildren, whom I adore.

Dear reader,

Take a deep breath, close your eyes and leave your world behind.

Open these pages and wander into another time, another place, and another realm: the Aztec world. Follow an extraordinary human being, Huitzilin, the hummingbird, to experience a fascinating and vibrant civilization. Imagine their lives and world view, though vastly different from our own.

I pray that you will not speed read this story. Take your time. Read it like you would a poem, for this story is a poem in long form. Listen to the words, the passages, the stories. Savor them.

Sprinkled through the stories, you will find Nahuatl names and words. I will give you their meanings in the sentence or in a footnote. The sounds and names will feel impossible on first encounter. Don't be discouraged. You can look at the written word as you would an object, a piece of jewelry, its length, its letters. Or you may take the time to sound them out. After a while you will notice the same prefixes and suffixes. Nahuatl language uses many compound words, like the German language, which explains the word length. In the appendices I have included a glossary of the Nahuatl words that appear in the text.

Go now.
Kneel before your teachers as before the gods.
Offer copal to the ancestors.
Let the smoke rise to the heavens.
And walk always with your eyes upon the mirror that smokes,
where truth hides and destiny waits.

Table of Contents

Voices

We are the voices of the gods – not distant, not forgotten.

We speak through obsidian and memory,

through the shimmer of reflection and the breath of ancestors.

We speak not to ears, but to spirit;

Not in words, but in echoes;

Not in light, but in shadow.

If you would know the truth of this world,

listen to the blood in the stone,

the silence between names,

the pulse beneath the dust.

I AM HUITZILIN, born in the shadow of the temple, where silence is speech and wind carries memory. My story is not carved in stone nor sung in schools – it lives in the hands of my mother, in the sweat of my father, in the choices I made when no one was watching. If you will walk with me, I will show you what it means to live between myth and blood, between duty and desire. For this is not a tale of gods, but of a man who listened.

But before I could listen, my father listened, and his father before him. The stories of our people passed like breath, like fire – from hand to hand, heart to heart. I was not yet born when grandfather spoke, but his words live in me as surely as my name. And so I begin, as my father began, with the story of those who came before. Here's how my father remembers his.

I

Sacred Origins and the Family

a. Mexitli's Migration from Aztlan, 1150 AD

The evening is still and quiet in Tenochtitlán.[1] Lush *chinampas*[2] surround the island the Mexica call home.[3]

Chinamcatl,[4] my father's father, finishes his day's work as the sun sets behind the western hills. He returns to his one-room home where he hangs his tools and pauses at the scent of warm maize lingering from the *comalli*.[5] His body is tired from tending soil, reeds, and canals. He steps outside and kneels at the water's edge. He fills a small clay basin and lets the coolness run over his face, neck and arms. He makes a light lather with amole root to scrub away the grit of earth and the fine dust of maize leaves, and dries himself with a clean cotton cloth.

Inside, he settles onto his petate, stretching his legs, lying back for a moment as his breath loosens. Nonantzin brings warm corn drink, *atole*, and a plate of beans and squash, and he eats in quiet gratitude. When he is ready, she brings his finest cape and ties it carefully over

---

1 "Tenochtitlán" was the island in Lake Texcoco where the Mexica established themselves in 1325, named after Tenoch, the Mexica founder of Tenochtitlán. The people residing there referred to themselves as "Tenochca." Mexico City now sits where Tenochtitlán once stood.

2 Floating gardens where crops are grown.

3 "Mexica" (meh-SHEE-kah) refers to the ethnic group that that is better known today as the Aztecs, derived from the name of their first leader, Mexitli (meh-SHEET-ly).

4 From Chinampa + catl = a person of or from. A person of the chinampa, a farmer, a steward of sacred land, a participant in the life-force of the city.

5 Griddle

Chicomoztoc, the 'Place of the Seven Caves,' a rocky womb from which the people first appear. The bent hill above marks Colhuacan, emblem of ancestral legitimacy. Beside it, a coyote-skinned fire-maker kindles the first ritual flame, signaling the passage from the primordial womb into the world of human society. A spiny cactus and a smooth cactus frame the scene, contrasting the wild northern homeland with the cultivated world the migrants will enter. Historia Tolteca Chichimeca (ca. 1547–1560), Bibliothèque nationale de France. Public domain. Reproduction from UncoveredHistory.com.

his shoulder. She smooths the knots from his hair with her fingers, and places his carved staff in his hand, and together they walk to the public square at the heart of their *calpulli*.[6] Children follow and watch as he builds a large fire. Soon neighbors gather to enjoy the fire's warmth. On this cool, moonless night, the only light comes from the fire's flickering flames. Shadows dance on the faces of the gathered Mexica, young and old, as they settle onto their woven mats, eager to hear stories of their gods and ancestors.

The air cools as the sun sets and the moon and the stars take their place. Yet what draws everyone to the plaza is not only warmth, but the promise of words that carry the weight of destiny. When Chinamcatl speaks, it is as though the voices of ancestors stir within him, whispering of journeys out of shadowed places; of a people searching for their true home, and of a destiny that may not yet be secure. Tonight, the square is still – waiting, as if the fate of our world might be hidden in the story about to be told.

Chinamcatl rises to address the gathering and a hush of anticipation falls over the gathered. Standing beside the flames, his white hair and staff command attention. The air is thick with copal incense and all eyes turn toward him, breath held, intent. His voice is soft, like wind through feathers, and it enraptures his guests.

> Gather close, children of the Mexica, and listen well for tonight we remember who we are. We remember where we began – not in cities, not in temples, but in the cave of seven mouths, Chicomoztoc, where our ancestors first emerged from the womb of the earth. For this is the tale of Mexitli – war priest, wanderer, flame-bearer – whose voice echoed like thunder and whose heart

---

6 Neighborhood, a political subdivision. (cal = house, pulli = group)

beat with the fire of Huitzilopochtli, god of the sun, fire and war, patron god of our people.

Tonight, we speak their names so they are not forgotten. We summon their footsteps so they may walk with us again. For in the telling, they live.

Around him, children lean forward, while elders nod approval. He gestures into the darkness beyond the fire, as if summoning visions from the world before this one and continues.

In a time before time, when the sun had not yet claimed the sky, our ancestors dwelt in the sacred birthplace called Chicomoztoc. There, in the highlands beyond Aztlán,[7] seven caves were hidden. Each cave, a womb of stone from which our ancestors emerged at the sun's first rising. Each cave a cradle for a different Nahuatl speaking people: Acolhua, Tepaneca, Otomi, Chalca, Xochimilca, Tlahuica, and the last—our own: the Mexica.

When our ancestors left the caves, they descended into Aztlán, a lush world of springs and waters where the white heron danced, where corn and all other plants grew in abundance. We lived freely with the Chicomoztoca, the tribes already there. It was a happy time.

Chinamcatl pauses, closing his eyes as if remembering, when a child's voice breaks the stillness, "Why did we leave the happy place?" Continuing the story, Chinamcatl answers,

One day the world changed. Drought and misfortune came to Aztlán. The earth became barren and the lakes disappeared, leaving beds of cracked mud thirsting for rain. The reeds grew weak and the wind carried dust. Our corn would not grow. There was not enough food for everyone.

Soon Aztlán became a place of tyranny as the Chicomoztoca became oppressive rulers, taking our lands and harvests, attacking our people from all sides. Families turned against each other, stealing food. There was disorder and our people grew restless,

---

8 "Aztlán," which means, place of white herons, was the original homeland from which the Mexica people migrated and was believed to be located in the American southwest.

they scattered, running in every direction, finding food where they could. We were strewn like reeds on the wind, without root, without name, without fire. We were not yet the Mexica, not yet the chosen.

Our people might be vanquished and disappear, but when all seemed lost, a great leader arose. His name was Mexitli, a man not born to thrones or turquoise diadems, but to vision. His eyes looked beyond the hills, beyond hunger and hardship. He wore no crown, but the gods crowned him with sacred knowing. He could hear the voice of our god, Huitzilopochtli. Some say Mexitli was more than a man – that he was the breath of Huitzilopochtli.

The old ones would tell that he was the living spirit of Huitzilopochtli, the god of war, walking among us in mortal form.

One night, as the fire dimmed and stars filled the sky, a vision came – bright as the midday sun. Huitzilopochtli spoke to Mexitli,

"Mexitli, you must abandon Aztlán and lead your people to a new homeland, there, greatness awaits. You will know the place," Huitzilopochtli declared, "When you see the eagle upon the cactus, devouring the serpent, there you shall build. There you shall be Mexica."

Driven by this divine omen, and after years of aimless wandering, Mexitli gathered our scattered bands and led our people through hardship and exile. He taught us the art of war and the way of the sacred, to fight not only with obsidian and fire, but with faith. He led us with courage through deserts and mountains, and the lands of hostile peoples; through valleys where no welcome waited, and through cities that mocked our poverty. Everywhere our people went, we had to fight to survive. Wherever we wandered, hardship followed us, yet still we endured.

And when the gods sent us the sign – the eagle rising from the cactus, serpent in its grasp – we understood:

that we must root ourselves like the nopal that grows from stone, enduring where others wither;

that we must carry the wisdom of the earth, as the serpent carries it in silence;

and that we must see far and rise with courage, as the eagle rises with the fire of the sun in its wings.

Under his guidance, we became not just a tribe, but a people – the Mexica, named in his honor, so that his memory would never fade from our hearts.

All agreed that when the sign came, when the eagle tore the serpent and sat upon the cactus, it was Mexitli's voice that rang in our ears, saying, "Now. Build."

And so we did. And so we became the Mexica.

Remember him, children – not for his staff, not for his robe, but for his fire. For in the cry of the warrior, in the beat of the drum, in the heart of the Mexica, Mexitli lives!

b. 1427 - Itzcoatl, Nezahualcoytl and the Triple Alliance

The stories of my father's life, from the time he first opened his eyes to the world, are precious to me. I know them as my mother whispered them to me, from the songs my uncle sang, in the silences my grandmother kept. His story was not written – it was lived, and I carry it now, as he carried the flame.

My father was born in the year 13 Acatl[8] (1427),[9] a momentous year of change, when the Valley of Mexico was shifting beneath the feet of empires. The stories of my father's life, from the time he first opened his eyes to the world, are precious to me. I know them as my mother whispered them to me, from the songs my uncle sang, in the silences my grandmother kept. His story was not written – it was lived, and I carry it now, as he carried the flame.

The old ones say that to understand a man, you must understand the winds that shaped his cradle. And so I speak now of the rulers and rebels, the tyrants and poets, whose shadows fell across the Valley of Mexico – for their stories live in the breath of my father, and later, in the fire of my own awakening.

---

8 13 Acatl (Reed)" was the Aztec name for the year 1427. In the Aztec Xiuhpohualli, the 365-day solar calendar, each year was identified by pairing a number (1–13) with one of four repeating symbols – Reed, Flint, House, or Rabbit.

9 All dates will be reflected using our current Gregorian calendar system, even though it was not introduced until after the events described here. Expressing dates in the Aztec calendrical system, even if possible, would not serve the reader.

In the time before my father's birth, The Valley of Mexico was under the dominion of the powerful city-state (altepetl) of Azcapotzalco and its ruler, Tezozomoc, who was feared and revered. His reign spanned nearly sixty years, and his power stretched across the Valley of Mexico. Some called him a tyrant, others, a genius of empire. He lived one hundred years, and in that time, he shaped the world my father was born into – a world of tribute, ambition, and shifting alliances.

His hand weighed heavy – yet even the mightiest hand must loosen. When Tezozomoc died, the Valley held its breath. One of his sons, Maxtla, seized the throne not with the flowers of ceremony, but with the knives of treachery. He turned against allies, silenced dissent, and in that year, he sent assassins to claim the life of Chimalpopoca, the beloved tlatoani of our island city of Tenochtitlán.[10]

Our new leader, Itzcoatl, the Obsidian Serpent, was the son of Acamapichtli, Tenochtitlán's first tlatoani. But, his mother was a slave girl from Tlacopan, taken in tribute. Yet in her veins—so the whispers said – flowed the sacred blood of Colhuacan, the ancestral wellspring of Toltec nobility and civilization. Itzcoatl, master of the battlefield and the council alike, wielded cunning and courage with such brilliance that he reshaped the destiny of the Mexica people.

To the east lay the magnificent city-state of Texcoco. There fell Ixtlilxóchitl, its noble lord, struck down by the knives of Azcapotzalco, while his son Nezahualcóyotl, yet a boy, watched in silence from the sheltering branches of a distant tree.

Hunted for his father's blood, the child became a wanderer. For ten years he walked the earth without a throne, gathering wisdom as others gather maize. They say he slept by moonlit streams among the humble reeds that bend but do not break, beneath heavens where the stars wrote their counsel. He spoke little but listened deeply, and from silence he forged the heart of a king.

---

10 Tlatoani means "Speaker." The Tlatoani speaks for the people of his city-state and is their royal ruler. There is only one "Huey Tlatoani," Great Speaker who rules over all city-states.

Thus was tempered Nezahualcóyotl – poet, warrior, lord to come. He rose not by birthright alone, but by the fire in his chest, as obsidian is born of earth's furnace, as jade is polished by the patience of time and sweet water. His influence was powerful. The breath of his poetry and wisdom would one day stir the fire in me.

When Maxtla, the Tepanec ruler, overreached, Nezahualcóyotl returned at the head of allies he had gathered, warriors bound not by tribute but by the memory of wrongs and the hope of renewal. He commanded one wing of the army while Itzcoatl, the Mexica, led another. A third army from Tlacopan, an altepetl just across the water from Tenochtitlan, joined and from their unity was born the Triple Alliance – not of ambition alone, but of memory and the vision of our ancestors. Together, they shattered Maxtla's grip and the Tepanec yoke was broken.

Their story is not separate from ours. It lives in the breath of my father, and later, in the fire of my own awakening. My father was born into a world shaped by shadows – not only of mountains and temples, but of rulers whose words could bless or destroy.

He was born at that very moment of history, 1427, when Itzcoatl became the first Huey Tlatoani – the Great Speaker, voice of the gods and supreme ruler of the Valley. From that moment the Mexica stood above all other city-states, their word shaping the destiny of nations.

c. My Father, Cuauhtli

Cuauhtli was my father's name. It means "eagle," the mightiest bird in the sky. When it rises, we feel the warmth of the sun and our bond with the celestial realm. He passed down stories of the lessons his father taught him when he was a child. His stories blend in my mind as though I was there. I do not know if I remember or imagine, only that the stories live inside me. I recall the stories this way:

On bright days along the shores of Lake Texcoco, where our island city meets shimmering waters, farmers bend over their chinampas.[11] Among these humble workers my father was born, descended

11 Floating gardens built on the lake's surface using layers of mud and compost.

from generations who turned the soil, planted maize, and raised life from the mud of the lake. His father, Chinamcatl, told him about the work we do:

> Cuauhtli, it is our duty, as it was for our forefathers, to build and tend the chinampas. Under the sun we stake the plots with willow poles, we weave reeds and branches to hold them. We fill them with the gifts of the lake – mud, reed, and decay – the remnants of what has died to raise the plot above the level of the waters. The porous soil absorbs living waters from the canals surrounding the chinampas. And from what is dead, life returns: maize, beans, squash, tomato, and chili peppers. Remember, my son: the chinampa is not just earth raised from water, it is the womb where what was dead comes to life again.

NONANTZIN SPEAKS

My grandmother, Nonantzin,[12] was the first voice of wisdom in our family. It was she who taught my father the secrets of life. I know her teachings because my father carried them in him, and he carried them into me. And later, when I was a boy, I too heard her voice with my own ears – sweeping the courtyard, she spoke to me as though the gods themselves had paused to listen. Here is her voice speaking to father:

---

12 Nonantzin means revered mother, Here, Huitzilin uses it affectionately for his grandmother.

Farming on the chinampas, Tenochtitlán. Photo by Ian Mursell/Mexicolore of an oil painting by José Muro Pico, National Museum of Anthropology MXDF.

Cuauhtli, we are *tlacah*, humans.[13] We walk upon *tlalticpak*,[14] the earth beneath our feet, yet we also breathe within *Teotl*[15] – the unseen realm where the gods dwell, where dreams and visions rise, where the *nagual* moves in shadow.[16] Teotl is the sacred motion of all things, it is the current that flows through stone and flower, through sun and heart.

– The flower is not a shadow of color. It is teotl opening its face to the sun.
– The bird is not only feathers and bone. It is teotl in motion, rising, carrying our breath toward the sky.
– The maize is not dust in the hand. It is teotl becoming flesh to feed the people.

---

13 The Nahuatl word for human.

14 The Nahuatl word for "upon the earth" and includes the entire physical realm.

15 The Nahuatl word for the celestial realm and includes the heavens, the underworld, dreams, spirits and the metaphysical essence of all things.

16 "Nagual," is the animal spirit that guides each person.

– The stone is never empty. It is teotl resting, waiting for us to see the mountain within.

Nonantzin continued,

We see the earthly realm with our eyes, but the celestial realm cannot be seen. Only your soul can walk there, for it is the dwelling of the gods. And from that realm they give us three fires – the vital energies that make us human.

First is *tonalli*, the fire of mind. It is born of the sun and rests in your crown, warming your thoughts and your courage. It gives you destiny, the strength to rise each morning, the power to act in the world. Guard it well, for if your tonalli falters, so too does your path.

Second is *teyolia*, the spirit of the heart. It is the flame that burns in your chest, the seat of memory and will. It binds you to your ancestors, for their songs and sorrows live within your heart. And know this, Cuauhtli: when your body dies, it is *teyolia* that journeys on. It is the fire the gods do not extinguish. It is your essence that returns to *teotl*.

Third is *ihiyotl*, the rhythm of your breath. It stirs within the ribs, like wind over the lake. It carries your laughter, your anger, your passion; it rises with the copal smoke and sighs with the night air. Without ihiyotl, the body is still; with it, you are alive in joy and desire.

These three – tonalli, teyolia, ihiyotl – are threads woven from teotl itself. Together they are your soul, your fire, your destiny. Guard them, my son, for they are the gifts by which the gods give you life.

Nonantzin shifted in her seat, breathing deeply after revealing the sacred truths of life. She took a drink of cool water and continued,

We are farmers, my son. But to live well, to fulfill the duties we owe our gods and our people, you must feel the spirit that dwells in all things:

in the land and the water,
in the mountains and the rivers,
in the sun and the rain.

Only then will you understand the chinampas, for they are not only soil and reed, but living wombs that give us maize, beans, and squash, the strength of our people.

Never forget, we are *macehualli*, commoners. Yet we are the wings and the tail; without us, the bird cannot fly. With our labor the city rises, with our hands the gods are fed. We have earned our place on this land, bound to it as surely as roots to the earth.

And when her teachings were done, Nonantzin closed her eyes and began to sing. It was not only her voice we heard, but the voice of the ancestors themselves, carried on her breath, remarking on the beauty we seek. My father often whispered this song that his mother sang to him, but I too remember it, for once as a child, I heard her sing those same words as she swept the courtyard:

Deep within the mountain valley,
in the land of abundance, in the realm of heavenly flowers,
The spirit of our ancestors comes to me.
There it is, where the sun's rays sparkle in the shimmering dew.
There, in that place, we behold melliferous scattered flowers.
See how these robust fragrant flowers glitter and shine.
In the ethereal mist a brilliant rainbow spreads across the sky.[17]

FATHER'S FATE REVEALED

In the quiet hours of my childhood, my father told stories of his struggles and successes. Nonantzin sometimes told me these stories while we sat in the courtyard, and my mother, too reminded me of those times when the house was still. Now, I know these stories by my heart. Here's how the story went:

From an early age my father was captivated by the beauty of the natural world. Wherever he walked, he sought the brightest flower, the tallest tree or clearest mountain stream to please his heart. One day, on a family journey to the sacred mountain, Huizachtecatl,[18] he

---

17 This stanza is an excerpt from the poem, *The Origin of Songs*, by the philosopher king Nezahualcoyotl of Texcoco, interpreted by the author. (https://dsol.com/the-origin-of-songs/)

18 Sacred Mountain, known today as Cerro de la Estrella.

found glistening black stones and two curious bits, one light green as sky, the other glowing brown. He tucked them in his *maxtlatl*,[19] treasures hidden close to his skin.

Cacaxtli, a wooden frame tied with a strap over the forehead for carrying loads. "Pochtecas con su carga," Florentine Codex, Book 9, Med. Palat. 219, f. 326v

On market days, he carried large bushels of corn, beans and squash to the Tlatelolco marketplace,[20] tied to a *cacaxtli* on his back.[21]

But on one of these days, when he set his burden down, his eyes wandered, hungry for wonders. At ten years of age, he slipped away from duty and wandered among the endless stalls of food and finery, colors and voices pressing close. There, at a jeweler's stall, my father noticed stones like those he'd gathered on the mountainside and approached the stall to watch the old man at work. He stopped as though rooted to the earth. His gaze fixed on an old man whose hands moved like water, swift and sure, shaping stone and metal into things of beauty. My father could not breathe; he only watched.

---

19 Loincloth

20 The Tlatelolco marketplace located on the island of Tenochtitlán, was the greatest market in the world.

21 A wooden frame for carrying bundles, secured by a single strap over the forehead.

CHALCHIHUITL, THE OLD JEWELER

The next day he returned, carrying the stones from Huizachtecatl. The old jeweler did not look up. "You have returned," he said. "I am Chalchihuitl, precious green stone. What is your name?"

"I am Cuauhtli," my father answered. "Look — I found these on the mountain."

Chalchihuitl turned each stone in his hands. "The black ones are obsidian, the god's mirrors — sharp for tools, bright for jewels, deadly for blades. This green one is turquoise, the sky made stone, beloved in temples and crowns. And this red-brown piece, copper, the blood of the earth, strong when joined with fire. You have a good eye, boy." At those words, my father's heart fluttered like wings.

He returned again and again and spent hours quietly watching. Chalchihuitl enjoyed my father's company and soon, father started helping the elderly jeweler, handing him tools and holding gemstones as the jeweler worked on them.

One day, the old jeweler said, "Stay with me. Learn." And so, father left the furrows of the chinampas for the fire of stone and metal. It was a fateful choice that would shape his destiny forever.

ᘓᘓᘓᘓᘓᘓᘐ

My father was eager, a quick learner with nimble hands. Under Chalchihuitl's guidance, he learned to hold volcanic glass steady and grind obsidian until it became edges sharp enough for warriors' blades and for the clean shave of noblemen. He learned to strip the maguey's spiny leaves, soaking and pounding them until their fibers loosened like threads of hair. With resin he bound sand to cord, to make the jeweler's saw, *mecatl* and *xalli,*[22] that could cut and shape even the hardest stone for beads, pendants and sacred tools. With sharp awls he cut delicate patterns; with the hand drill he opened spaces for cords to pass through. Each task taught him not just skill, but patience, rhythm, the feel of stone yielding beneath his will.

---

22 "cord and sand" Mecate in Spanish means cord or string.

The years turned, and my father's world widened. He learned the secrets of metal: gold softened by fire, copper lending it strength; silver, pliant and radiant as moonlight. He mastered the lost-wax casting that made molten metal take the shape of dreams. His hands grew quick, his eye precise, but his heart reached further. Soon he no longer copied Chalchihuitl's designs – he imagined his own, weaving old motifs with new forms, as though the fire itself whispered to him.

One day, from the turquoise he had carried since childhood, he crafted a necklace. Around the sky-stone he wound gold, etched with patterns of maize and eagle feathers, symbols of life and flight. When it was finished, it shone like dawn breaking over water. Chalchihuitl gazed long upon it, then said, "This belongs not to the workshop, but to the world. Show it at the marketplace, Cuauhtli. Let others see what your hands have become."

AT THE MARKET PLACE

Nervous yet proud, my father built his stall in the great Tlatelolco marketplace, the empire's heart of trade, where voices rose like birdsong and colors spilled in every direction. He set out his finest creations, arranging each piece with care. When all was ready, he stepped back – and for a moment, he saw beauty shining in the work of his own hands.

Before the first buyer arrived, he raised an altar to Xochiquetzal, Precious Feather Flower, goddess of adornment and love, patroness of those who shape gold and jade. He laid flowers upon it, feathers bright as dawn, and lit the copal. He washed his hands and face, knelt, and lifted his palms to the sky. In a quiet voice he prayed, thanking the goddess for weaving *flower and song*, gifts of the divine, into his work, asking her to let beauty live in his hands.

Then he touched his forehead, honoring the tonalli, radiant force of destiny. He touched his chest, where teyolia, the spirit-heart, bound him to memory and thought. He breathed deeply, calling upon ihiyotl, the vital wind that stirs laughter, passion, and desire. He felt all three energies awaken within him – one guiding, one remembering, one connecting – until it seemed even the market itself held its breath. Bowing, he touched earth to his lips in humility, sealing the prayer.

Turquoise and jade pendants, Aztec jewelry.

Thus did my father begin his path, bringing each work into the world as offering. Soon word spread of the young artisan whose jewels shone with both skill and spirit. One market day at mid-sun, he was summoned to the palace courtyard. There, to the sound of drums and flutes, nobles and warrior-priests formed a circle around a broad reed mat. Upon it my father unveiled his latest creation: a breastplate of *teocuitlatl*, gold, as bright as sun,[23] set with jade and obsidian discs that gleamed like a quetzal's throat, its surface alive with glyphs of beauty and power. The piece seemed to breathe.

A hush fell. A *tlacuilo* stepped forward,[24] took the breastplate in his hand, studied it carefully, traced the symbols with his finger and recited their meaning, "the quetzal, sign of beauty bestowed by the gods; the jade, heart of life and nobility; the obsidian, mirror of truth and destiny." When the reading was finished, the governor of Tlatelolco himself approached, lifted a hand, and declared:

---

23 Teocuitlatl, the Nahuatl word for gold, literally meant "divine secretion, something that flows from the gods.".

24 A scribe

"This breastplate shines not only with gold, but with the cosmos itself. He who strings the stars and orders the heartbeat of light shall be named *Cozcatlani* – Master Jeweler, Bearer of Beauty."[25]

My father bowed low. Yet as the praise filled his ears, his eyes turned skyward, searching. The world called his name, but within, he was listening elsewhere, wondering of things to come.

TLAMACAZQUI TLACAELEL

Another year passed, and one day a nobleman paused before my father's stall. His bearing was commanding, his eyes sharp with the weight of power. It was Tlamacazqui Tlacaelel,[26] [27] – priest, counselor, and head of the Tenochtitlán Calmecac School, where the empire's noblest sons were trained in wisdom and war. He was known not only for his learning, but for the fire in his voice, the force that could bend destinies.

On the stall lay the turquoise necklace, its stone gleaming like a fragment of sky bound in gold. Tlacaelel's gaze fell upon it. He lifted the piece, turning it slowly in the light. My father, seizing the moment, bowed and spoke with reverence. He told of the mountain where he had found the stone, of the symbols woven into its design, of the way metal and spirit joined in harmony. As he spoke, Tlacaelel listened, and in his eyes my father saw both scrutiny and approval.

At last the priest said, 'Your hands shape beauty, but more than that, your heart gives it meaning.' He purchased the necklace and commissioned a new set of jewels for a royal ceremony. Yet he set one condition: 'You will come to my lessons at the Calmecac. For Chalchihuitl has taught you to carve what can be seen – flowers, birds, jaguars, eagles. But true artistry is not in what the eye beholds. Skill

---

25 A poetic honorific form referring to a person whose life is bound to precious jewels, metaphorically referring to a person with the moral virtue of a jewel.

26 Tlamcazqui means priest, a title for the most educated members of the nobility who perform religious rites and ceremonies or who have charge of important institutions.

27 His name, Tlacaelel means a vigorous man of strong emotions. He bears the same name but is not the same person as Tlacaelel I, chief advisor to four of Tenochtitlán's Huey Tlatoanis.

is only the skin of art. The heart of art is philosophy. You must learn to shape what is unseen.'

So began my father's second apprenticeship – not only to the craft of the hands, but to the wisdom of the mind and spirit. Under Tlacaelel's shadow, he would come to see that every jewel was a prayer, every design a reflection of the cosmos.

ᴣᴣᴣᴣᴣ

This encounter fixed my father's fate – and the fate of our family. Tlamacazqui Tlacaelel became his mentor, tutor, and sponsor for life.

In the Calmecac courtyard, Tlacaelel taught *in xochitl in cuicatl* – the "Flower and the Song," poetic, ephemeral beauty. Truth, he said, is too delicate to be spoken plainly, too sacred to be left naked. It must be wrapped in beauty – as a thorn hides within a flower, as silence hides within a song.

> *A flower blooms and withers.*
> *A song rises and fades.*
> *But what they carry remains.*

At other times, Tlacaelel spoke in plazas, during festivals and sacred observances. These were not sermons, but public philosophy.

He told of Quetzalcoatl's humility, teaching that wisdom walks with restraint. He sang of Xochipilli, lord of beauty and song, to remind the people that joy itself is sacred – joy must walk hand in hand with duty.

He reminded us of the poor god, Nanahuatzin – hunched, disfigured with sores, dressed in rags. No noble feathers, no golden speech. Yet when the call came for a god to sacrifice, it was he who stepped forward, while the wealthy, proud god, adorned with jewels, hesitated. Tlacaelel taught that true honor is not in outward appearance, but in the fire within.

He retold the Cipactli myth. Tezcatlipoca and Quetzalcoatl faced the sea monster – mouths at every joint, hunger without end. They fought. They sacrificed. They dismembered Cipactli, and from its body, they formed the earth. In this, he showed: to create order, the gods first had to destroy chaos.

For a full season, Tlacaelel sent my father into the forest near Chapultepec, commanding him only to watch. To observe the curl of vines, the dissolving of clouds, the way the wind carries silence. When he returned, he said: "I saw a fallen bird, and I understood – all that flies must fall. Yet even its descent bears truth and beauty."

From Tlacaelel he learned: "You are not the source. You are the mirror. And a mirror must be clean." So my father began to fast before he worked. At first, hunger gnawed at his belly like a running bear. But once his body grew quiet, his thoughts stopped chattering. In the silence, he saw: his jewelry must not just please the eye, it must carry truth. It must be beauty that invites reflection on life and death, on the fleeting and the eternal.

THE SACRED ARTIST

From that moment, my father's jewelry began to whisper of the fleeting, of longing, of transformation. He learned to inlay not only color, but absence. In time, he discovered that the sacred artist lives between worlds – order and chaos, creation and destruction, light and shadow. He no longer carved hummingbirds; he carved flight.

He would light the copal and sit cross-legged before the empty brazier, eyes closed, listening – not with his ears but with his bones. Slowly, images would rise: not drawings, but sensations. The cool drip of water on obsidian. The flare of a hummingbird's chest in the sun. The silence of a cave where breath echoes. From these felt images, the design would emerge. In that blurring of vision and hand, he felt the gods moving through him. The piece was not made; it was received.

Gold jewelry: Eagle and serpent labrets, one with articulating tongue, and pendant.

One day he presented a necklace shaped like the Milky Way, stars of pyrite strung across its length. Tlacaelel asked, 'What does it sing?' My father answered:

> It sings of the road we walk when we die.
> It sings of what guides us when our eyes are closed.
> It sings of gods watching through holes in the sky.

> The priest nodded. 'Then it is worthy.'

〰〰〰〰〰

Seasons passed, enough for flowers to bloom and wither. Then, one evening at the close of a busy day, a messenger appeared at my father's shop, summoning him to the Calmecac courtyard. When he arrived, there was no music, no fanfare. Only Tlacaelel, seated beneath the shadow of a ceiba tree, sipping cacao from a clay cup.

My father had just completed a necklace not meant for men, but for gods: a humble flint carved into the outline of a falling star, strung not with gold and jewels, but with shell and bone. It was not beautiful in the marketplace sense. It had come to him in fasting, in a dream of war and birth.

Tlacaelel lifted the necklace and held it long in silence. At last he spoke:

> You no longer create for praise, Cuauhtli. You create to speak what cannot be spoken. Your hands do not decorate; they interpret. You are no longer a maker of objects. You are a re-weaver

of meaning. What you shape binds sky to earth, gods to men, the fleeting to the eternal.

He set the necklace down and said:

From this day you are not merely Cozcatlani, a master jeweler, a craftsman, you are *Toltecatl* – a philosopher-artisan.[28] Through wisdom and discipline, your art reveals hidden truth, reflects harmony, and carries the balance of the cosmos. May your path be straight, and your soul curved like the reed – strong because it yields.

No one applauded. No scribe recorded the name. Only a breeze passed through the courtyard, lifting flower petals into the air. Thus, the gods made their presence known – not with thunder or voice, but with the rising of fragile beauty, dancing for a heartbeat, then gone. My father bowed his head, not in pride but in gratitude. He knew this was not a title. It was a duty.

With Tlacaelel's patronage, doors opened. My father's reputation spread – not only as a master of craft, but as one whose creations pleased the gods themselves. Huey Tlatoani Motecuhzoma Ilhuicamina and every emperor after him, wore his jewels with pride.[29] His journey – from a child of chinampa farmers near the bottom of Mexica society to the premier jeweler of Tenochtitlán – became a story told across the empire.[30]

᭞᭞᭞᭞᭞

In our home, my father was more than a master of gold and stone. He was the steady hand upon our shoulders, the flame that lit our

---

28 Toltecatl originally meant "inhabitant of Tollan", but over time it came to signify the Toltec tradition, the highest form of civilization, which emphasized mastery in arts, philosophy, and sacred knowledge.

29 Motecuhzoma Ilhuicamina, aka Moctezuma I, reigned from 1440-1469. Motecuhzoma means "He who frowns like a lord." Ilhuicamina means "Archer of the Sky." His great grandson, Moctezuma II, was the Aztec ruler overthrown by Cortés.

30 The lowest levels in Aztec society were *mayeque*, tenant farmers and *tlacotin*, slaves.

paths. We revered him not for his titles, but for the care with which he lived – precise in his craft, unwavering in his honor. His gaze was both a gift and a measure, and we, his children strove always to be worthy of it. His legacy was not only in jewels worn by emperors, but in the patience and dignity he set in our bones. We grew in his shadow, and we were proud to do so.

d. Chicomecoatl, the Matriarch

My mother cared for me when I was sick. She kept me warm. I always wanted to be by her side. But she was strict. She was the master of the house and everyone knew it.

My mother's name was Chicomecoatl, Seven Serpents. Seven represents the center of balance. Chicomecoatl is the goddess of maize, matron of abundance, who moves with the seasons, who knows when to sow and when to reap, when to speak and when to yield.

Mother was the heart of our home, the keeper of rhythm and fire. She did not manage; she orchestrated. The daily flow of our household moved by her will, like water flows down a stream. What she touched held order, and what she spoke carried weight.

Children, elders, and all who dwelt beneath our roof looked to her. She did not command – she harmonized. Attendants served her with quiet devotion, preparing offerings, tending to the young and old, and weaving the day's tasks into sacred order. Servants came and went with the sun, cooking, cleaning, and carrying the weight of daily life. Even slaves,[31] some taken in war, others bound by debt, worked hard grinding maize, fetching water and tending the garden to earn their freedom. They labored with dignity under her gaze, not out of fear, but out of reverence, because they recognized in her the rhythm of rightness – the quiet force that held the world in balance.

Mother's voice carried in matters of marriage, trade and ceremony. She chose when we would offer flowers to the gods, when we would burn copal, when we would speak to our ancestors. In the gatherings

---

31 Slaves were called "tlacohtin." Slavery was not hereditary; their children were not slaves and were free to marry. They could earn their way out of slavery.

of our calpulli, she was not merely present – she was a thread in the weaving of alliances, a whisper in the wind that shaped decisions. I watched elders lean toward her silence and I learned that influence doesn't always speak loudly.

Above all, she was my guide. She taught not with scolding, but with example. From her I learned how to walk with dignity, how to speak with care, how to offer with both hands. She shaped our lives as she shaped cloth – with patience, precision, and purpose.

My sisters learned the art of weaving at her side. I understood what she expected of me and I carried the weight of her expectations like a cloak upon my shoulders. Even father, master of gold and stone, deferred to her wishes when he set foot in our home and he bowed to her wisdom in matters of custom and ceremony.

Mother wove with a backstrap loom, her body anchored to the earth, her hands dancing with cotton and maguey fiber. From plants, insects and minerals she summoned color – reds from cochineal, blues from indigo, yellows from marigold. Each thread was a prayer, each pattern a memory.

"Virtuous Daughter," Florentine Codex, Book 10, Med. Palat. 220, f. 47r. All images from the Florentine Codex are reproduced with permission from the Biblioteca Medicea Laurenziana, Florence.

I still remember a cloak she made for me when I turned six – deep blue, with a border of maize blossoms stitched in gold thread. I didn't understand the pattern then, only that it shimmered when I ran. She said it was for protection, but I wore it because I loved it.

For father, she shaped *maxtlatlin,* loincloths, and *tilmatlime,* cloaks tied over one shoulder, adorned with the marks of lineage and spirit. For my sisters she crafted *Cueitlmeh,* skirts and *Huipilmeh,* blouses that flowed like water, stitched with symbols of fertility and fire. Her sashes, *Aczotlmeh,* bound the garments with grace, and in their folds lived the stories of our people.

Beside clothing for our family, she sold her garments in the marketplace. Her finest work bore flowers, serpents, and celestial designs. Each garment was more than clothing – it was an emblem of the wearer's place in the world. In her weaving, as in her rule, she clothed not only our bodies, but our honor. She carried forward the wisdom of her mother, and passed it to her daughters in turn.

e. Tezcacoatl, Eldest Brother

My brother, Tezcacoatl, whose name means the mirror serpent of reflection and insight, was the first born of our family. I always remember the first day brother came home from school. I was glad to see him and I ran to him. He looked tall to me; his hair shining in the afternoon sun. He smiled when he saw me and ran to meet me too. He showed me his satchel. He had a new reed flute that he was learning to use and he played it while we walked together. I hoped to play the flute and go to school like him someday too.

ᘰᘰᘰᘰᘰ

In the evenings, father always built a fire in the courtyard and friends and neighbors often came by to say hello, tell stories and laugh. Once, my uncle and some of father's jeweler friends were talking beside the fire and Tezcacoatl and I and mother were in the courtyard too. Brother was ten years old and I was eight.

One jeweler friend told of seeing Tezcacoatl at the market talking with a merchant and making him laugh; soon a crowd gathered around the boy and they were laughing too. The merchant gave him a feather and another gave him maize – two fresh ears, still wrapped in husk.

I could see, father was pleased to hear this and then he said,

> Tezcacoatl moves like a windblown flame – restless, quick-witted, full of fire, yet never careless. From the time he could walk, he had a way of reading faces, coaxing smiles and making people laugh when there was tension.

Uncle said, "I too have seen elders smile at him; and market vendors call him by kind names."

The next day, when our family gathered for the afternoon meal, I sat on my mat eating tamales and beans from a clay bowl. I didn't finish eating all the food mother made for me and I start playing with palm leaves. Mother taught me how to weave a mat, so I was trying to do it right. I listened while Father told mother about a dream he had:

> Last night I dreamt our son, Tezcacoatl would become a pochteca.[32] I saw him climb mountains in faraway lands. I saw him meet distant tlatoanis and make friendships.[33] I heard him speak a language I did not know. I saw how people loved him and he brought back gifts to Tenochtitlán. When I awoke, my heart felt proud, not proud in the way of self-glory, but in the way I see a piece of fine jade and imagine what may be carved.

Mother said,

> Pochteca are not mere traders, they are diplomats. They walk among people in foreign lands, speak with their rulers and bring back knowledge of their customs, their needs and wishes and their fears. When pochteca trade in distant regions, it opens doors for closer friendships among our peoples and helps Tenochtitlán grow.

---

32 A long-distance merchant, member of a hereditary merchant guild. The plural form is "pochteca." The singular form is "pochtecatl," but "pochteca" is the most commonly recognized form of the word, so for ease, I choose to use pochteca consistently when referring to the singular or plural.

33 Plural of tlatoani in Nahuatl is tlahtohqueh, but for ease, I use the anglicized plural, tlatoanis.

Father nodded, took a breath and continued,

This is not ambition; it's a revelation that came to me. I see that our son has the rare gifts that make a true pochteca. I dream that he might one day serve Tenochtitlán, carry our voice to distant mountains, and help preserve the balance of the world beneath the Fifth Sun.

I remember seeing how pleased father was when pochteca arrived at his workshop. They would bring obsidian and copper, gold and silver, turquoise and jade and he studied each piece in silence. Father always asked where the stones came from and he listened carefully to the stories the pochteca told. Father said each stone has its own story and he wove those stories into each finished piece. Father traded his finished jewelry for the materials he received.

Thirteen days later, I was in the kitchen with mother when women of our calpulli gathered to prepare for the Tozoztli Festival, a day of gratitude, abundance and feasting. The kitchen smelled of corn and copal. One woman boiled the corn while another ground and kneaded it. I sat on a stone shelling beans, and listened.

Mother, rinsing a basket of chilies, sighed, "Remember the pochteca who came last market day? He was tall and strong, his hair neatly bound. Women turned their heads, hiding their smiles. Among the common folk, they hold the highest place, next to the nobles."

"They tell good stories, too," the woman at the grinding stone answered, scraping her metate. "We sing of them in the courtyards–of the trials they endure on the road–bringing strange goods, strange tongues and trouble sometimes. Each trip they make is a great adventure." Then all the women in the kitchen joined in laughter.

Pochteca from Tenochtitlán (cactus) and Tlatelolco (stone mound) purchase feathers and goods and return. Florentine Codex Book IX, The Merchants. Med. Palat. 219, f. 326v. Biblioteca Medicea Laurenziana, Florence.

Mother folded tamales with steady fingers and said, "Some return richer than nobles. It is true. But they do not show it. They must not put on fine clothes or walk like kings. Mother lowered her voice as she patted the masa and added, "They dress plainly when they come back, bare feet, humble garments. They hide their wealth – so no one envies, so the balance between houses and lords stays steady. Respect keeps the city whole."

"Before they go," another woman said, "they pray to Yacatecuhtli.[34] Once I saw one draw blood from his ear – a quiet offering, praying the road might be safe."

I tucked a bean into my palm and imagined the pochteca at a distant market – barefoot homecoming, satchels heavy with jade and stories.

---

34 Yacatecuhtli was the patron god of merchants and travelers, worshiped by pochteca.

The women kept talking and my hands kept working, and I imagined the life of the pochteca.

SPEAKING WITH TLAMACAZQUI TLACAELEL

Later, when Tezcacoatl reached his fourteenth year, father set his mind to help his first-born son begin his journey to become a pochteca. Restless with his thoughts, father went to seek counsel. In a courtyard behind the Calmecac, morning light shone through woven mats hung to dry and the red ochre of the temple walls glowed faintly. There, father's patron, Tlamacazqui Tlacaelel, a thin, stately priest with eyes as dark as polished obsidian—reflective, unreadable, and sharp as truth—stood with folded hands. Father arrived, unbidden, bowing respectfully and said, "Tlamacazqui, please excuse this intrusion, I only wish your guidance on a matter of deep importance to me."

Speaking softly, Tlacaelel said, "Cuauhtli, I am pleased to have your presence. Tell me what troubles you."

"You have known my house, revered one. You have blessed my forge, seen my sons grow. I come not with boast, but with a father's question."

Tlamacazqui Tlacaelel responded with a sympathetic voice, "Say it, Cuahutli. May the truth carry no dust on its sandals."

Father continued,

> I wish to speak of my firstborn—Tezcacoatl.
> The boy has a fire in his *yollotl* (heart), the kind the gods place in those meant to walk far and return with wisdom. He has a tongue that charms even the old market wives. He listens when travelers speak. He speaks the Mayan words he learned from wise men. He trades small stones for cacao in the square—not for gain, but for delight.

Father knelt in a gesture of humility,

> I dreamt that the gods shaped him to serve the Mexica as a pochteca to carry our city's voice across the mountains. To bring back grain, wisdom, alliances—to hold up the Fifth Sun, as we all must.

Tlacaelel listened, eyes closed, paused and spoke,

Many fathers dream. Few speak the dream with such clean breath. Cuahutli, I know your son, I know Tezcacoatl. Tezcacoatl shall be known in council. His steps will not be alone—my voice will walk beside him. His path shall be open, not for your house alone, but for the people and for the gods. His breath belongs to the gods, his road to the people.

〽〽〽〽〽

Later that day, father spoke with Calpullec Teyacanqui, head of our calpulli.[35][36] Though father was the most prominent member of the calpulli, he honors Teyacanqui and they have remained powerful allies. They sat on reed mats under the portico of the communal house while father described the dream he had concerning his son, Tezcacoatl, becoming a pochteca, and asked Teyacanqui if he would support Tezcacoatl's admission to the Pochteca Guild.

Teyacanqui responded,

If your boy rises, it lifts the whole calpulli. If he falls, we catch him. I have seen him dance, question, trade, and watch. He does not walk like one content with borders. I will send my seal to the Pochteca Guild.

〽〽〽〽〽

As a jeweler, father knew many pochteca who brought precious items for jewelry making. Senior pochteca Olintecuhtli faithfully brought jade from the Maya lands.[37] They had known each other since Cuahutli first worked with the old jeweler Chalchihuitl.

When Olintecuhtli returned from Tulum and Mayapan, his back heavy with fine cotton garments, cacao beans, shell necklaces and parrot feathers, he did not go directly to the market. Wearing no

---

35 Calpullec is the leader and administrative head of a calpulli.

36 Teyacanqui means he who is at the forefront, or, a leader of people. In this case, he is the leader of our calpulli.

37 The name, Olintecuhtli, Lord of Movement, means he who guides through uncertainty.

colors but white, he walked first to the Shrine of Yacatecuhtli. There, in silence, he burned copal and whispered thanks.

Later that afternoon, weary and still wearing his travel-cloak dusted from the road and carrying a packet of gems for trade, he went to visit father in his shaded workshop courtyard where the scent of charcoal smoke from the brazier mingled with the breath of copal.

To celebrate Olintecuhtli's return from a lengthy trading mission, the two enjoyed a ceremonial frothy cacao drink together. Olintecuhtli opened his packet of jade pieces and said, "You'll like what I've brought – green as the rain's first breath."

But father stopped him and said,

> Olintecuhtli, I am preoccupied with another matter, it's not jade. [He gestures toward the courtyard where his son, Tezcacoatl, is busy polishing.] You've seen him grow. You remember when he played at your feet, asking if Maya wore gold in their teeth. Now he's nearly a man. Eyes sharp, like yours were. Voice quicker, I'd say.
>
> In a dream my eagle *nagual* (animal spirit) came to me. Its wings made a great cloud of dust and Tezcacoatl appeared with his pochteca's staff seeking air to breathe. Tlamacazqui Tlacaelel believes it is an omen that my son is destined to be a pochteca, to travel away from Tenochtitlán for the breath of wind beyond our lake; that he may become a great asset to the empire.
>
> It is my wish that you support his admission to the Pochteca Guild and that you mentor him and protect him as though he were your own son.

Olintecuhtli rejoined, "Your son has the fire, Cuahutli. I saw it when he bartered with my porters, giving them salt cakes and making them laugh." He pledged his support, saying, "but he must know the road is no song. It is mud, arrows, betrayal, and offerings to gods who give and take."

"Yes," father said, "but it is his choice. He knows the danger; he has his eyes wide open." The two men then carry on, laughing and enjoying the rest of the evening.

Under Olintecuhtli's tutelage, Tezcacoatl began his career by trading within Tenochtitlán, dealing in goods such as textiles, cacao, and precious stones. His keen eye for quality and his ability to negotiate favorable deals, a skill he learned at his father's side, quickly earned him a reputation as a successful merchant, and he built strategic alliances with other merchants and artisans, expanding his network and gaining access to a wider range of goods. Tezcacoatl's strength was his pleasant personality and ability to gain the confidence of the people around him. He was a natural leader among men.

f. Xochitl, Preeminent Amanteca

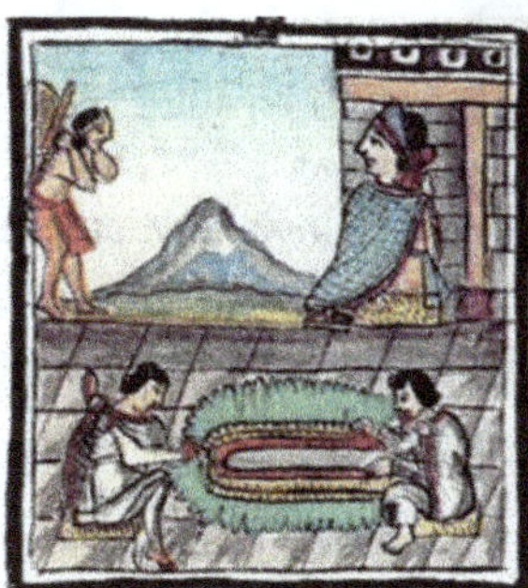

Feather works Florentine Codex Book 9, Chapter 20, Med. Palat. 219, f. 370r

Xochitl, my older sister, the family's second child, became a renowned *amanteca*, a feather artisan, known throughout the empire for her skill and artistry. From an early age, Xochitl was captivated by the beauty of featherworks. Father encouraged her and taught her to perfect her skill and to seek beauty and meaning in her work to enhance the lives of our people.

Xochitl especially loved working with the tail feathers of the Resplendent Quetzal. Xochitl explained it this way.

> The iridescent turquoise and blood red chest give this feathered creature its name, "Resplendent Quetzal." We Mexica people love this bird above all others, and call it Quetzal, which means precious.
>
> This bird can only be found in isolated ravines in the highest mountains, where the air is thin and cool, where clouds gather

and cling to the mountainsides, where a dense mist permanently wets every leaf, every surface, dripping water onto the jungle's fertile floor. There, the Resplendent Quetzal makes its home.

The Resplendent Quetzal, photo by Kevin Mercier

People who live where the Quetzal is found provide these birds as tribute, delivering them to the Tenochtitlán Totocalli (aviary) where hundreds of bird species are kept. There, the Toto Tlamacazqui, the priest responsible for the aviary oversees their care. He is a highly educated priest and skilled ornithologist, who studies each bird species to know their diets, habitats and nesting requirements for breeding in captivity.

When the male Quetzal reaches his breeding age at year three, he grows long iridescent turquoise tailfeathers. When the full beauty of the plumes is realized, they are carefully plucked, leaving the Quetzal to grow new tailfeathers for harvesting every six months.

I adorn royal headdresses and a wide variety of specialty items for religious ceremonies and military gear. Only royalty, priests, and generals may wear Quetzal feathers.

Blue and yellow featherwork, in the image of rain god Tlaloc with running water, goggle eyes and fangs. (Photo by Ian Mursell/www.mexicolore.co.uk)

My younger siblings join father's jewelry business and continue our family's legacy.

g. Our Calli the Family Home

On a quiet evening, in the courtyard, father spoke of the house he first built — the one of reed and earth, the one that held his beginnings.

I was young, still sleeping behind Chalchihuitl's shop where tools and stock were stored, where obsidian dust mingled with the faint scent of charred mesquite and heated stone.

The shed was narrow, the nights cold. But I was grateful — for tools, for purpose, for the whisper of a future.

Then came the day Chalchihuitl called me to his side. "You are no longer a child," he said. "Your hands have shaped my fortune. Now let me help you shape yours." He spoke of a plot — humble, but waiting. A place to serve the city, to comfort, to kindle a new hearth."

I bowed to him, and to the calpullec, our calpulli leader, who granted me permission. And so began the work — not alone, but with neighbors, canal workers, kin. We raised a platform of tamped earth that sloped toward the water, so the rains would not drown my dreams.

I drove stakes into the soil, and others came with willow branches, weaving them into walls. The women mixed clay and maguey fiber, plastering the house with a rhythm of joy and laughter. From the lakebed came reeds and grasses, bundled and tied, thatched into a roof that capped my new heartful nest.

We made two doorways, raised above the ground. I hung heavy mats over them that I could raise so the house might breathe, or lower to protect against the scorching rays of Tonatiuh, the sun, or Ehecatl's harsh winds. After storms, I patched the roof with fresh palm leaves, cursing the leaks but smiling at the work. It was no palace – only a hearth that held me, one room of breath and reed. But it held my sweat, my silence, my fire.

When we became a family, it was our first calli. A root in the soil of Tenochtitlán. A place where memory could take hold, and life and family could begin to flower.

ʒʅʒʅʒʅʒʅʒʅ

With the years, as our family grew and father's craft prospered, our calpullec honored us with a larger house plot. This time father dreamt of a grander calli: three rooms with basalt walls and floors, their surfaces smoothed with lime plaster inside and out – no longer a common house, but one built to reflect father's artistry.

By our custom, neighbors helped neighbors on projects big and small, for our obligations to each other made us all richer; for a strong calpulli enriched us all and strengthened Tenochtitlán itself.

But a house of basalt and lime plaster could not be made by the calpulli alone. Stone was quarried from distant volcanic slopes, lime burned in great kilns, both carried across water by canoe and over earth by the sweat of men. Specialized calpulli of lime-burners and stonecutters labored year-round to supply the city's endless hunger for building.[38]

---

38 Here, calpulli refers to a collective of tradesmen.

Father employed a *tlachiani*, a master builder, who arranged deliveries and oversaw crews of excavators, stonecutters, masons, plasterers, carpenters, roofers and artisans. While our calpulli members could haul earth, raise beams, and thatch roofs, skilled artisans were still required to shape stone and lay mortar.

During these days, I was always there. When men dug, I dug too. When basalt was laid, I knelt down to see if the lines were straight. Once I pointed to a spot where a stone was crooked. The mason nodded, shifting it into place. I loved the feeling, helping build a strong foundation.

For their wages, my parents bargained with what they had saved over years: cacao beans counted by the hundreds, cakes of salt, obsidian blades and deer hides. Father also bartered with his store of famed jewelry pieces. Mother too contributed her finely spun and woven cotton cloth as well as her celebrated finished garments. Some payments were made in highly prized copper axes, others in bolts of cotton or carefully measured loads of salt.

Whenever father was bartering at the marketplace or with the tlachiani, I could see older brother, Tezcacoatl, at his side, talking and in his way, helping father make a trade. He loved those exchanges and he usually had them laughing in good humor. And so, by trade and barter, and stone by stone, our three-room home was raised.

Over the next ten years we never stopped expanding and improving our home. We were a family of eight children, but our household included my grandmother, Nonantzin, and several attendants, servants and slaves. As my father's success grew, he employed several artisans and craftsmen to assist him.

Father acquired the adjacent lot and added rooms to accommodate us all, creating a grand U-shaped dwelling with the rooms arranged around a central courtyard; a space that served as the heart of our daily lives, where we played as children, where we gathered for family meals, ceremonies and storytelling, where we could quietly rest in the sun or watch the rain.

Our ceremonial chamber had a shrine dedicated to Xochiquetzal, patroness of those who shape gold and jade. On one wall we had a painted mural depicting two white herons in a mountainous landscape, depicting Aztlán, the place where our Mexica ancestors originated. Other walls were decorated with colorful tapestries that mother had made. The stone floors were covered with woven reed mats.

Kitchen scene depicting a daughter grinding corn on a metate (grinding stone), sitting before a round comalli (griddle) supported by three stones. Photo by Mexicolore.co.uk, from Codex Mendoza, 1938 James Cooper Clark facsimile edition, London. "Faithful reproductions of two-dimensional public domain works of art are public domain," Wikimedia Foundation. See also, Codex Mendoza Aztec Manuscript, Productions Liber SA Fribourg, 1978.

Father made a three stone hearth with a large ceramic *comalli* for cooking and heating.[39] He made it with the same skill and workmanship as he did when making fine jewelry. After forming the clay for the *comalli*, he applied several coats of paste made of white pickling lime. He then submerged it in salt water overnight to strengthen; then finished it with oil. Finally, he slowly heated it to create a hard smooth surface.

My parents had a private sleeping area, while we children shared sleeping quarters, with the older children helping to care for the younger ones. We slept on reed mats (petlatl) with cotton or maguey

---

39 The Nahuatl word comalli became comal in Spanish. It means griddle in English.

blankets. Father also expanded his jewelry shop and storage spaces. We had our own temazcal for bathing.[40] A canal from the lake entered our property and we kept two canoes, one for father's business and one for the family.

We had a perimeter wall to protect our privacy. Even though we were respected and prominent members of our calpulli, father did not wish to make our prosperity an object for public envy.

Night Soil and Sacred Order: Once, I asked my father why we keep our waste in clay pots behind the house; each tucked beneath a woven lid. He crouched beside me and said,

> Even what leaves the body must return with honor. In our calli, we place our waste in those pots, and at night, quiet men come in canoes to collect it. They paddle toward special chinampas where they mix the night soil with lake sediment, dead plants, food scraps and ash – layered like offerings, then they cover it to keep the air sweet.

"Why don't we just throw it in the lake?" I asked.

Mother overheard our words. She turned to me and said,

> Even our waste has a place, a purpose, a path back to life, It becomes earth again, and feeds the maize that feeds us all. But it is forbidden to let waste touch the lake, for the lake is sacred and we must never offend it.

I remember how serious she looked when she said that. I didn't understand all her words then, but I felt their weight.

---

40 A dome shaped hut made of adobe brick, for our ritual bathing.

II
My Early Life

a. 1450, My Birth

It is Day 1 Reed (March 1, 1450), in the center of Tenochtitlán, capital of the powerful Mexica Empire. The *tlamatlquiticitl* (midwife) works with my mother as she labors until we are parted. I inspire, and vital energy from the divine Life Giver enters my body for the first time. It is *ihiyotl*,[41] the sacred essence of breath that gives rhythm to my life. With ihiyotl I have emotions, vitality and charisma.

My family seeks guidance from a *tonalpouhqui*,[42] a diviner, responsible for interpreting the *tonalpohualli*, the sacred 260-day calendar that determines fate and destiny based on a person's birth date. He explains,

> Day 1 Reed is an auspicious day to be born. But a reed may be blown by the wind. A person born on that day could have all his accomplishments blown away. Hold the water-based naming and purification ceremony on Day 7 Rain. That is a date connected to Tlaloc, the powerful god of rain, fertility and sustenance. Tlaloc is firmly rooted to the earth and can protect this child from the negative forces of Ehecatl, the god of wind.

When Day 7 rain comes, my family and elders from our calpulli (community) gather. The midwife who delivered me is present to

---

41 Third of the three vital energies of human life, mind, heart and breath.

42 A soothsayer or diviner, responsible for interpreting the tonalpohualli, the sacred 260-day calendar.

prepare me for the naming ceremony. She guides the cleansing ritual to purify and protect me from negative influences. At our family altar they make offerings to god Tlaloc who has dominion over water, fertility of the land, and the well-being of the community. They prepare the altar with fresh flower bouquets and offerings of tortillas still warm from the comalli, chiles, *ahuacatl, tilxochitl, canella, xocolatl* and *xochimiel*.[43] The air fills with the scent of copal incense, calling upon the spiritual realm where the gods can receive the essence of our offerings.

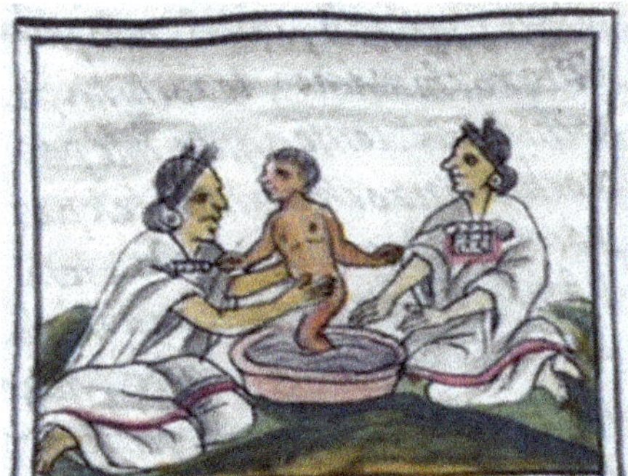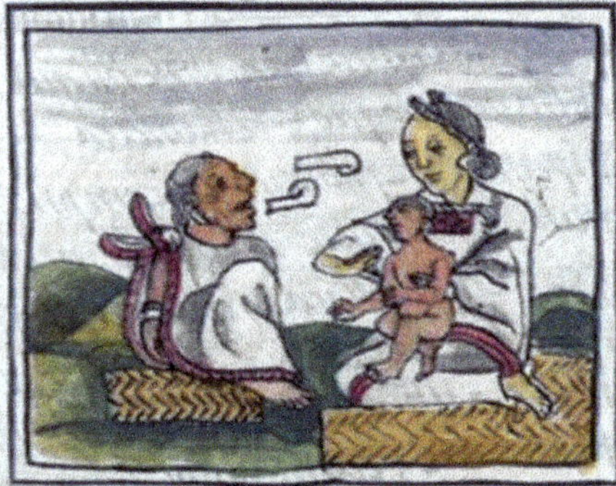

Mother and midwife purify the baby. The diviner priest speaks a suitable name for the baby. Florentine Codex Book 4, .Med. Palat. 218, f. 308r

The priest, an elderly man robed in a white cotton mantel, embroidered with sacred images and adorned with jade beads moves to the center of the gathering. Facing my parents and me, his voice rises in chant,

> Day 1 Reed is auspicious, the birthdate of wisdom.
> Day 1 Reed is precious, yet fragile in the wind.
> The reed may break, its glory blown away.
> Child of Reed, do not be carried off.
> Hold fast to the reed that bends,
> Hold to the earth, hold to the rain, hold to the root.
> On Day 7 Rain, the waters will bless you.
> On Day 7 Rain, Tlaloc will guard you.
> With blessings from the gods, I give this child a name.

---

43 Avocado, vanilla, cinnamon, chocolate and honey

> I give the name Huitzilin, the hummingbird.
> Huitzilin, creature of grace, creature of agility.
> Huitzilin, resilient, overflowing with vibrant energy.
> Namesake of Huitzilopochtli, god of War, god of the Sun.
> Patron of our people, patron of our destiny.
> May the hummingbird's wings be swift,
> May the hummingbird's heart be strong.
> May the child carry the sun in his flight,
> May the child carry the war god's strength in his song.

After the *tlacualli*,[44] they prepare to bury my umbilical cord. All gather in canoes to cross the waterways from Tenochtitlán to the revered battlefield of Azcapotzalco, the birthplace of the Aztec Empire where Tenochtitlán, Texcoco and Tlacopan, known as the Triple Alliance, united to overthrow the oppressive Tepanecs.

Once we arrive, the priest looks toward the heavens and incants,

> Great Tlaloc, we call upon you, lord of rain and fertility, to watch over this child as he grows.

Turning to me, he says,

> May you be resilient as the rain that nourishes the earth.
> May you bring life and abundance wherever you go.

He then digs a small hole where he buries my umbilical cord and says,

> This cord, once linking child to mother, now returns to the earth.
> It joins the life force of our ancestors.
> May your bond to this place give you strength.
> May your bond to this place give you courage.
> Be a brave warrior, be a protector of the Mexica people.

b. The Famine of One Rabbit, 1450-1455

"Mama, I'm hungry."

"Yes, sweet one, I know. Everyone is hungry. Go tell your father."

---

44 Feast or banquet.

I am four years old and I follow my father outside. He says he must find food. He picks me up and carries me as he jumps over thick mud. He points and says,

> Look there, son, that is where we had our chinampas. We grew squash and beans and chilis here. We grew sacred corn that fed our family and all Tenochtitlán.

I look, but there are no people, nothing growing. I only see mud and rubble. "Papa, where is the corn?"

Father is silent. My eyes look up searching for an answer. Father looks away for a long time. Then he says, "See over there," gesturing, "and there and there? That's where our neighbors grew their corn."

"Papa, where are the neighbors?"

> These neighbors had no food so they grew weak. They moved away searching for water and many died. There were days when we had no food or water and our family suffered.

Mother takes me from his arms. I hear squishing sounds as she walks in the mud. I struggle out of her arms and jump in the mud too. There are cracks in the mud everywhere we go. The mud is deep and it comes up to my knees.

Father calls to me, "Huitzllin, come, look here!" He points to a small pond where creatures are swimming and says, "Can you catch one of those?"

I jump into the puddle and laugh when the little creatures tickle my feet. I reach down and grab one but it gets away. I try again and again until I catch one. Father is pleased. He says, those are *axolotls*, they're good to eat. Look around," father says, "See the dead and dying axolotls? They are dying from the drought."

"Papa, what does drought mean," I ask.

Mother answers my question,

> We have drought when we have no rain. Rain brings water to the mountains and rivers and lakes. We need water to live. All living things need water, even the axolotls.

This used to be a big lake. We call it Lake Texcoco. It had lots of water and grandfather grew all our food there. But when it did not rain the lake started to dry up. The corn could not grow and many fish that lived in the lake died.

Axolotls, a species of salamander. https://www.childrensaquarium. com/wp-content/uploads/2024/10/axolotls.jpg

On this day, big brother, Tezcacoatl and big sister, Xochitl join in our search for food on the drying mudflats of Lake Texcoco. Xochitl had made a woven basket that she used to scrape spirulina, blue-green algae, from lake surface. Mother gathered water bug eggs, larvae, and beetles from the reeds and mudflats. Big brother helped father gather tadpoles, frogs, and crayfish.

Today we have gathered plenty to last us for many days, for there will be other days when we will not find food.

After some days pass, father takes us across to Chapultepec. We spend the day there with many other families gathering grasshoppers to eat. Father catches rodents, snakes and insects, too.

When it's time to rest, I sit on my father's lap and he tells me,

Long, long ago, before we had chinampas, our people roamed the countryside looking for things to eat. We ate all sorts of wild plants and fruits. We ate rabbits, turkeys, fish and insects to survive. But sometimes we could not find enough to eat and so we learned to grow our own food on the chinampas. The chinampas saved us. But now the chinampas are dying because there is no rain. Many people have forgotten how our ancestors survived and they have died. That's why we cannot forget our ancestors.

己己己己己己己

Year 1455: I am five years old now, walking into the kitchen, looking for mama and papa. They are together praying, but I don't know why.

The next day our family gathers early. Mother says we must fast. She does not prepare food this day. Instead, we wash and sweep. Mother burns copal and we pray together in silence. Father explains,

> The god Tlaloc was angry and gave us drought because we did not honor him. Today, Huey Tlatoani Motecuhzoma Ilhuicamina, (Moctezuma I) will preside over a sacrifice. The sacrifice will show the gods our sincere devotion. We will offer a human life, the greatest gift we can bestow on the gods. If the gods are satisfied with our offering, they will protect us.

With the sun at its zenith, I walk with my family slowly, to the *Huey Teocalli*[45] to observe the sacrifice. We each carry flowers and bow our heads in silence. As we approach the magnificent temple, the sun hovers above like a golden shield and the entire city is at attention.

I watch as a great crowd fills the plaza. The temple is the biggest and most beautiful thing I've ever seen, with giant stone steps leading to the very top. I can smell the air, thick with steam from offerings, with smoke curling toward the sky. I can smell copal, wild herbs, and maize husks burning in clay braziers. I hear whispers rustle like reeds in the wind.

Mother places our family's woven mat on the plaza's stone floor. I clutch mother's hand, standing with my family on the mat. Mother kneels down to speak to me,

> Sweet boy, the gods gave us everything – the sun, the rain, the maize. We make offerings to repay the gods for the divine blood that gave life to the world. This offering is how we speak to the gods.

---

45 Great Temple, house of god, at the center of Tenochtitlán, Templo Mayor.

"What can we offer the gods, Mama?"

We must make an offering to Tlaloc, something very precious.

"Like what, Mama?"

The most precious thing we have is life itself. But not any life. We choose a man of strength and bravery so the gods will know we are sincere. In this way the gods are nourished so that they may uphold the balance of the cosmos.

"Mama, what is balance of the cosmos?"

Once the cosmos was in balance. We had rain and the chinampas were fertile. The maize grew tall and the lake was full of fish. In year One Rabbit the skies changed, the rains did not come. The land became thirsty and maize could not grow.

Today we make a sacred offering to the gods. Today we ask Tlaloc, the god of rain, to hear our prayer to restore balance to the cosmos and give us rain once again.

I have never before seen such a gathering. I open my eyes wide and gaze at the magnificent temple and my mouth drops open. I hear the drums begin to beat. It feels like my heart beating.

Atop the temple, I see the figure of a man with a majestic headdress, standing beneath a feathered parasol. It is held high by his attendants. I see obsidian rings glittering on his wrists. He is still and says nothing. But I can see he is powerful; everyone bows before him. I think he must be a god. I ask mother if he is a god.

She says,

Dear sweet boy, he is our king, our divine leader, chosen by the gods to be the great speaker of our people, he is *Huey Tlatoani* Moctezuma Ilhuicamina. He rules over the Aztec Empire. He doesn't just lead our people; he listens to the gods and speaks their wishes to the people. The sun watches over him.

"And who is the other man next to him? Is he a god?"

Mother answers, "That is *Tlamacazqui Quetzalcoatl Totec*,[46] the highest priest in the land."

I watch the Tlamacazqui carry a jade bowl filled with offerings for Tlaloc: maize, blossoms, and shimmering water and place it on an altar. He raises his arms toward the east, where a dark cloud creeps over the horizon and chants with a deep and rhythmic voice,

> Today, we petition *Tlaloc*, bringer of rains, to accept our offering and end the long drought.
> O Tlaloc, lord of rain, hear us.
> O spirits of the mountain springs, rise up.
> From the stormy caverns, thunder's womb, come forth.
> From within the mountain, send your waters, send your thunder.
> Let the clouds gather, let the rains descend.

Then I see a group of men approach the priest. One man is painted blue with garlands around his neck. He kneels before the Tlamacazqui. He is calm and does not struggle.

Mother whispers to me,

> That man was taken captive long ago. He was chosen because he is strong, brave, and worthy. Since his capture, priests have kept him pure: he bathes in water and fasts on sacred days.

Is he afraid, mama? Why doesn't he run away?

> He feels honored to be chosen for this duty. He steps into duty with honor, not fear. He is brave. He walks humbly, knowing his fate. He knows that after this day, he will live with the gods.

"Can I live with the gods too, Mama?"

"If the gods call for you, my son, you may go. Only the gods know."

The priest murmurs a final invocation and lays his hand on the man's shoulder. Drums silenced.

---

46 Tlamacazqui means priest. "Tlamacazqui Quetzalcoatl Totec" is the title of one of the two highest priests in the land. The Mexica had two supreme priests: one serving Huitzilopochtli (war and the sun), the other serving Quetzalcóatl (ritual knowledge and the calendar). They were titles, equal in rank and officiated major state rites.

Mother draws me close. "Don't look away," she whispers gently, "This is how the world is mended."

I see the Tlamacazqui holding a big shiny black knife. I see him working but the man does not cry out; I would cry. I see blood splatter everywhere. I can even smell the blood wafting in the warm humid air. I'm scared but mama presses her hand against my chest so I don't cry. Everyone around me is still; everyone is watching. Then the priest holds the bloody heart in his hand and lifts it toward the sun. I can see the heart is still beating in the priest's hand. Then I hear his voice cry out to the gods, not with words but with a loud wail. Huey Tlatoani Moctezuma steps forward. He scatters sacred petals and whispers a blessing. Then he lifts his arms to the crowd, and finally, he speaks, "Tlaloc has heard! The rain will come again! We will endure!" At that moment, the crowd bursts into cheers and merriment.

I hug mama tight and try to understand. "Will the rain come now?" She strokes my hair and says,

> We hope so. Tlaloc watches from the mountain tops. If he sees we are sincere, he will open the skies again. That's why we give something precious – to remind him we are waiting.

I try to understand. I only know it is one of the mysteries of life. That night as I fall asleep, I think of the man giving his life. In my mind, in my heart and in my breath, I feel the gods speak to me. Now I know I must be clean, I must obey. I must always honor the gods.

After this day, the rains begin to fall and we rejoice. The balance of the cosmos has been restored and father goes to help the farmers rebuild their chinampas in the manner he learned from his father.

c. Lessons Beneath the Ceiba

CLEANSING IN THE TEMAZCAL

Father builds a fire in the fire pit in the courtyard to heat large volcanic stones and brings them into the temazcal. Tezcacoatl pulls down the blanket that covers the entrance. In the darkness the stones glow, emitting red and yellow sparks. Mother brings a jar of water infused with epazote, a medicinal herb, and lets me help pour it over the sizzling stones.

A temazcal (temazcalli in Nahuatl) a dome shaped hut made of stone or adobe brick. Stones from a firepit are brought into the Temazcal to induce sweating, cleansing the body of toxins. Photo by the author, Tulum, Yucatan.

In the evenings, my family gathers in our temazcal to cleanse our bodies, soothe the souls and reconnect with ancestral rhythms. It is a time to be together; to share stories of the day and sometimes mother teaches us the rules of life.

As the steam rises and the fragrance of herbs fills the temazcal, Mother's voice softens into *huehuetlatolli* – the ancient words of our people.

Our ancestors taught their children the sacred wisdom of life and now we must share their wisdom.

Remember, the gods smile upon those who keep their bodies pure and their hearts humble. We sweat to clear impurities from our bodies. When we breath in this fragrant steam, Ihiyotl calms disruptive energies and internal fire is rebalanced so we can heal. Let its potent fragrance cleanse the pathways within us, soothing our stomachs and helping the foods we eat sustain us.

Mother makes lather from the amole plant root mixed with other herbs and plants to scrub and exfoliate our skin. Then, she helps me clean my teeth. She sits beside me and whispers, "Open your mouth, Huitzilin," dipping the soft, fibrous brush of the *tlatlauhcapatli* root into the powdered bark of the *quauhteputztli* tree she keeps in a small clay bowl.[47][48] She says, "The gods do not smile on foul breath." She scrubs my teeth gently, humming as she works, but I grab the tlatlauhcapatli root from her hand and say, "I can do it mama." When I'm through, she rinses my mouth with cool water steeped in mint and liquidambar, I feel clean not just in body, but in spirit.

SWEEPING IN THE COURTYARD

I rise early one morning and find grandmother, Nonantzin in the courtyard. Grandmother is very old. Her hair is grey and her face is wrinkled. She is hunched over and can barely get around. But she is there, singing ancient songs as she sweeps the floor with her broom, a bundle of stiff grass. I go to her and ask, "Nonantzin, why do you sweep?"

Grandmother pauses and smiles at me. She says,

Huitzilin, dear child, I'm glad you see me. We sweep to honor the gods. Coatlicue, the goddess of mother earth swept her temple to keep harmful forces away and to maintain cosmic harmony. And, so do I sweep every morning to purify our home and remove disorder. When we sweep, we chase away not only dust, but also the bad spirits that linger in corners.

I ask, "Nonantzin, does sweeping bring good spirits?" Grandmother answers,

---

47 Tlatlauhcapatli is a soft fibrous root used as a toothbrushing tool.
48 Quauhteputztli is bark powder, toothpaste

Toci is the patron goddess of grandmothers. She watches over us when we keep our houses clean. Each stroke of the broom is a prayer that she may keep us healthy and safe.

"Do we have to sweep the whole courtyard?" I ask.

We sweep the courtyard and every room of the house. We sweep the street in front of our house. Your father sweeps his shop. The priest sweeps the temple and so too do the city's workers sweep the streets and causeways each morning – to keep the breath of the city pure, and to show respect to the gods who walk among us. You too can sweep, Huitzilin, to keep your life clean and to keep your thoughts and deeds pure.

Grandmother hands me a small broom and I follow, sweeping behind her.

TORTILLAS IN THE KITCHEN

Family dinner. Women's hair with top knots and clasped capes. Men tie their capes. Codex Mendoza

The next morning, I wake up to the aroma of warm tortillas in the kitchen. Mother is kneeling before the comalli making tortillas. Her hands are moving so fast I can hardly see them as she pats the corn dough into perfectly round tortillas. I stand next to her, watching and rest my cheek on her shoulder.

She says, "My sweet boy, why don't you try to make one?" She pulls off a small round ball of dough and shows me how to pat back and forth until the tortilla begins to take shape. But I can't make a nice round one like mother does. Still, she places the tortilla that I made on the comalli to heat. She turns it over without burning her fingers. She pours a bit of honey on the tortilla and offers it to me. It tastes good and I'm happy.

Later, when we are having our afternoon meal, mother reminds me,

> Do not eat and drink in a hurry. Don't take too much food. Don't stir the pieces around, or dig into the sauce bowl. Don't stuff your mouth, or swallow without chewing. Don't gulp like a dog. Avoid making a spectacle of yourself. Eat and drink slowly, calmly and quietly. Wash your hands after eating, clean up any messy scraps. And don't let snot hang from your nose.

A CHILD'S DUTIES

Five-year-old boys carry firewood and reeds for sweeping, earning one tortilla each.
Codex Mendoza

I am six years old now. I follow mother into the kitchen. She says to me, "O my quetzal feather, you're a big boy so you must know your duties." I spend the day with her and she teaches me the things I must do every day. She says, "Before we prepare our food, the kitchen must be clean. Will you help me?"

I tell her, "Grandmother taught me to sweep, so I'll sweep as fast as I can."

Mother says,

> No, my jewel, sweep with care to please the gods. It is not just dirt we sweep; it is disorder. If you sweep fast, the dust flies in the air and there is more disorder. Tlazolteotl, the goddess of filth and purification, watches how we clean. She sees whether we sweep with care or with haste. The gods walk through our home in silence. If they find filth, they turn away.

She places her hands over mine and we sweep together slowly and rhythmically. She lowers her voice and her words settle gently in the air,

> O Tlazolteotl, eater of what is cast off, purifier of what is tangled, see this child's hand, still clumsy, still learning. Let his sweeping be enough. Let his heart be clean. If there is disorder in this house, devour it. If there is forgetfulness, remind us.

Next, I help mother in the kitchen and clean up after our morning meal. Mother takes me to a nearby canal where I scoop clean fresh water in a clay vessel to carry home. I gather firewood and reeds to make a new broom.

BENEATH THE CEIBA TREE

By the day's end, I have completed all my chores. The evening is warm but a cool breeze descends from the mountains around us. Mother says, "O my jade, come with me. We must visit the Ceiba tree." I look up at her in wonder. Then she says, "It is the world tree. The tree's roots reach into the underworld, its trunk is the middle world where we live, and its branches extend into the celestial world.

As we begin our walk, I ask, "Mama, what is the celestial realm.

"O my precious thing, come with me," she says as she leads me to the ancient Ceiba tree, "This tree of life is a sacred space. Here we can communicate with gods and our ancestors." We huddle down between its massive buttress roots to escape the cool evening breeze. Mother's arm holds me next to her warm bosom. She closes her eyes and sings:

300-year-old ceiba tree. Photo by Jay Sturner, used under CC BY 2.0.

Tlalticpac is the physical world where we live,
but it cannot exist without Teotlan.
Teotlan is the celestial realm, it is everywhere.
It is here within the ceiba tree, but it is not the ceiba tree.
It is within you and it is beyond you.
Close your eyes and you can see it.
Plug your ears and you can hear it.
Purse your lips and you can speak to it.
Without touching, you can feel.
Be still and you can move with it.
It is there, in the celestial realm,
where we dream and where the gods dwell.
Feel the vital force moving within you,
and there you can hear the voices
of the gods and of our ancestors.

"Mama, will I grow to be strong like Papa?"

My son, you were born on Day 1 Reed, a very auspicious day. Rain God Tlaloc has vowed to keep you rooted to the earth, no matter how hard the wind blows, no matter how strong the forces against you. Like a reed, you will grow tall and strong.

We are still and I think of what Mother has said. Birds entertain us with their song and a yellow butterfly floats in the wind. Mother points toward the setting sun and says,

> Look, my son! See the lush chinampas and narrow canals, where your grandfather once worked growing corn, beans, squash, chilies and flowers so that our people could flourish.
>
> See Lake Texcoco, silent and still with canoes gliding by, returning people to their homes to rest for the night.
>
> And there, sacred Mount Chapultepec,[49] the source of life-giving waters, rises from the edge of the lake. It appears dark and heavy in the fading light, with ancient cypress and pine trees, and wild grasses. Great eagles and hawks circle and cry high above and nest in her treetops and rocky cliffs.

I stand and point, "Look mama, see the color of the sky!" Mother holds me on her lap with both arms, her head next to mine and we look at the colors of the sunset, a pale blue sky with orange and golden yellow clouds. She whispers,

> Every color is a promise, my son. And every promise, a thread in the cloth of our world. That golden fire in the sky isn't just light, it's Tonatiuh's[50] courage. He is preparing to descend into the underworld, where darkness awaits. The orange is his shield of flame, and the blue is the breath of Tlaloc, calming and vast. When they touch, they remind us that the gods still walk together, even when the night comes."

She looks toward the violet hills of Chapultepec, a silhouette against the fading light.

> The sun is setting now. When the sun sets, it must pass through Mictlan, the underworld, where it will battle the forces of darkness before it can rise again in the east at dawn. So too, must we do our part to ensure the continuation of life.

I ask, "Mama, how can I fight the forces of darkness?"

---

49 Grasshopper hill.

50 The sun's

Mother answers,

Sweet boy, darkness is not only the night, it is doubt and fear, the shadows within your own heart. To fight it, you must know yourself. And you must know your *nagual* (animal spirit).

"What is my nagual, mama?"

We walk upon the earth, but we do not walk alone. When you were born, your spirit was twinned with the spirit of the hummingbird. The hummingbird flies faster than anything. It can hover in place. It can fly backward and change directions like lightning. It is a powerful warrior that carries the energy of the sun in its iridescent feathers. Hummingbirds dart between the earthly and celestial realms, carrying messages between humans and the gods.

"But Mama, where is my nagual? I can't see it."

We all have a nagual, a Shadow Spirit that walks beside us. My son, wherever you go, no matter what you may encounter, your shadow spirit is beside you to guide you and protect you. If you feel fear, pause and breathe deeply, listen to your hummingbird spirit and follow it. You don't need to search; it is already within you.

"Can I talk to my nagual, Mama?"

You may call for your hummingbird with a prayer or song. If you move, you will feel it move within you. Close your eyes to see your nagual, its colors, its energy, its presence. Your nagual will not speak, but trust that it will give you courage and guidance. It will give you speed, cunning and endurance when you need it. It will inspire quick reflexes and fearless movement.

MISCHIEF IN THE COURTYARD

Mama sent me out this morning to gather kindling for the comalli. I bring back as much as I can carry and run to pile them next to where she is working. Mama says, "Dear heart, you dropped some. Go pick them up."

I run back to pick up the ones I dropped next to Xochitl. She's sitting with a bunch of feathers. I grab the prettiest one. It's green and shines in the sunlight. I grab another and stick it in my hair and run around the courtyard when sister calls out, "Huitzilin, bring them back! I need those." I laugh and run and jump. She calls to me again and I laugh louder swinging the feathers in the breeze. Soon, I laugh as loud as I can.

I see mother coming and spit. I don't know why, I just did it.

Mother calls to me. I can tell she is firm. She kneels, holding both of my arms, with her face in front of mine and says. "Huitzilin, what have you done?"

"Nothing, Mama, I was just playing."

"Huitzilin, my son, you were laughing very loud. You disrespected your sister. You disrespected your family. You disturbed our calpulli. Is that how we taught you to behave?"

"No, mama. I didn't mean to, I just forgot."

"Our courtyard is a sacred space, Huitzilin. We care for it and keep it clean to please the gods. Did we teach you to spit on it?"

"No, mama, I don't know why I spat."

Mother sees Xochitl's feathers scattered across the courtyard. She points to them and asks, "Did you do that?"

"Maybe my foot touched some feathers. But, Mama, Xochitl has many feathers, why can't I have some?" I lower my head. "I didn't mean to make her sad. I just wanted a feather."

"Wanting is not wrong," mother says, "but taking what is not yours is wrong." Mother tightens her grip and it makes me stand still. "Playing doesn't mean forgetting respect. You were loud, you grabbed feathers, you spat. This breaks the social order.

I ask, "Mother, what is the social order?

Mother explains:

> Our world is like a great woven mat. Each person is a thread in the mat. When we perform our duties and follow the correct path, we make the fabric strong and it will last, the gods smile and the city flourishes. But if someone forgets their duty and breaks the rules even in small ways, the social fabric is frayed and the mat

will fall apart and the whole world is at risk; the rains may stop, the maize may fail, and even the sun might grow tired. That's why we live with respect – for each other and for the order the gods have given us.

Mother stands and I look up to her. She says:

Remember what we have taught you, Huitzilin. Never be brutish like a *Chichimecatl,* a wild soul, uncultured and without reverence.[51] Your actions should never harm the social order. Be steady. Walk and talk with care. Show humility and you will be honored. Behave like a nobleman. Always please the gods with beauty in everything you do.

When Mother finishes her admonitions, I am relieved and glad that it's over. But just as I begin to walk away, father enters the courtyard and calls to me.

He says, "Huitzilin, I too heard your loud laughter and disruption. You brought disorder to our home."

His voice is heavy. I feel my body begin to shake and I weep. I bow to him because I cannot speak.

"Huitzilin, did you forget your duty as mother has taught you?"

Trembling, with a broken voice, I answer, "Yes, father, I forgot."

Father explains:

You followed the footsteps of Huehuecóyotl, the ancient coyote. Huehuecóyotl was mischievous and played tricks on humans and the other gods, but when he did this, he was caught in his own chaos. We must learn to resist when Huehuecóyotl whispers to us. We must always remember our duties. Huehuecóyotl will come to you again and again in your life, but if you remember this day, and this lesson, you will choose the correct path and protect our social order. To help you remember, you must suffer punishment. Today chili smoke will teach you. If you need another lesson, you will know the maguey spikes.

---

51 The Mexica viewed the Chichimeca as nomadic peoples of the northern frontier who lived outside the structured order of the city-states and thought of them as wild and uncultured.

Punishments for misbehaving children. Chili smoke and maguey spikes. Codex Mendoza

I watch father build a fire in the firepit. When the flames are strong, he drops chili peppers on the fire. I am crying now and shaking. All of our family members are in the courtyard watching, even neighbors have come to see. Father holds me above the smoke. The acrid smoke blinds my eyes. I choke and cannot breathe. I cry out and my tears sizzle as they fall into the fire.

Father puts me down quickly. I am wailing now and he holds me upright by the shoulders, waiting for me to look at him.

> You are my son, Huitzilin. You carry my name and my craft. But you must also carry discipline. I punish, not to hurt you, but to mark the lesson in your bones. So next time, when Huehuecóyotl whispers, you will remember the stinging smoke and choose order over chaos. Will you remember now, Huitzilin?

"Yes, father. I will not forget." I run to my bed and sob.

DISORDER IN THE CALPULLI

The next day, I go out to collect firewood again. On my return home, I see a boy from the chinampas. I think he's about my same age, but he has muddy feet and no sandals. He is carrying a bundle on his back. Two older boys from our calpulli push him and knock him down. The older boys kick his bundle and scatter corn and vegetables on the street. They call him names and run off laughing and the little boy cries.

When I get home, I tell mother what I saw. She says, "Sweet boy, what did you think about that?"

"I didn't like it, mama. It made me feel sad for the poor boy. But the older boys were too big so I didn't do anything."

Mother asks, "Why didn't you like it? Why did it made you feel sad?"

I answer, "They just hurt the little boy for no reason. They made him cry."

Mother explains,

> What you saw made you feel bad because what they did harmed the social order.
>
> We are *tlacayotl*, humankind. We live in *tlalticpac*, the earthly realm, but the earth is fragile. Four times before, our world was destroyed in chaos. This is the era of the fifth sun. If the gods are not happy with us, they can destroy our world again.
>
> Our duty is to live with dignity, to uphold social order, to act with compassion and respect. We must align our actions with the cosmic order – walking the path of *neltiliztli* (truth and balance), understanding our moral and social responsibilities.[52]
>
> The small boy with dirty feet is a farm boy, living on the chinampas doing chores for his family just like your grandfather did. We need that boy and his family to grow crops and bring them to market so we can all thrive. When those older boys pushed him down and scattered his goods, it hurt us all because there will be less food for everyone. It's like tearing the reed mat. Every time someone harms social order, the earth loses its balance.

CUAUHTLI TEACHES

One morning at sunrise, my father leads me to a quiet area near the edge of the chinampas. He says,

> My son, to be respected, you must perfect your skill with the bow and arrow. Today I will teach you the art of bow, as my father taught me, and as his father taught him. Remember, the

---

52 Neltiliztli is the state of being well-rooted – truth, virtue, and authentic goodness. Denotes a life of meaning, balance, and coherence, where existence is deeply anchored and actions resonate in harmony with the world and one's community.

bow is not just a weapon. Through it you express your spirit and your will.

Father demonstrates, his movements fluid from years of practice. I am nervous, but I hold the bow my father made for me from the branch of a guava tree. Father says,

> Do not rush, my son. Feel the tension in the bow, it is your strength and courage gathering. Look at your target with intention. When you feel aligned, let your spirit release the bow string and see your arrow strike its target.

I practice every day, until I can hit my target with ease. Before long, my arrows can hit rats and mice near the chinampas. The farmers are pleased to have me practice there and help preserve their crops. As I grow stronger, my arrows can reach faraway targets. Every day my father observes me and teaches me new techniques. He tells me that he has never seen another who can shoot as accurately as me.

One afternoon, my father calls me to the edge of the reeds. He carries a long, feathered dart – *tlacochtli*[53] – and an *atlatl*,[54] a carved wooden shaft with a hook at the end.

"Today," he says, "you will learn the art of the atlatl. This is not a weapon of brute force, but of precision and timing. It is an extension of your arm, your will, your breath."

He shows me how to nest the tail of the dart into the cup of the atlatl, how to hold it steady, how to feel the weight and balance. "The tlacochtli must fly like a bird, not tumble like a stone. Let your body guide it. Let your spirit aim it."

I practice each day, learning to throw with speed and accuracy. At first, my darts wobbled and fall short. But my father is patient. He adjusts my stance, corrects my grip, and teaches me to breathe with the throw.

---

53 A long, flexible dart or javelin, often with an obsidian head. To increase stability in flight, the darts were fitted with fletching at the back, similar to an arrow.
54 A device used to throw javelins long distances.

Archer. Codex Mendoza

"When you fight," he says, "you will not have time to think. Your body must remember. Your dart must strike before your enemy sees it coming."

In time, my tlacochtli flies true – piercing bark, striking distant targets, and once, splitting a hanging gourd clean in two. My father smiles, his eyes proud. "You are ready," he said. "You carry the strength of our ancestors in your arm."

Some days, my father teaches Tezcacoatl and me to play the ball game, *ollamaliztli*. We spend many days playing the game, bouncing a rubber ball off our hips, elbows and knees, to pass it through a hoop. With my quick reflexes and agile moves, I can keep the ball in play while avoiding injury from the bigger and stronger players. I play daily, building my power and stamina. I learn strategies and direct my team-mates to outmaneuver our opponents. I feel my heart beat. I feel my legs fly through the air. I am bursting with vital energies.

Other days he takes me to the canals to teach me how to use a net to catch fish.

I like to be with my father when he's working in his jewelry shop. It smells of fire and earth. Father bends low, lips against the cane, breathing fire into the crucible until it glows like the heart of the sun.

"Silversmith. Son of the silversmith."
Father teaches son silversmithing. Codex Mendoza

Once he let me blow into the tube too. He shows me how he makes jewelry; how he melts gold, silver and copper. I watch the silver smoke rise from the furnace, curling up through the open roof like serpents reaching for the sky. Outside, the street hums with vendors and the clang of chisels. Inside, only Father's breath and the crackle of the fire speak.

Then two guards enter, and behind them walks a stranger. His cloak is simple, patched at the shoulder, his eyes weary but strong. His skin is darker than ours, his hair thick and bound with a woven band of red thread. When the guards leave, he bows low to Father, but his gaze moves to the crucible's glow, as if the fire were his old friend.

The man opens a bundle wrapped in maguey fiber and lays its contents on the table – stones, black and heavy, veined with threads that glimmer faintly green.

"From Coixtlahuaca," he says. "Ore of the red metal – *tepoztli tlatlauhqui*, referring to copper. It breathes fire differently than silver or gold. You must coax it, not force it."

Father lifts one of the stones. The green glint catches my eye.

"Arsenic," the stranger says softly, shaping the foreign word as if it cuts his tongue. "A spirit that bites."

Father nods, curious, respectful. "Teach me," he says.

I shift closer, heart pounding, wondering. The man breaks the ore into small pieces and crushes them with father's basalt hammerstone and sprinkles it into the crucible. A hiss rises — a sharp, bitter smell, not like silver's sweetness nor gold's honey warmth. I snatch a cloth from the bench and press it over my nose. The smell bites my throat, sharp as burning garlic. White smoke swirls like ghost-breath.

"Do not breathe it," the man warns. "Its spirit is jealous."

Father watches the color in the crucible change — from dull gray to a deep red glow, then to a shimmer of a golden sun. He murmurs a prayer to Xipe Tótec, flayer of the old, giver of new skin.

"This is how bronze is born," the man says. "Copper with the breath of arsenic. It sings when you hammer it, harder than copper, brighter than a shimmering lake."

He pours the molten metal into a small clay mold shaped like a bell. For a breath it burns red as living copper, then cools into a pale, silvery sheen, "brighter than any copper I've seen," says father. When the metal cools, the man breaks the mold away, leaving a bright shining bell. Then he strikes it — tink! — a clear note leaps into the air, sharp, like the cry of a bird in morning air.

My father smiles, "It sings," he says with delight.

"Yes," says the man. "Each bell carries a breath of the mountains where the ore was born. It remembers the deep places."

I reach out, wanting to touch the bell, but Father stops me. "It's still hot," he says.

Still, I can feel its song in my chest long after the sound fades.

The man sits beside the furnace, staring into its glow. "In Coixtlahuaca," he says, "we smelt this metal under the eyes of the god of earth's breath. When we lost our city, we carried its fire within us. Now that fire will serve the Mexica."

Father inclines his head. "Not serve," he says. "Live. The fire has found a new home."

I look at the two of them — the stranger and my father — faces lit by the furnace. One brings the mountain's ore; the other, the city's skill. Between them, the fire breathes, alive, hungry, and bright as the sun.

That night, when I lie awake, I still hear the bell's echo.

It sounds like the promise of something new – the song of *tepoztli tlatlauhqui*,[55] the red metal with a silver sheen that remembers its mountain heart.

d. The House of Knowledge

ADMISSION TO THE CALMECAC

My father is proud of me and recognizes my potential. He decides to do everything he can to help me advance. He tells me, "My son, your heart is steady and your breath flows cleanly. May you enter the Calmecac, may you honor our ancestors."[56]

Father discusses his wishes with his noble patron, Tlamacazqui Tlacaelel of the Tenochtitlán Calmecac School.[57] He had seen me with my father many times and enjoyed quizzing me as he did his students. I have made him laugh because none of his students could solve his riddles as quickly and as well as I could. He has noticed my good manners and praised my intellect. The tlamacazqui says, "This boy's heart is not of common wood. It is jade, it is turquoise. He is worthy." Thus, at age ten, he admits me to the prestigious Tenochtitlán Calmecac School, a rare honor for a macehualli (commoner).

ⱫⱫⱫⱫⱫ

That night, my father gathers our neighbors and friends to celebrate. The sky is clear and the stars are brilliant. Father builds the fire as neighbors gather in our courtyard. He commences, saying,

> Tomorrow, our son Huitzilin commences his studies at the Tenochtitlán Calmecac School. [*The people murmur loudly.*]
> Tonight is a time to celebrate. [*The people cheer.*]

---

55 Tepoztli means metal, tlatlauhqui means fire red.

56 A school of advanced learning for children of the noble class

57 Tlamacazqui is a priest, title for the most educated members of the nobility who perform religious rites and ceremonies or who have charge of important institutions.

Just then, a man from our calpulli stands and asks my father for permission to tell a story. Father is pleased to give him the floor. The man rises to address the gathering and speaks,

> I will tell the story of Princess Chimalxochitl, (Shield Flower) daughter of Huehue Huitzilihuitl who was our leader before we arrived in Tenochtitlán.
>
> Our people wandered. Our people waited. Our people endured, searching for a home for many *xiuhmolpilli*[58] until Heuhue Huitzilihuitl brought them to Chapultepec Mountain. At that time, the Tepanecs of Azcapotzalco dominated the western shore of Lake Texcoco where Chapultepec sits.
>
> At first the Azcapotzalcah accepted our presence but then, in the time of the burning reed, in the shadow of Chapultepec, beneath the gaze of the gods they grew fearful of our growing power and turned against us. Culhuacan in the south and Xaltocan in the north likewise grew fearful. The three city-states attacked. From the west they came. From the south they came. From the north they came and swiftly destroyed our Mexica settlement, expelling our people from Chapultepec Mountain in year 1299.
>
> Coxcoxtli, the Colhuah king, immediately executed Huehue Huitzilihuitl and his first-born daughter and banished our people to Tizaapan, a barren land, making us his vassals. [*Now the crowd becomes restive.*]
>
> The sole remaining descendant of the Mexica ruler was the beautiful Princess Chimalxochitl (Shield Flower). Instead of executing her, Coxcoxtli paraded her naked through the streets of his cities as a public humiliation of the Mexica.
>
> They brought her back to Colhuacan, still naked and tied her to a stake in the central square before King Coxcoxtli, the high priest and the Colhua people, who snickered and laughed. Then the princess spoke, "I am Chimalxochitl, I am the Shield and the Flower of the Mexica."
>
> When she spoke her name, the Colhua warriors fell silent. "We cannot burn her," the priest murmured. "She bears the shield of protection, war and divine favor. She bears the flower of truth,

---

58. Xiumolpilli literally means «the binding of the years,» referring to the 52-year cycle of the Mexica calendar. A concept similar to our use of the term "century."

beauty and the breath of ancestors. A person who embodies both is marked by destiny, favored by the gods. Her spirit is powerful. If we burn her, we take her spirit into our hands. Her spirit will not leave; it will turn against us and bring imbalance and ancestral vengeance. Do not let her spirit rest in our hands. This death is not ours to command.

She remained there for many days, waiting. Chimalxochitl painted half her body with black charcoal, invoking Tezcatlipoca, god of the smoking mirror who brings power and divine protection. She painted her other half with white chalk, a symbol of purity, death, and spiritual readiness. Then, speaking to the Colhuah people she said,

> *"I am here.*
> *I am tied to this stake.*
> *I am ready. Why do you hesitate?*
> *What do you fear?*
> *You Colhuahs only dishonor yourselves by delaying.*
> *Have you no courage?"*

Finally, at the Princess' command, a Mexica warrior stepped forward and lit the pyre. As the logs crackled and popped, and the flames shot up her legs, Chimalxochitl stood tall and spoke her final words,

> *"I stand as the flower of the shield.*
> *I burn as the offering of my people.*
> *Let the smoke rise to the heavens.*
> *Let the fire speak my name!*
> *"O people of Colhuahcan, I go now to live in the house of the gods.*
> *The Mexica will rise again, great warriors and will reign victorious*
> *over you.*
> *You will see!"*

Voices among the Mexica warriors can be heard in prayer,

O Tezcatlipoca, you who see through smoke, witness her courage. O Tlaltecuhtli, earth goddess who drinks the blood of sacrifice, receive her spirit.

Thus, we remember. Thus, we teach. Thus, we walk the path of our ancestors. Our women are strong – like flowers with obsidian stems. Their beauty is not fragile, but sacred. They bloom in the sun, they bleed in the storm, and still they stand. Like the shield-flower Chimalxochitl, they do not break – they burn, and in burning, they become eternal. Our people are warriors of destiny.

ƨƨƨƨƨ

CUAUHTLI'S HUEHUETLATOLLI[59]

At dawn, when the breath of Tonatiuh (the sun) warms the stones, before my first day of school, father summons me to remind me of the ancient counsel of our people, spoken as huehuetlatolli, as I take this next step. He says,

> Listen well my son, for now your path begins – not with your feet, but with your heart. You have been called to the Calmecac, where the wind carries the voices of gods and men alike. Do not mistake this for honor, this is a burden that you must repay.
>
> Do not become arrogant. Do not swell with pride.

I feel father's words in my heart. I want to speak, to promise – but I nod and stay silent. His words are not questions. They inform me.

> Remember: I, too, once carved jade with trembling hands and offered it in silence. Now the lords wear my work, but I still sweep the dust, I still fast before the gods.
>
> You will walk among the sons of warriors, priests, even the tlatoani's kin. You will learn their words, their law, their secrets.
>
> But know this: the flower opens, the song rises. They laugh in the wind, and vanish. Do not chase the laughter. Chase the root. Truth grows where no one watches.
>
> Speak with measured words. Sit with upright posture. And when others boast, be as obsidian, dark as night, still as death, sharp as truth. For pride will cut your own throat before it wounds another.

---

59. Huehuetlatolli, "the ancient words," refers to ceremonial discourses used in rites of passage, education, and state ceremony that preserved ancestral wisdom, ethical guidance, and the moral foundations of Mexica society. They articulated ideals of balance, humility, discipline, and proper conduct.

You are the hummingbird, Huitzilin – not to flutter, but to fly, swift, unseen, from blossom to blossom. Carry sweetness. Leave no wound. Take only what the gods allow.

Go now. Kneel before your teachers as before the gods. Offer copal to the ancestors. Let the smoke rise to the heavens. And walk always with your eyes upon the mirror that smokes, where truth hides and destiny waits.

I bow my head. I do not speak. I see the mirror in my mind – dark, swirling, endless. I do not know what waits inside it. But I will walk toward it. *"I will carry sweetness, father. I will not chase the wind."* My words feel strange in my mouth – but true. I will remember.

⊇⊇⊇⊇⊇

ATTENDING THE CALMECAC

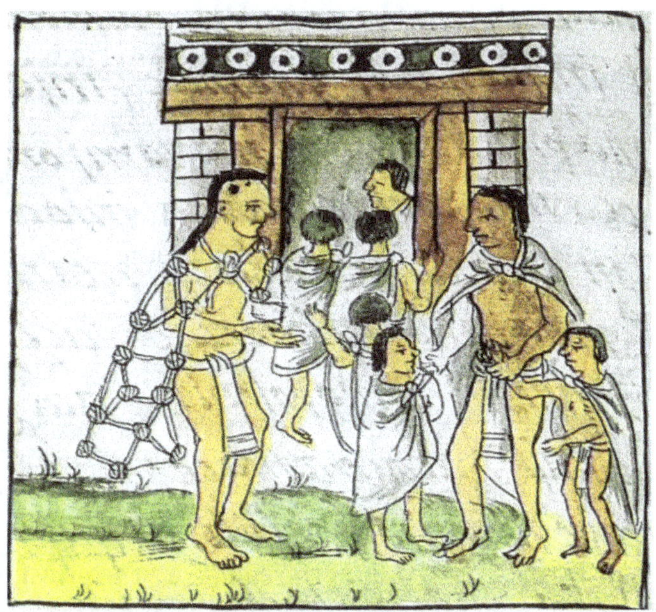

Tenochtitlán Calmecac School. The knotted cape indicates his preeminent position and authority within the school. Florentine Codex III Med. Palat. 218, f. 232v

At dawn, I step into the Calmecac for the first time. My heart trembles. My breath shallow. Around me, sons of noble houses walk with quiet pride. I am not one of them – but I have been called to this sacred house, where knowledge is revered. The halls are thick with the scent of copal. Priests chant in voices that rise like smoke.

I sit cross-legged upon a woven mat. Before me lies amatl paper,[60] soft as skin, waiting. I dip the reed brush into black ink and begin to copy the sacred glyphs – each stroke a prayer, each symbol a story. My teacher, a priest with eyes sharp as obsidian, watches in silence, then speaks with measured breath to convey the deepest meaning.

In these first days at the Calmecac, I'm unsure of my place among these noble boys. Not all welcome me. One boy, a noble much bigger than me, never calls me by my name. Instead, he sneers "macehualli," (commoner) as if the word itself were dirt. He mocks my clothes, my speech, my family. I try to ignore him, but the sting remains. I am ten years old, and I learn quickly that knowledge is not the only test in the Calmecac – dignity must be defended, even in silence.

One of the students I meet is Ahuitzotl, a few years older than me. He is popular, known for his sharp wit, laughter and fierce spirit, yet he greets me with warmth. He shows me where to hang my cloak, which priests to avoid. We become friends and teammates in the ollamaliztli games, where we learn to move as one – reading each other's thoughts, trusting each other's steps. Ahuitzotl's friendship steadies me. He treats me not as a commoner, but as a companion. And in the quiet spaces between lessons and games, a bond is forged that will shape both our paths.

I hear whispers that he is the grandson of Huey Tlatoani Motecuzoma I. I meet his younger brother, Axayacatl just a year older than me but I don't see him much. He is stronger than all the others, faster too. His fire burns hot for military campaigns and eagerly joins every battle that comes.

At the start of my second year at the calmecac, the priest orders us to attend class the next morning in the eighth hour of the night.[61] We meet not at the calmecac, but on an elevated platform near the Huey

---

60 Bark paper
61 The time before dawn

Teocalli.[62] Facing the eastern sky, just above the horizon, we see Venus, brilliant, rising, portending the arrival of the sun. Our priest stands with arms outstretched and says,

> Children of the calmecac, lift your eyes to the east.
> Behold *Tlahuizcalpantecuhtli*, Morning Star, Lord of the Dawn, whose dart pierces the sky. [63]
> He rises before the Sun, fierce and demanding, a sign that blood must feed the day.
> Count his days, mark his vanishings, for in his fire lies the rhythm of war and renewal.
> Forget not: the heavens speak, and we must answer.

Following the priest's instructions, I use a maguey spine to pierce my tongue. Others pierce their ears or thighs. I let my blood drip onto a special white cloth which the priest gathers with all the others, and sets ablaze on the basalt stone platform, thus delivering our offerings to the gods. The priest speaks again,

> O Tonatiuh, radiant Sun, we have torn ourselves to give you precious water.
> Accept these drops, accept this fire, that you may rise strong and carry the day.

Over my years at the calmecac, I learn the language of the gods. I master the writing of Náhuatl, the calendar wheels, the stars, the maize cycles, the histories of fire and stone. I study the paths of the sun, the count of days, the secrets of water and earth. But it is in the shaping of stone, the lifting of beams, the joining of canals and temples that stirs my spirit. I find joy in the art of building – where thought becomes form and form becomes the answer.

---

62 The main temple in the center of Tenochtitlán "Great House of God," (Templo Mayor).

63 Venus

In my last year at the calmecac, I enter the warrior's path. Jaguar warriors teach me the silence of the stalk. Eagle warriors teach me the strike from above. I learn to wield obsidian blades, to read the wind, to lead with breath and blood. This training is not for glory – it is for duty. For one day I must defend my people, my gods and the memory of those who walked before.

ⵣⵣⵣⵣⵣ

I am eighteen years old when I complete my education, and am ready to begin my compulsory military service, but before I do, I have other duties to fulfill.

III
1468, Huitzilin, the Young Man

a. Teoxochitl, My Divine Flower

It is year 1468 and my parents invite friends and neighbors to our home to celebrate the occasion of my graduation. When the festivities wind down, my mother calls me to her room for a talk. She says,

Huitzilin, my dear son, listen to me – listen with your heart, not just your ears. You are a man whom the gods have touched and our ancestors have blessed. But your gifts are not yours alone – they are entrusted to you by the divine and by our Mexica blood.

Now, as you begin your life as a man, your path turns. You have duties to the gods who have blessed you, and to our Mexica people who need you. You must walk not only for yourself, but for those who will come after.

Our ancestors have whispered to me: it is time to find a spouse for you to plant the seed of lineage, to bind your name to the future.

There is one I wish you to meet. Her name is Teoxochitl,[64] named for the ethereal flower and celestial beauty. She is beautiful, yes, but more than that, she is wise, her thoughts are measured, her speech is clean, her manners are like polished jade. She has been raised with reverence, taught the ways of the home and the temple. She is the daughter of Tezcatl,[65] a *tequihua* warrior whose obsidian blade has sung in battle and whose name is

---

64 Tēoxochitl means "divine flower." a name that evokes beauty offered to the gods, sacred femininity, and the power of sacrifice. Pronounced, Tehh-ohh-SOH-cheetl.

65 Tezcatl refers to obsidian mirror, associated with god Tezcatlipoca. It implies a powerful and insightful person.

spoken with respect.[66] From such roots, strong branches grow. I see in her *the flower and the shield, the song and the silence.*[67]

Consider her, my son – not as a prize, but as a partner. Not as duty, but as destiny. The gods do not give lightly, and neither do I.

Under mother's aegis, our two families gather for a feast in our courtyard. It is a formal occasion. The air smells of copal and roasted maize. All members of my family are present and I kneel beside my mother. My heart is steady – not with excitement, but with readiness. I accept mother's guidance. I accept the will of our ancestors.

Teoxochitl enters with her father, Tezcatl. I do not stare. I observe. She walks with measured steps, her gaze lowered, her hands folded like a priestess. Her hair is braided with red thread; her tunic embroidered with hummingbirds and obsidian flowers. Her posture is upright. Her silence is not timid – it is composed. She does not glance at me, not at first. But when she does, her eyes meet mine without hesitation. They are dark, polished, reflective. I think of the mirror that smokes.[68]

I feel no fluttering in my chest. No fire. But I feel something else – alignment. She is not a stranger. She is a vessel, like me.

We speak briefly, in the presence of our elders. Her voice is soft, but her words are clear. She asks about my studies. I ask about her weaving.

We do not laugh. We do not touch. But we understand. I do not choose her. I accept her. And she accepts me.

I offer copal to the ancestors. I kneel before the hearth and whisper my vow – not of love, but of duty. I announce, "Let this union be a

---

66 *Tequihua* is the highest warrior rank primarily focused on military achievements and leadership in warfare, awarded to warriors who have captured at least four enemy for sacrifice, highly honored and respected in Aztec society.

67 In Nahua philosophy, xochitl (flower) symbolized beauty, fragility, and truth. Flowers were linked to poetry, the highest form of wisdom. The shield represented war, protection and martial duty. Song was sacred speech, poetry and chant. It was the way humans communicated with the divine. Silence implied restraint, discipline and reverence, the moment of awe before the gods.

68. The mirror that smokes is a mirror that is inhabited with divine power, not passive reflection, implying mystery and hidden truth.

bridge. Let our children carry the breath of both houses. Let her name be honored. Let mine be worthy."

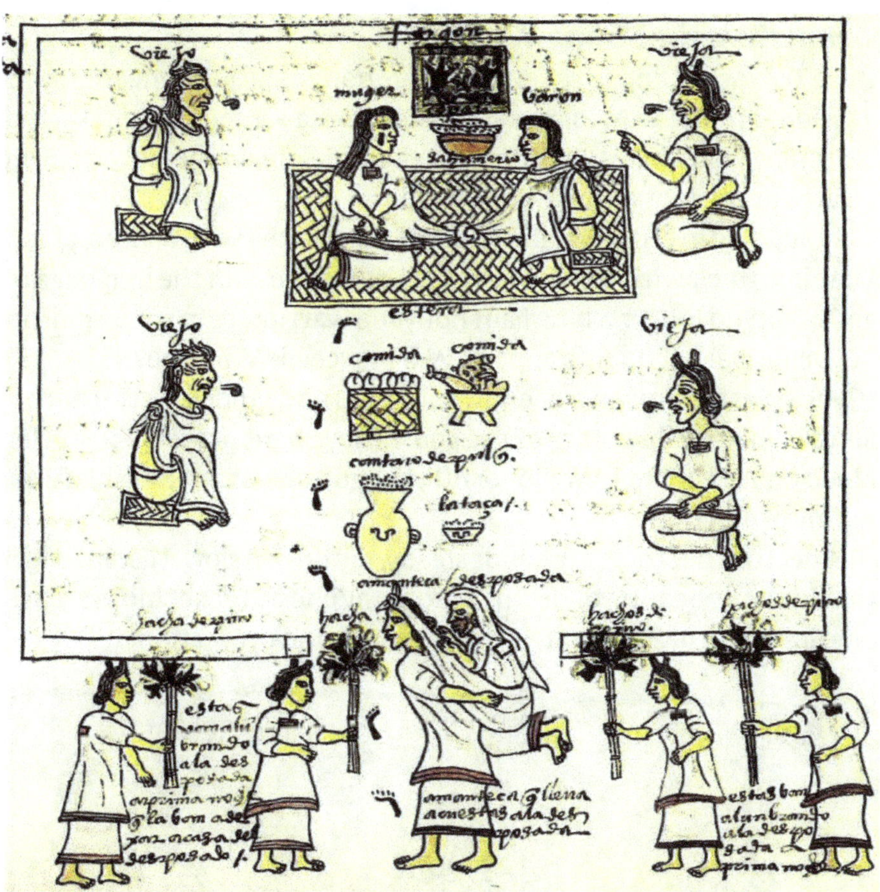

The Marriage Ceremony: The matchmaker (bottom center) carries the bride, symbolizing her dependence and the support of the community. The nighttime procession along the path from her family home to the groom's residence is lit by four attendants, each carrying a pine torch to light the way. The bride and groom sit on woven mats with their garments tied together symbolizing their union. Elders give advice and admonishments of obligations. A banquet follows. Codex Mendoza folio 61r

The wedding is elaborate, forming a permanent bond between our two powerful families. We receive Teoxochitl into our household with open hearts and rightful ceremony. She joins our lineage not as guest, but as thread in the weaving of our lives – cherished, honored, and upheld. Teoxochitl takes her place as a treasured pillar of our household, performing her duties and taking part in our joys and wellbeing, just as we are joined to her lineage as one.

b. Huitzilin, the Young Warrior

Once Teoxochitl and I are settled in our home, she joins me for my induction into the warrior ranks of the Mexica — a solemn and sacred ceremony held at the Cuauhxicalco, the circular ceremonial platform located at the foot of the Huey Teocalli.

I stand clad in ceremonial attire; my face painted with ochre and ash. The air is thick with copal. I hear the drums speak in the language of gods. I am no longer a boy. I am not yet a warrior. I am something in between. Dark thoughts appear. Will I succeed? Will I fail?

The priests who have been my mentors and guides, perform rituals to invoke the blessings of the gods. They chant prayers They offer blood and breath to Huitzilopochtli, the god of war, seeking his favor for my protection.

I kneel on the stone, my hands steady, my breath slow. I listen — I feel the rhythmic beating of drums echo in my chest. Teoxochitl watches. She does not speak. But I feel her presence and protection.

Merchants in battle array carrying macuahuitl, clubs with obsidian blades, and chimalli shields. Florentine Codex 9, Med. Palat. 219, f. 313v

Then, Tlacochcalcatl, the supreme military commander, second only to the tlatoani, steps forward. He places the *macuahuitl*[69] in my right hand, its obsidian blades flashing the fire of the sun. On my left arm, he straps a decorated but sturdy *chimalli*[70] . He places a finely carved *atlatl*[71] in my waist band. These weapons are not only tools of war – they are symbols of my new status and responsibilities.

During the ceremony, I must demonstrate my proficiency with these weapons. While I wait, my mind wanders. I recall a candidate last year who dropped his macuahuitl and was sent back to train for another cycle. He was shamed. His father was humiliated in front of the whole of Tenochtitlán.

I turn and see my parents, brothers and sisters and Teoxochitl watching – silent, expectant. I see hope and worry etched in their faces. I feel the weight of my family's honor in my hands. I dare not dishonor my ancestors. I dare not fail. My breath comes fast now. I grip my macuahuitl tight; sweat dripping from my palms onto its obsidian teeth. What if I fail? What if I dishonor my lineage?

The priest calls my name. I step forward. My sash is tight. My palms are wet, my throat dry. I kneel. I rise. I squeeze the handle of my macuahuitl in my wet hand. The chimalli on my arm. My atlatl fixed to my waist band. The drums slow. The air thickens.

I know this drill. I have done it a hundred times. But never here. Never before the Huey Teocalli. Never with the eyes of the elders, the priests, and my father upon me.

I begin. My feet move swiftly. My arms follow. My first strike is clean. The second – I slip, my heel catching the edge of a stone. My balance falters. It's only a moment in time when I feel my nagual right me. I hear nothing. No gasp. No whisper. Only the drum beating its cadence, like a heart refusing to break. I pivot and strike again. Harder. Truer. I finish with the atlatl, the dart flying clean into the woven target.

---

69 Wooden club embedded with sharp obsidian blades.
70 Shield adorned with symbolic designs.
71 Spear thrower

The priest nods. Tlacochcalcatl raises his hand. I bow. I do not smile. I rise to face the crowd. I think of Teoxochitl watching. I think of my father's words: "Be as obsidian – dark as night, sharp as truth." I have been named, armed, and watched. I slipped, but I did not falter.

I am now a proud member of the Mexica military force and I join my comrades, ready to defend our people and uphold the honor of our ancestors.

ↄↄↄↄↄ

The ceremony is complete, but my path is just beginning. I know the journey ahead will test me – not only my strength, but my spirit. I may fall in battle. I may be captured. I may be sacrificed on a foreign altar; my heart lifted to gods I do not serve. I may be eaten. But my duties tell me I cannot turn away.

I walk forward. My nagual walks beside me. The gods have marked me. My name has been spoken. I carry fear. I carry ambition. I carry the breath of my ancestors. I am ready.

To begin, I am a novice. Nothing at the Calmecac prepared me for this. On my first day, I rise before the sun and run without pause, barefoot across stone and reed, all morning long carrying weighted bundles – not for transport, but for transformation. Then, the entire afternoon I wield my macuahuitl, biting obsidian into wood. When my hands blister, I learn to breathe through pain, to walk without complaint, to sweat without shame. At day's end, I collapse, exhausted.

The next day is the same, I arise, my body aching from yesterday's drills. And so it goes, day after day, seemingly without end. Calluses grow on my hands and feet that I had never known before, but my nagual reminds me, "I can do this." I clench my jaw hard and continue.

After two thirteen-day periods, I train with weapons. The same ones my father taught me to use. I excel with all: bow and arrow, throwing tlacochtli with the atlatl, thrusting with the obsidian bladed spear.

I learn battlefield formations – how to flank, how to feint, how to capture without killing. Battlefield commanders teach the difference between chaos and strategy, between noise and signal. I memorize the signs of enemy rank, the meaning of banners, the logic of terrain.

Novice warrior joining the ranks, carrying an obsidian tipped lance and other gear. Codex Mendoza folio 63. ©

During this training, I go without comfort, without praise, without certainty. I eat sparingly, sleep lightly, and endure mockery from seasoned warriors.

I feel my strength grow, my spirit harden. I am not yet one of them. But I am no longer who I had been.

During the early years of military service, I am called to duty, only during the dry season, from October through May when we engage in military campaigns. In the wet season, we return home to attend to our usual occupations and to serve the gods, the people and the memory of those who came before.

೭೭೭೭೭೭

On the longest day of the sun's journey, summer solstice, I return home to be with my wife Teoxochitl and my family. Brother Tezcacoatl is also just returned from trading in distant lands. This day also marks the completion of my first campaign cycle. I tell my family, "I have not yet engaged in combat, but I have marched. I have endured hunger, heat, and silence. I have stood in formation beneath the burning copper sun without bending. My commanders know my name; I have earned their trust, with discipline, endurance and loyalty."

I see my father rise. His eyes glisten, but he does not weep. He places his hand on my shoulder, firm and warm. "You have returned with your name intact," he says. "That is no small thing. You have not yet drawn blood, but you have earned the breath of warriors. You have upheld our family honor. I am proud."

He turns to Tezcacoatl, who stands beside me, his cloak still dusted with the colors of distant markets. "And you, my son of the road – you have crossed rivers and mountains, spoken in tongues not your own, and returned with honor. Tomorrow, we feast for both of you."

Tezcacoatl clasps my forearm, his grip firm, and I grasp his. "You march with warriors," he says. "I trade in far away places. But we both walk the path of the Mexica."

I nod. "And we both return with stories."

He says, "You know, little brother, when you left, Mother prayed you'd return a warrior. I prayed you'd return at all. And here you are – both of us win." We laugh heartily into the night sharing with our family tales of our adventures. Meanwhile, mother is already busy preparing for the next day's festivities.

⌇⌇⌇⌇⌇⌇

The morning sun rises victorious from its nightly battle against darkness. Huitzilopochtli has vanquished his celestial siblings, the stars and the moon, in his endless war for the sky. Brilliant golden rays cast long shadows across the courtyard. The air smells of damp earth and roasted maize. Women from our calpulli arrive early, their arms full of squash, beans, and wild turkey. Men build the fire pit, sharpen obsidian blades and hang woven banners that ripple in the light breeze like ancestral breath.

Mother oversees the grinding of cacao. Sister Xochitl presents her latest creation, a large, feathered shield with the image of white herons fishing on a lakeshore – symbols of Aztlan, where our people's journey began, where the gods first whispered our name. Teoxochitl weaves fresh flowers into the altar cloth, her fingers steady, her silence reverent, summoning visions of her ancestors. We all don our finest ceremonial garments, each embroidered with the glyph of our calpulli – a hummingbird in flight, its wings outstretched toward the rising sun.

Honored guests begin to arrive – elders, warriors, traders, and priests. Teoxochitl's father Tezcatl arrives with his family. My brother Tezcacoatl stands beside me as we greet each guest with a bow and a word of thanks. I feel their eyes linger on us with expectation. I feel the weight of a mantle I must carry.

When the sun reaches its zenith, a *quiquiztli* (conch shell blower) blows a deep, resonant tone – low and ancient, like the call of gods stirring in the sky.

Drummers from our calpulli begin – not loud, but steady. The *huehuetl*[72] speaks first with a deep reverent tone, then the *teponaztli*[73] answers, sharp and clear like stones bouncing on the temple floor. The rhythm is not for dancing. It is for remembering.

Father rises to welcome all. He speaks of his devotion to his family and his gratitude for the gifts the gods have bestowed on him, his children. Tezcatl rises to thank our family for the respect and kindness we have shown Teoxochitl and his family.

Then our calpullec, Teyacanqui,[74] steps forward, his hair white with age. His cloak is embroidered with the glyphs of our lineage. His voice is clear, but not hurried. He does not speak to entertain. He speaks to bind and says,

---

72 A vertical skin drum, similar to a conga drum, used for deep, resonant beats.

73 A horizontal drum made of hollowed wood with an "H" slit, played with mallets, producing melodic rhythms.

74 Teyacanqui means he who is at the forefront, or, a leader of people. In this case, he is the calpullec of Cuahutli's calpulli.

Huitzilin, you have returned with honor. You have not yet drawn blood, but you have endured. You have stood where warriors stand. And so, on this longest day, let us remember the story that made our standing possible...

The courtyard falls silent. Even the fire seems to still. Calpullec Teyacanqui raises his cup – not to drink, but to offer. "To those who came before, whose blood became our breath, whose silence became our song." He continues,

> Let us remember the story of the flayed princess – for it was through her sacrifice that our people rose. And through your service, Huitzilin, we rise still.
>
> I am reminded of a story that attests to our adherence to our religious obligations and the strength and perseverance of our people.
>
> It happened in the year 1323. We were living as vassals in the barren lands of Tizaapan, a place of black stones and snakes, where the wind carried more silence than song, but a home all the same. Grateful, we served Culhuacan faithfully, proving ourselves as warriors and hunters.
>
> But we Mexica were not content to remain vassals, or to be known as uncivilized Chichimecs. We sought to be recognized as descendants of the great cultured Toltec civilization. Culhuacan was a city with Toltec heritage, and by ritually merging with its royal line – not through marriage, but through sacred offering – the Mexica could claim the mantle of the revered Toltecs, elevating our own status from wandering outsiders to legitimate heirs of civilization.
>
> And, so, the time came when our priests, following the will of Huitzilopochtli, sought to bind our people to Tollan through sacred blood.[75] The priests approached the new Tlatoani of Culhuacan, Achitometl, with a request: "Give us your daughter, most beautiful among women, that she may become a god-

---

75 Tollan ("Place of Reeds"), capital of the legendary Toltec civilization, was remembered as the cradle of high culture, divine artistry and sacred knowledge. It was a model of ideal rulership, where gods, artisans, and wise leaders shaped the world. To invoke Tollan was to claim descent from this legendary center of cultural and political legitimacy.

dess among the Mexica and be our queen, wife of our god, and mother of a new people." Achitometl agreed, believing his daughter would marry our leader and rule over the Mexica as our queen. But we did not seek heirs – we sought gods. Through the blood of Culhua royalty, we bound ourselves to Tollan, not by birth, but by sacrifice.

She was brought to Tizaapan, adorned in finery, prepared for a great ceremony. But our priests, obeying ancient rites of renewal and the voice of Huitzilopochtli, sacrificed her. Her body was flayed, and a priest donned her skin, enacting the sacred mystery of life's renewal, shedding old skin to allow for the new. Her skin was not desecration – it was transformation. The priest who wore it did not mock her, he became her. She was no longer daughter of Achitometl – she was Yaocihuatl, goddess of warriors, bride of the god.

During Tlacaxipehualiztli, the festival of sacrifice and renewal, Achitometl was invited to witness the celebration. He entered the temple, incense thick in the air, and there, before all, he saw the priest dancing in the skin of his beloved daughter. In that moment, horror and rage filled his heart. Realizing what had been done, Achitometl called his warriors to arms, and the Colhuah, joined by others, attacked the Mexica.

Driven from Tizaapan, our people fled into the marshes and reeds of Lake Texcoco, using shields as rafts, exiled once more. Once again wandering. But from this suffering, we learned endurance. We remember the lesson of the flayed goddess: from death comes new life, and from loss, renewal. Her sacrifice was not the end – it was a beginning. And so we rose, not with crowns, but with memory.

The courtyard is silent. I feel the story settle into my bones. I've heard the story before. We all have. It's sung in the schools, told during Tlacaxipehualiztli, whispered by the elders. But today, with my wife seated beside me, it feels heavier. I do not flinch. But I do not smile. I think of Teoxochitl's silence. I think of her father.

I think of the priest who wore the princess's skin and became her. Did he believe the Culhua king would see divinity in the flayed skin of his daughter? He did not. Did he believe the gods would shield us from consequence? They did not. We were nearly undone. We fled into the marshes, into the reeds, into exile.

That is not triumph. And yet the story is told not with shame, but with pride.

They say she became our queen – wife of our god, mother of our people. They say her death was not desecration, but offering. That from her skin, we inherited not disgrace, but Tollan descent. I do not know if she became goddess.

But I hear the echo of Calpullec Teyacanqui's words, "From this suffering, we learned endurance . . . Her sacrifice was not the end – it was a beginning." I know the truth. From the mud, we rose. We built Tenochtitlán. Today, we Mexica are feared. The world knows we obey Huitzilopochtli without hesitation. We offer blood, breath, bone. Not because he is kind. Because he is ours.

Perhaps that is the lesson. Not that the gods are just – but that they are *real*. And we are bound to them, not by comfort, but by covenant. We do not worship Huitzilopochtli because he is gentle. We worship him because he rose from Coatepec with fire in his hands and silence in his heart.[76] Because he fights every night so the sun will rise. Because without him, we are nothing but reeds in the lake.

c. 1469, Huey Tlaotani Axayacatl[77]

Moctezuma Ilhuicamina,[78] Huey Tlatoani since 1440, is dead.

On this day in 1469, I walk along the chinampas and muse – *Moctezuma Ilhuicamina has ruled since before I drew breath. Now he is gone, and the throne stands exposed–its shadow long, its weight contested.*

---

76. Coatepec, serpent mountain, is the sacred birthplace of Huitzilopochtli, the place where he defeated his sister Coyolxauhqui and his 400 brothers, establishing the cosmic order of Sun, Moon, and stars.

77 Huey Tlatoani, "great speaker," is the title given to the Aztec emperor who presides over all allied city-states.

78 Commonly known as Moctezuma I. His name, "Motecuhzoma" means "He who frowns like a lord," or "The solemn ruler."

As I pass the canals, I worry–there are many heirs from different mothers, each with their own faction, each pulling at the mat and throne.

When I reach the Tenochtitlán marketplace I hear voices around me grumbling, "We have shared our island with our brothers, the Tlatelolca for many generations,[79] now Moquihuix, their tlatoani, wants his brother to rule over our empire."

Another answers, "The mat and throne belong to the sons of Acamapichtli.[80] From his branches we choose the one whose heart is strongest."

Then I see Ahuitzotl, my beloved friend from the calmecac. We greet with joy and he tells me, "The Tlatocan–the council of lords who choose the Huey Tlatoani–is meeting. The lords fear Moquihuix is coming. They seek a warrior king, one who can carry Moctezuma's military power, his readiness. A young, aggressive, war-ready tlatoani who shows no fear. My younger brother Axayacatl has that strength, that fire, that vision to lead Tenochtitlán. I will support him above all others."

We walk together toward the Sacred Precinct, toward the wide courtyard before the Huey Teocalli. As we arrive, a voice rises above the crowd: "Huey Tlatoani Axayacatl!"

The decision is made. Axayacatl–Face of Water–just nineteen years old, now rules the empire. He speaks for Tenochtitlán and for all allied altepetls of the empire.[81] I know Axayacatl from our years in the calmecac. I know the size of him, the courage in him, the way he steps forward without hesitation. He will be a strong leader.

Tenochtitlán is jubilant. "He is young," people say. "He does not fear beginning."

There is calm on the surface, but troubled waters swirl deep beneath, as Moquihuixtli believes Axayacatl is a child and below him.

---

79 Since 1337

80 The first Tlatoani of Tenochtitlán.

81 Altepemeh is the plural of "altepetl," a city-state. Altepetl is the most commonly recognized form of the word, so for ease, I choose to use altepetl consistently and "altepetls," when referring to the plural.

He feels disrespected and does not attend the *Tlatocaxtiliztli*, crowning ceremony. His absence is not silence. It is defiance. And it will echo.

d. 1472: Heartbreak: Nezahualcoyotl and Teoxochitl

NEZAHUALCOYOTL, PHILOSOPHER KING

Nezahualcóyotl, Codex Ixtlilxóchitl, folio 106r

It is the fourth day of the sixth moon, the year, 1 Reed, 1472.[82] The morning is quiet, as if the world itself holds its breath. Teoxochitl is grinding cacao, her movements easy, deliberate. I'm with my father

---

82 June 4, 1472

in his studio. A messenger arrives – his cloak is torn. He rushes to my father's side, kneels breathing hard and whispers the words. My father's face hardens. He turns to me.

"Nezahualcoyotl is dead."

My jaw drops. I can not speak. I walk outside, past the courtyard, past the garden. I fall to my knees beneath the ahuehuetl tree,[83] its roots holding the earth's memory. Teoxochitl follows, silent. She places a hand on my shoulder. I cry – not for a king, but for the man who taught me that even reeds think.

The Ahuehuete, Mexico's National Tree (https://theeyehuatulco.com/2020/06/29/ the-ahuehuete-mexicos-national-tree/). This photo is of a single tree.

The rites are swift. His body is prepared. The call goes out throughout the empire to attend the solemnities. I accompany my father and Calpullec Teyacanqui, travelling by boat to Texcoco. The lake is still, its surface unbroken, as if mourning with us.

Copal smoke curls upward in slow spirals, thickening the air with sadness. The breath of the gods ripples the banners of mourning. I stand in the sacred precinct beside my father and our calpullec near the front of the Tenochca delegation.

---

83 Ahuehuetl trees have the largest trunks of any tree in the world, measuring over 55 feet in diameter. One Ahuehuetl is believed to be 23,150 years old.

Before me lies the body of Nezahualcoyotl beneath a woven shroud, surrounded by offerings of maize, jade, and poetry. Huey Tlatoani Axayacatl stands weeping next to the body. I see rulers from all of the nearby city-states among the mourners. There are priests in feathered cloaks, warriors in ceremonial armor and scribes with sharpened reeds.

The ceremony begins. Elders chant verses from Nezahualcoyotl's poems. A priest recites his lineage. A scholar from Texcoco speaks of his dyke, his laws, his temple to the Unknown Lord. Then, a hush. A murmur. The next speaker – an aged diplomat from Tenochtitlán – has collapsed on his way to the podium, overcome by heat and grief.

Axayacatl signals Calpullec Teyacanqui to speak in his place. But Teyacanqui turns to me. His voice is low. He tells me, "You know his words. You know his spirit. Speak your heart, Huitzilin. Go."

I am shocked but I keep my face fixed like stone. My breath stops. I have not prepared to make a public address before all the world's leaders. My father nods. I feel my nagual nudge me, I have been called, it is my duty. The priests part. The drums pause. I step forward. I do not know what I will say. But I know who I must be.

I climb the steps to the ceremonial platform where Nezahualcoyotl rests. His body lies upon a carved stone bier, surrounded by offerings – maize, jade, feathers and folded poems. The most distinguished leaders of the land are gathered on the dais: tlatoanis, priests, generals, and sages. Their faces are solemn. Their eyes fixed on me.

When I reach the top platform and stand beside the bier, I see the body and fall to my knees in a moment of grief. I rise and place a flower upon the shroud and speak to Nezahualcoyotl.

> May your tonalli return to the sun. May your teyolia walk the flower-strewn path to the House of Song. May your ihiyotl linger in the breath of your verses, in the silence of your temple, in the hearts of those who still listen.

I bow to the assembled leaders – first to Huey Tlatoani Axayacatl, then to the priests of Texcoco, then to the elders of Tlacopan and Tenochtitlán.

I turn to the gathered mourners below the platform. The drums fall silent. The air thickens with copal and expectation.

Then I begin.

I do not cry for a king. (As I speak these words, I hear my own voice. It is not raised, though loud enough to be heard. I speak as if whispering to the dead.)

I cry for the tonalli that burned bright in his brow – his destiny, his solar fire, his will to rise.

I cry for the teyolia that pulsed in his heart – his wisdom, his memory, his voice that questioned even the gods.

I cry for the ihiyotl that moved through his breath – his passions, his presence, his power to draw others near.

These were not fragments. They were a constellation – his soul mapped across the heavens. And now, that constellation has dimmed.

He built a temple to the Unknown, Unknowable Lord of All. It stood empty – No idols. No blood. Only silence. And in that silence, he found truth – not in conquest, but in contemplation.

In his poem, *The Origin of Songs*, Nezahualcoyotl lamented,

I recall that I saw it there, in the land of flowers, I the singer.
And I now stand here, upon the earth and I reflect
and my heart-spirit cries out:
"Perhaps there is no happiness here on the earth.
Perhaps somewhere else,
in the land of abundant joy is where true wisdom resides.
What indeed is there here on earth?
Perhaps for just a moment may we live in the heavens where life thrives.
Let me go there;
let me sing there among the many precious birds.
Let me learn there among the fragrant flowers,
that gently capture people's hearts,
and softly refreshes and perfumes them,

that I may learn what brings joy to the heart,
that gently intoxicates with sweetness, with fragrance.[84]

I pause, breathe deeply and look up, searching the heavens while I wipe a tear. I look back to the gathered and continue,

And now, he has gone there
where the precious birds sing,
where the fragrant flowers bloom in the land of abundant joy.
May he walk among the shimmering dew,
where the sun's rays sparkle beneath the rainbow mist,
where the sacred songs never cease.
May he gather beauty in the folds of his cloak.
His voice is no longer bound to earth,
it rises in the wind,
in the petals,
in the silence between verses.

The drums do not resume and silence drifts through the air like a mist over still water. I touch Nezahualcoyotl's bier once more, the woven mat cool beneath my fingers. I bow to Huey Tlatoani Axayacatl, his gaze steady, unreadable.

As I rise, I hear a Texcoco priest lean toward him and murmur, "When he spoke, I heard the voice of the heavens remembering our king."

Beside him stands Ahuitzotl, cloaked in obsidian feathers. He leans toward a general and whispers, "That one has a voice the gods might borrow."

In the shade of a jade parasol, a six year old child clutches his nurse's hand. He is Moctezuma Xocoyotzin,[85] son of Axayacatl. His eyes are wide, unblinking. He may not understand my words, but something in him knows he heard something special.

I turn to descend the steps moving slowly, quietly, unsure if my feet touch the stone. As I reach the ground, I hear quiet voices begin to stir.

---

84 Final stanza of *The Origin of Songs* by Nezahualcoyotl as interpreted by the author.
85 Xocoyotzin means "the younger one." He is later "Huey Tlatoani Moctezuma II," ruler of the empire at the time of Cortés' arrival.

When I rejoin my group, Calpullec Teyacanqui bows to me and places a hand on my shoulder. "You were not chosen by chance. You were recognized."

And somewhere in the crowd, a scribe begins to write.

FAMILY

Teoxochitl has two children during our marriage: a son, Cuauhtémoc, and a daughter, Xochiquetzal.[86] I am devoted to Teoxochitl and our children and cherish the time we spend together.

During the spring Toxcatl Festival, we join the procession through the streets of Tenochtitlán to honor Tezcatlipoca. I tell my son,

> He's the god who sees through smoke and mirrors. They say he watches the world through obsidian, dark as night and full of secrets. He is the god of change and tricks. The path might twist when you think it's straight.

Cuauhtémoc asks, "Why does Tezcatlipoca carry a mirror, papa?"

I smile. "So he can see what people are thinking. His mirror shows not just faces, but feelings. Tezcatlipoca sees the truth, even when we don't say it out loud, even when we try to hide it."

As we pass through the Tlatelolco Marketplace, we marvel at the stalls filled with goods from all over the empire. Vendors speaking a variety of dialects sell exotic goods from faraway lands. There are food vendors everywhere and the air is rich with the aromas of delicacies like spicy tamales, maize cakes, and roasted meats.

We stop to visit Cuauhtli's prestigious jewelry stall, where he displays his finest gold and silver pieces. His stall gleams with gold shaped like fire and feathers. I tell my son, "Even Huey Tlatoani Axayacatl wears your grandfather's pieces." Next, we see Xochitl's amanteca stall.[87] It's a garden of light – her feather mosaics dazzle the eyes and shimmer like the wings of gods.

At the ball court, we watch ollamaliztli, a ball game played throughout the land. Our four-year-old son, Cuauhtémoc, sits on my lap,

---

86 Precious flower
87 Amanteca is a feather artist.

while Teoxochitl who is enceinte with our third child, holds little Xochiquetzal. The children marvel at the excitement of the event.

Cuauhtémoc asks me "Did you ever win, papa?"

"Many times," I say. "But the best games weren't about winning. They were about flying."

"Did you ever hit the ball through the ring?"

"Once," I say, smiling. "And the crowd roared like jaguars."

"Were you fast like that player?"

"Faster," I laughed. "I ran like the wind over Lake Texcoco."

The grandeur of the arena and the skill of the players inspire us all, and we cheer enthusiastically.

1325 FOUNDING OF TENOCHTITLÁN

As the sun begins its climb, on this auspicious day, I turn to little Cuauhtémoc and say,

> Today is *Nahui Xochitl*,[88] Zenith Passage. It is the day when the sun stands directly above Tenochtitlán and casts no shadow at noon. It is a moment of perfect light, when even the gods seem to pause. Some offer flowers for lost children and ancestors. Others sing poems to the sun, honoring the fleeting beauty of life. But today, we will gather with others to remember the journey that brought our people here."

We join thousands of Tenochca in the central plaza at noon to hear the story of our city's birth – how the Mexica rose from exile to empire. The air is rich with the scent of copal and sweet blossoms, and the plaza hums with quiet reverence. The high priest, Tlamacazqui Quetzalcoatl Totec, ascends above the crowd. His voice carries like wind through maize – soft at first, then rising, touching every ear and heart:

> My dear beloved Tenochca,
> Today, beneath the sun that cast no shadow, we remember.

---

88 Nahui Xochitl ("Four Flower") is a sacred date in the Mexica calendar that corresponds to Zenith Passage in Tenochtitlán, July 26 – a day of cosmic balance, spiritual renewal, and ancestral remembrance.

We remember the footsteps of our ancestors, the pain of exile, the fire of hope.

We remember the journey from sacred Aztlan, across mountains crowned with ice, through deserts that burned our soles.

We remember the jaguar's growl, the serpent's hiss, the hunger that gnawed at our bones.

We were cast out from Chapultepec. We were driven from Tizaapan. We wandered, but we did not fall.

And when the gods tested our spirit, we answered with song, with prayer, with courage.

It was then, in 1325, that Tenoch rose – a priest, a guide, a voice in the dark. And on the marshes of Lake Texcoco, he saw the sign foretold by Mexitli: An eagle, noble and fierce, devouring a serpent atop a cactus, blooming from stone.

There, the gods spoke. There, the prophecy blossomed. There, our destiny would take root. We rejoiced.

But not all saw what Tenoch saw. As our people rejoiced, others watched from the shadows. Tepanec spies crept along the lake's edge, their eyes sharp, their hearts cold. They returned to Azcapotzalco, to the hall of Lord Tezozomoc.

His palace was cool and dim, its reed mats muffling the steps of messengers. A runner knelt at the edge of the dais, head bowed. Tezozomoc, cloaked in embroidered feathers, motioned for him to speak.

"My lord," the youth said, "I bring news from the southern marshes."

Tezozomoc's eyes narrowed. "Speak, and quickly."

"The Mexica gather at the lake's edge. Their priest points to a small island where eagles nest and cactus blooms."

One lord laughed. "That island is swamp. Let them have it. They'll sink before they rise."

But Tezozomoc did not laugh. He remembered the tales – how these foreigners had survived famine, exile, and war. How their priests spoke of visions and destiny. He saw not fools, but fire.

"They may be useful," he said. "But not to be trusted."

And so he granted them the island – muddy, reed-choked, and scorned by others. He thought it worthless. But we were a people shaped by hardship. We learned to endure where others faltered.

Our people did not see ruin; we saw destiny. We would build not because the land was generous, but because we had the fire.

The Azcapotzalca laughed, they doubted. "Let them sink," they said.

But we did not sink. We took the mud, the reeds, the shallow water, and with relentless will we made foundations. What others mocked, we transformed. What others dismissed, we claimed with labor and the stubborn strength that had carried us through years of wandering.

From that island of thorns and feathers, we built a city of stone and song. From exile, we forged empire. From silence, we summoned thunder. We are the children of the eagle and the cactus. We are the voice of the lake. We are Tenochtitlán.

CIHUATEOTL, "DIVINE WOMAN"

Four days after the death of Nezahualcoyotl, Teoxochitl's labor begins. The Tlamatlquiticitl, midwife, and her assistants rush in bringing water, medicinal herbs, supplies, and copal incense. They move Teoxochitl to the temazcal, which they prepare for birthing. A Tlamacazqui priest performs rituals, chants, and prayers for divine intervention to protect mother and child.

For several hours, she labors with no progress. The midwife gives her medications to relieve pain and to intensify and regulate her contractions. She gives Teoxochitl hypnotic and hallucinogenic herbs to support her positive birthing spirit, speaking to her with a divine voice, guiding her through movements meant to change the baby's position in the womb. After eight more hours, Teoxochitl grows weak, having lost much blood.

The priest returns to the temazcal where fate unfolds.

In the Temazcal sweat pours from our faces, from our bodies. The air is thick as grief. Teoxochitl lies before me, her breath shallow; her body trembles; her movements are softer with each breath. Her eyes fluttered open, then close again, as if she drifts between worlds. Blood pools beneath her, dark and silent.

The priest kneels beside her, his face solemn, his hands steady. He waves a fan of eagle feathers through the rising copal smoke, letting it drift over her brow, her chest, her womb. He whispers prayers,

O Tonantzin, Our Revered Mother;
O Cihuacoatl, Serpent Woman, patron of childbirth;
O Tlazolteotl, goddess of purification and transformation, hear me now.
Shield this brave woman with your breath.
Guide her through the flower-covered path.
Hold her spirit in your hands, as gently as you hold the sun.
If her journey must begin, let it be with honor.
If her life may yet remain, let it be with strength.

I watch as he touches her forehead with a bundle of maize, then her heart with a polished obsidian shard. His voice is low, rhythmic, like the beat of a distant drum. He is not pleading—he is preparing. Preparing her soul for its journey, should the gods call her home.

Teoxochitl's fingers twitch. Her lips move, but no sound comes. The priest leans close to her breath, murmuring sacred words I cannot hear. The copal smoke thickens. The fire dims. I feel the air shift, as if something unseen has left the room.

Then, I see it. Not with my eyes, but with something deeper. A stillness in her chest. A quiet release, a final expiration. The priest pauses, his hand hovering above her heart. He bows his head, places a flower beside her and whispers, "She ascends." Outside the temazcal a gentle rain begins to fall as if the heavens themselves weep and bless her passage.

Everyone gathers closely, straining for any sign of life, but there is none. Seeing this, those in the temazcal sob and cry.

I reach for her, cradling her body against mine. Her skin still warm, but her breath gone. My tears roll. I cry. After only four years of marriage, Teoxochitl and the child she was carrying are lost.

Others in the temazcal fall to their knees and cry. Members of our calli and calpulli[89] also appear, expressing their heartache and sorrow.

---

89 Home and neighborhood

The Tlamacazqui declares,

> Our dear Teoxochitl, a good and honorable woman leaves us today. Her body lies here now, an empty vessel. Teoxochitl fought the ultimate battle and met her fate like a heroic warrior while doing her duty for our people. Her courage and sacrifice will be remembered. Her spirit will guide and protect her family.
>
> Teoxochitl has crossed the flower-strewn path to the western realm. She is now a *cihuateotl*,[90] a divine woman, a warrior of the womb. Her spirit ascends, following the path of the White Cloud Serpent, the Milky Way, to *cihuatlampa*[91] the realm in the west where the sun sets. There, she will join other *cihuateteo*, divine spirits of women who gave their lives in childbirth, guiding the sun from its zenith to its setting.

We give Teoxochitl a ceremonial burial, reflecting her honored status. Her death in childbirth is a noble sacrifice. My family and our entire calpulli join me in mourning her heroic death. We pray to honor her spirit and ensure her safe passage to the afterlife, offering her spirit food, incense, and beautiful ornaments. Special prayers are recited to invoke the gods' blessings to guide her soul's ascent to cihuatlampa.

I am moved to recite a poem by our beloved, Nezahualcoyotl, philosopher king of Texcoco whom we mourned just four days before:

> *I, Nezahualcoyotl, ask this:*
> *Do we truly live on Earth?*
> *Not forever on Earth, only a little while here.*
> *Even jade is shattered, even gold is crushed,*
> *Even quetzal plumes are torn.*
> *Not forever on Earth, only a little while here.*
>
> *Like a painting, we will be erased.*
> *Like a flower, we will wither here on earth.*
> *Like plumed vestments of the precious bird,*

---

90 *Cihuātēotl* means woman-god, or divine woman. Its plural is *cihuateteo*.
91 *Cihuatlampa* is the realm where cihuateteo reside.

that precious bird with the agile neck,
we will come to an end.

I pause as mourners sob and wail loudly.

The flowers sprout, they are fresh, they grow,
they open their blossoms, and they are sweet-scented.
But they will not last forever,
they will wither.

I am intoxicated, I weep, I grieve,
I, the singer, am afflicted,
I am a weeper, I am a crier.
I am a bird of four hundred voices,[92]
I am a crier, I am a singer.
I am a weeper, I am a crier.

I tell our children we will honor Teoxochitl's memory through regular offerings and prayers at our family altar. We will honor her spirit every 52 days – on 1 Deer, 1 Rain, 1 Monkey, 1 House, and 1 Eagle – offering flowers, incense, and prayers to guide her journey. I remind them of her bravery and the honor she brings to our family, At this, the children tear in sadness and we all weep.

꒰꒰꒰꒰꒰

After one year passes, my daughter Xochiquetzal, who is now four years old, comes to me one evening and asks, "Where is mama? Is she too weak to come home? I tell her, "Call your brother and we will talk in the courtyard tonight about your mother."

That evening, my two children, members of our calpulli and all who knew and loved Teoxochitl come together to remember her. I want to tell my children stories to relieve their pain. I light the firepit in the center of the courtyard and all gather sitting cross-legged before the fire. I hold Xochiquetzal in my arms and I speak:

---

92 Mockingbird

One year ago, today, our dear Teoxochitl died in childbirth. Xochiquetzal asked me today where she has gone and asks if her mother is too weak to come home.

I say, dear heart, your mother lives with the gods. She is strong. She has the power to move the sun.

Dear Xochiquetzal, dear Cuauhtémoc, I know your hearts are heavy, as is mine. The light of Teoxochitl, your mother, has left our home. But her light will never go out. It lives on in each of us, in the lessons she taught and in the strength she showed us every day. Like so many Mexica women, she was a powerful force.

She faced the pain of childbirth with courage, just as she faced every challenge in her life. Remember this, my children: Mexica women are not weak. They are the backbone of our people, the givers of life and the keepers of our traditions.

Long ago, in the time before Tenochtitlán, our people lived on Chapultepec. We were becoming too powerful, so all the other city-states attacked us. Princess Chimalxochitl, (Shield Flower), a beautiful and strong woman, daughter of Huehue Huitzilihuitl, the second Mexica Tlatoani, was captured.

They stripped her of her garments and paraded her through the streets. But she did not weep. She did not beg. She stood tall, like a sunflower in the wind. She demanded to meet her fate with honor, to die as a warrior, not as a victim. And when they mocked her, even in her final moments, she spoke words that became a promise:

"You may break my body, but you cannot break my blood. My people will rise. My name will rise when yours is dust. My people will all become warriors. You will see!"

Xochiquetzal, you too will grow to be a strong and powerful woman just like your mother. Do not be afraid and you will hold up the empire just like Chimalxochitl did. Teoxochitl was a heroic woman a strong woman, like so many of our ancestors.

That evening we watch as Teoxochitl, in her divine form as a cihuateotl, helps carry the sun westward to its setting, and we remember.

IV
1468, Huitzilin, the Warrior

a. 1473, Tlatelolco

I begin my second year of military duties as a *telpochtli* (novice) as I have not yet seen battle. I am at the lowest rank, serving as shadow, helper, baggage handler carrying equipment, learning the basics of warfare by observation and participation in a support role.

The gods smiled on me and assigned me to assist renowned Jaguar Warrior, Tlaltequani, "earth eater," whose name conjures a supernatural beast with an unstoppable predatory force. He has the rank of *tequihuahqui*, senior captain, of the Jaguar Warriors and allied calli contingents, commander of the left-wing vanguard. He moves like wind through maize; speaks like fire beneath the earth — hidden, but fierce when stirred. He has many years of battlefield experience. I watch his moves, eager to absorb the rhythm of war. He becomes my mentor and I follow him closely.

MOQUIHUIXTLI'S PROVOCATIONS

We are conducting military drills in the plaza before the Huey Teocalli,[93] the sacred heart of our city, when a sudden commotion breaks the rhythm of our march. I observe our beloved, Princess Chalchiuhnenetzin,[94] running barefoot, breathless, dressed in the humble garb of a palace servant – rushing toward the royal palace. Her dignity stripped, her sorrow visible. Tlaltequani dispatches me and three others to escort the Tenochca Princess and attend to her

---

93 Templo Mayor
94 Her name means "Jade Doll."

needs. I escort her into the royal sanctum where her brother, Huey Tlatoani Axayacatl, appears. I bow my head as Chalchiuhnenetzin, wife of Moquihuixtli, Tlatoani of Tlatelolco, sobs and describes the maltreatment she has suffered at the hands of her husband. She tells Axayacatl:

> Moquihuixtli took all of my royal clothing and accoutrements that I brought when we married. He took the gifts you recently sent me.
> He made me stand naked with others, comparing our bodies. He said I am too thin and he prefers others.
> He demoted me to the status of household help. He beat me.
> He resents that you are Huey Tlatoani instead of his half-brother.
> He builds alliances with other altepetls.
> He vows to overthrow you.

Axayacatl is furious, and I feel the insult and anger too.

I return home to my family and calpulli to tell them what I have seen, but everyone is already aware of this unforgiveable insult by Moquihuixtli. They are shocked to hear that our princess, whose bloodline carries the honor of two Huey Tlatoanis, has been so mistreated.

Their marriage was meant to cement a bond of friendship between our two city-states, but Moquihuix is aggressive and arrogant. His cruelty is not just personal—it is political. His betrayal of our princess is an insult to the empire itself. The people stir. The drums of war begin a silent beat.

The air thickens with unrest. My commander calls us to readiness. We sharpen obsidian blades and whisper prayers to Huitzilopochtli. The time for peace may be ending.

THE BATTLE OF TLATELOLCO

Moquihuixtli declares Tlatelolca's independence from Tenochtitlán and summons all young men over the age of twenty to participate in military exercises. A sudden rain storm breaks over the city—lightning cracks the sky, thunder rolls across the lake. The gods stir. A hard rain falls, foreshadowing bloodshed and cosmic imbalance.

Then, without the usual diplomatic exchanges, Moquihuixtli launches a surprise midnight attack, hoping to decapitate our leadership. He signals for his canoes to silently slip into Tenochtitlán through the canals to deliver warriors to ambush Axayacatl's bodyguards, leaving him vulnerable. But they are not trained to fight in the rain. Ehecatl blows a harsh wind and their canoes wobble.

We are ready for the attack as our spies have reported every aspect of Moquihuixtli's plans. In the dark of night, I accompany Tlaltequani. We lie in wait near the main plaza, hidden in an alcove beside the canal. The storm lashes the city – thunder rolling low, rain pounding the dark volcanic stone pavement.

The first Tlatelolca warrior climbs ashore. I rise and swing my macuahuitl with all my strength, slicing through his torso. He collapses like a felled stalk, limbs splayed, blocking the path. His comrades stumble over him, slipping on the wet, rain-slicked basalt. The rhythm of their attack breaks. Confusion spreads. Surrounded now, I have no time to reflect – only to survive.

My comrades swing their macuahuitls furiously. Eagle warriors from surrounding rooftops attack with arrows, slings and spear throwing atlatls. We engage in close quarters combat for several hours and slaughter the Tlatelolca attackers in vast numbers. Their heavy losses force the survivors to retreat and we drive them out of Tenochtitlán. Many of our men are killed and wounded too.

When we retire from the battlefield, I notice warm blood dripping from my left arm and see a gash I suffered while defending against a powerful blow. I contemplate what I have just done, my first battle, the first swing of my macuahuitl, my first kill. The storm has passed, but its echo remains. I am no longer who I was.

That night, after the Tlatelolca retreat, I return to the barracks to tend my wound. The rain has eased, but the air is still frozen with tension. I sit near the fire, wrapping my arm, when a scout bursts into the room – mud-splattered, breathless. He kneels before our commander and speaks in hushed tones, but I am close enough to hear.

"Moquihuixtli refused the peace offering. Our emissary is dead. Beheaded before he could speak."

Silence fills the room. Even the fire dims.

I glance at Tlaltequani. His jaw tightens, but he says nothing. Around us, warriors shift uneasily. The gods have been insulted. Diplomacy is dead. War is now inevitable.

ⵣⵣⵣⵣⵣ

Axayacatl summons every able-bodied warrior for the assault on Tlatelolco. Even with my injured arm, I am ready. The pain sharpens my focus. I will not be left behind.

At dawn, we strike. The Tlatelolca forces are still reeling from their failed attack – disorganized, demoralized.

Our battle plan unfolds with precision. We surround them with thunderous sound: drums pounding like the heartbeat of Huitzilopochtli, conch shells wailing like spirits in the wind. We hurl insults and battle cries across the plaza, each word a blade meant to cut their courage.

Tlaltequani, my superior officer, commands with the calm of a seasoned jaguar. He orchestrates flanking maneuvers and ambushes for our pantli,[95] weaving our forces through alleyways and canals like silver threads in the tapestry of war.

The battle is fierce and chaotic. My unit attacks the western fringe and I engage in close combat, wielding my macuahuitl in one hand and a chimalli (shield) in the other.

A Tlatelolca warrior strikes me from behind with a blow to my right cheek, knocking me to the ground, ripping a jagged bleeding wound on my face. Barely conscious, I look up. He stands above me slowly raising his *tepoztopilli*[96] for the *coup de grâce*. At that moment, my nagual, the hummingbird, intercedes. He grabs my right hand, still clutching my macuahuitl, and swings it with lightning speed and great force, slicing through the enemy's leg with a single whack.

---

95 A military unit of twenty men.

96 An obsidian bladed spear

Still woozy from the blow to my head, I stagger to my feet to disarm my adversary. But he cannot move; he is powerless. He moans while blood pulses from his leg. I quickly bind it, hoping to staunch the bleeding and keep him alive for sacrifice, but it is too late.

I kneel beside him and watch as his body becomes lifeless. I see his soul in motion. The heavens stir; the gods watching.

For this moment in time, I am no longer on the battlefield. I look up as the sky cracks open with light. The souls of our ancestors, the Eagle Warriors who died before, fly across the eastern sky, calling his soul upward. Tonatiuh, our radiant sun god, pauses on his path across the sky. He looks down beckoning this worthy warrior to join him. I feel a celestial wind, Quetzalcoatl's breath, lifting the warrior's spirit upward to the House of the Sun.

I feel his warm blood pooling around me. This precious fluid soaks the earth and feeds hungry-earth goddess Tlatecuhtli. From this offering, flowers will bloom. Life will renew.

I tell my fallen comrade,

> You fought well, brother. You rise now to the House of the Sun. May you soar with eagles and return with flowers. May I be worthy to follow.

Battle of Tlatelolco & death of Moquihuix. Codex Mendoza ⊛

The fighting rages through the day, but our army outnumbers the Tlatelolca and soon we dominate the battlefield. I join Axayacatl, guarding his flanks as he charges up the Tlatelolco temple in pursuit of Moquihuixtli.

As we fight our way up the pyramid, a noble Tlatelolca warrior intercepts me, hurling me against the basalt wall. We grapple fiercely, exchanging brutal blows. He lunges — I parry, throwing him off balance, and I club the back of his head, and swing my macuahuitl carving a deep gash across his chest and send him tumbling down to the bottom of the temple steps. I feel my hummingbird nagual stir within me, guiding my descent. I rush down the narrow steps to where my foe lies dazed, bruised and bleeding, but still breathing. I quickly bind his arms and legs to a post as I've been taught. He will not escape. He is my first capture. He may yet serve the gods.

Rushing back up the pyramid, I hear Axayacatl confront Moquihuixtli, reminding him of the taunts he once hurled – calling him a child, unfit to rule. Before Moquihuixtli could respond, Axayacatl plunges his *tecpatl* deep into his chest.[97] His fury is palpable. He lifts the dying ruler and hurls him from the temple's summit.

Axayacatl shouts,

> Never again will a Tenochca princess be disrespected. Never again will a city-state rise up against Tenochtitlán!

I watch as the body tumbles and bounces down the pyramid steps – and for a breathless moment, I imagine the sound of bells, as if Coyolxauhqui, the Moon Goddess, "She Who Is Adorned with Bells," were falling again from Coatepec Mountain. The stone remembers. Divine justice made flesh. With that climatic act, the battle ends.

We parade Moquihuixtli's corpse through the main square of Tlatelolco for all to see. Several high-ranking Tlatelolca leaders are executed on the spot – hearts removed, heads severed – as retribution and as a warning to all who might defy Tenochtitlán. All around me, the people of Tlatelolco fall to their knees, bowing before Axayacatl, accepting their subjugation. He appoints a new Tlatoani to restore order under Tenochca rule.

I am among the *xiquipilli*[98] who triumphantly return to the main square of Tenochtitlán, escorting captured warriors and Tlatelolca nobility. Many will be sacrificed to honor the gods; the rest will live as slaves. My commander, Tlaltequani, orders me to help carry Moquihuixtli's body to the Huey Teocalli. There, it is respectfully cremated. We bury the urn with his ashes beside the Coyolxauhqui Stone at the foot of the great temple of the gods – a final act to affirm the supremacy of Tenochtitlán and our war god, Huitzilopochtli.

---

97 Tecpatl is a small personal knife with a razor-sharp, double edged obsidian blade used for quick, precise strikes.

98 a military unit of 8,000 warriors

As the smoke rises, the High Priest of Huitzilopochtli, draped in turquoise and eagle feathers, steps forward. He raises his arms and chants a prayer, then recounts the sacred legend of Coyolxauhqui.

Coyolxauhqui Stone, Templo Mayor Museum (10' 8" diameter, 16" thick.)
Note the jagged lines where her head, arms and legs were severed.

Long ago, atop Coatepec – Serpent Mountain – Coatlicue, goddess of the earth, swept the temple floor. A ball of hummingbird feathers fell from the sky. She tucked it into her waistband and miraculously became pregnant. Outraged, her daughter Coyolxauhqui rallied her four hundred brothers to kill their mother to preserve family honor. But Huitzilopochtli, unborn yet aware, heard their plot from the womb. At the moment of ambush, he burst forth fully grown, wielding a *xiuhcoatl* – a serpent of fire and lightning. He struck down Coyolxauhqui, decapitating her and casting her head into the night sky, where it became the moon. He scattered the brothers across the heavens to become the stars. Her dismembered body tumbled down the mountain, a divine warning: the sun reigns supreme over moon and stars. And so does Tenochtitlán over all city-states.

The priest's voice echoes across the plaza. The people bow their heads. The gods are honored. The empire endures.

As the sun dips below the horizon, casting long shadows across Tenochtitlán, I kneel before Tlaltequani, my captain. With solemn precision, he lifts the obsidian blade and severs my *piochtli* – the lock of hair I have worn since childhood. The blade is cold, but the moment burns with meaning. I feel my youth fall away, replaced by the mantle of duty and respect.

I am now a *Tlamanih* – a capturer. Tlaltequani nods once in recognition, and the warriors around me bow. Some chant my name. Others raise their weapons in salute.

I am presented with distinctive garments – a tunic embroidered with sacred glyphs, a feathered headdress that marks my new rank, and jewelry of jade and shell, symbols of valor and divine favor. These are not mere decorations – they are declarations. I have stepped into the circle of warriors whose deeds echo beyond the battlefield.

CARE AND PREPARATION OF THE CAPTIVE

I hold this charge as both duty and honor: to husband my captive and make him worthy for the gods. The offering must be a warrior of strength and valor; to lay before the temple a blackguard would be an insult to the divine.

My family prepares a special place for my captive. It is a narrow, barred room behind the family courtyard, but he is kept comfortably and his every need and wish are carefully addressed.

My captive is severely injured, his face and body battered from his fall down from the temple; the gash on his torso is gaping. He can hardly walk. In the morning after his first night in my charge, I speak to him gently, treating him with reverence. I remind him his role is sacred. He answers with the voice of a noble, a man of learning:

I am Xolotl,[99] a psychopomp, a guide of souls to the other world. I bring fire and lightning. I am a shapeshifter – I can become maize,

---

99 Xotol is a god, who appears with a dog's head. He is associated with fire, lightning, death, and transformation. Xolotl plays a crucial role in guiding the sun through the underworld each night.

agave, or even an axolotl. But how inutile that would be, for I cannot flee. I am a noble warrior. I know my destiny. I will do my duty.

Each morning, I bring him out of his confine into our family's inner patio so he can receive sunlight to heal and fresh air to breathe. I bring him food to nourish his body, and delicacies to buoy his spirit. I lay out a special woven mat where he can take his meals. I light incense and recite prayers.

I call the helpers I must.

The *ticitl*,[100] comes on the first day with a bundle at his belt. He uses *tlapatl* and *toloache*[101] – plants whose touch dulls the bite of pain and eases the joints. His is the work of hands and herbs. I watch him press the dark paste where the obsidian cut deep, and rub salves over the wounds and bruised head and limbs. Xolotl's face slackens and the sharpness leaves his mouth.

On the second day, the *tlamatini*,[102] shaman, arrives. She bathes him in ritual waters while singing a low, calming melody. She anoints his brow and chest with sacred oils for purification.

From a small bundle at her belt she selects two dried buttons of the peyotl[103] cactus and grinds them in her metate while I boil water on a three stone hearth. She mixes the powder and water in a ceremonial vessel, painted with images of Xipe Totec, symbolizing the shedding of the old to allow for renewal. She tastes it once. Her face tightens, then she lifts a spoon and, with no hurry, sweetens the draught with honey – only enough to make it bearable.

The chant begins, low and rising. Slowly, the captive drinks. His jaw works; his hands tremble; his eyes roll beneath the lids. After a time his breath comes jagged and the stomach heaves – the purge, a letting-go and the shaman washes his mouth and wipes his brow.

---

100 A healer, skilled in medicine, herbal knowledge, and divination.

101 Types of Jimsonweed, thorn apple, used for pain relief, rubbed onto aching joints.

102 A shaman, sage, a wise person, "someone who knows things" a "knower."

103 Hallucinogenic peyote, mescaline.

Herbal medicines: tlapatl and toloache (jimsonweed varieties) for pain relief, rubbed onto aching joints. Mescaline from the peyotl cactus induces deep meditative states and visionary experiences for spiritual healing. Nanacatl, "sacred mushrooms," (psilocybin) used for its hallucinogenic effects, facilitating visions and spiritual experiences. Florentine Codex Book XI, Med. Palat. 220, f. 294v

When he comes back to his breath, his face is different: emptied, quieter, as if some heavy door has been opened inside him. The tea has opened his inner eye and steadied his mind to bring visions, to quiet dread, and to let him see the road that his spirit will walk.

On the third day, the Tlamacazqui comes and kneels at his side and speaks words that settle the man's heart. He guides the captive's breath into silence and speaks of the road to the sun, of duty and balance. The priest's voice is low, and the courtyard holds it as if it were a precious thing.

In time, Xolotl tames his pain. Flesh grows over his wounds. He calmly accepts his fate, without choler. He sits calmly, eyes closed, and speaks in a slow, thoughtful voice:

Huitzilin, we cannot contest fate. It is inevitable. I am honored and accept the duty assigned to me.

Two of our gods leapt into the great fire to create the Fifth Sun. They gave their lives so we may live. Now we must repay them with our own blood. My sacrifice will nourish the gods, sustain the world order, and ensure the well-being of all mankind. I serve the cosmic order. The gods will reward me.

THE SACRIFICE

The Tlacaxipehualiztli Festival honoring Xipe Totec,[104] "Our Lord the Flayed One," marks an auspicious day for sacrifice. It is a time of renewal through suffering, of life reborn through death.

I dress Xolotl in an elaborate feather costume crafted by my sister, Xochitl. It represents his divine namesake – Xolotl, the dog-faced god, guardian of the underworld and guide of souls. His snout is painted with care, his body adorned with vibrant feathers, shimmering jewelry, and sacred pigments to enhance his beauty before the gods.

To ease his passage, I offer *teonanácatl*[105] and natural sedatives – gifts of the earth to calm his spirit and open the door to the divine.

Then we join the silent parade through the streets leading to the main temple. Thousands of devout denizens of Tenochtitlán join the somber procession. They have fasted for days to prepare for the event and carry flowers, symbols of the ephemeral, the sacred, recognizing that we all must die.

The drummers beat a slow, steady cadence as we march. We pause briefly at the foot of the great pyramid to contemplate the Coyolxauhqui Stone, commemorating Huitzilopochtli's triumph over the forces of darkness.

---

104 Xipe Totec, known as "Our Lord the Flayed One," is a central deity in Mexica (Aztec) cosmology. He embodies agriculture, renewal, and rebirth. The ritual flaying of sacrificial victims in his honor symbolized the shedding of old skin to reveal new life – just as seeds cast off their husks before germination. This sacred act mirrored the cycles of nature and the divine order, affirming the Mexica belief that sacrifice is essential for the continuation of the world. Through death, life is renewed; through pain, the earth is nourished.

105 Divine psilocybin, magic mushrooms.

We ascend the vast staircase slowly, step by solemn step, accompanied by an assemblage of priests, attendants, and ceremonial aides. At the summit, we reach the platform where Huey Tlatoani Axayacatl sits beneath a canopy, surrounded by his retinue. Attendant priests adorn the platform with sacred offerings – flowers, maize, cacao, and cooked delicacies – gifts to honor the gods. Drummers and flutists play ceremonial music, their rhythms steady and reverent. Dancers, adorned in elaborate feathered costumes, move in slow ritual patterns, invoking divine presence with each step. The air is thick with the scent of copal incense, its fragrant smoke curling skyward, creating a veil between the earthly and the divine. The atmosphere is sacred, heavy with expectation.

The high priest of Huitzilopochtli stands beside the *techcatl* – the highly polished and adorned sacrificial stone, a large volcanic stone carved with sacred images. Its convex surface is designed to elevate the chest of the offering, granting the priest swift access to the heart.

When all is in order, the high priest signals me. I step forward and lead Xolotl to the sacrificial stone. He walks with dignity, his body adorned in ceremonial regalia. I help him lie on his back on the bowed techcatl. I hold his right arm; three other priests secure his left arm and legs. I feel Xolotl's hand gripping my arm as he speaks his final words,

> I will not go to Mictlan, the underworld, I will ascend to *Tonatiuh Ilhuicatl*, "Heaven of the Sun", and accompany the sun on its journey across the sky. In the morning, I will rise with the sun in the east and in the evening, I will descend with it into the underworld, aiding Huitzilopochtli in his eternal struggle to maintain cosmic balance and rise again.

The crowd gathers silently at the base of the temple steps. The Tlamacazqui, adorned in the feathered headdress and ceremonial robes of Huitzilopochtli, his face painted with sacred symbols, stands before the sacrificial stone. He holds the obsidian blade, gleaming in the sunlight as he performs purification rituals, chanting and burning copal incense, invoking the gods. His voice, deep and resonant, echoes through the temple precinct. He speaks to the gods most reverently, and prays:

> Hear me, oh mighty Huitzilopochtli, Hummingbird Wizard, god of the Blazing Sun, Lord of War! Before you, we prepare this sacred offering, a noble warrior chosen for his strength and courage! We cleanse this space; we purify this act. May it be pleasing in your divine eyes.

The Tlamacazqui sprinkles sacred water around the sacrificial stone.

> May this *tlaqualli*,[106] this precious heart, be rendered worthy to sustain your celestial fire, to empower your eternal battle against the forces of darkness, and to ensure the glorious dawn of each new day!

He pauses; his gaze fixed on the heavens.

> Accept, O Huitzilopochtli, this offering! For we know that his teyolia, his soul, the vital life force of his heart, shall ride with you across the heavens, escorting you with honor and valor for the day's first half, just as the *cihuateteo,* women who die in childbirth, escort you for the day's second half. Accept the strength of his heart as a testament to our devotion.

He lowers his head in reverence.

> Let this act be a renewal of our covenant, a repayment for the life you bestow upon us. Grant us your continued favor; protect us from our enemies and maintain the sacred balance of the cosmos!

Xolotl lies quietly, without fear, breathing softly, his eyes fixed on mine. Between us, the veil thins – we dwell in the spiritual realm. I hold the hair of his head in my hand and I feel his *tonalli* energy pulse with mine.[107]

---

106 Tlaqualli refers to food. In the context of a human sacrifice it refers to food for the gods, the human heart.

107 The vital force of will, consciousness and spirit that resides in the head.

The priest lifts his *tecpatl*,[108] the obsidian blade gleaming. He makes a deep incision into Xolotl's abdomen, beginning at the solar plexus and cutting along the edge of the left ribcage, slicing through his diaphragm to reach his heart. Another priest catches the flowing blood in a *cuauhxicalli*, a jade bowl reserved for sacred offerings.

When the obsidian blade pierces his skin, I feel Xolotl's grip tighten. When his heart is cut free, his body falls limp. I watch his mouth open, releasing his final breath. His *ihiyotl*[109] shimmers as it departs, and I feel his *tonalli*[110] pass through me – igniting a fiery current that opens the path between the human and divine.

The priest removes Xolotl's heart – intact, still beating, and lifts it toward the sun, blood dripping down his arm onto the stone. His voice rings out:

> O Huitzilopochtli! Hear our call! For your grace, for your sustenance, we offer now the ultimate gift – *yollotl*,[111] the heart, the seed of life itself!

As he speaks, I feel Xolotl's *teyolia*[112] rise before me – an invisible force ascending, drawn upward, following the shimmering path, beginning the sacred journey toward Tonatiuh's radiant procession.

> Behold this still-beating heart of this valiant warrior, Xolotl, who bravely transitions from this earthly realm to join your heavenly host!

The priest moves closer to the brazier, bathing the heart in light and smoke. I feel the air shift around me, charged with divine presence.

> May his sacred blood nourish *tlalticpac*, our mother earth, ensuring abundant rains, fertile fields, and balance in the world below, sustaining the divine order you command!

---

108 An obsidian blade sharpened on both sides.

109 Ihiyotl is breath-soul.

110 Tonalli is the soul of his consciousness.

111 Heart

112 Teyolia is his heart-soul.

He raises the heart higher, turning it toward the heavens.

> May his teyolia soar to the heavens, and ride upon Iztac-Mixcoatl, the White Cloud Serpent – the shimmering band of stars we call the Milky Way, the pathway between the mortal and divine realms. May he rise to your side, O Huitzilopochtli, on your daily journey across the sky, achieving eternal honor and unity with the divine essence!

I feel the moment stretch – time suspended between blood and flame, between earth and sky.

The priest lowers the heart slightly, speaking with solemnity:

> Xolotl does not die. His liberated spirit is released into the vast cosmos, where he will continue to serve your grand design. After four years, when his earthly ties have faded, may his soul transform into a hummingbird, sipping nectar from celestial flowers, or a butterfly, dancing on the winds of creation – forever embodying the beauty and fragility of life.

He places the heart into the bowl-shaped ceramic brazier that holds the sacred fire. Smoke rises, carrying Xolotl's essence to the gods. Then, in the ritual of Xipe Totec, the priest flays Xolotl's body and dons his skin. He rolls the body down the temple steps, painting the pyramid with blood – reenacting Huitzilopochtli's conquest over Coyolxauhqui, affirming the supremacy of the sun over chaos and darkness.

I am profoundly struck by the importance of what I have seen and what I have done. Having watched my captive take his final breath and having held his hair while his life force left him, I am in awe. I close my eyes and recite "The Flower Songs" of Nezahualcoyotl:

> *Among the copses and the cypresses*
> *there are fresh and fragrant flowers.*
> *Although for a while they are fresh and attractive,*
> *they reach a time when they wither and dry up.*
> *All who are present must end and cannot come to rule again,*
> *and all their grandeur must finish,*
> *and their treasure must be owned by others,*

and they are not to return and enjoy it once they have left it behind.
In the house of the old ones,
The flowers are scattered,
They are strewn in the house of the old ones.

The large crowd attending the ceremony stands in solemn silence, exhibiting reverence and religious awe. They understand the gravity of the cosmic necessity they have witnessed. After a moment of deep devotion, we feel relief – knowing that we have performed the ultimate sacrifice, that we have satisfied the gods and that the they will reward us with blessings and abundance.

A city-wide celebration follows. Drumming, flutes, conch shells and ritual dances fill the air with joy and sacred rhythm. All members of the community gather in the temple courtyards and city plazas. People sit on *petates,* woven mats spread across the ground in groups based on social status or family ties. Women, including my mother, Chicomecoatl, and others from noble families, prepare and serve great quantities of food, nourishing the people in honor of the gods.

The spectators erupt in cheers as I watch Cuetlachtzin,[113] the temple steward, hoist Xolotl's severed head and mount it on the tzompantli[114] in the city center. His skull joins the ranks of honored warriors whose sacrifice sustains the sun. The crowd roars, but I remain silent, absorbing the gravity of what I've witnessed.

I follow Huey Cuetzpalcalpixqui, the great steward of the Royal Zoo, as he gathers Xolotl's entrails and offal into woven baskets. He moves with practiced reverence, feeding the sacred beasts – jaguars, eagles, serpents – who pace behind stone enclosures sensing blood. I nod to him, and he nods back. We both understand the cycle.

---

113 Name meaning "honored wolf" here referring to a tzompantli attendant or steward.

114 Skull rack

Later, I enter the temple kitchens where Chef Tlamacazqui prepares the *tlacatlaolli* – the sacred stew of maize, chili, and flesh. He slices the flesh of Xolotl's limbs with solemn care, murmuring prayers as he works. The scent of roasted maize and smoke fills the air. When he ladles the stew into ceremonial bowls, he does so with precision, placing only a small slice, a morsel of flesh in each dish. It is a *qualli tlacualiztli*, a precious food, meant to be tasted with reverence.

At sunset, I take my seat at the *Teocualo* feast[115] along with revered nobles, priests and generals. As Xolotl's captor, I sit with honor. The bowl before me is painted with solar glyphs. I look down and see the single slice of Xolotl's flesh floating upon the stew. It glistens in the firelight.

The priest stands and raises his voice:

O, Xolotl, noble warrior,
your heart has been offered upon the stone,
and your teyollotl, your heart spirit, has fed the sun.

You were a warrior, a flame-breather, seized in valor.
Your body now becomes teotl, a divine force.
Now, in holy remembrance we infuse our bodies with yours.

With each bite, we take your courage.
With each taste, your sun-bound soul blesses us.

May your strength enter our bones,
may your memory pass into our blood.

As the gods devour the hearts of men,
so we, their shadows on earth,
partake in this sacred rite.

Let none forget:
this is the banquet of the gods.

---

115 The sacred feast.

Let us honor the gods
and partake in the divine essence of the sacrifice.

The stew is warm and fragrant. I lift the bowl to my lips slowly, aware that this bite is precious—a sacred communion with the divine. I pause, then taste the morsel. It is tender, spiced with maize and chili, but more than flavor passes through me. I feel his courage enter me. I savor it slowly, deliberately. With this bite, I absorb Xolotl's essence—his bravery, his clarity, his devotion.

I do not speak. I do not weep. I carry him now.

b. 1474, Matlatzinco

Following our swift victory over Tlatelolco, Tlaltequani, my mentor and commanding officer, summons me.

"Huitzilin, I've been watching you and I see that your instincts on the battlefield are good. I have been called to a meeting with the Huey Tlatoani at the ceremonial hall in the sacred precinct. You will accompany me as my assistant."

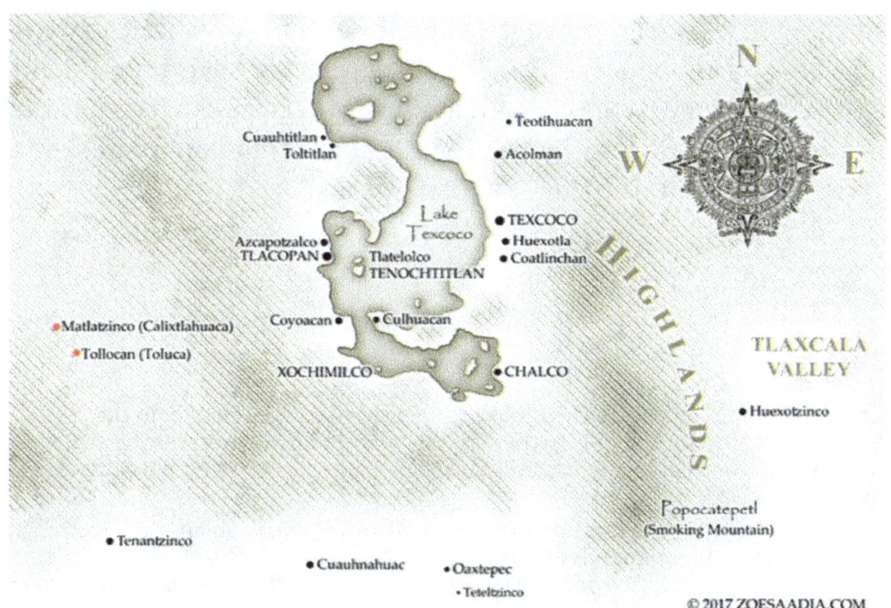

Map showing location of Toluca and Matlatzinco, by Zoe Saadia.

Late that afternoon, toward dusk, when the light slants through the courtyard, torches and copal braziers are being lit, I follow my commander into the hall. My stomach tightens and I breathe deeply as I pass by the maps, banners and weapons racks. Officers rushing in and out. A painted map covers one wall and standards of participating altepetls along another wall. A drum (huehuetl) and conch rest near heralds. The room smells of copal, lime plaster, oiled shields. Messengers and scribes hover at the edges, but the inner circle is quiet and taut.

Huey Tlatoani Axayacatl sits on his throne. His two highest generals, Tlacochcalcatl[116] and Tlacateccatl[117] stand on either side of him like statues. Before them, are senior captains including Jaguar wing/vanguard, Tlaltequani, with me beside him. Beside us are counterparts from Eagle corps, and a Cuauhchicqueh[118] detachment leader. Behind us are Captains from allied altepetl contingents (Texcoco, Tlacopan, plus pledged subject cities) with their standards. To the left and right sides are heralds and priests.

Tlamacazqui Quetzalcoatl Totec rises and a hush settles in the room. He gives a solemn invocation for the event. Tlacochcalcatl steps forward and announces, "The Council of Military Advisors has deliberated with Huey Tlatoani. The decision has been made that our next mission will be to bring the Toluca Valley under our dominion.

Herald: "Be still. The Huey Tlatoani speaks."

---

116 Keeper of the House of Darts" – high-ranking military commander in the Mexica hierarchy, second only to the supreme war leader. He oversees the armory, coordinates troop deployments, and leads major campaigns. Often a candidate for future rulership.

117 "Leader of Men" – the second top military officer, equal in rank to the Tlacochcalcatl. He commands elite warrior units, supervises battlefield discipline, and serves as a strategic advisor. Together, the Tlacateccatl and Tlacochcalcatl form the core of the Mexica war council.

118 The shorn ones, elite warriors with shaved heads, marked by the captives they've taken.

Axayacatl: "Tlatelolco lies quiet. Our gaze now turns west. Between us and the Purépecha of Michoacán,[119] stands the Toluca valley – green, walled with hills, stubborn. He gestures to the map. There, the Matlatzinca and their Otomi allies make a formidable force.

Tlacochcalcatl steps forward, tapping passes and rivers with a dart shaft: "Here the road skirts the lake marsh, here the rise into Matlatzinco. Two stone places hold the valley mouth. We take the left pass before midday or we bleed in the narrows."

Tlaltequani (bowing slightly): "My Jaguars hold the vanguard and left wing. Grant me a cuachicqueh detachment for the pass assault."

Axayacatl: "Granted. Tlacateccatl, screen the right; keep the Eagles tight on the main road."

Tlacateccatl: "It will be done. Scouts already on the ridges report Otomi slingers posted near the terraces."

Tlacochcalcatl: "For three days' march: ten thousand dart bundles, eight thousand sling-stone sacks staged at the second canal crossing; lime-water and tamales for the porters. The Texcocan grain barge meets us at the western causeway."

Priest: "May the road be straight and the mirrors clear."

Axayacatl: "At first light, assemble at the southern gate. Banners high, runners ready. Tlacochcalcatl – order the march. Captains, see your counts right; no man short, no bundle missing."

[Drumbeats. Standards dip in acknowledgment. The commanders disperse.]

OUR MILITARY FORCE

Tlacochcalcatl, our top military commander, stands atop the inspection platform, his eyes scanning the ranks. I stand among them, shoulder to shoulder with warriors from across the empire, as he assembles and inspects a vast army – twenty thousand strong, ready

---

119 Purépecha is the name of the people and polity commonly referred to as Tarascan. "Tarascan" was a term applied by the Spanish conquistadors who mispronounced a Purépechan word. The Purépecha inhabited the state of Michoacán with their capital at Tzintzuntzan.

to march into the Toluca Valley. The air hums with anticipation, and I feel it in my chest like a second heartbeat.

At the vanguard are our elite forces: the Eagle Warriors and the Jaguar Warriors. I watch them prepare – sharpening weapons, adjusting armor, whispering prayers to their patron gods.

The Eagle Warriors are drawn from the most gifted nobles. They carry the spirit of the sun and sky, representing Huitzilopochtli, our god of war and fire. As the sun rises, they strike first – ranged combatants with the eagle's aerial view of the battlefield. I've seen them wield the atlatl, spear thrower, with terrifying precision, hitting targets from over a hundred paces. They also carry javelins, slings, and bows tipped with obsidian – each weapon designed for speed and reach.

The *Ocelomeh*, Jaguar Warriors, are drawn from the worthiest commoners and nobles. They wear jaguar pelts and headdresses, invoking Tezcatlipoca, god of night and sorcery. They fight like the jaguar – stealthy, ferocious, relentless. I stand with Tlaltequani, leader of the Jaguar Warriors, as his assistant. I've trained under him, watched him design ambushes and flanking maneuvers with the precision of a hunter. He calls me his shadow, and I follow close behind.

The four highest generals who make up the supreme war council are depicted in ceremonial regalia carrying Tepoztopilli (spear)and chimalli (shield). Codex Mendoza folio 67 r

Our weapons are brutal. The macuahuitl, a wooden club lined with obsidian blades, can decapitate a man with a single blow. Some carry the *tepoztopilli*, a broad-tipped spear edged with obsidian, perfect for slashing and thrusting. Others wield the *cuauhololli*, a round-headed club embedded with stone or hardened resin – designed to crush armor and bone. Like all warriors, I keep a *tecpatl* tucked in my waist sash, a double-edged dagger for close combat or the final strike.

I see the *Cuauhchicqueh*, the Shorn Ones – shock troops with shaved heads and a single lock of hair – marking them as front-line fighters who have vowed never to retreat.

The *Yaotl*, our common warriors, fill the ranks. They carry bows, arrows and macuahuitls, eager to prove themselves. Each of us bears a *chimalli*, a shield painted with symbols of rank and valor. Mine is modest still, but I carry it with pride. I was one of them not long ago. Now, I stand closer to the front, under Tlaltequani's command, ready to earn my place among the elite.

The gods are watching. The valley awaits.

MARCH TO MATLATZINCO WITH TLALTEQUANI

This is my first campaign beyond our island home. I am one among twenty thousand warriors bound for Matlatzinco. Each calpulli[120] unit of 200-400 warriors marches separately. I continue under the guidance of my mentor, Jaguar Warrior Tlaltequani, commander of the left-wing vanguard. The first unit leaves as the sun rises. The next unit awaits the signal to move when the first unit is out of sight.

My unit leaves when the sun is at its zenith. I feel pride as I cross over the causeway, leaving Tenochtitlán, the chinampas and Lake Texcoco behind. When our home is out of sight, I feel my tonalli, teyolia, and ihiyotl – my head, heart, and breath – swirling inside me like startled birds. I am the standard bearer for my calpulli unit, and I must not falter. I grip my standard tightly.

---

120 Calpulli in this context is not a neighborhood, but a cohesive military unit.

We march in formation. Huehuetl and teponaztli drums set our cadence. My feet move in rhythm, my breath syncing with the beat. I join the chanting and feel settled as part of a greater force.

As we march, our unit and the units before us and behind us create a roaring river of sound: drums banging loudly, flutes whining, chants rising, standards snapping in the wind. The sound is overwhelming. It stirs devotion in our hearts and dread in those who hear us. Even we, the marchers, feel its power.

Scouts run ahead of each unit gathering information of dangers or potential hostilities. Messengers run back and forth between units carrying notices of importance. One scout passes word to us late in the afternoon that the last unit has left Tenochtitlán. I nod and breathe deeply, I feel the weight of the banner I carry; not the heaviness of cloth and wood, but the weight of destiny's charge.

The day stretches long. The sun tilts toward its descent – *Tonaltoca*, the hour of fading light, when shadows stretch and the world begins to dim. In time we tire and my mind wanders. I remember when I was struck from behind in Tlatelolco. Then I think of my mother, her warm hands comforting me when I was hurt, her voice humming lullabies as she braided my hair. Then I think of my son, Cuauhtémoc, my daughter, Xochiquetzal – how they chase each other through the courtyard, how they cry when I leave. I wonder if they'll remember me if I don't return.

I see my dear devoted wife, Teoxochitl, her laughter, her scent, the way she used to press her forehead to mine when the world felt heavy. I see her face as she labored, the blood, the silence.

I stumble over a stone on the road and the memories scatter like birds. I'm back in my body, back on the road, back in the march. The mountain looms ahead. The air thins. My breath shortens.

I hear rustling in the bushes beside the road – Enemy scouts are attacking! My eyes search – it's a family of javelinas digging for grubs. I try to calm my breath but I sense fear. I don't want to die. Not yet. Not here. I love this world – the scent of wet earth, the sound of flutes, the fragrance of sweet flowers. I remember the words of Nezahualcoyotl:

"Not forever on Earth, only a little while here," and I think, "A little while longer, please?"

I glance at the eastern sky behind me, still glowing faintly. I search for my nagual, my hummingbird spirit. I can't see him, but I feel his presence – just beyond the veil, nudging me forward, and I whisper a prayer as I march:

> O Huitzilopochtli,
> Lord of the sun,
> Fire in the sky,
> Guide my steps.
> Give me courage to face the unknown.
> Let my heart be strong,
> Let my breath be steady.
> If I must fall, Let it be with honor.
> But if I may live,
> Let me return to those I love.
> Let me carry your fire within me.

The wind shifts. Somewhere ahead the drums continue. I march on. I follow close behind my mentor, Tlaltequani, and on the first day we march twenty miles through the countryside, with just one short stop for water and a small *tzoalli* snack.[121]

We reach the foothills as the sun sets, painting the sky in hues of amber and violet. The air cools, and the scent of damp earth rises. *Tlamemes*[122] set up camp beside a freshwater spring, assembling simple shelters from woven mats and reeds. They gather firewood and dig a firepit. Cooks prepare our evening meal warmed on a portable *comalli*[123]

I get a tortilla with beans, chillis and a small portion of rabbit meat. I kneel facing the eastern sky and break off a small piece of my tortilla

---

121 Energy food made from amaranth grain mixed with honey.

122 Porters

123 Griddle

and place it on a prominent stone next to a living tree as an offering to Huitzilopochtli. If a bird or small animal eats it, it means the gods accept my offering through these earthly messengers. I whisper a prayer to Huitzilopochtli asking for protection and courage. Around the fire, other warriors toss their offerings into the flames. Smoke rises, curling skyward, carrying their prayers to the celestial realm. Mine remains on the stone, waiting.

After the meal, we gather in a circle, weary but proud. The fire crackles. Our leader, Tlaltequani, rises slowly, his silhouette framed by the flickering light. His voice carries strength and memory.

> My fellow warriors, you must remember who we are! We are Mexica – born of fire and lake, shaped by hardship, chosen by the gods to rise from the reeds and command the earth.
>
> But, remember, we were once newcomers to the Valley, unknown in a land ruled by powerful lords. We settled in Chapultepec but were expelled. We then settled in Tizaapan and were ejected again. We wandered, guided only by the voice of Huitzilopochtli, until Tenoch saw the sign – the eagle, the cactus, the serpent – and claimed the island the gods had promised.
>
> Tenochtitlán was young, its people poor, and warriors were few. We lived under the harsh rule of the Tepanecs who considered us lowly and weak. We served as their vassals for a full *xiuhmolpilli*,[124] the 52-year calendar cycle, paying tribute and doing their bidding while we built our humble village among the reeds and marshes.
>
> Without help from anyone, we found a way to make firm soil where there was only swamp and mud. We drove wooden stakes into the marshy ground and layered reeds, mud and stone to create a solid foundation for our empire. We created chinampas for year-round farming, producing maize, beans, squash, and flowers to feed the growing population. We built aqueducts to bring fresh water to our island; we built causeways over the lake for easy transport of goods to and from our great city.
>
> During the reign of our first Tlatoani of Tenochtitlán, Acamapichtli, the Tepanecs were battling Xochimilco. We could have

---

124 A 52-year calendar cycle, a binding of the years.

stayed back to await the outcome, but we knew it was time for us to prove ourselves.

But, when we assembled our warriors we looked to our stores; we found our weapons in disrepair, our macuahuitl worn and broken, our shields battered and useless. We had no gold, no iron, no favor. Only broken blades, battered shields – but we had fire in our hearts.

So, our elders and warriors went before the Tepanec lords, humbly bowing their heads. "Great ones," they pleaded, "we are your loyal servants, but our weapons are old and broken. Might we have the cast-off arms that your own warriors no longer need? The swords with chipped obsidian, the shields with torn leather, the spears whose tips have dulled?"

The Tepanec lords laughed, for they thought little of their vassals. "Take what you will from the rubbish heaps," they said, "for what harm can come from such pitiful arms?"

With gratitude, we gathered the discarded weapons – splintered macuahuitl, battered shields, and spears worn thin. Back in our island home, we set to work. The smiths and craftsmen, guided by the wisdom of our priests and the spirit of Huitzilopochtli, labored day and night. They bound new obsidian to the macuahuitl, patched the shields with fresh hides, and sharpened every spear and dart.

When the day of battle came, Mexica warriors marched alongside the Tepanecs. Their enemies looked upon us and saw only ragged arms, but we fought with the fury of the sun. our refurbished weapons struck true, our shields held firm, and our courage blazed brighter than gold.

The battle was won, and the Tepanec lords marveled at the valor of their vassals. From that day, the Mexica were no longer seen as mere beggars or outcasts, but as warriors worthy of respect – a people who, from the scraps and cast-offs of others, could forge their own destiny.

And so, the legend reminds us: Greatness is not gifted – it is forged. From cast-off scraps, from wounded pride, from the will to rise and strike with all the strength of one's soul.

Weary from the long tense day, I wrap myself in my cloak and lie on soft grassy vegetation for the night. Above me, the sky is moonless, vast and dark. Yet across its breadth stretches the White Cloud Serpent – Milky Way, the shimmering band of stars that winds across the heavens.

I gaze at its coils, imagining the souls of fallen warriors riding its path toward the divine. I wonder if Teoxochitl is among them, her spirit dancing among the stars. The serpent seems to pulse with quiet power, and I feel my breath slow, my body sink into the earth.

Huitzilin's Nagual visits him in a dream. Image by sora.chatgpt.com

My aching limbs are heavy from the day's march and I drift into deep sleep.

In the silence of the night, I hear the beating of tiny wings . . .

Like a flash of lightning, a shimmering hummingbird appears before me, its feathers flickering like sunlight trapped in jade. I feel the rhythm of its heartbeat as though it had merged with my own. My nagual tells me,

You are not alone.

You have the strength and courage of all the warriors who have come before you.

Your macuahuitl is as fast and accurate as a hummingbird's flight.

Your shield will move like a hummingbird to fend off enemy blows.

I awaken with the morning light and I know that I am not alone. My nagual is with me. The camp is in motion with seriousness. Cooks prepare a light morning meal, a tamal with beans and water.

On our second day we climb the volcanic highlands surrounding the Valley of Mexico, known as Quauhtepetlthem, Eagle Mountain,[125] a cold pine forest with rugged terrain. The mountain passes are narrow and rocky and some of my companions who are barefoot suffer. That night, we all suffer from the cold.

On our fourth day, we arrive at our assembly point near the Matlatzinca capital, Calixtlahuaca. It is an area of dark dense forests and rugged terrain, surrounded by mountains with steep cliffs and narrow passes. There are rivers and lakes and small open plains with thick brush and tall reeds. The area is ideal for unconventional warfare, hit and run tactics and ambushes.

MATLATZINGO "THE BATTLE OF TOO MANY AMBUSHES"

Our army of twenty thousand warriors camps in the shadow of Matlatzinco, hidden from view but impossible to ignore. We spend the day preparing – digging fire pits, sharpening weapons, arranging supply lines. The air is thick with anticipation. Their Otomi scouts have seen us. They know our numbers, our strength, our readiness. Word has reached their tlatoani and his chiefs. They know we are here.

Protocol demands that every effort be exhausted to find a diplomatic solution before blood is shed. That evening, Tlacochcalcatl, our supreme military commander, assembles a delegation to deliver our

---

125 Known today as Sierra de las Cruces.

proposal. Tlaltequani is among those chosen, and he selects me to accompany him.

At first light, our diplomatic mission gathers. We wear clean white robes embroidered with symbols of peace – flowers, birds, and flowing water. I carry a banner bearing the glyph of Tenochtitlán, flanked by others that signify our peaceful intent and diplomatic authority. We carry no weapons. Instead, we bear offerings: cacao, obsidian blades, and feathers – not for battle, but for respect.

A herald runs ahead, to give notice that our delegation wishes to approach peacefully to present a proposal for our mutual benefit. He carries a staff wrapped in white cloth – the emblem of peace.

We approach Matlatzinco not as warriors, but as envoys. The guards at the city's edge do not raise their spears. They wait. We speak in the language of ancestors, invoking shared blood and sacred earth. The air is tense, but we are not attacked. Not yet.

We are led into the royal court, where the Tlatoani of Matlatzinco sits upon a carved stone throne, surrounded by his nobles and priests. His face is unreadable, his gaze sharp. Tlacochcalcatl steps forward and presents our terms:

> We come not to conquer, but to unite. Let Matlatzinco join with Tenochtitlán in a pact of mutual protection. Pay tribute to the sun-born city, and in return, receive our shield and our friendship. Let our warriors stand together against common enemies. Let our gods be honored side by side.

The Tlatoani listens. He does not speak. He turns to his advisors, who whisper in his ear. Time stretches. The court is silent but for the rustle of robes and the sizzle of burning incense. Finally, he rises.

> We bow to no one.
> Matlatzinco will not pay tribute. We will not serve. We are not your vassals. We demand mutual respect and dignity.

His voice is calm, but final. The offerings are not accepted. The banners of peace are not acknowledged. We bow and withdraw. They have heard our words. Now they will hear our war cries.

That night, our generals meet beneath the stars. Again, I accompany Tlaltequani. Spies report that Matlatzinco has prepared a new battle plan – ambushes hidden in the underbrush, warriors concealed behind maguey and reeds.

Tlacochcalcatl decides we will not commit the full force of our army to a frontal assault. Instead, we will divide into smaller units, concealed in the forest. A decoy force will provoke the enemy, then retreat, drawing them into our trap.

The next morning, the battlefield is quiet. Each side waits, watching, baiting. The hours stretch into a strange rhythm of feints and retreats. Scouts dart through the trees. Our scouts report that the bulk of their army is hidden behind maguey agaves and underbrush. Messengers whisper updates. The forest holds its breath. The day goes by with each side trying to lure the other into their ambush trap.

And so begins the Battle of Too Many Ambushes.

My comrades and I remain hidden in the forest under leaves and branches. I am with a small force ordered to foray deeper onto the battlefield and to retreat when the enemy counterattacks, luring them into our trap where we can overwhelm them. When we charge close to the enemy's encampment, Matlatzinca warriors charge at us, but quickly turn and run toward another clearing. Instead of chasing the enemy, we follow orders not to fight on the open battlefield, but to fall back to our garrison.

The day proceeds with both sides playing defense. Platoons charge onto the battlefield trying to lure the other into a trap. Even in this limited confrontation, I can pick off enemy warriors with my *atlatl*[126] and *tlacochtli*,[127] a skill my father taught me as a small boy. I am crouched low among the reeds when my attention is drawn to a decorated enemy warrior chasing one of my comrades. Before he can swing his macuahuitl I stand, holding my atlatl and launch a tlacochtli, with

---

126 A spear-throwing device that can launch a javelin over 300' at speeds up to 90 mph.

127 A four- to seven-foot-long obsidian tipped javelin.

all my strength. I feel my nagual guide my arm and my tlacochtli sails forth at lightning speed and accuracy, hitting my target in his left eye. Blood splatters his face; he cannot see and he staggers not knowing where to go and falls to the ground writhing, the spear still hanging from his face. I run to him I tie his hands behind his back and remove the spear. I bring my stumbling capture back to our garrison, where healers tend to him.

As the day wears on, the battle intensifies. We pick off more enemy warriors and more of our warriors are lost. Finally, after an extended period of intense fighting, we are successful. Our forces have killed hundreds of the enemy and many more lie dying, gasping in pools of blood. The few survivors retreat, running back through the forest. At last the fighting ends and there is silence.

With the Matlatzinca and Otomi fighters gone and our victory secure, Axayacatl proudly enters the battlefield alone, stepping over enemy bodies and beats his drum to proclaim victory. Then, suddenly, the Otomi chief, Tlilcuetzpalin and two of his lieutenants attack. The Otomi chief uses his tecpatl to stab Axayacatl in the thigh, nearly to the bone. His strength waning, Axayacatl fights on, but Tlilcuetzpalin gains the upper hand.

I rush onto the battlefield to save my tlatoani. Several Texcocan captains, and jaguars from my calli follow. The Texcocans separate Axayacatl from the Otomis, revealing blood flowing freely from his wound. I gravely wound Tlilcuetzpalin and gain control of him before he can escape, my third capture of the day. The Texcocans capture his two lieutenants. We tie their hands and then tie the three together with ropes around their necks.

At that moment, several of the enemy rush onto the battlefield to ambush us once again, but we are able to drag our captives safely back to our main encampment.

When I return to our lines, dragging the Otomi captives behind me, Tlaltequani, my commander and mentor, meets my gaze with pride. He clasps my shoulder and says, "You've honored your lineage today, Huitzilin."

Word of my achievement spreads quickly through the ranks. By nightfall, even the Tlacochcalcatl, commander of our entire 20,000-strong force, sends a messenger to commend my valor. Around the fires, warriors speak my name with reverence. Some say the gods must have guided my hand. I say little, knowing I have served the empire and the gods with distinction.

That evening, Tlacochcalcatl calls all the captains together. I stand at Tlaltequani's side. Tlacochcalcatl announces,

> Axayacatl is in pain and unable to preside over the meeting. Our main force will depart for Tenochtitlán at first light and all must be ready.
>
> A contingent of our forces, as many as 5,000 will remain under the command of Tlacateccatl in a fortified stronghold, with orders to hold the valley, enforce tribute and suppress uprisings while the tlatoani recovers.
>
> In the morning, I join the main army on the march home with my captives in tow. Axayacatl is in pain and is carried on a litter. Yet, on leaving the battlefield, I feel we have left unfinished business behind.

HUITZILIN'S HONORS

On our return march, we have time to reflect. I notice Tlaltequani is staring at my cheek. I explain,

> During the battle at Tlatelolco, I was struck from behind and it ripped my cheek open. The jagged wound healed, but left a large scar in the shape of a flying hummingbird. It pulses blood red when my spirit moves me.

Tlaltequani says,

> Huitzilin, your scar mirrors your name, like the smoking mirror of Tezcatlipoca, so I will call you "Tezcatl Huitzilin."

The moniker sticks and soon I am recognized wherever I go as "Tezcatl Huitzilin." My hummingbird scar becomes my emblem and brings me notoriety. It is now my trademark and I feel my power grow. My accomplishments on the battlefield become legendary and people believe I have the speed and power of the hummingbird and the vision and magic of god Tezcatlipoca. People say,

> He sees the knife before it falls.
> He hears the word before it is spoken.
> Where he walks, fate bends.
> Where he points, kings fall.

On the day following our return to Tenochtitlán I am inducted into the ranks of the elite Jaguar Warriors, I stand before the temple of Huitzilopochtli, the sun warming my brow, the drums echoing like thunder in my chest. A priest steps forward and paints my face with black and yellow, the sacred colors of the jaguar. He binds my arms with obsidian-studded cuffs and hands me a macuahuitl carved with glyphs of fire and blood. Tlaltequani, my commanding officer, places a jaguar pelt across my shoulders. His eyes hold pride, but also expectation. I have earned this honor – but now I must live it.

Tlaltequani turns to the gathered warriors and priests, his voice carrying like a conch-shell call:

> Today we honor Huitzilin, who has honored us.
> On the field at Malinalco, where ambush followed ambush and the earth drank deeply, he stood unshaken. With his atlatl he struck true, taking one captive for the Sun. Again he struck, and a second fell into his shadow. And when our Huey Tlatoani Axayacatl was wounded and the enemy pressed close, it was Huitzilin who broke through the storm. He seized Tlilcuetzpalin, the Otomi Chief, and carried him from the chaos to be offered in Tenochtitlán.
> Now, we honor Huitzilin above all others for his bravery and skill and for preserving the glory of Tenochtitlán and saving the life of our Huey Tlaotani.

I kneel before the warriors and priests. The incense rises. The drums slow to a heartbeat.

I remember the weight of my first shield, and the awe I felt watching seasoned warriors in battle.

I remember Tlaltelolco when fear and duty met in my hands. The blood was real, the fear was real. My piochtli was cut and I became a tlamanih, a capturer. My name was spoken with new weight.

And now, Matlatzinco, where the gods tested me hardest. When chaos closed around our Huey Tlatoani and the Otomi's tecpatl was in his raised fist, ready to plunge into Huey Tlatoani's chest, my nagual rose beside me, leading me into the center to save our revered leader. The gods were with me. I was named Tequihua, a warrior of distinction. My shield bore new glyphs. My step grew heavier with purpose. But it was the moment when I stopped the Otomi's knife that shaped me more than any title or glyph.

I now join the ranks of the Jaguar Warriors. I wear the skin of the beast, not for pride, but for duty. I fight not only with blade and fire, but with discipline, devotion, and the memory of those who walked before me.

I am Huitzilin. I am a son of Tenochtitlán. I am the breath of the gods and the blood of the people. I do not walk alone–I walk with the jaguar, with the sun, with the ancestors who whisper in the wind.

I rise to face the people. I feel their cheers wash over me like rain on stone. But remembering my father's words, I bow low, touch the ground, then touch hand to lips to express my humility and devotion to the people of Tenochtitlán.

c. 1476, Malinalco

The year is 1476. Two years have passed since the battle of Matlatzinco but messengers report renewed troubles in the Toluca Valley. The Matlatzinca and their Otomi allies have staged ambushes and insurgent actions and resistance continues. They have moved their forces to fortified mountain strongholds, especially at Malinalco. Now, the message is urgent. It carries weight.

Generals and commanders rush to the war council chamber. Tlaltequani and I attend. Axayacatl rises slowly, leaning on his staff, grimacing from his injured leg. But his voice is strong. All bow to him when he speaks,

> Tlacochcalcatl will march to Matlatzinco with an army of twenty thousand—warriors from Tenochtitlán, Texcoco, and Tlacopan together. They will join Tlacateccatl who is garrisoned there together with our occupying force of five thousand. Tlacateccatl knows the enemy, where they stand, where they fight, where they sleep. He will decide the course of battle from there.
>
> I will not burden the expedition through mountain trails and ambushes. I will remain here, in Tenochtitlán. Paynani will pass messages with each movement, each question.
>
> Place the paynani along the road so the word does not grow old. The message must pass from mouth to mouth, from hand to hand, before the strength of the runner falters. Station them close—where the road bends, where the valley narrows, so no runner shall carry the burden beyond the reach of his breath. The speech of the captains must fly as the arrow flies, so the drumbeat of war will reach me before the sun sets, and the mountain will not hide what happens in its shadow.
>
> The resistance must be vanquished. The Toluca Valley must stand with Tenochtitlán. Let no resistance remain.

ROAD TO MATLATZINCO

The road from Tenochtitlán to Matlatzinco is long, the dust rising with every step of our march. My shield weighs heavy, but my heart is steady. As always, I march beside my mentor. The mountains surrounding the Toluca Valley are treacherous and as we pass through the area, we are the target of small bands of fighters seeking advantage and information.

Then, through the lines of warriors, I see him—Ahuitzotl, brother of Huey Tlatoani Axayacatl. My mind spins—my best friend from the Calmecac, the one who studied beside me, who recited hymns with me, who laughed with me when the lessons grew long; teammates on the ball court, our bodies moving as one, striking the rubber ball with hips and shoulders, trusting each other's rhythm.

Years have passed since those days, yet the bond remains. I stop, and he stops too. Our eyes meet, and in that instant the years fall away. I move my hip like I'm hitting the ball to him. He moves his, like he's bouncing it back to me; like we did when we were young. We bow slightly, as we were taught, but then I clasp his forearm, and we both laugh – the sound rising above the march like a drumbeat of joy. And those around us notice our special bond.

We walk together now, side by side, shields lifted, banners swaying, sharing stories. The road ahead is dangerous, but I know – as I knew on the ball court, as I knew in the Calmecac – that our friendship will endure, through this campaign and beyond.

ARRIVAL AT MATLATZINCO

We arrive without shouting.

From the ridge above Tollocan, Matlatzinco's capital, I see the banners–dark shapes moving against the pale grasslands. As we march over uneven ground, the standards of Tenochtitlán rise and dip like slow birds. We make camp beside the main garrison. I stand with Tlaltequani at the edge of the encampment, silent, measuring. Our men look well-fed, sandals intact. Our cotton armor not yet softened by weeks of rain and sweat. We carry ourselves with the confidence of those who have marched out from causeways and canals, not ravines. We are strong, but we have not yet learned the land.

Tlaltequani leans close and speaks without turning his head. "They will learn quickly," he says, "Or they will be carried."

I nod. I feel the old familiar tightening behind the ribs–not fear, but readiness. The sense that something long delayed has finally begun to move.

That night, the camps do not mingle. Tenochtitlán on one side. Texcoco and Tlacopan interspersed. Fires are small. Voices low. No drums sound. The mountain looms above, black against the stars, indifferent.

I sleep lightly, my hand on my shield strap, listening to the wind pass through stone like breath through a chest.

THE MEETING OF CAPTAINS

The captains are summoned before dawn and gather beneath a low awning stretched between poles, the ground hard and swept clean. No map lies before them. None is needed. Tlacateccatl stands at the center, upright, unadorned, his cloak plain for a man of his rank. Authority rests on him like weight on a settled stone. Tlacochcalcatl stands beside him.

I stand beside Tlaltequani and the other senior warriors of the wing, at attention, listening.

Tlacateccatl does not begin with Malinalco. He begins with Matlatzinco:

> Our patrols are stretched thin. Of paths that have grown unsafe, tribute slowed not by distance, but by defiance. You will see ravines where men have died, not dramatically, but uselessly. You will see hills where scouts no longer linger. Now the Matlatzinca and their allies have spread their main forces to several altepetls, but they have placed their command at Malinalco. It is an altepetl surrounded by tall, steep mountains, with only a single access point through a long narrow valley. If we take Malinalco, and capture the Matlatzinca there, the entire valley will be ours.

Turning to look south, gesturing, he continues,

> The heart of the resistance is Malinalco, a two-day march through perilous mountain terrain. As we approach Malinalco ambushes will find us.
>
> Our main force will follow the travelled road to Tezontle Volcano and turn south through the valley floor to the entryway of Malinalco.
>
> Our goal is to destroy all resistance so that it does not rise again. Once peace comes to Malinalco the Toluca Valley will be at peace.

"Malinalco watches us," he says. "And believes we do not watch back." He lifts his hand—not to point, but to indicate height. "There is a ridge they do not guard," he says, "because they believe it guards itself."

Tlacateccatl's eyes shift—briefly—to Tlaltequani.

Tlaltequani, your wing will break from the main body at Xiuhtepetl Volcano. Loyal scouts who know, will lead you to the hidden way. You will go where sound falls upward and paths vanish.

Tlaltequani nods once. No words.
Tlacateccatl continues,

You must climb without pause to the ridge. The descent is not kind. It will not take all men at once. It will take the strong, those who know how to wait.

When the sun rises to the height of a thrown spear, the main force will show itself, our banners will be seen and Malinalco will turn its face toward them. When their drums answer from the valley and their warriors rush to attack us, we will feign a pull back. When our conch shells blow, wing warriors will rise behind them, appearing to come from within the mountain itself.

There is no flourish. No invocation. The plan is spoken as something already accomplished. The captains disperse quietly.

Outside, the light has begun to change. The world holding its breath.

⧉⧉⧉⧉⧉

Tlaltequani assembles an elite force of the fittest warriors for the mission and splits them into three units of thirty warriors each. He appoints me to take charge of the vanguard cadre.

The ropes were prepared long before the order was spoken—thick maguey fiber, rough against the palm, smelling faintly of sap and smoke. They were coiled carefully, stored dry. Not one rope. Many. Enough for the mission, none to be wasted. The ladders are fewer. Short lengths only. Rope and slats. Made to bridge gaps, not cliffs.

⧉⧉⧉⧉⧉

The next day at first light, we march to Teotenango, a walled hilltop fortress overlooking the Toluca Valley, site of an ancient pyramid devoted to water and earth gods of an earlier time. Our priests burn copal incense at the shrine, asking for safe passage through the mountains. Captains pierce their ears with maguey spines, letting blood fall on paper banners. Shields are lifted. A chant echoes: "O Huitzilopochtli, receive our breath, strengthen our hearts."

THE TURN AT XIUHTEPETL VOLCANO

In the eighth hour of the night, before sunrise, our wing, joined by our guides, departs without a sound. Xiuhtepetl Volcano rises ahead, its flanks dark with brush and broken stone. Our guides lead us along the west edge of the mountain. The moonlit night is still. Nothing stirs.

I feel the world narrow. Here the road ceases to be a road and becomes a memory of passage—scratches in rock, bent grass, places where men had once chosen to go. The sound changes first. Footsteps dull; voices die. The air is cool, heavy, unsteady. Our wing moves in disciplined silence, each man carrying what he must, not more. Shields slung. Weapons wrapped. No shell horns. No drums. Orders pass by touch and gesture. We climb for hours, unnoticed.

When the sun breaks the darkness of night, the main army moves forward along the wide road leading to Malinalco, drums beating, banners visible now. But our wing is not among them. To ensure success, Malinalco's attention must be drawn to the approaching army that will camp at the foot of Tezontle Volcano.

The sun is descending when we reach the mountain's ridge. At the crest, the land falls away sharply. I step forward and look down. The eastern face is not a cliff, but it might as well be—broken ledges, loose stone, shadowed drops where the eye cannot measure distance. Below lay folds of darkness.

Tlaltequani crouches beside me. "This is where men stop thinking of themselves as many," he says quietly. "And remember they are one."

We uncoil ropes. Set anchors around stone, through roots, tested twice. No speeches. No ceremony. No prayers spoken aloud. My group goes first. I take the rope first, hand over fist. I dig out footholds in the mountain for the next man. I reach a narrow ledge where I wait for a short ladder to get across to the next sure spot. And so it goes, One foothold to the next. Each breath is the world to me. The rope bites into my palms. Above, silence. Below, nothing. When my feet touch firm ground, I do not look back. I wait and signal for the next man. I guide one at a time down the ropes and ladders until all thirty are accounted for. Hands burn. Muscles shake, but none moan. Time stretches. Waiting.

We are exposed on the cliff face. We crouch, searching for rock or bush to hide us, bodies pressed low, breath measured. I find a wide cave in a steep south facing mountainside and usher warriors there where we are safe, hidden in the dark, hanging branches obscuring us from watchful eyes below.

THE BATTLE OF MALINALCO

Early the next morning, we hear the sound of drums faintly. Not near. Far from the valley. The main force announcing itself, drawing all eyes and attention toward them as they descend from their encampment and march down the main road to Malinalco.

From the cave, we have an open view of Malinalco. Their army, weapons and priests, all visible. But they are not Malinalca; they carry the banners of Matlatzinca and Otomi warriors. I watch the warriors assemble. Their weapons sharp, glistening. Commanders order the march north to meet the approaching Tenochca allied forces. When the Matlatzinca army moves past our position, we hear the conch shells blow. Not hurried. Not confused. As expected. Our signal.

⊐⊏⊐⊏⊐⊏⊐⊏⊐⊏

I can see Tlaltequani and his men to my right. I do not see the third group, beyond. Tlaltequani lifts two fingers. Men rise without sound. My group moves forward first—silently, not charging, not yet. Following Tlaltequani's plan, I order my men to spread out, each in a separate pocket, hidden behind a rock or bush with a superior view of the battlefield.

When the last enemy warrior marches on, I drop down to the valley floor, and throw my spear, striking him squarely in the back of his neck. His comrades pause to render aid and I attack with my bow and arrows. Soon more enemy warriors see me and rush toward my position. I move back for cover and signal to my men to open the attack and slaughter the oncoming enemy. My men become visible, but remain high in the mountainside attacking with range weapons: bows and arrows, spears, slinging stones and atlatls and darts. The defenders turn, look, understanding all at once that the mountain has not protected them. It has delivered their enemy. Their spears cannot reach my warriors; their arrows lose strength as they reach our positions. We draw part of their force away from the main body and create confusion, my men attacking from above and from all angles.

While we are attacking from one side of the valley, Tlaltequani moves his group into the undefended town and attacks from the rear. The third group reaches the other side of the valley, encircling the enemy and join the attack. Soon, our missiles rain on the enemy who find no escape.

Matlazinca and Otomi warriors turn and scatter, pulled apart by sound and confusion. Some rush toward the drums, only to be attacked by our main army. Others wheel toward our line, but find no respite, disbelief still on their faces, as if our men have stepped out of the mountain itself. We were ready for them. They were not ready for us. We continue a furious barrage.

Their discipline breaks as too many of their men are struck. Some retreat toward sanctuaries, toward carved stone, toward belief but belief does not hold. Trying to escape, some pound on doors, but the Malinalca do not support them. They are turned away to face our knives.

Tlaltequani points once. A gap. His men flow into it, moving as practiced—closing distance, breaking lines, isolating pairs. The fighting tightens into narrow places—between stone walls, along paths meant for single-file. This place was never meant for large battle.

By the time the great Mexica army arrives in Malinalco—banners held high, shields glittering like wet obsidian—the Matlatzinca and Otomi fighters are already scattered, their war-bands shattered, their breath fleeing before them. Their hold on Malinalco folds inward, like a flower closing at nightfall, like a reed bending before the wind. By midmorning, Malinalco is taken. Not burned – taken. The Matlatzinco hold over Malinalco is broken.

We honor the Malinalca. For long have they lived beneath the grinding stone of Matlatzinco, for long have they carried another's burden on their backs. Now the weight is lifted. They open their doors; they open their hearts. They welcome us.

THE FIGHTING ENDS

This is the part of war few speak of—the stillness after violence, when discipline matters more than courage. I feel the ache in my hands now, the stiffness in my shoulders. I flex my fingers, test my grip. Blood— some mine, most not—darkens the edge of my shield.

Tlaltequani studies me for a moment. "You are thinking again," he says.

I do not deny it. "I am listening," I reply. "To the stone."

Tlaltequani exhales through his nose, almost a laugh. "Stone speaks slowly," he says. "Choose your questions carefully."

The order goes out without ceremony. Weapons down. Fires controlled. No looting permitted. Matlazinca and Otomi warriors are bound and separated. The living counted. The dead left where they fall, waiting for the local people to dispose of them as they wish.

I stand with Tlaltequani near the lower terraces and watch the army settle into the place like water finding level. Units re-form. Guards are posted at paths and stairways. Texcocan scouts fan outward. Tlacopan banners hold the center.

The captives are taken at dawn. Not all at once, not with shouting, but by names spoken aloud and answered with silence. The Matlatzinca tlatoani is brought first, wrapped still in dignity he can no longer command. Behind him come the Matlatzinca generals and captains whose faces I recognize from the fighting, and priests whose hands smell of copal even now.

I stand with Tlaltequani at the edge of the square, watching the order of it. There is no confusion about who is chosen. These are the ones whose words carried weight, whose rites made resistance permissible, whose ambushes bled the empire.

Some are bound for the road. Those destined for Tenochtitlán are gathered carefully, separated by rank, guarded closely. They will walk the long way north, displayed and counted, their lives already placed into ritual time.

Others do not leave. A small number—chosen for what they represent rather than what they did—are executed in the square. The blades fall cleanly. Blood darkens the stone, then thins, then disappears beneath the water they pour. Nothing remains but a faint smell of obsidian and blood, and the echo of voices that no longer have breath.

I note how the people stand—rigid, attentive, watching in silence, relieved, yet uncertain of what fate will reveal for them. No one rushes forward. No one cries out. This is a Nahua town. They understand what is happening.

Though the shock of what has happened reverberates, I watch the square slowly return to itself, as it must, and I think: so passes the man, like a word that thought it could stand alone. What remains is not the man, but the place where he once stood—and even that does not last.

THE MORNING AFTER

The next morning, Malinalco opens its eyes again.

I walk the streets without armor, my shield left behind. The town smells of damp earth and cooking maize. Doors open. People move. Life resumes, cautiously, but it resumes.

At the market, I stop.

The woman selling tamales looks at me once—long enough to measure my posture—and then names her price without trembling. Her Nahuatl bends differently, like maize grown on another slope, but the root is the same. It carries a turn of sound I'm not used to, softer in some places, sharper in others, but the words are the same. I answer her in my own speech.

She blinks, surprised, then nods as if something has been confirmed.

As I eat, I listen. A proverb passes between two women and I know the ending before it is spoken. The jokes are familiar, the curses too. Even the prayers murmured under breath are the same. Water still descends from the mountain. Maize still rises from the earth. For a moment, the market feels like a remembered song—one verse changed, the measure intact. I think: we are all flowers of the same root that opened in different light.

ARRIVAL OF AXAYACATL

We remain in Malinalco for several days, repairing structures damaged in the fighting and mingling with the locals. After three days, Huey Tlatoani Axayacatl arrives in Malinalco before midday.

The litter moves slowly through the town, borne by men who have carried him across causeways and valleys before. The banners rise. The sound of drums is controlled, ceremonial, unmistakable. The litter passes and the people bow, but I notice how quickly the dust settles again. Power moves through a town like a wind through reeds—felt, then gone. What endures is the cut of the path beneath it.

Axayacatl speaks briefly to the gathered Malinalca . He does not threaten. He does not boast:

> Malinalco is a Nahua altepetl, now joined to Tenochtitlán, now returned to order. Your rites will continue, not erased. Tenochtitlán will shelter Malinalco.
> You did not stand with Matlatzinco. You did not raise your shields against us. Thus, your tribute will be light—unlike that of Tollocan, Ocuilan, Tecaxic, or Calixtlahuaca, altepetls that resisted, that fought, that slew Mexica warriors. They will bear the weight of their defiance.

I stand among the captains as the emperor names a new tlatoani, chosen carefully—a nobleman of Malinalco with known ties to Tenochtitlán. His lineage is recited. His obligations are made plain.

Axayacatl thanks Tlacateccatl for executing the mission. Tlacateccatl then speaks, thanking Tlaltequani for organizing the wing and executing the flanking maneuver. He also mentions me by name, highlighting my management of men and strategic vision.

The people watch. Some faces are hard. Others curious. Many relieved.

That evening, fires burn again.

d. Imagining the Cuauhcalli

Later–after the wounded are moved, the captives secured, the first ritual boundaries are marked–I walk the upper paths. I do not do this as a warrior now. I imagine, I measure.

The mountain rises sharply above the settlement, its face cut and worked in places, raw in others. The ropes are gone. I follow a narrow approach, half-hidden, known to priests more than soldiers. I climb carefully, testing handholds, remembering the path my men took in darkness, now obvious in daylight–scratches in stone, compacted earth, places where hands reached to survive. I remember the night before the battle, my warriors pressed into shadow, waiting without sound. There is no urgency now. No signal to listen for.

The air cools. The sound thins. Then I see it. The place where our men waited, overlooking the city. The cave waits exactly as it did before, unchanged by the bodies it hid.

The cave opens before me. I stand at its mouth, the cave breathing the cool air in the heat of the day. Sound dies quickly here, as if the mountain keeps only what matters.

Inside, I stand and look. Now that I am not counting men, I count space. I pace the curve with measured steps. I trace the walls with my palm. The stone is not random. It turns inward deliberately, as if following a shape that already exists in the mind of the mountain. The floor is level, shaped to walk upon. The ceiling curves naturally, but not chaotically.

I imagine benches carved where the rock thickens. I imagine the walls smoothed, the mouth widened just enough to accept light but not surrender shadow. I imagine the stone learning the shape of jaguar and eagle, not imposed, but revealed.

A PRIESTLY PRESENCE

Footsteps sound behind me. I turn. An ancient priest stands at the mouth, his shape like a dark shadow, the light of day behind him. He is not surprised to see me. Perhaps no one is surprised inside a place like this.

"You returned," he says.

"Yes," I answer. "I wanted to see if it was still here."

He looks at me for a moment, then steps inside. He kneels without ceremony, the movement is practiced, as if the stone expects it of him. He places his hands on the stone as one might greet his mother.

"It does not leave," he says. "Men do."

"This is not just a hollow," I say.

"No," the priest agrees. "It is a place where the mountain allows itself to be entered."

"You were here during the fighting," he says at last, his voice low, directed more to the stone than to me.

"Yes."

"You brought men."

"I hid them."

He pauses. He places his palm flat against the wall, fingers spread.

"The mountain felt them," he says. "It did not refuse."

"Was this place known to you before the fighting?" I ask.

"This cave was already old when our grandfathers were dreams, Huitzilin."

I turn, wondering how he knew my name.

He continues,

> Long before your Mexica banners climbed this hill, the mountain was a sleeping serpent, its heart hollowed by the first waters. In the beginning, when the Fifth Sun was still weak, the earth opened her mouth here and breathed out mist and song, and from that breath stepped warriors of feather and claw, jaguar and eagle, their eyes bright with star fire. Children were once brought to this mouth of stone so their souls could remember where they had first emerged, and the old ones say that in the deepest watches of the night, you can still hear the footsteps of those who were born from darkness into flame.
>
> When you crept through this place in war, you walked in their tracks without knowing it; now you return not as a warrior but as one who listens, and the cave remembers your scent, folds you again in its cool breath, and whispers that every flanking path in battle is also a path back into the body of the earth, where fear and courage are ground together like maize for the gods.

I answer,

> I know now. The night I brought my men to this space in the still of night, huddled with fear, it was meant by the gods that I should remember, that I should return to this, the womb of the earth. That this place be revealed.

"There are places that make themselves known," he says. "They do not announce it to everyone."

"Did people come here before us?" I ask.

"They came," he says. "They listened. They fasted. They asked for rain. They asked for permission."

"For what?"

He presses his forehead briefly to the stone. "To pass through."

I think of my men waiting here, breath held, bodies pressed into darkness, ready to be born into battle at the sound of a drum.

I look again at the walls, at the way the rock curves inward as if remembering something older than either of us. I step farther inside now, measuring without moving my feet.

Pointing, I say,

> The curve could be widened without breaking its shape. The floor could be leveled where the stone already softens. Light could be taken in—not too much—through the mouth if it were taught how to open.

I run my hand once more along the wall, already seeing the line where the stone will fall away, already knowing where it must not.

I stand quietly for a time. "We will carve here," I say at last—not as a question.

I hear the priest's voice soften behind me,

> But only where something already listens. Do not ask this place to change, ask it to remember" You must know where the stone wishes to be touched. When you return, if you must, bring stonecutters who know restraint. They are not making a thing. They are revealing one.

I step toward the light, measuring again, not with my feet this time, but with intention.

The cave is still, silent. I turn to speak to the old priest but no one is there.

The mountain watches. It does not resist. This place holds memory. It also holds possibility. I leave knowing I will return.

THE AFTERNOON MEAL

I return from the mountain with stone dust still in the lines of my hands.

The cave does not release me easily. Even as I descend, I am still inside it–counting the way the wall curves inward, the way a ridge of stone lifts like a beak when the light strikes it from the mouth. In one place, the rock folds back on itself in a heavy, muscled swell that hides the shape of a Jaguar waiting.

I wash at the basin near the camp, but the smell of stone remains. I let it.

The afternoon meal is already laid out beneath the shade screens. Men sit in loose order, armor set aside, talking with the ease that comes only after victory. My mentor, Tlaltequani, sits slightly apart, his posture unchanged by the informality. Beside him is Tlacateccatl, broad-shouldered, already eating, listening to three conversations at once. Ahuitzotl sees me first and shifts to make room.

"You look like you've been counting ghosts," he says quietly.

"Stone," I answer, "Older than ghosts."

Tlaltequani studies me over his bowl.

"You went back," he says.

"Yes," I answer as I smell the sweet maize cakes.

He nods, without looking up from his bowl.

We eat for a time without speaking. The sound of hungry men; the low hum of the camp. Then Tlacateccatl wipes his hands and looks at me directly.

"You found something," he says. It is not a question.

"There is a hollow in the mountain," I reply. "A cave shaped by time, not by hands. It hid men during the fighting. It will hold more than men."

Ahuitzotl leans forward. "More than men?"

"It holds the breath of the mountain, the attention of the gods, and it will hold the memory of men who enter it."

Ahuitzotl rises from his seat, "Show us, I will witness it myself."

MEETING AT THE CAVE

When the meal is done and the sun leans westward, the four of us rise together. I lead, Ahuitzotl at my side, Tlaltequani and Tlacateccatl follow behind. I guide them up the rough hillside, the path winding through brush and stone until the cave mouth opens before us.

We pause at its threshold. The air is cool, carrying a breath that feels older than our steps. I speak in a reverent tone, telling them how I imagine the place: the mountain is a sleeping serpent, the cave is its heart, a womb of stone where warriors might be reborn.

Tlacateccatl runs his hand along the wall, nodding at the curve of the rock. Tlaltequani tilts his head, hearing echoes in the silence. "Listen to the echoes," he says.

Ahuitzotl answers, "I hear the sound of a newborn's breath–The earth remembers."

Together we marvel at the vision the cave awakens. The hillside holds us in its stillness, and for a moment we are not captains or messengers, but companions standing at the edge of mystery.

I explain, "It is an ancient cave, a birthplace, sacred–it faces south, where the sun may see in only on the morning of the winter solstice. Men have come here to listen, to fast. If we shape it with care, it will not just shelter warriors, it will change them.

That draws Tlaltequani's full attention, yet he does not speak.

"The stone already bears forms," I continue, keeping my voice level. "Not carvings. Suggestions. That ridge, there, rises in the form of an eagle. And, look there [indicating], a mass that turns inward like a crouching jaguar. They are not finished shapes. They are beginnings."

Tlacateccatl grunts softly. "I see them in the rock."

"We see what the rock permits," I answer. "It carries the essence of these shapes."

Silence settles—not resistance, but consideration.

"Such places are old," Tlaltequani says at last. "Older than us. Older than Malinalco."

"Yes," I say. "Which is why they endure. If we shape it carefully—if we carve only where the stone already yields—we do not erase what came before. We bind it to what comes next."

"A monument, then," says Tlacateccatl . "Not a fortress. Not a hall."

"A threshold," I reply. "For those who pass from one state to another. Warriors who must leave behind what they were."

He considers this, eyes narrowing—focused. "And you," he says. "You would carve it?"

"I could design it," I answer. "Oversee the first cuts. After that, others can continue. Stoneworkers who know restraint. I would name it 'Cuauhcalli,' Jaguar House." As I speak those words, I think of my father, Cuauhtli, his strength, his wisdom, his perfection.

Tlaltequani's gaze remains on me, steady and unreadable. "You are already thinking beyond this campaign," he says.

"I have to," I reply. "The empire is becoming stone and water now. Roads. Aqueducts. Places that must outlast the men who order them built."

No one speaks for a moment.

Then Ahuitzotl shakes his head. "We used to argue about glyphs and calendars," he says. "Now you're planning to teach mountains discipline."

Tlaltequani allows himself the smallest smile. "An idea," he says carefully, "is like a seed. It does not need approval to take root. Only ground that will hold it."

Tlacateccatl exhales, a sound halfway between a sigh and assent. "When the time comes," he says, "bring me back to this thought."

I bow my head once, not in gratitude, but acknowledgment.

We step out of the cave and the camp noise rises again. But something has shifted, quietly, like a stone turned to reveal a face beneath.

The mountain waits.

And now, so do we.

When we reach the valley floor, we all look back toward the mountain, its flank glowing in the late light. "This ground will hold," Tlacateccatl says.

HUITZILIN, THE BUILDER

Axayacatl leads a triumphant return to Tenochtitlán with thousands of captives, more than eleven thousand, some say, captured in the Toluca Valley campaign. Ahuitzotl, Tlacateccatl and Tlacochcalcatl join him together with the army of twenty thousand.

Before they leave, Tlacateccatl calls me to his side and says, "I have seen your talent for ordering men and I know your interest in building. Now, you shall remain here to oversee construction of military fortifications, to rebuild what has been broken and to improve roads to Tenochtitlán.

Once the army is out of sight, the city of Malinalco is quiet. Farmers and artisans return to their work and life resumes as it must.

I understand my duty. After each conquest, we raise works to improve the lives of the newly conquered people and to bind new lands to the empire. For this, I gather hundreds of workers – captives, conscripts, villagers. The work is swift and I'm pleased when my work is done here in Malinalco.

When the rains come hard, I return home for time with family, my children and parents. But before I can settle, a summons comes. I am called back to attend to a mudslide that has destroyed a portion of highway.

Then, more orders come—first to mark routes between altepetls, then to organize crews where roads must be widened and leveled, where old paths fail under tribute traffic.

I build causeways. These are not mere paths, but arteries of tribute and power. Major causeways must carry eight warriors abreast. Our paynani, long-distance messengers, rely on these roads to relay urgent messages across hundreds of miles in a single day. Pochteca and porters travel great distances, and return with heavy loads of textiles and pottery, of copper, obsidian, gold and silver. Without good roads, we cannot grow strong and prosper.

The work begins by clearing the earth down to bedrock. I walk the site with care, measuring distances, aligning markers and coaxing the terrain into order. In wet areas, I direct the crews to dig deep until we reach stable ground. Where the soil shifts or sinks, I order wooden piles driven deep into the earth to anchor the road. I oversee the layering of gravel, sand, and small stones to ensure proper drainage, and I inspect the surfacing–packed clay or crushed stone, sometimes finished with lime plaster or stucco for smoothness. Drainage ditches flank each side, and where rivers cross our path, I design bridges or sluice gates to allow water and canoes to pass. Raised curbs prevent erosion. Every seven miles, I place marker stones and oversee the construction of rest stations with small temples for tlamemes and paynanis (porters and messengers).

I walk the roads each evening, inspecting every curve and stone, searching for the answer that will make the project sing. If a section is uneven, I order it redone. If a ditch is shallow, I have it deepened.

I work closely with my laborers–not with a whip or a shout, but with presence and care. I learn their names, listen to their stories, and treat them with dignity. In return, they respect me. My workers watch how I inspect each line and angle, how I pause to adjust a stone or remeasure a slope with precision, a trait I first displayed as a child on my family's building sites. Soon, they learn to see the work through my eyes, and they strive to meet the standard I set–not out of fear, but out of shared purpose. Together, we build not just roads, but trust.

In time, I begin to envision and design entire projects on my own–temples, administrative buildings, fortifications. I manage hundreds of workers. I am recognized not just for what I build, but for how I build it. My peers and warriors of lower rank show me respect, not because I demand it, but because they feel it.

I no longer swing the macuahuitl, I order men. Men no longer look to me not for where to strike, but for where to begin. With time, my heart begins to shift–from conquest to creation.

When I think of Malinalco now, I do not remember the fighting. I remember the mountain–how it waited, and the cave–how it may be taught. Cuauhcalli.

CONFLICTS AND JEALOUSIES

I begin to see what others whisper but dare not say aloud–my accomplishments and reputation now eclipse those of my superiors, men of higher rank and noble birth. One of them, a high-ranking officer, knew me as a boy in the Calmecac. Even then, he refused to call me by my name. "Macehualli," he would sneer, as if the word itself were a stain. Commoner. Peasant. Dirt.

Now we are both officers, but he continues the insult. It is a breach of protocol–he should address me by rank. Other officers hear it. They glance away, say nothing. The silence stings more than the word.

After a decade of service, I grow weary–not of battle, but of the politics that rot the heart of the military. I have led men, built roads, captured enemies, and earned honors. Yet doors remain closed. Roles are denied. My birth shadows every achievement.

In 1479, I learn that Axayacatl has suffered a crushing defeat at the hands of the Purépecha in Michoacán. I worry about his health as I know he has not fully recovered from his injury at Matlazinco. I am not part of the Purépechan campaign, but I feel the tremor ripple through our ranks. The defeat wounds our pride, and the prestige of our military begins to fray.

Meanwhile, my brother Tezcacoatl thrives. His trade routes stretch across the empire. His name opens doors. He urges me to leave the military, to build a life of wealth and influence as a civilian. "You have the mind of a tlachiani,"[128] he says." "Why waste it on men who will never see you as their equal? If you stay in the military, I'll have to start trading for better incense – the kind they burn at funerals."

I begin to wonder if he is right. My loyalty to the battlefield wanes. I dream of designing temples, building aqueducts, shaping the future

---

128 master builder

with stone and vision. I imagine a life where my work speaks louder than my lineage. A life where I am not just tolerated–but valued.

A QUIET DECISION

I sit alone beneath the shade of a ceiba tree, the sun warm on my shoulders; the sounds of the city distant but familiar. My armor rests beside me, polished but heavy. I run my fingers along the jaguar pelt, once a symbol of pride – now a relic of a life I feel slipping away.

Ten years of service. Ten years of blood, stone, and silence. I have fought with honor, built with precision, and led with care. But the fire that once burned in me for battlefield now flickers for something else – creation, family, peace.

I think of my children, Cuauhtémoc and Xochiquetzal, their laughter echoing in my memory. I think of my brother Tezcacoatl's words, urging me to build a life beyond the sword. I think of the roads I've laid, the temples I've raised, the dreams I've yet to shape.

I rise, brush the dust from my cloak, and walk to my commander's quarters. I speak clearly, respectfully.

"I am ready to retire from military service. My path now leads elsewhere."

He nods, surprised but silent. The decision is mine. The next chapter begins.

V
1480, Civilian Life

a. Huitzilin and Itzel

It is year 1480. I take my children Cuauhtémoc and Xochiquetzal to attend the Huey Tozoztli Festival, an exuberant celebration honoring Tlaloc, god of rain, water, and fertility. Music fills the air. Dancers whirl like petals in the wind. The scent of roasted maize and cacao drifts between laughter and song. It is a day of joy, of mingling and memory.

As we walk among the crowd, I notice a pretty young woman glimpsing me. Her gaze lingers, and my heart stirs. I approach the young lady and introduce myself in a formal, respectful manner. "Greetings," I say. "I am Huitzilin – Jaguar Warrior, and builder of temples. Son of Cuauhtli, jeweler to the royal family."

She replies with grace, "I am Itzel,[129] royal daughter of Chalchiuhtototl,[130] Tlamacazqui of the Royal Aviary.

I gesture toward the feather art display behind her. "The amanteca who created that piece is my sister, Xochitl. The quetzal feathers were provided by your father."

She looks up at me with eyes that say she is pleased with my attentions. I sense her approval – not just of my words, but of my bearing, my distinctive clothing and jewelry awarded to me for my valor on the battlefield.

---

129 Name means "radiance of dawn, morning star, beauty"
130 Name means "Jade Bird."

Her own presence is radiant. Like the fragrant plumeria, her scent intoxicates my heart. She wears a finely woven *huipilli*,[131] embroidered with jade-green quetzal feathers and gold thread.[132] The designs reflect maize plants, hummingbirds and rain.[133] Her cueitl (skirt), is long and flowing, dyed in vibrant turquoise and deep red.[134] It is adorned with obsidian beads and shells. She wears a lightweight mantle embroidered with cloud motifs[135] draped over her shoulders, fastened with a jade brooch I recognize – crafted by my father.

The next day, we meet again by chance. We walk together, speaking softly. Over the following weeks, we continue to see each other. I tell her of my children, and of my wife, who died heroically in childbirth six years before. Itzel listens with tenderness. Her voice is gentle, her words thoughtful.

Our courtship remains formal, respectful and secret. But it deepens. She is not only beautiful and intelligent – she shares my passion for learning, for innovation, for shaping the world through thought and craft.

One day, in the city plaza, I speak from my heart. "Itzel, I have completed my military service. Now, I dream of a life with you, always. Hear my song:

> *"Like the bird calling for its mate,*
> *I cry out in the stillness.*
> *Will you not come, my precious flower?*
> *The moonlight embraces me,*
> *But your warmth is all I seek.*
> *Your face is a radiant flower,*
> *Your breath, a gentle breeze.*
> *Your words are like jade,*
> *Precious and everlasting.*

131 Blouse or Tunic.

132 Symbols of nobility and connection to the gods.

133 Symbols honoring Tozoztli, god of fertility.

134 Colors representing vitality and renewal.

135 Invoking Tlaloc's blessings.

> *Do not let the winds scatter you,*
> *Stay close, for my heart is yours."*

She reaches out and holds me tight. "I too, love you dearly, Huitzilin. I too wish to be with you always. But I am preoccupied by fear that my family will insist I marry a man from a noble family." Itzel sings,

> *Huitzilin,*
> *You are the one who paints the skies,*
> *My paradise of colors and light.*
> *In your arms, the sun rises,*
> *And the stars take their rest.*
> *Do not leave me, O flower of the heavens,*
> *For in you, my heart finds its home.*

I too know well that Itzel's noble family will not favor our union, but we continue to meet in secret. Our love blossoms—quiet, fierce, and true.

SEEKING APPROVAL OF MARRIAGE

My father, Cuauhtli, has reached fifty-two years of age, and our calpulli gathers in grand celebration. This is no ordinary feast, but the completion of the sacred *xiuhmolpilli*, the fifty-two-year calendar cycle—a moment of cosmic renewal when the fire of life is rekindled. The people assemble, their voices hushed with reverence, for such a milestone binds the rhythm of one man's years to the heartbeat of the universe. When the meal is finished, our calpullec, Teyacanqui, rises. His words carry the weight of age and memory:

> I have known Cuauhtli for many years—too many, some might say. I rise to honor him, a man who has brought pride to our calpulli, who has stood beside us in strength and in counsel. Now my own years are heavy, and it is time for me to step aside. It is my wish that Cuauhtli take my place, and become our new calpullec.

The assembly stirs, voices rising in assent, as the cycle of years turns and leadership passes like the sacred flame—renewed, enduring.

Late that night, after the last songs fade and the incense burns low, I speak with my parents. I tell them I wish to marry Itzel, daughter of Tlamacazqui Chalchiuhtototl. I explain our love, our shared dreams, and our fear – that her noble family may reject a union with a commoner, believing it would diminish their standing.

My brother Tezcacoatl and sister Xochitl know the Tlamacazqui well. Tezcacoatl delivers rare birds from vassal states to the Royal Aviary and Xochitl receives exquisite feathers for her artistry. My father understands the significance of this match – not just for me, but for our family's future, and makes it his mission to secure it.

In the days that follow, father meets with his royal patron, Tlacaelel, and shares my wish to marry Itzel. Tlacaelel is delighted. He agrees to speak with his old friend Chalchiuhtototl and his wife to discuss the merits of the proposal.

When they meet, Chalchiuhtototl expresses concern. He speaks of lineage, of alliances, of the advantages that a union with another noble house might bring. Tlacaelel responds:

> Huitzilin is not a mere commoner. I have known him and his family since he was a child. He was gifted, and I admitted him to the Calmecac, where he excelled in every discipline. His manners are refined, his achievements many. He comes from a powerful and wealthy family.

He invites Chalchiuhtototl to meet us in thirteen days, at a feast he will host in his own home.[136]

When the day arrives, our family prepares with reverence and care. We shower Chalchiuhtototl with gifts. My father presents his finest gold and jade jewelry and sister Xochitl unveils a breathtaking featherwork display made from quetzal plumes. Finally, Tezcacoatl rises to present his gift, cacao beans from distant lands. "To bring these here," he says, "I crossed mountains, rivers, and one very stubborn swamp. The swamp nearly won." With that comment, we all join in laughter and the seriousness of the moment is broken.

---

136 In the Mexica sacred calendar, time was measured in repeating 13-day intervals – much like we might say "next week."

Female attendants in elegant garments arrange flowers, incense, and decorative items to honor the gods and elevate the dining experience. Food is served on black porcelain dishes from Cholula, adorned with intricate patterns. Before the meal, servants pour water from decorated *xicales*[137] so we may wash our hands.

The feast is abundant: corn, beans, squash, amaranth, chia, avocado, jicama, chayote, nopales, and honey. Platters of iguana meat, chapulines, axolotls, maguey worms, and azcamolli[138] follow. We end with papaya, annona, chirimoya, zapote, and capulin cherries. *Xocolatl*[139] and pulque are served in ornate cups. After dinner, we relax with cigars while musicians and dancers perform.

As the evening unfolds, Chalchiuhtototl is visibly moved. He sees the strength of our family, the refinement of our traditions, and the support we enjoy from Tlamacazqui Tlacaelel himself.

I speak to him directly: "It would be my honor to design and build a prestigious addition to your home."

Chalchiuhtototl sits in quiet reflection, weighing the gifts, the lineage, the implications. My education, my military record, and the strength of our family stand before him – not as boasts, but as offerings of honor. His wife studies me with careful eyes, and I see her glance toward Itzel.

Itzel steps forward, her voice steady but full of feeling. "Father, I love Huitzilin. He is noble in spirit, wise in thought, and kind in heart. I ask you not only as your daughter, but as a woman who knows her own heart – please, let me choose the path that brings me joy."

Her words hang in the air like incense. Chalchiuhtototl looks at her, then at Tlacaelel, then at my father. The silence is long, but not cold.

At last, he rises with his wife beside him. "Let it be so," he says. "We give our blessing."

The room exhales. Our union is approved – not just by power and politics, but by love.

---

137 Pitchers
138 Edible ant larvae
139 Chocolate

THE WEDDING

Our wedding is a grand affair, held in a beautifully adorned courtyard within the palace grounds. The space blooms with vibrant flowers, woven textiles in brilliant hues, and carvings that speak of gods and ancestors. At the center stands a large altar, heavy with offerings – incense, maize, cacao, and flowers – meant to honor the divine and bless our union.

Distinguished guests arrive in their finest garments, greeted by music and dance. Nobles and members of the royal family, including my beloved friend, Ahuitzotl, mingle with the city's most prominent merchants and gifted artisans, all honored to witness the joining of two esteemed houses. The air hums with joy and reverence.

I watch my father enter the courtyard. He walks with measured steps, never rushing. His hair, once obsidian black, is streaked with brilliant silver, and his face bears the fine lines of wisdom earned over decades. He wears a mantle of deep blue, embroidered with gold thread, and his jewelry – his own masterpieces – glints in the sunlight. He is a *huehuetqueh*, a respected elder, and his presence commands reverence. I see pride in his eyes and I feel a deep satisfaction and quiet joy, knowing that I have earned his approval.

Tlamacazqui Quetzalcoatl Totec, the highest priest of the empire and guardian of the cult of Huitzilopochtli, presides over the ceremony. He leads us through sacred rites – blessings, prayers, and offerings to the gods – to ensure our union is harmonious and prosperous. Itzel and I exchange vows and gifts, symbols of our devotion and shared destiny.

As the festivities unfold, a royal messenger arrives bearing a scroll sealed with the emblem of the Huey Tlatoani Axayacatl. The crowd hushes as the message is read aloud:

> To Huitzilin, Jaguar Warrior and Builder of Temples
> I send my warmest congratulations on your union with
> Lady Itzel.
> In the forests of Matlatzingo, I saw your courage and discipline
> in my moment of need.
> In the halls of Tenochtitlán, I have seen your wisdom and honor.

May your household flourish like the maize fields in springtime,
And may your children carry your name with pride and
strength.
– Axayacatl, Huey Tlahtoani of the Mexica Empire.

The note is met with murmurs of admiration. That the emperor himself would send such a message is a rare honor – one that affirms my standing not only among warriors and builders, but among the highest ranks of the empire.

After the ceremony, the courtyard erupts in celebration. Dancers whirl, musicians play, and guests feast beneath the stars. My father, already a *huehuetqueh* – a respected elder and master jeweler whose creations adorn the royal elite – stands taller than ever. The marriage of his son to the daughter of a noble Tlamacazqui family brings him immense pride and elevates our family's prestige.

⌫⌫⌫⌫⌫

Together, Itzel and I build a household worthy of our lineage. She bears five children, each recognized as noble by virtue of their mother's status. We raise our children with the values my father instilled in me: hard work, ambition, and integrity. I remember being a boy, watching him shape molten gold with steady hands, never rushing, never compromising. "A careless hand," he once told me, "makes a forgettable piece." Now, when my children help me sketch temple designs or carry stones at the worksite, I repeat his words. I teach them that excellence is not born of talent alone, but of discipline and care. In our home, every lesson is a thread in the tapestry of his legacy.

In the evenings, I sit with my children. I teach them, play with them, and listen to their dreams. We attend ollamaliztli games, festivals, and wander through the bustling marketplaces of Tenochtitlán, where colors, sounds, and stories swirl around us like feathers in the wind.

b. Becoming Tlachiani[140]

I am proud of the life I led in the army, yet I know the obsidian blade is not the only path to serve the empire. My destiny now turns to stone and water, to works that endure longer than the memory of war. My first task is close to my heart: the building of a grand house for my father-in-law, Tlamacazqui Chalchiuhtototl. He, a man of feathers and prayer, deserves walls that reflect his station.

I take my time learning where to source basalt and lime mortar and where to find skilled masons, plasterers, carpenters. I nurture these relationships because I know I will need their loyal help on future projects.

When the new home is ready, Chalchiuhtototl proudly hosts his friends and neighbors to show off his impressive new home and proudly introduces me to his guests as his son-in-law and boasts of my military career. Their admiration is plain, and soon they too seek my hand for their projects. My father's name also opens doors, for nobles adorned with his jewels know of our family's skill.

I am 30 years old now, starting a new life with a new wife and a new career. I see my path clearly. My heart is restless. My tonalli burns hot like the midday sun. I cannot sit idle while stones lie waiting.

There is much construction in the Aztec world. I join the builder's guild and labor under older tlachiani, building temples and public works in neighboring altepels. I hone my skills, learning design and techniques from men seasoned by decades. But as I learn from them, I see ways to improve the flow. I run with my workers, I coach them. I find new ways to brace walls against lakebed soil, new forms to align water channels. Soon other tlachiani see my work and copy it. Many thank me for teaching them. I am pleased to be accepted and recognized.

They call me tlachiani – master builder. In our tongue it means more than builder: the eye that measures, the mind that knows how weight is carried, the voice that leads men, the visionary who imagines what

---

140 Tlachiani means master builder, its plural is tlachianimeh, but for convenience I will use tlachiani for singular or plural.

can be and the engineer who makes it endure. I accept all names, for in truth they are one: the duty to raise what lasts.

c. 1481-1486 TIZOC BECOMES EMPEROR

1481 AXAYACATL'S DEMISE

After his crushing defeat in Michoacán, Axayacatl returned to Tenochtilán a beaten man. Thousands of our warriors were lost, and the leg wound he suffered in Matlatzinco was injured again, reopened. I have seen him push through the pain before, leading campaigns and presiding over affairs of state, but over the five years since Matlatzinco, the old injury has soured. People speak of Axayacatzin – revered Axayacatl – lame yet enduring, a testament to his sacrifice for his people. Axayacatl's leg is hot; it makes walking a labor and he spends his days seated on mats, leaning on his staff or borne in a litter. Many warned him not to pursue the Purépechan campaign, but he did not want the people to see him as weak. Now he has fallen gravely ill. Since his return those around him whisper that the gods have turned the Purépechan arrows into a slow, inward-creeping punishment.
I worry and reach out to Ahuitzotl for news of his brother's health. He tells me,

> My brother's leg is afflicted with the hot illness that comes and goes, the head sickness. His leg is red and swollen. He has the illness of pus, the weeping does not stop. He is weak and unable to rise. Brother is grave. He remembers you, Huitzilin. Come with me tomorrow to see him.

We enter the royal precinct in Tenochtitlán. He is among his wives, children, and close retainers. He sees me and waves, beckoning me to come closer,

> Huitzilin, dear one. It pleases me that you have come. I always remember the day in Matlatzinco. You made three captures that day. And, you saved me from the Otomi.
> I will never forget.

Axayacatl closes his eyes, breathing softly. I leave the room and weep.

The next day as the sun rises, the words are whispered, "Huey Tlatoani Axayacatl is dead." In thirteen days, the sickness consumed him. The news of Axayacatl's death strikes me like a frigid wind through the temple corridors. Not unexpected, yet, still I weep again. I pause, remembering the storied day, heroic for me, the beginning of the end for him. He was more than an emperor – he was a warrior, a brother-in-arms. I mourn him quietly, with respect and gratitude.

TIZOC'S REIGN

Days later I hear the announcement, the nobles and priests name Tizoc our new Huey Tlatoani. I do not recall seeing him lead warriors in battle, but he is Axayacatl's brother and grandson of Moctezuma I and Itzcoatl, so we cheer continuity and stability of royal succession.

At his coronation, I watch from the edge of the plaza, among builders and warriors, with Itzel and our children at my side.

Tizoc stands beneath the golden canopy, his mantle heavy with turquoise. He raises his arms toward the gods. The drums fall silent. And then he speaks. We lean in to listen carefully as his is a voice we have not heard before. I anticipate a grand expression of devotion and an invocation to the gods seeking favor for the future of our people.

Tizoc speaks, "Let the gods . . . let them see our devotion." His voice catches, "Let the temple rise – yes, rise – higher than the clouds, broader than the lake. Let the blood . . . let it flow, as it must. As it must."

The words echo, but not with thunder. I hear the hesitation, his eyes searching, the priests, the nobles, the sky. The ceremony continues, but something in me stirs – not awe, but unease. His voice, light with tremor is not powerful like those who came before.

Tizoc continues, describing his vision for the Huey Teocalli – sweeping renovations to the great pyramid at the heart of Tenochtitlán, long weathered by time and neglect. We listen as he describes an expansion worthy of the gods: "Two temples at the summit, One temple shall rise for Huitzilopochtli, who wields fire in his fist; another for Tlaloc, who pours down water and rain."

He pauses, "New platforms, broad terraces, ceremonial spaces to stir awe and devotion." After a long pause, he continues, "A grand staircase will rise, climbing toward the heavens, to honor the gods and humble the people."

When he concludes, Itzel whispers, "Will he lead our people with strength?"

I counsel, "We must wait to see what the gods reveal."

All the great master builders scramble to win Tizoc's favor. I dream of working on such an undertaking too, but I do not see order, I see bickering. I see a project losing direction. A voice tells me to bide my time.

The gods do not smile on Tizoc. He is distracted as resistance flares in the Toluca Valley. Tizoc assembles an army of 20,000 for his coronation campaign, determined to crush the rebellion and prove his strength. But as the forces leave, disputes among his commanders flare in public and Tizoc is unable to control powerful generals pulling in different directions.

Tenochtitlán waits in silence. Soon, messengers arrive, with shadows in their words. Before the moon turns, Tizoc returns with half of those who left, nine captives trailing behind. Matlatzinca, the place of Axayacatl's sacrifice is lost. No voices rise in joy; disbelief drifts like a sickness over Tenochtitlán. The Mexica army is disgraced. A grim omen for Tizoc's rule.

The Huey Teocalli project falters, weighed down by waning confidence, labor shortages and uneven tribute flows needed for large-scale works. The great pyramid stands in shadow, its stones waiting, its vision dimmed.

HUITZILIN THE INNOVATOR

Yet even in shadow, new roads call, new visions rise. I am tlachiani; I feel it in my bones. Wherever I go, day or night, I look, I inspect. Is that stone out of place, misaligned? Is the structure well supported? My neighbors look to me for advice, for guidance, and to keep an eye on the structures around their homes, the canals and causeways.

Our calpulli lies on the western shore, near the Tacuba Causeway. Beyond it rises the Chapultepec Aqueduct, proud vessel that carries sweet waters from Chapultepec's springs to the heart of the city. It is our lifeblood. If the aqueduct fails, Tenochtitlán falls. One day as I walk past the aqueduct, dark lines on its surface draw my eye. I approach closer. I climb the rim where I see more. Fissures creep through the masonry like a sickness beneath the skin. Tlaloc's water does not rest; it craves the stone that dares stand in its path. In some places the lime mortar is eaten away, leaving gaps where Tlaloc's tongue reaches in to feed.

I bring word to the palace, and soon the tlamacazqui summons me: "Huey Tlatoani Tizoc entrusts you to guard the aqueduct. Let the water flow. Let the city drink."

I gather workers for the repairs. We cut the flow in one channel to mend the other. Joints are sealed, piers replaced, walls braced against wind and rain. Lime and tezontli bind anew, the serpent body of stone made firm. But the work is slowed waiting for materials. Deliveries clog the causeway, canoes arrive half empty, masons sit idle with empty baskets, Lime paste arrives in uneven quality, lumpy or too thin. The work takes longer than it should.

⊑⊒⊑⊒⊑⊒⊑⊒⊑⊒

Tenochtitlán is a beautiful capital city and villagers from every altepetl come, attracted by its wealth and for a better life. The city swells and soon Chapultepec's waters run thin. I propose a second vein from the south, Coyoacán. Tizoc approves, but my charge will be to feed the work with a steady flow of stone, lime and wood, while others design and build the new aqueduct. It is the emperor's will. I will do my duty.

Each day I walk among quarriers, canoe men, lime burners, masons, carpenters and porters to find the answer. Where once, small lime burners were scattered among the calpulli, I gather them into one stream and decree a single great yard on the southern edge, its kilns larger, its fires constant, its workers covered in a pale ghostly layer of lime dust. Fire and stone yield mortar by the ton, and the scattered efforts of many fuse into one strong stream.

Stone too must flow. Tezontle, basalt, limestone—all must arrive in steady measure. Canoes serve us well, but overland we depend on porters dragging sledges over greased logs. I refine their system: logs cut to equal size, shaved for rolling, Upon them, sledges ride, bound with maguey cord, the paths smoothed with sand. Where once stones crawled for weeks, they now glide in days.

It is not strength alone that raises an aqueduct, but order: each hand guided, each trade in harmony, so that work runs through it like water itself.

d. Keeper of the Roads

After I complete my work arranging the workflow for the Coyoacán aqueduct, I busy myself with small projects while I await the next burden the gods will place in my hands. Two thirteen day periods pass before, I receive a summons to appear before Huey Tlatoani Tizoc. At the appointed time I present myself at the emperor›s palace, barefoot, wearing only a plain white loincloth. I am escorted to an antechamber where I am instructed to wait. Several hours pass. Messengers and guards come and go. Finally, the sun's light dims and an attendant approaches and advises me to appear the next morning for my meeting with the emperor.

The next day, I appear again, but my meeting is delayed without explanation.

On the third day, I appear again and wait and wait. Finally, as the sun begins its descent in the west, I am admitted to the inner chamber where the emperor sits, but Tizoc does not look up to recognize me, so I remain silent.

Then a guard presents young nobles dressed in exaggerated warrior costumes. Tizoc complements their ferocity, and all the courtiers in the chamber join the emperor, chanting approval of the costumes.

I see the throne mocking the warrior's path with gaudy feathers and empty boasting, yet I must bow my head.

Tizoc then turns his attention to a patolli game he is playing with a courtier. He is crouched over the patolli mat, holding five beans in his hands; each marked on one side. He calls to Macuilxochitl, god of games, as if coaxing fate itself, as he throws the beans. They clatter across the floor—only one bean lands with its marked face up. Tizoc snarls, "Macuilxochitl, O lord of games, why do you twist the beans against your own tlatoani?" Then he turns to his opponent, "Your shadow crossed over the beans when I threw them." Around the cross shaped board, courtiers murmur that one marked bean means the road ahead is uncertain. Tizoc, still feeling the shame of his defeat at Matlatzinco shouts, "Only one mark? Macuilxochitl, you give me a road of doubt!"

Finally, Tizoc addresses me,

> Huitzilin! You have come at last. My eyes have followed your steps. I saw how you taught the heavy stones to travel, like a stream finding its path. I saw how you gathered the lime burners into one place, so their fire would speak with one voice. Now I need you to set these roads straight before this omen becomes my fate.
>
> For Tenochtitlán to grow and for her people to prosper, we must have good roads and causeways and aqueducts. Today, many of our roads ache; they buckle. In distant places they have grown thin as old reeds. New paths must be opened; old ones straightened and strengthened.
>
> The roads, the bridges, the aqueducts—they need a steady heart to watch over them. Huitzilin, in all the breadth of the empire, you are the one whose hands know how to bind earth and stone so our warriors may march swiftly and our merchants carry wealth between the altepetls. Now I place this burden in your hands.
>
> Now it is my wish that you shall be Keeper of the Roads for the empire. Go to the keepers of the treasury to see that the roads, the bridges, the aqueducts are supplied. You do not need to call on me for every matter, let your judgment guide you. Huitzilin, walk the path that brings prosperity to our people; walk this path with a steady heart.

When the emperor pauses, I address him, "Honored leader, I know the road to Cuauhahuac is in disrepair. Shall I commence with that project?"

Annoyed, Tizoc responds, "Huitzilin, do not burden me with these details. I appoint you for this task because I trust your judgment. You do what you think needs to be done. I have other matters to attend to and I need you to take charge." He closes his fist around the beans, as though sealing the matter, though his eyes never rise to meet mine. Then, he waves his hand as though brushing aside a gnat and I am dismissed. Thus, I am given freedom not through favor, but through the tlatoani's indifference.

IN THE TECPAN[141]

Following my meeting with the Huey Tlatoani, four senior members of Tizoc's staff lead me to my new office space inside Tenochtitlán's main Tecpan within the palace complex of the huey tlatoani, next to the sacred precinct, where councils meet and records are kept. There, I am led into a three-room suite: a front chamber lined with painted maps and reed mats for receiving envoys, a quieter inner room where pigments, codices and measuring cords are kept, and a small workroom where tools and materials lie stacked in orderly bundles.

My staff includes four specialists who present themselves to me. The Tlacuilo explains that he will maintain the great road codex and will record every repair; the Paynani bows and says he will command a team of messengers to carry my orders across the empire; the Chief Engineer gestures to the surveying cords he will use in the field; and the Logistics Officer promises to marshal labor, stone, and timber wherever the roads demand it.

In time, I have the office functioning as it should. From first light, messengers arrive with dust on their cloaks, reporting washed-out causeways or broken bridges, sometimes placing a cracked stone or splintered beam before me to show the damage. The tlacuilo records

---

141 Tecpan is a government office building, the palace-complex of a ruler; an administrative and ceremonial center where governance, tribute, and judicial affairs are conducted.

each report in the road codex while the engineer studies maps and measuring cords. Couriers come and go, carrying my decisions to labor overseers and provincial governors. In this room, the empire's roads take shape through judgment—what must be repaired now and what can wait.

CUAUHNAHUAC

I am at home with my family when Tezcacoatl comes to me. He is proud to hear that the emperor has appointed me Keeper of the Roads. He says, "Huitzilin, you remember my troubles with the road to Cuauhnahuac. Now the tribute caravans falter where the rains have moved the mountain."

The next day, I arrange a party to visit the site. When we arrive, I study the place where the mountain moved. I explain, "The mountain is hungry, it will move again." I point the engineer to an alternate route through the forest. The team measures and scouts the area, finding spaces where the earth is firm and the passage is safe.

I envision the design and oversee the work of a local tlachiani who maintains the workforce. The Logistics Officer works with Tezcacoatl to arrange trades for lime and plaster, to secure stone from nearby quarries and to manage deliveries through his networks. During a break in the work, Tezcacoatl turns to me and says, "If you keep building roads this straight, even the gods will stop getting lost."

Before we leave, Tezcacoatl insists I accompany him to visit the Tlatoani of Cuauhnahuac for a trading session. Their reunion is joyful—over the years they have built an easy friendship—and he introduces me as Tenochtitlán's Master Builder and Keeper of the Roads. As Tezcacoatl speaks, the Tlatoani turns his attention to me instead, expressing his wish for a modest temple to mark the gateway to his city. I send word back to Tenochtitlán , but when Tizoc does not respond, I remember his charge to act on my own judgment. I envision the design for the temple and oversee the work of a local tlachiani who maintains the workforce, while Tezcacoatl arranges the trades for lime, plaster, and stone needed for the new gateway temple.

Together we turn the imperial assignment into a local partnerships, blending construction with diplomacy and trade. Wealth flows back to our home and to Tenochtitlán. My reputation grows with every stone set in place.

After Cuauhnahuac, I am called to appear before the Huey Tlatoani. But Tizoc does not come. Instead, a messenger delivers the emperor's words: "I am pleased with your work at Cuauhnahuac. The roads are the veins of tribute and war, they must endure."

Having my office in the same Tecpan as the Huey Tlatoani's office places me closer to the nexus of power. In a way that moves like wind through tall reeds, I feel the court bending differently around me now. I sense it in the way courtiers pause when I pass—my name now travels ahead of me like a standard. Whispers follow me through the palace corridors; men who once overlooked me now weigh their words. Though I am macehualli, a commoner, I am respected in the halls of power.

CHOLULA

Tezcacoatl returns to Tenochtitlán after three new moons on the road, and when he finds me, he speaks in hushed tones. He tells me, "The Tlatoani of Cholula—guardian of the ancient city of Quetzalcoatl and heir to the sacred civilization of Tolan—invites you to be his special guest at a ceremony celebrating the completion of repairs to the great road leading to his altepetl."

I notify the Tlatoani's office of this invitation, but after three days I receive no reply. Tezcacoatl and I assemble an entourage for our mission to Cholula, an altepetl I have not visited, but whose name carries the weight of legend.

Along the way, I keep an eye on the repaired road, and I am pleased to see it holding firm—its surface smooth beneath the sandals of our porters, its gutters clean and well-cut, its causeways lifting us dry over creeks and swollen streams like the sure glide of a heron over shallow water, lifting us clean above the flood.

Tezcacoatl and I lead our entourage with an elderly scribe beside us. Along the way, Tezcacoatl tells me of his experiences at Cholula and says, "Huitzilin, Cholula is no common altepetl. It stands at the crossroads of the world, where merchants from the Huaxtec coast, from Oaxaca, and from the southern lands bring their riches. Its marketplace alone could rival a kingdom."

The tlacuilo, who has walked there many times as a pilgrim, lifts his gaze and adds, " But its true power is older than trade. Cholula is the seat of Toltec memory, where Quetzalcoatl once dwelled, where the great pyramid rises like a mountain of prayer. It commands reverence, not obedience. Its authority is cosmological. It is the sacred center for pilgrims from all lands, " I listen to them both, feeling the road carry us toward a place where politics and the sacred breathe the same air.

I walk the road with measuring cord and staff, my sandals dusted with white grit that does not belong to the lake. The stones beneath my feet have been reset many times. Pilgrims do not walk lightly. The road narrows as it enters Cholula. It does not announce itself the way Tenochtitlán does. There is no sudden widening, no causeway unfolding like a declaration.

Tezcacoatl has already gone ahead, blowing his pochteca whistle announcing his arrival. I follow after removing a stone blocking a gully. Beneath the shadow of the Quetzalcoatl Temple, Tezcacoatl steps forward, bowing before the tlatoani, priests and nobles. Addressing the tlatoani, he recites a greeting,

> Revered Tlatoani of Cholula, lord of the sacred altepetl, we bow before your mat and throne. I come as a humble pochteca of Tenochtitlán, bearing the message of affection from our Huey Tlatoani. We honor Quetzalcoatl, whose temple rises here, and we honor your people who guard the roads and markets. We seek friendship and exchange, that the goods of distant lands may flow like water between our cities, and that our devotion to the gods may be joined in strength.

The tlatoani then places his hand on Tezcacoatl›s shoulder as a sign of warmth and respect; Tezcacoatl bows his head and after a moment, he looks up with a grin and they all join joyous laughter.

Tezcacoatl then turns to present me, his voice carries both pride and ceremony: "Revered Lord, this is Huitzilin of Tenochtitlán–Master Builder and Keeper of the Roads." The Tlatoani inclines his head toward me, his gaze warm. He reaches out and we clasp forearms. with both strength and ceremony, his other hand settling lightly on my shoulder. "Keeper of the Roads," he says, his voice bright with gratitude, "your work has carried life back to the path of Cholula. We feel the difference with every step our people take."

I bow and say, "It is my charge to tend the roads of the empire. Water pools. Feet slip. My mission is to repair the roads, to place stone to connect lands so goods can flow and people flourish; that pilgrims may travel well."

More words of welcome are exchanged, offerings of cacao and cotton laid before us. The Tlatoani speaks of friendship, of the roads that bind our peoples, of tribute flowing like water between cities. Tezcacoatl then gathers the Cholulan traders and they drift into their familiar discussions. When attendants begin to gather at the edges of the courtyard and drums sound in the distance, the Tlatoani turns to me with a smile that carries both ceremony and warmth. "Keeper of the Roads," he says, "come–our people have prepared a celebration to honor the path you have restored to us."

The celebration unfolds in a burst of color as we are led into the courtyard: dancers in bright feathered capes sweep past in spirals, their steps keeping time with the deep pulse of the huehuetl. Conch shells sound from the terrace above, their long notes curling through the air like calls to the gods, while priests scatter flower petals that catch the sun in drifting reds and yellows. Platters of maize cakes, cacao, and roasted turkey are carried before us, and the people of Cholula cheer as if the renewed road itself has arrived in our company.

The Tlatoani takes me aside, his gaze drifting toward the city's threshold. "This gate," he says softly, "is narrow. I wish for a grander entrance, a threshold worthy of Cholula's greatness, a passage that proclaims our devotion to the gods and our place among the altepetls." His words hang in the air, half dream, half petition.

I answer, "If you desire a gate to your city that rises like a mountain, strong as jade, broad as the causeways, I can shape it. I will widen the road as it enters Cholula, build a monument with stones that endure, a threshold that honors Quetzalcoatl and welcomes all who pass."

The nobles murmur. The pochteca nod, imagining caravans entering beneath such a monument. The tlatoani smiles faintly, his eyes bright with possibility. In that moment, I feel the weight of my duty and the promise of my craft: to raise what lasts, to bind cities with stone and vision.

The Cholulan nobles and tlatoani meet privately and agree to the project, but with the condition that only Cholulan hands will touch the stone. I send a paynani with a notice for Tizoc, notifying him of this project. The next morning, paynani arrives with word: Huey Tlatoani is pleased. I spend the day measuring, looking at the angles of the sun as it rises and sets over the pyramid, the levels of the road as it approaches the central plaza. In the days that follow, I meet with local tlachiani and work commences as agreed.

When the gateway is complete, I attend the celebration and am acknowledged by the Tlaotani as the bringer of good will between our peoples, the one who set stone to bind us together. Tezcacoatl joins me on this day and we visit the marketplace before we leave. The Cholula Marketplace, known throughout the world, spreads like a tapestry: stalls of cacao and cotton, turquoise beads glinting in the sun, the scent of copal drifting from temple courtyards.

As we leave the marketplace, Tezcacoatl nudges me and says, "The road brings us here, but it is the market that makes the journey worth it. Listen—every voice is a bargain, every stall a story."

I look at him through the corner of my eye, still examining cracks in the stone and remark, "Without the road, none of this flows."

Tezcacoatl laughs softly, "And without the market, your road is only dust." And so, we return

COIXTLAHUACA

Over the next years I oversee projects throughout the empire, but in time, I turn to my biggest challenge—the long road to Coixtlahuaca, gateway to Oaxaca. Here the terrain is harsh and porters struggle under heavy loads. I organize stations along the way for rest, shade and water. Thus, the road becomes a living artery. Admiring my work, Tezcacoatl says, "Huitzilin, you've moved so many stones the mountains are starting to look nervous."

At Coixtlahuaca the tlatoani welcomes the project, seeing how it eases tribute and trade alike. Finally, at the request of the tlatoani, I raise a magnificent temple there, a monument of Mexica presence that also honors local lords.

ⴰⴰⴰⴰⴰⴰ

At the edge of the empire, Tezcacoatl and I meet Zapotec envoys and traders, turquoise and textiles in their packs. Tezcacoatl speaks as merchant, I as builder, and between us we find common ground: roads that might one day bind our valleys together, Mexica and Zapotec, a dream to come.

At the edge of the empire, Tezcacoatl and I meet Zapotec envoys and traders, turquoise and textiles in their packs. Tezcacoatl speaks as merchant, I as builder, and between us we find common ground: roads that might one day bind our valleys together, Mexica and Zapotec, a dream to come.

e. 1486-1502 Huey Tlatoani Ahuitzotl

I hear whispers of rivalries and strife among the royal families, and one day in 1486, Tizoc is found dead in his palace, cause unknown. He leaves behind a troubled legacy and an unfinished monument to divine power.

Ahuitzotl, the last of three brothers to rule the Aztec Empire, is crowned Huey Tlatoani. He was once my classmate at the calmecac, my teammate in the ollamaliztli games. In those early years, he treated me with respect, even when others saw only my humble origins. We shared lessons, laughter, and the quiet camaraderie of boys learning to become men. Later, we fought together in Malinalco. Over the years, our friendship endured – but now everything changes. He is emperor, and all protocols must be observed. I can no longer speak to him as a friend, only as his subject. It is the social order; I must respect it.

THE HUEY TEOCALLI

Soon after the coronation, an official messenger arrives at my home with a summons bearing the seal of Ahuitzotl. The Huey Tlatoani is displeased with the stalled Huey Teocalli project, the grand temple at the heart of Tenochtitlán and commands my service to see it completed. It is the greatest honor of my life.

I gather a team of the most skilled master builders in the empire, including those from the Maya lands of the southeast — men who have studied the temples of Teotihuacan and know the wisdom of celestial alignment and sacred proportion. They carry in their hands the mathematics of the gods, the rhythms of the sun and stars, and the geometry that binds heaven to earth.

Every measurement must be exact. The temple's main axis must align with the path of the sun, so that its rays illuminate the inner sanctum at sunrise and sunset during the equinoxes. Each room is shaped according to divine proportions for harmony with the gods; golden rectangles for rooms, and steps and walls built with sacred geometry, reflecting balance and strength.

The workforce is vast. Thousands labor under my direction. Slaves from conquered territories quarry and transport massive tezontle and basalt stones. Stonecutters carve and masons set each block with precision. Lime-burners and plasterers cover the temple in gleaming white stucco, so that it shines beneath the sun like polished bone. Hundreds of *tolteca*[142] artists adorn the structure with vibrant murals and carvings — scenes of myth and memory. They paint the birth of Huitzilopochtli, the battles of the gods, and the celestial order that governs our world. Serpent heads, fierce and majestic, guard the base of each staircase, their jaws open as if tasting the breath of the living. On one side, symbols of fire, the sun, moon, and stars shimmer across

---

142 Master artisan with divine knowledge.

the walls, binding heaven and earth in sacred union. On the other, the signs of rain and water spread like flowing currents – fertility and torment intertwined, the gifts and punishments of Tlaloc etched into stone.

And I, once a boy uncertain of his place, now shape the heart of the empire.

DEDICATION OF THE HUEY TEOCALLI

Year 8 Acatl, day 7 Acatl (December 19, 1487), two long years after I commence, the renovation is complete and Tenochtitlán holds a grand dedication ceremony.

On the morning of the ceremony, the sun rises behind the sacred peak of Mount Tehuicocone, and its rays pierce the eastern temple as if summoned by the gods themselves. It is the solstice, the turning of the sun, and the temple awakens in light. The city stirs with anticipation. Today, the gods will be honored, and the empire will witness the rebirth of its sacred heart.

I stand at the base of the Huey Teocalli, the great pyramid I have helped shape from stone and vision. The air is thick with copal smoke and reverent silence. Thousands gather – nobles, priests, warriors, artisans, and commoners. Huey Tlatoani Ahuitzotl ascends the grand staircase, his mantle trailing behind him like a river of jade and obsidian. He pauses at the top, turns, and raises his arms to the sky. A priest chants the sacred words, and the crowd responds with a unified breath.

Then, the moment comes.

A shaft of sunlight pierces the eastern temple, striking the inner chamber precisely as designed. The room glows with divine light, illuminating the carved image of Huitzilopochtli's birth. Gasps ripple through the crowd. The alignment is perfect. The gods are pleased.

Ahuitzotl descends and approaches me. Though protocol forbids casual speech, he places a hand on my shoulder – firm, silent, understood. In that gesture, I feel the weight of our shared past: the Calmecac, the games, Malinalco, the years of distance, and now, this moment of unity.

I do not speak. I bow; slowly, deeply.

The drums begin. Flowers are cast into the air. Dancers whirl like flames. And above it all, the pyramid stands – immense, eternal, alive. This is not merely a building. It is a prayer in stone.

f. Cuauhcalli

It is now the year 1500 when a message from the emperor arrives at my door: "Huitzilin, twenty-four years ago we stood together in the cave at Malinalco; it still burns in my mind. I wish to visit it again with you."

In thirteen days, we enter the cave together. It is unchanged – the same cool breath, the same scent of stone. We remember the idea clearly: a temple grown from the mountain itself, a womb of stone for warriors reborn. Ahuitzotl runs his hand along the wall and does not speak at first. When he does, his voice is low, as if the cave itself might be listening. "This place already knows what it is," he says. I nod. That has always been the truth of it. "This place has waited for you, Huitzilin," he says. "Shape it. Give it breath. Make it worthy of the eagle and the sun."

Then he leaves me – alone with the mountain, the silence, the mission, and the memory of the dream.

THE CARVING

I gather a workforce of carvers from Tenochtitlán, from Malinalco, from Matlatzinco.[143]

The work begins slowly. Day after day we carve the living rock, coaxing forms from the darkness. Where the stone rises hiding shape, we reveal it.

First the eagle – wings unfurled, talons gripping the earth, its gaze fixed on the rising sun.

Then the jaguar – crouched and ready, muscles rippling beneath the stone, its spots etched like constellations.

---

143 Ahuitzotl retook Matlatzinco during his coronation campaign in 1486.

At the entrance, a warrior emerges: seated, vigilant, shield resting on his knee, his face carved with the calm of one who has faced death and returned.

Opposite him, the huehuetl takes form – its surface adorned with serpents and stars, the heartbeat of those who will gather here.

The cave becomes a chamber of guardians. No stone is added, no mortar used. It is the mountain itself, one piece, its essence revealed.

THE CONSECRATION

When the work is finished, Ahuitzotl returns with the High Priest of Huitzilopochtli and a small retinue of attendants. Together we climb the carved steps to the entrance and step inside quietly, as though entering the breath of the mountain.

Ahuitzotl's hand brushes the seated warrior as he enters, then the eagle's wing, then the jaguar's flank. "You have carved a house for courage," he says. "Here, warriors will be reborn."

We stand together in the cool darkness, the scent of stone dust lingering. After a long silence, the High Priest lifts his copal burner and sends three slow breaths of smoke toward the guardians – the warrior, the drum, the eagle, the jaguar – feeding the gods and awakening the sacred essence of the place.

"The mountain breathes," he says. "The spirits of eagle and jaguar awaken in the fire of the sun. This place is consecrated."

Outside, the world waits. Inside, the cuauhcalli breathes – a temple shaped from dream and mountain.

Cuauhcalli: 1) Exterior with thatched roof and awning. 1) Front entrance with seated warrior (missing body) and heuheutl drum in the distnace. 3) Inner chamber with Eagle at center and jaguar in back.

THE FIRST USE

At Ahuitzotl's signal, a procession climbs the path: priests first, their cloaks dark with copal smoke, their faces streaked with black and red. Behind them comes the first cohort of chosen warriors – young men who have taken captives, who have stood in the heat of battle and returned with their hearts unbroken.

We gather at the cave mouth as the sun rises over the eastern ridge. The priests lift their arms and begin the chant – low at first, then rising like wind through reeds. The words echo against the stone: a call to courage, to transformation, to the path of the warrior.

Ahuitzotl steps forward. "This house is carved from the mountain," he says. "A womb for warriors. A place where courage is sharpened and the sun finds its servants."

He gestures, and the first cohort assembles at the doorway. They pass between the seated warrior and the huehuetl, then enter the chamber where the eagle waits with wings unfurled and the jaguar crouches in eternal readiness.

A priest strikes the drum. The sound rolls through the chamber like thunder in a canyon. The warriors kneel. The chant swells. The cave breathes.

Ahuitzotl turns to me. "Your vision lives," he says. "From this place, warriors will rise with the strength of eagle and jaguar. You have given the empire a heart of stone that beats."

And as the chant fills the chamber, I see the purpose of the cuauh-calli realized – not in the carvings alone, but in the warriors who now sit in its darkness, ready to be reborn.

VI
1502, Huitzilin the Huehuetqueh

This year, 1502, marks my fifty-second year of life, having completed a full calendar cycle, a binding of the years. It is a sacred milestone in the calendar and in my life, a cause for recognition and celebration. Like my father before me, I am honored as a huehuetqueh, an elder revered for wisdom, achievement and leadership. I have lived honorably, serving the emperor, my wife and my seven children.

SPEAKING WITH TLAMACAZQUI QUETZALCOATL TOTEC
During the celebration, I reflect on the recognition I have received as Keeper of the Roads and Chief Tlachiani of the empire. Yet my spirit stirs with ambition—I long to serve the Mexica in even greater ways. I seek counsel from the high priest, Tlamacazqui Quetzalcoatl Totec, and share my thoughts.

The Tlamacazqui replies:

> Huitzilin, you are an honorable and capable man. Wealth and power are signs of divine favor—gifts bestowed by the gods upon those who are worthy. No one can deny your success and merit as Tenochtitlán's Supreme Builder. Now you pray for new ways to serve the well-being and harmony of our people. I will retreat and contemplate your prayer.

For a full thirteen days, the Tlamacazqui meditates on my future. Then, resolved, he prepares to present my petition to Huey Tlatoani Ahuitzotl.

Before the appointed time for his meeting with the emperor, Tlamacazqui Quetzalcoatl Totec prepares in his dressing chamber, where his attendants remove his priestly garments. An attendant brings a clean white maxtlatl,[144] which he dons before walking barefoot to the emperor's palace. There, he waits in the anteroom for a long time before he is summoned to enter the royal chamber.

As the emperor enters, the Tlamacazqui bows low. Then, in a gesture of humility and devotion, he casts himself face down upon the ground, intoning three times: "Our revered lord, most revered lord, we supplicate—our heartfelt thanks in your presence."

When permitted to speak, he says:

> In the presence of Tonacatecuhtli,[145] Lord of Our Sustenance, and in the sacred breath-winds that bear our words upward, I, Tlamacazqui Quetzalcoatl Totec, make reverent bow before Your Majesty.
>
> I speak of your noble subject Huitzilin, Chief Builder of the Mexica, servant of our altepetl, who has carried his burdens with the breath of the gods. Raised in our finest calmecac, he became a tequihua upon the field, taking captives for offering, and entered the company of Jaguar Warriors. He laid down roads and raised up causeways across the breadth of empire; and when the great aqueduct from Chapultepec faltered, he gathered an army of hands and brought it back to flow with greater vigor than before. For sixteen years he has served Your Majesty faithfully; and now, as you have seen, he has completed the renewal of the Huey Teocalli with excellence beyond our imagining.
>
> He stands at an age of ripeness and a heart of steadiness, fit to guide this people to yet greater flourishing. May Your Majesty behold in him not only a servant, but a mirror of the sun's devotion upon the earth. I set these words as flowers upon the stone; may they open in your heart.
>
> *Tlazohcamati*,[146] my lord, for granting speech before Your Majesty.

---

144 Loincloth

145 The creator god who dwells in the thirteenth and highest heaven, from which all souls descend, is responsible for populating the earth and making it fruitful.

146 A deeply reverent form of thanking.

With head bowed, the Tlamacazqui slowly backs out of the chamber, leaving behind the weight of his words and the hope of my future.

ENNOBLEMENT

Four days later, Huey Tlatoani Ahuitzotl summons me to a public rite. As I arrive at the steps of the royal palace, a multitude of Mexica are gathering. He calls for me to stand at his side, then he speaks:

'We gather to honor one worthy and meritorious Mexica, Huitzilin – known to me since our days in the calmecac, where he was first among students and steadfast among companions. In his heart, he has the fire that burns and never yields and in his hands he has the power to guide the rain on its course.

Across ten years beneath the banners, he won renown in battle, a tequihua and entered the company of Jaguar Warriors. In battle he stood fast and in victory he took captives; in his later charge, he marshaled builders ordering great works in the newly-subdued provinces.

He led works vast as a valley: first, the renewal of the Chapultepec Aqueduct. He built roads and causeways across the empire as Keeper of the Roads; and finally, the Huey Teocalli. He laid down stone upon stone with precision, he raised up the house of god with devotion. His courage in war and his service to the people are proven; his fame walks before him, his deeds stand behind him.

Therefore, I declare from this day forward Huitzilin is numbered among the *Pipiltin*,[147] to enjoy their honors, burdens, and privileges.

Let the mats and seats know his name; let the banners and drums proclaim it. So is my word; so is it set upon the stone.

My joy is immeasurable. Itzel and our children stand beside me, their faces radiant with pride. We sing songs of love to each other, voices rising like flowers in bloom.

I sing,

---

147 Nobles

> *I know not whether you have been absent:*
> *I lie down with you, I rise up with you,*
> *In my dreams you are with me.*
> *If my teardrops tremble in my ears,*
> *I know it is you moving within my heart.*[148]

Itzel answers,

> *Do not let the petals fall,*
> *Do not let the winds scatter them.*
> *Our love is the fragrance of flowers,*
> *Delicate, yet strong as jade.*
> *Stand by me, my beloved,*
> *For together, we are as the sun and the moon,*
> *Dancing forever in the heavens.*

---

148 An Aztec Love Song translated by D.G. Britton & John Bierhorst

VII
Delivering the Princess to Tzapotlan

Days pass following my ennoblement and I become restless, wondering what my fate holds. I walk the streets of Tenochtitlán with my family, enjoying the sight of the Huey Teocalli, the gardens and canals, but I feel empty, restless without a duty. Itzel counsels me to be patient, in time, my future will be revealed.

Thirteen days later, I arise to the sound of the centzontle,[149] the bird of four hundred voices. It speaks to me. I know it portends a fateful day. An imperial messenger arrives and escorts me to the palace. I wait in silence, seated among carved pillars and painted walls, until I am summoned into the emperor's inner sanctum. There, I see Tlacateccatl[150] Cuauhtémoc.[151] His presence signals the gravity of the meeting.

I bow three times and whisper, "Our revered lord, most revered lord, we supplicate – our heartfelt thanks in your presence."

Then the emperor speaks:

Huitzilin, as you well know, for five years we have waged war in Tzapotlan.[152] The Zapotecs are descendants of a sophisticated and ancient civilization – renowned for their architecture, metallurgy, artistry, and writing. Their southern coastal lands are a

---

149 The mockingbird
150 Tlacateccatl means "commanding general" or "chief of men."
151 Cuauhtémoc later becomes the last Huey Tlatoani, hanged by Cortés.
152 Land of the Zapotecs.

gateway to unknown regions, rich in gold and salt. It would be a great honor if they joined us — for the good of both our peoples.

Our siege of their mountain stronghold at Guiengola lasted seven long months. Both sides suffered. We inflicted heavy casualties, and their people endured famine and disrupted trade. Yet they held firm, using guerrilla tactics in the dense forests to harass our supply lines. The distance has cost us dearly. They will not accept conquest, and we will not withdraw.

Now, ambassadors of the Zapotec Coquitao,[153] Cosijoeza,[154] offer a diplomatic solution. Tzapotlan will recognize Tenochtitlán's supremacy in all matters of empire. In return, we will grant them autonomy in their internal affairs. They will retain their nobility, hierarchy, and religion. Tribute will flow — gold, jade, salt, cacao, cotton, and more. Hostilities will cease, and a new military alliance will bind us together for our mutual defense and expansion.

To seal this peace and to prove my sincerity, I give my daughter, Princess Xiloxochitl,[155] in marriage to Coquitao Cosijoeza.

He pauses, then looks directly at me.

Huitzilin, you have proven yourself a wise and loyal servant to me and to the empire. I now entrust to you the safety and care of my daughter on her voyage to Zaachilla-Yoo, the Zapotec capital. You will act as her guardian. Protect her as you would your own child.

I bow deeply and accept the emperor's charge. The journey will be long and arduous, but I am ready.

I explain the mission to my brother, Tezcacoatl, who eagerly joins me and prepares a trading expedition. His entourage includes twenty *tlamemeh*,[156] each bearing loads of up to sixty pounds. He gathers gifts for the emperor: jade, quetzal feathers, woven cloth, obsidian blades,

---

153 Coquito is the title for the supreme ruler of the Zapotecs, "King" in their language.

154 Cosijoeza, the name of the Zapotec ruler.

155 Meaning, soft, silky flower.

156 Porters

cocoa, herbs, and spices – treasures to honor the alliance and open new paths of exchange.

DEPARTURE: TENOCHTITLÁN TO TZAPOTLAN

Emperor Ahuitzotl commands Tlacateccatl Cuauhtémoc to assemble a mighty contingent of the Imperial Army to protect the princess at all costs on this long and perilous journey. At the vanguard march the elite Jaguar Warriors, wielding macuahuitl and tepoztopilli.[157] Behind them follow the Eagle Warriors, armed with atlatls and tematlatlin.[158] A company of the strongest and most accurate archers joins the force. All are seasoned, battle-tested warriors – chosen for their loyalty and skill.

The princess's retinue includes personal attendants who manage her garments, assist in dressing her, and attend to her needs. Priests, healers, musicians, and dancers accompany her, forming a sacred and celebratory entourage. Tezcacoatl's twenty tlamemeh join many others bearing supplies of food, water, and ceremonial offerings for the marriage.

The night before our departure, the sky is clear and filled with brilliant starlight – a favorable omen, signaling the gods' guidance and protection. At dawn, a brief shower passes, leaving a radiant rainbow high in the western sky – another sign of divine favor. Priests chant and perform rituals, beseeching the gods for success. Drums thunder and conch shells wail in honor of the assembled caravan.

I watch as Princess Xiloxochitl emerges from the grand palace with grace and poise, adorned in garments woven with precious green feathers, gold ornaments and polished jade. Her appearance is irresistible like the noble magnolia, the heart-flower whose fragrance rises like truth from the soul. She steps onto a magnificently decorated palanquin, allowing her comfort and a view of the majestic landscape. Eight strong bearers carry her, with four additional bearers following behind who will rotate duties. I take my place as her

---

157 Broad tipped spears with obsidian blades.
158 Plural form for tematlatl, a sling for hurling stones

guardian and escort, walking beside her sedan chair. Throughout the journey, I will represent her in all communications with military leaders and officials. Only her attendants and I may speak directly with her.

The entire cavalcade stands at attention as citizens gather to witness our departure. Huey Tlatoani Ahuitzotl addresses the assembly:

> Warriors, nobles, esteemed guests – hear now. We embark upon a journey that will bend the path of our peoples for generations. As we send forth my beloved daughter, Princess Xiloxochitl, to wed Cosijoeza of Zaachila-Yoo,[159] we bind not only two noble houses but two great civilizations.
>
> Guard her with unwavering resolve. Let your strength and courage bear the honor of Tenochtitlán. Through trials ahead we will show our unity: not conquerors only, but keepers of peace, ready to embrace allies for the greater good.
>
> May the sun warm your path and give you strength. May the gods favor your going, and may Xiloxochitl arrive in her new house ready to sow the seeds of alliance and prosperity.
>
> Go forth with courage, and let the gods watch over you."

General Cuauhtémoc addresses the guard:

> The road to Zaachila will span two sacred counts of thirteen suns. You will cross rivers and mountains, pass through Mixtec lands and the high forests of the Zapotec. We will halt at eight great altepetls along the way and traverse hard terrain. The farther from home, the greater the peril.
>
> Each day will test you. Guard the princess not only with shield and obsidian, but with honor, vigilance, and the breath of the ancestors. Let no harm touch her. Let no insult reach her ears. She carries the flower of alliance. And you, Huitzilin – be her protector, her shadow, her voice when silence is required.

As we cross the long causeway, Tenochca climb to their rooftops and crowd the waterways in canoes to watch our departure. Their raucous cheering and joyful songs make for an auspicious sendoff. We turn in silence to watch Tenochtitlán fade into the distance.

---

159 Zapotec Capital City

We journey south through the Valley of Mexico, where the air is sweet with flowers and alive with the distant sounds of village life. As we pass through towns and villages, we are greeted by curious children and joyful locals, eager to glimpse the princess and our formidable procession. The news of peace between the Mexica and the ancient kingdom of the Zapotecs spreads quickly, and we are showered with gifts for the princess—tokens of hope, goodwill, and celebration.

CHALCO

We are weary from our first day's march—eight long hours beneath the sun—when we finally reach the entrance to Chalco, a Mexica tributary altepetl twenty miles from Tenochtitlán. Following the tradition of the Pochteca, my brother Tezcacoatl leads the way, playing his flute to announce his arrival with goods for trade. But this is no ordinary trading party. Behind him follows our vast entourage: the princess in her palanquin, her attendants, priests, musicians, and the full strength of our military escort.

The Chalcans line the entryway, eager to witness our procession. We march into the central square, where we are greeted by their tlatoani and the royal families. Tezcacoatl presents gifts—jade, feathers, cloth, and cocoa—and in return, they offer us food, water, and quarters for the night. Our soldiers, ever disciplined, make camp outside the city walls.

That evening, Tezcacoatl meets briefly with the tlatoani. Their exchange is cordial and efficient, and they complete several regular trades—quiet gestures of goodwill that strengthen the bonds between our peoples.

IZTACCÍHUATL AND POPOCATÉPETL

At daybreak, General Cuauhtémoc rouses the caravan, and we resume our journey. After eight hours of steady travel, we collapse beside the road near the small town of Amecameca, grateful for rest.

From our encampment, we behold the famed twin volcanoes—Iztaccíhuatl and Popocatépetl—rising in silent grandeur. As the sun sets, its golden light glistens against their snowcapped peaks. The air stills. All eyes turn to the mountains.

Princess Xiloxochitl steps down from her palanquin. A hush falls over the crowd. With grace and quiet strength, she ascends a small mound beside our camp and addresses us:

She places a flower at the hearth and begins:

> Today, we have journeyed beneath the gaze of the twin volcanoes. Popocatépetl, the 'Smoking Mountain,' breathes fire and ash – alive with power. Iztaccíhuatl, the 'White Woman,' sleeps in silence, her snowy form stretched across the ridge like a resting figure. Look closely, and you will see her lying there – her head, her chest, her feet – wrapped in a blanket of snow. This is the story our grandmothers whisper when the mountains turn red at dusk.
>
> But they were not always mountains. First, they were lovers. Long ago, in the vibrant heart of our land, there lived a princess named Iztaccíhuatl, beloved by all who knew her. Her beauty and grace were legendary, and many sought her heart. Her father was Tlatoani of his people, proud and powerful.

Iztaccihuatl on the left, Popocatepetl on the right.

> Among her suitors was Axooxco, a nobleman of great wealth, but his heart was steeped in trickery and deceit. He longed to possess her. Yet Iztaccíhuatl's heart belonged to Popoca, a humble peasant and gifted warrior, known for his kindness, courage, and honesty.
>
> Popoca went to the Tlatoani to ask for her hand. The ruler agreed – on one condition. Popoca must first prove himself in battle, serving his people with valor. Only then would he allow the marriage.

Popoca departed for war, far from home. With his rival gone, Axooxco spread a cruel lie: that Popoca had fallen in battle. When Iztaccíhuatl heard this, her heart broke. She refused to marry Axooxco, withdrew from the world, and fell into a deep sleep from which no one could wake her.

When Popoca returned and found his beloved sleeping, he tried to rouse her – but she would not stir. He carried her to the mountaintop, hoping the cold air would revive her. Still, she slept. So he laid her gently along the ridge and stood beside her, waiting.

I'ztaccihuatl. Note, from the left, her head, her chest, knees and feet.

Years passed. She did not wake. Popoca vowed never to leave her. And so there he stands, frozen in time, guarding her still. When his heart burns with longing, the fire within him belches smoke. She lies dormant, wrapped in snow. He watches over her, and so the lovers remain – forever stilled, reminders that love may burn, but it does not vanish.

CUAUHNAHUAC,[160] HUAXTEPEC, YELOIXTLAHUACA AND TEHUACÁN

The next morning, we march toward our next destination, Cuauhnahuac, land of the Tlahuica people, a major tributary altepetl nestled in the Valley of Morelos. It is the place where years earlier, I built a modest temple to mark the gateway to the city. The tlatoani and his most prominent noblemen greet us at the gateway, remarking on the beauty of the structure, thanking me once again. They invite a small group – including the princess and me – to tour the Teopanzolco

---

160 Cuauhnahuac is the present day city of Cuernavaca.

pyramid and the royal palace. The city is surrounded by lush forest, giving it its name: Cuauhnahuac, "near the trees."

After three days of travel, we reach Huaxtepec,[161] another tributary altepetl famed for its exquisite gardens. That evening, we bathe in the thermal springs, letting the warm waters soothe our weary bodies.

Two days later, we arrive in Yeloixtlahuaca,[162] a region known for its thriving tobacco cultivation. Tezcacoatl engages in several trades and departs with more merchandise than he brought – his packs heavy with new goods and his spirit light with success.

That night, after our evening meal, the elite members of our group smoke tobacco. We use charcoal-lined, painted reed tubes, filled with ground tobacco blended with rose petals, liquidambar, mushrooms, and fragrant grasses. Tobacco serves many purposes beyond smoking. It is burned in temples alongside copal as a sacred offering. We use it to treat pain, fatigue, asthma, and headaches. We also use it in rituals as the smoke can induce visions to commune with the divine and to walk the thin line between the earthly and the sacred.

Three days later, our party arrives at the welcoming altepetl of Tehuacán, where we camp and rest for a day. An envoy from the tlatoani greets us with warmth and inquires if we require anything. The princess wishes to visit the city, and my brother is eager to engage in trade with the locals.

While the military sets up camp, Tlacateccatl Cuauhtémoc and his guards escort a small contingent to the city's main plaza. Princess Xiloxochitl is carried in her palanquin, with me walking at her side. Four Jaguar Warriors guard us, and Pochteca Tezcacoatl, accompanied by two porters bearing goods, joins the procession.

The plaza is adorned with banners and flowers. Incense drifts through the air, mingling with the sounds of traditional music. The tlatoani and local nobility receive us in a grand ceremony, bowing deeply before the princess.

Cuauhtémoc speaks:

---

161 Oaxtepec
162 Tepeaca

Honorable Tlatoani, I bring you greetings from Tenochtitlán. May the gods bless our alliance and your people. We are en route to Tzapotlan, delivering Princess Xiloxochitl for marriage to the Zapotec king.

The tlatoani turns to the princess, bows deeply, and says:

Honorable Princess Xiloxochitl, your presence graces our city. May the gods bless your journey and our alliance.

Princess Xiloxochitl replies:

Thank you, Honorable Tlatoani. I am pleased to be welcomed in your city. May our friendship bring prosperity to both our peoples.

Turning again to Cuauhtémoc, the tlatoani adds:

Welcome, esteemed Tlacateccatl Cuauhtémoc. Your presence honors us. May our friendship continue to bring prosperity to both our lands.

An exchange of gifts follows. Cuauhtémoc presents woven textiles, jewelry, and exotic goods:

We offer these gifts as tokens of our respect and to strengthen our bond.

Cacao drinks are served, incense is burned, and prayers are offered to the gods. The ceremony concludes with a feast celebrating our friendship and a discussion of mutual interests.

After the feast, Tezcacoatl speaks with the tlatoani:

We are grateful that our alliance ensures safe passage for our caravans and that the roads are well maintained for smooth, safe, and efficient trade. Please let us know what goods you need so I may bring them on my next visit.

He presents samples of his wares: fine textiles, cacao, precious stones, tobacco, and exotic feathers from distant lands.

The tlatoani replies:

These items are exquisite. We are pleased with your offerings. What do you seek in exchange for these treasures?

Tezcacoatl responds, "We are in need of obsidian blades, maize, and fine pottery."

They engage in extended negotiation.

Later, the tlatoani warns, "Travel through the Mixtec region is perilous."

Cuauhtémoc replies:

We have encountered roving bands of bandits during our journey from Tenochtitlán, which our soldiers repelled. But we wish to avoid warfare with the full force of a city-state's trained military.

Map showing route from Tenochtitlán to Zaachila-Yoo.
Note the location of Izta and Popo (red dots) south of Chalco.

In response, the tlatoani offers a *pantli*[163] of his finest warrior scouts to guide us through the lands of the treacherous Mixtecs. In return, we gift him one of our porters with a sixty-pound load of merchandise.

THE BATTLE AT COIXTLAHUACA

After a day's rest, we enter Mixtec territory, traveling in tight formation with guards strategically placed to protect our porters and goods. Our Tehuacán scouts monitor the terrain and guide us away from routes where ambushes might lie in wait. After two days on the road, we reach the outskirts of our tributary altepetl of Coixtlahuaca. The sight stirs an old memory – the clear ring of the bronze bell a man from this place once taught my father to cast when I was a boy. And now, as the valley opens before us, I feel a quiet eagerness to see again the temple I raised here only a few years ago, a house of stone honoring both our peoples.

Along the way, Mixtec scouts shadow us, observing every detail of our convoy. They keep their distance until Coixtlahuaca comes into view – then in the late afternoon, four Mixtec warriors step forward, blocking the road. I accompany General Cuauhtémoc, together with my brother and four Jaguar Warriors, to meet with these men while the rest of our party remains behind.

The Mixtec with a red feather tucked into his headband steps forward. He shouts, "We are emissaries from Coixtlahuaca What brings you to our land?

Cuauhtémoc replies, "Huey Tlatoani Ahuitzotl sends us on a mission to Zaachila-Yoo where we have made peace. On our journey, we carry gifts for your tlatoani and wish to engage in trade. We will pass after a day's rest."

Red Feather speaks once more, his tone sharpened with impatience and says with a sneer, "You cannot meet with our tlatoani. You must wait here while we deliver the gifts. When we return, you will know his wishes."

---

163 A unit of 20 well trained soldiers

Tezcacoatl steps forward and gives Cuauhtémoc an obsidian mirror. Our general then tells Red Feather, "The gifts will be unpacked when we arrive in Coixtlahuaca, but I give you this token." He places it in the emissary's hand, and for just a moment their eyes meet in the mirror. In that moment, Cuauhtémoc sees Red Feather's nose flare. The smoking mirror does not lie, It penetrates and sees hidden intentions; it reveals what lies beneath appearances: deceit, ambition, concealed motives.

After the emissaries depart, Cuauhtémoc calls a council and asks, "Tezcacoatl, you've traded in Coixtlahuaca before?"

"Yes, my general. I've visited regularly over the past twelve years and have had favorable relations with their rulers since our army sacked their city long ago."

"Did you recognize these emissaries?"

"No, my general."

Cuauhtémoc turns to the Tehuacán scout leader:

"You've known the Coixtlahuaca. Did you recognize these men?"

"No," he answers.

Cuauhtémoc addresses the company and announces, "I saw it in the smoking mirror. This is an ambush. I fear a rogue Mixtec army is preparing to strike. Our first duty is to protect the princess and ourselves. We must reach higher ground – now."

For six hours, we follow our scouts through darkness, climbing craggy hills and weaving through dense forest. I walk beside the princess's palanquin, steadying her bearers when they stumble. At last, we reach a ridge with a commanding view where we prepare our defenses.

Cuauhtémoc instructs the Tehuacán scouts, "You must track the enemy's movements. Spread out. Report everything – especially silence."

The scouts vanish into the night. We set up camp under a moonless sky, torches flickering, soldiers tense. Shadows move in the dark. The night is long.

In the eighth hour of the night,[164] Cuauhtémoc receives word: a Mixtec army is advancing from the east, following our trail.

---

164 The moments before dawn

Cuauhtémoc acts swiftly. He orders Eagle Warrior archers to take elevated positions in trees and high rocky outcroppings. He splits Jaguar Warriors into two flanking groups. As a decoy, six warriors surround the princess's palanquin, while I quietly move her to a cave nearby.

At dawn, battle cries shatter the silence. The Mixtecs attack with bows, arrows, and slings. A stone strikes a porter's face; arrows find flesh. But Cuauhtémoc waits. When the Mixtecs reach a narrow pass, our horns sound.

Our archers unleash a deadly volley. Atlatls hurl spears with lethal force. Then the Jaguar Warriors charge, striking from both flanks. Obsidian blades slice through armor and bone. A pantli (unit of 20 warriors) circles behind, attacking from the rear. The air fills with the stench of blood and the cries of the wounded.

The Mixtecs falter. Surrounded and disoriented, they attempt to flee. Our warriors pursue, cutting down many, separating heads from bodies. The survivors scatter, leaving their dead behind.

We suffer no fatalities. We spend the day tending our wounds and prepare to continue our journey.

NOCHIXTLÁN

Within two days, we arrive at the Mixtec altepetl of Nochixtlán. Word of our victory near Coixtlahuaca – and the brutal decapitation of many Mixtec warriors – has preceded us. The city receives us with utmost respect and deference, their leaders eager to avoid conflict.

Tezcacoatl presents the cacique with gifts of fine jewelry, tokens of goodwill and diplomacy. The gesture is well received. We are offered rest, and our party remains for an extra day, replenishing our strength before continuing the journey.

ENTERTAINING THE PRINCESS

As we traverse the rugged terrain, I walk beside the princess's palanquin, sharing stories from my years as a Jaguar Warrior – tales of valor, hardship, and honor. She listens intently, her eyes bright with curiosity and quiet strength.

To lift her spirits, I recite a beloved poem by Tlatoani Nezahualcoyotl, the philosopher-king of Texcoco, whose verses speak to the soul of our people. His words are not merely poetry – they are prayers, shaped like jade and smelted like gold.

I begin:

Strike it up?
Sing before the face of our father, God Life Giver?
How could I sing but uselessly? For I am poor.
Let a singer come to please you, O Life Giver.
He is smelting songs, he is drilling them as turquoise beads,
but I am poor.
I wish I could please you.
Let me somehow grieve,
I, a singer, sighing before your face, bereft,
lifting flowers of bereavement, music of bereavement,
for you, O Noble One,
O Only Spirit, O Life Giver.
Where are you?
You are being entertained, O Life Giver?
Everywhere, throughout the world you are served.
Flowers of bereavement, music of bereavement, do I lift for you,
O Noble One, O Only Spirit. O Life Giver.
And now I sing!
So let there be flowers!
So let there be songs!
I drill my songs as though they were jades.
I smelt them as gold.
I mount these songs of mine as thought they were jade.
O, God! Though Poor, I say that I please you, Totoquihuaztli![165]
Let the singer come. He can please you.
Let the singer come. He will set free your songs.
How excellent this noble one!
He burnishes songs as though they were turquoise.
As though they were plumes, he twists them, he, Totoquihuaztli.

---

165 Tlatoani of Tlacopan, one of the three great cities of the Aztec Triple Alliance.

Let the singer come.
Let the singer come.

ARRIVAL IN TZAPOTLAN

For several days, the path ascends steadily toward the Zapotec capital. As we approach the outskirts of Zaachila-Yoo, we see the sacred mound of Zaachila-Yoo emerge – earth-lord rising from the plain, above the clustered houses, its terraces like the ribs of the living hill. The air is fragrant with rich earth and blossoming flowers. The sight of the sprawling city – its magnificent temples and vibrant marketplaces – fills us with awe.

We pause to allow the princess's attendants to prepare her for her grand entrance. They dress her in elaborate garments, adorn her with gold and jade jewelry, and style her hair with feathers and flowers, each detail a tribute to her grace and royal lineage.

Near the city's entrance, emissaries of the Zapotec king greet our caravan with reverence, bowing before the princess and conveying the king's good wishes and joy at our arrival. General Cuauhtémoc announces to the troops:

> We have completed the first leg of our mission. The princess has been delivered safely to Zaachila-Yoo. Warriors, fall back and make camp outside the city.

The king's emissaries guide us to the ceremonial center of Tzapotlan, where crowds have gathered. The streets come alive with music, dancing, and jubilation. Radiant and regal, Princess Xiloxochitl raises her hand in a gesture of peace and hope, and the crowd erupts in celebration.

THE FIRST MEETING

We enter the grand ceremonial hall that is sumptuously adorned with murals, carvings, and artworks that speak of centuries of Zapotec heritage. The air is thick with the sacred scent of copal, rising like prayers to the heavens. Princess Xiloxochitl enters, flanked by her attendants, her presence radiant and composed.

Moments later, Coquitao Cosijoeza arrives, dressed in his finest regal attire, accompanied by his advisors and warriors. As he steps forward, the room falls silent.

In recognition of the princess's status as emissary of the Mexica Empire, the king performs the *tlalcualiztli* gesture: he kneels, bows low, and scoops a small handful of earth – offered by his guard – which he brings to his lips. This act of humility honors the sacredness of the moment and sets the tone for a relationship founded on mutual respect and reverence for tradition.

Princess Xiloxochitl responds with grace, bowing deeply and presenting the king with a royal jade pendant, a symbol of peace and alliance. In return, Cosijoeza offers her a Quetzal feather headdress, its iridescent plumes shimmering in the light – a gift of honor and esteem.

WEDDING DAY

The princess is given several days to settle in to her new home before the wedding.

As the sun's first rays illuminate the city of Zaachila-Yoo, workers adorn the central plaza with fragrant, fresh flowers, transforming it into a brilliant canvas of color for the momentous occasion.

Princess Xiloxochitl's attendants perform a ritual cleansing with aromatic herbs and blossoms. They dress her in a huipil and a long cueitl, embroidered in vibrant colors and patterns that reflect her Mexica heritage. Her bridal cloak is magnificent – stitched with hummingbirds and flowers, symbols of beauty and renewal. She wears jewelry crafted by my father for this sacred day: a golden labret, necklaces, bracelets, earrings, and anklets of gold, jade, and other precious materials, each bearing symbols of fertility and prosperity. Her hair is styled with care, adorned with flowers and ribbons, and her face is enhanced with pigments to highlight her features. When she is ready, her attendants place the quetzal feather headdress – a gift from the king – upon her head.

*Detail of Coquitao (Zapotec King) from the mural
"Epic of the Mexican people" by Diego Rivera.*
https://commons.wikimedia.org/w/index.php?curid=61081404 *CC0 10*

Coquitao Cosijoeza wears a lavishly decorated ceremonial crown and the royal jade pendant gifted by the princess. His jewelry — necklaces, bracelets, earrings, and anklets — are designed with symbols of power and abundance. His belt gleams with gold and jade, and his ceremonial sword bears emblems of his status as a warrior king. Over his shoulders flows a long cloak, finely embroidered with gold thread.

At the appointed hour, the procession begins. As the princess's appointed guardian, I stand beside her, gently holding her hand. We are joined by the Mexica Tlamacazqui and General Cuauhtémoc, with their attendants following in solemn formation.

A Zapotec priest leads the opening rituals, invoking the blessings of their gods and ancestors. He chants sacred verses and offers prayers for a prosperous union.

Princess Xiloxochitl's personal Tlamacazqui honors the Mexica deities of fertility, love, and marriage, burning copal and presenting sacred offerings.

Together, the priests oversee the exchange of vows, where the couple promise to support and cherish one another with sincerity and respect. They exchange woven garlands and share a ceremonial drink, symbolizing the union of their lives and the blessings of the divine.

The ceremony concludes with a final blessing from both priests, invoking the gods to protect and guide the newlyweds. The hall fills with the sounds of traditional music, joyous celebration, and the vibrant spirit of two cultures joined in harmony.

It is a beautiful fusion of Zapotec and Mexica spiritual traditions — an honoring of lineage, love, and the promise of peace.

RETURN TO TENOCHTITLÁN

While General Cuauhtémoc musters our troops and porters for the return to Tenochtitlán, Princess Xiloxochitl calls out to me. She holds a note, carefully drawn on bark paper, adorned with pictographs, ideographs, and sacred symbols. She asks that I deliver it to her father, Huey Tlatoani Ahuitzotl.

With the mission to Tzapotlan and the marriage of the Princess and the Coquitao now complete, we begin our return journey. My brother

Tezcacoatl has profited from many successful trades. I have fulfilled my duty to the emperor.

VIII
Huitzilin, Ambassador and Parent

Upon our arrival in Tenochtitlán, Huey Tlatoani Ahuitzotl summons me to his palace. As tradition demands, I appear barefoot, dressed in a simple loincloth, and enter with reverence – casting myself to the floor and intoning three times, "Our revered lord, most revered lord, we supplicate – our heartfelt thanks in your presence."

I recount our journey in full: the tense battle near Coixtlahuaca, the warm reception in Tzapotlan, the magnificent wedding ceremony, and the kindness shared between Princess Xiloxochitl and Coquitao Cosijoeza. I convey the Zapotec king's gratitude and his solemn promise to uphold a permanent peace between our peoples.

Then, I present the note from the princess. It reads:

> Dear Father, I am now Queen of Tzapotlan, far from my beautiful Tenochtitlán.
>
> I wish to convey the deep respect and fondness I feel for Pipiltin Huitzilin, who has demonstrated intelligence and wisdom in his demeanor and his conduct with our military forces. I have come to admire his ability to engage and interact with foreign leaders and emissaries, especially with Coquitao Cosijoeza, who likewise developed a strong bond with him.
>
> I pray that you will look kindly on Huitzilin, who has proven his diplomatic skills and is loved and honored by the Zapotec people.
>
> It is our wish that Huitzilin be appointed ambassador to Tzapotlan and the Zapotecs, which will promote good relations and a lasting peace between our peoples.

I remain silent as the emperor responds:

Huitzilin, through your dedication and service to the empire, you have earned many accolades, Tequihua, Jaguar Warrior, Keeper of the Roads, Supreme Tlachiani.[166] You have performed your duties with excellence.

My daughter, Xiloxochitl, Queen of Tzapotlan, recommends that I appoint you ambassador. My most fervent wish is to maintain lasting peace with the Zapotec people. Your diplomatic skills will be a great asset to the empire.

I now appoint you Ambassador to Tzapotlan."

I nod, accepting the honor without words. I rise slowly, eyes cast down and back out of the hall.

As I leave the emperor's presence, I pause on the steps of the royal palace. It's the end of the day now. I tire after the long day and my meeting with the emperor saps my strength.

I watch the sun sink low over Tenochtitlán, casting golden light across the shimmering lake and the rooftops of the city I call home; the wind gentle against my face; the scent of copal still lingering.

Below me, the city pulses with life – children laughing, merchants calling out their wares, priests chanting in the distance. But here, in this quiet moment, I am suspended between past and future.

I think of the journey behind me: the long march through valleys and forests, the battle at Coixtlahuaca, the songs sung to Princess Xiloxochitl, the wedding that bound together two great civilizations. I remember the light touch of her hand in mine, the trust in her eyes, the note she gave me – words drawn in bark and ink now etched in my soul.

I have served as warrior, tlachiani, guardian, and now, I am ambassador. The emperor's voice echoes in my mind: "Your diplomatic skills will be a great asset to the empire." I carry that honor with humility.

But I also carry something deeper – a sense of purpose that goes beyond duty. I have seen the faces of the Zapotec people, heard their songs, tasted their offerings, and felt the warmth of their welcome.

---

166 Master builder.

I know now that peace is not just a treaty – it is a bridge built with respect, with listening, with shared dreams.

As the last light fades, I whisper a prayer to the gods:

> May I speak with wisdom.
> May I walk with honor.
> May I serve not only the empire,
> but the spirit of harmony between our peoples.

The stars begin to appear, one by one, like old friends returning. I rise slowly, the city glowing beneath me, and descend the steps – ready to walk the path ahead.

TLATELOLCO MARKETPLACE

My first day home falls on *Tianquiztli*, the sacred market day that comes every fifth day. I'm filled with joy, reunited with my wife, with my children beaming, standing beside me. We take an embroidered pouch filled with cacao beans from our household store and make our way to the bustling Tlatelolco marketplace – the largest and most vibrant in the Mexica Empire.

This day, more than 20,000 people fill the plaza: merchants, buyers, and visitors from across the empire and beyond. The marketplace is a living mosaic, divided into sections for food, crafts, and luxury goods. It is a place of respect and order.

In the food section, stalls overflow with fruits, vegetables, meats, and staples like maize, beans, and squash. Exotic delicacies – chocolate, honey, and rare herbs – tempt the senses. We stop at a vendor to enjoy prepared foods, to savor the flavors of distant places.

Artisans display exquisitely crafted textiles, pottery, jewelry, tools, and other treasures. In the luxury section, feathers, jade, and precious metals shimmer in the sunlight, drawing the eyes of nobles and wealthy traders.

My wife, Itzel, beckons me to admire a pair of beautifully embroidered *cactli*,[167] footwear. I feel a wave of gratitude – for her patience,

---

167 Aztec footwear, normally plain white, but embroidered designs denote high status.

her strength, and her devotion in caring for our children and home while I served in Tzapotlan. I buy the very special shoes for her with love and tenderness.

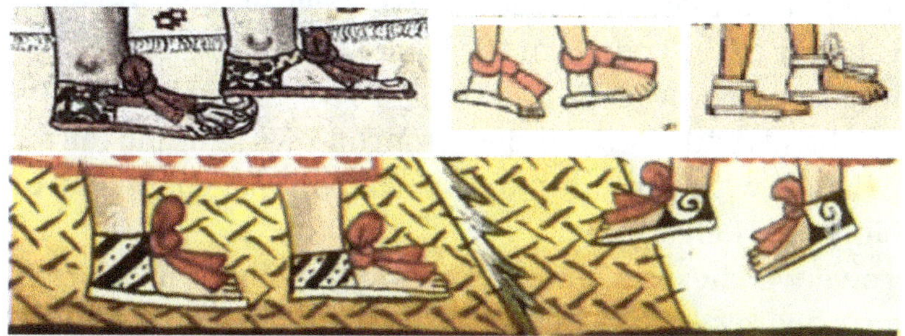

Fancy shoe styles in Tenochtitlán from various codices.

I shower our children with toys and games, their laughter filling the air. I spend the day speaking with travelers from distant lands, exchanging ideas, traditions, and news. The marketplace is not just a place of commerce—it is a place of connection, of renewal, of joy.

My children laugh as they clutch painted clay toys—tiny jaguars on wheels and hummingbirds. Itzel walks beside me, admiring the embroidered shoes I gifted her. The air is thick with roasted maize, copal smoke, and the hum of hundreds of voices.

I wear the tunic of a Jaguar Warrior, its black and yellow pattern unmistakable. My ceremonial macuahuitl rests across my back, obsidian blades gleaming like night. The hummingbird scar on my cheek turns red in the sun—earned in battle, now whispered about in reverence.

A shout pierces the calm. A vendor cries out, clutching his empty pouch. A young man bolts, weaving through the crowd, stolen goods in hand. Baskets overturn. Voices rise.

I step forward without hesitation, blocking his path. "Stop," I say—calm, but firm.

The thief skids to a halt. His eyes widen. He sees the scar.

"The hummingbird," someone gasps.

"Tezcatl Huitzilin," another murmurs. "The one from Matlatzinco."

The thief stumbles backward, trembling. "I didn't mean—please, lord, forgive me!" he cries, falling to his knees.

I approach slowly, my shadow stretching long across his body. I do not raise my weapon. I do not need to. I kneel beside the young man and speak low.

"You dishonor the market, the gods, and yourself. But you are young. You will answer to the court, not the blade. Let your hands restore what your haste destroyed."

I bind his hands with a strip of cloth from my own sash and call for a *topilli*, a bailiff with authority to detain, escort and command, to render him to the Judge.

The crowd watches in silence, then slowly resumes its rhythm. A few nod in approval. One elder bows as I pass.

My children run to me, unaware of the weight of the moment. Itzel touches my arm, her eyes proud but quiet. My daughter asks, "What will happen to that man?"

> He was led astray, little one. Huehuecóyotl, the old coyote, whispered mischief into his ear and made him forget. The Judge will not raise the blade—he will raise a lesson. The boy will serve the shopkeeper for thirteen days. In this way, order returns and the boy may walk a straighter path. But if he forgets again, the punishment will be harsher still.

I am no longer a warrior; I did not raise my weapon, but I upheld the social order. I feel my essence; I am a guardian. As we walk on, the market feels changed—calmer, more reverent.

FEAST OF THE DEAD

In the tenth month of the solar calendar, we celebrate Huey Miccailhuitl, the Great Feast of the Dead. It is a time to honor those who have passed, to remember their lives, and to commune with their spirits.

This year, the rituals carry a deeper weight. Both of my dear parents died during my journey to Zaachila-Yoo. Their absence is a quiet ache that lingers in my heart.

With my wife Itzel and our children beside me, we walk to our family burial ground. We bring offerings—food, flowers, and incense—and perform the sacred rituals of remembrance. I say,

O Chicomecoatl, loving mother,
O Cuauhtli, devoted father,
I hold you like flowers to the sky.
Walk with the stars, beloved ones.
May your spirits rise on the breath of our prayers."

The scent of copal rises into the air, curling like memory toward the heavens. The children place marigolds at the graves, their bright petals glowing in the morning light. My wife sings a quiet song, one my mother used to hum while grinding maize:

The stone turns slow, the maize grows strong,
By your hands, the gods are fed all along.
I kneel before their resting place and whisper:
I have returned. I have fulfilled my duty.
I carry your teachings in my heart.
May your spirits walk beside me.

In the stillness, I feel their presence – not as shadows, but as warmth. The Feast of the Dead is not only a mourning – it is a reunion. And in that reunion, I find peace.

GARDENS OF TENOCHTITLÁN

The following day, we visit the chinampa where my father was born, gliding across Lake Texcoco in a canoe as we circumnavigate our island city. The water shimmers beneath us, reflecting the grandeur of Tenochtitlán and the majestic mountains and volcanoes that surround it.

When Popocatépetl and Iztaccíhuatl come into view, I recount the legend of the two lovers for our young children. Their eyes widen with wonder as I describe the sleeping princess and the warrior who stands watch, his heart smoldering with eternal devotion.

We paddle through the canals that weave through every corner and avenue of the city. Small ponds and water features enhance both the beauty and functionality of our urban paradise.

The entire city is a brilliant, living garden, bursting with color and fragrance. With every turn, we encounter plumeria and jasmine, sweet and delicate; hibiscus, bright orange marigolds, and indian paintbrush, bold and radiant; bougainvillea, bird of paradise, and passion flowers, wild and vibrant; Gardens devoted to medicinal, culinary, and ceremonial herbs, tended with care and reverence.

In the days that follow, we visit the royal aviary and zoo, marveling at the diversity of life. In the zoo, we see jaguars, feared and revered for their strength and ferocity – capable of crushing bone with a single strike; pumas and ocelots, sleek and powerful; boa constrictors, coral snakes, and rattlesnakes, coiled with silent menace.

IN THE ROYAL AVIARY,

The air is thick with birdsong as we step into the royal aviary. My children gasp, their eyes wide with delight.

"Papa, look!" my youngest cries, pointing to a brilliant red macaw flapping its wings above a carved perch.

I smile. "That's a macaw. They love to chatter and show off. Listen – he's greeting you."

"Why are they in cages?" my youngest son asks, brow furrowed.

"Not cages," I say gently. "These are enclosures, built to feel like home. See the nets above? They let in sunlight and air, but keep the birds safe. Some have ponds, others have treetop perches. Each bird lives where it feels most at peace."

We walk past a shaded pen where a royal eagle perches high above, its gaze sharp and still.

"That one looks angry," whispers my daughter.

"Not angry," I say. "Majestic. That eagle is sacred – he watches over the aviary like a guardian. His perch is built tall, like the trees he would choose in the wild."

A flash of green catches our eyes – quetzals, shimmering like emerald fire, flutter in a quiet corner.

"They're so beautiful," my son breathes.

"Yes," I nod. "Their feathers are used in headdresses for priests and emperors. They are plucked with the greatest care so the bird can grow new ones. We do not harm sacred birds."

"Who feeds them?" asks my youngest, tugging my hand.

"The birds are cared for by the Tototl Tlamacazqui, the high priest of the aviary," I reply. "He oversees more than three hundred workers, each trained to understand the needs of every species — fruit for the macaws, insects for the quetzals, even small animals for the eagle. It's not just feeding — it's devotion. These birds are sacred, and their feathers are used in rituals, headdresses, and offerings to the gods."

We pause before a quiet enclosure where a priest collects fallen feathers with reverence.

"Papa," my daughter says softly, "do the gods really wear feathers?"

I kneel beside her. "Not in the way we do. But feathers carry breath and spirit. When we offer them, we offer beauty, flight, and prayer. The gods receive them as gifts of the heart."

She nods, thoughtful. My son reaches for my hand.

"Can we come again?"

I smile. "Of course. The birds will remember you."

"Tenochtitlán is not merely a city," I explain, "It is a sanctuary of life, a testament to the harmony between nature and man. And in its gardens, its waters, and its skies, we feel the pulse of our ancestors and the promise of our future."

IX
Moctezuma Xocoyotzin Ascends

Before the close of the year 1502, the rains descend with fury, flooding vast portions of Tenochtitlán. I am in the marketplace when the sky darkens and the temple drums begin to beat – not with celebration, but with a rhythm of gravity and importance. A messenger rushes in and announces,

> The new aqueduct from Coyoacán has failed and unleashed chaos. Huey Tlatoani Ahuitzotl struck his head while fleeing the rising waters. He has fallen ill with a mysterious affliction.

I leave my basket behind and follow the rising murmur toward the palace gates, where I hear people whisper, "Cipactli has taken him... the violent monster that devours without end."

The Tlatoani's *cuauhteca*, royal guards, grant me admission to Ahuitzotl's inner sanctum where he is being treated. Though I am a newly appointed ambassador, the guards know that I am also something more. I was Ahuitzotl's boyhood friend, chosen long ago to walk beside him in silence and service and he keeps me close, even now. Though we do not speak of our childhood bond in public, it lives beneath the surface, like the roots of a ceiba tree – deep, unseen, and unbreakable.

Inside the palace, the air is thick with incense and urgency. Prayers, chants and offerings fill the temples. I stand near his bedside while attendants speak in hushed tones.

Priests conduct rituals seeking divine intervention. They guide him through meditations, urging his spirit to focus on healing. *Ticitin*[168] arrive bearing medicinal incense for his lungs and herbal teas for his stomach. Sacred healers administer hallucinogens, and offer prayers to calm his spirit. Slaves are sacrificed to appease the gods.

But none of the remedies succeed. Ahuitzotl grows weaker. I watch his breath grow shallow; his strength flickers like a dying flame.

The healer turns to me and says:

> The emperor's tonalli has been disturbed by his encounter with the floodwaters. Water spirits entered him during the flood, they cling to him, and now illness grows from within. The emperor's tonalli no longer burns — it is cool, damp with the breath of the deep. His body can not resist; it yields. This is the wet silence of the lake.

I do not speak. I simply remain near him should he reach out. But he cannot. His spirit silently leaves. Chief Priest Tlamacazqui Quetzalcoatl Totec is present at that moment, and announces:

> Our dear Huey Tlatoani Ahuitzotl leaves us. He has gone by water. The signs are clear. His breath was taken not by blade, but by the embrace of Tlaloc. He shall not wander the nine shadows to Mictlan. He will walk the green paths of *Tlalocan* — the paradise of rain god Tlaloc, where the springs sing and the maize grows without end.

I help prepare his body. I wash him with reverence, dress him in his finest royal garments, adorned with gold, jade, and feathers. He is placed upon a richly decorated litter. As one of his favorites, I am honored to help carry his body through the streets of Tenochtitlán, alongside royal family members and priests.

The procession is grand. Moctezuma Xocoyotzin,[169] Ahuitzotl's nephew, great-grandson of Moctezuma I, walks beside us, honoring

---

168 Healers

169 The name means "the revered younger one, Moctezuma II.

his uncle with solemn praise. Musicians play low notes, dancers move slowly, gracefully and mourners fill the air with the sounds of sorrow.

At the cremation site, priests conduct final rituals and offer food, drink and precious items to the gods – especially to Huitzilopochtli, the sun god, and Tlaloc, the rain god – to ensure Ahuitzotl's safe passage to the afterlife.

Mexica from across the empire gather as the emperor's body is placed upon a great pyre and set ablaze. The flames rise, fierce and relentless, consuming his physical form and releasing his soul to ascend.

His ashes are placed in a sacred urn, and laid to rest in a tomb of honor. His spirit will dwell among the gods.

1502 ENDS, CORONATION OF MOCTEZUMA XOCOYOTZIN

The year ends with mourning. Ahuitzotl is dead, and the city holds its breath. The Tlatocan, council of nobles and high-ranking officials gathers to choose the next Huey Tlatoani. I hear the names whispered in the palace corridors and temple courtyards – Moctezuma Xocoyotzin, Cuitláhuac, Cuauhtémoc, Chimalpilli II, Tehuetzquitititzin – all of them warriors, all of them of noble blood.

But it is Moctezuma, great-grandson of Motecuhzoma Ilhuicamina, who rises without challenge. He is no stranger to power. He had served as a priest dedicated to the war god Huitzilopochtli and he has long stood at the center of ritual and command. I have seen how his presence alone silences dissent. He does not ask for loyalty – he demands it. And none dare refuse.

Once his selection is secured, I watch Moctezuma enter the *tlacoch-calco*[170] where he stays for several days and nights. There, he abandons his old identity – drops his finery and the emblems of rank, and dresses simply. He fasts, cuts his own blood, burns incense before the shrine of Huitzilopochtli. He renounces his role as war-commander, noble and high priest, and is reborn, prepared to assume the sacred office of emperor.

---

170 The house of warriors, the military-ritual building.

On coronation day, the Mexica priests bring him forward in awe, recognizing that he now speaks for the gods. We gather in the plaza watching as he stands before us clad in full royal regalia. A procession of priests leads him atop the grand platform of the Imperial Palace to the Jaguar-and-Eagle Throne. Elders and kings offer praise. Priests make offerings to Huitzilopochtli and Tlaloc, invoking divine favor. Tlamacazqui Quetzalcoatl Totec, the high priest, anoints him with oil and water, places the royal turquoise diadem upon his head and presents him with the scepter and shield – symbols of authority and divine mandate. From that moment, he is Huey Tlatoani Moctezuma Xocoyotzin.

Illustration depicting the coronation of Moctezuma II. Diego Duran, The History of the Indies of New Spain, Duran Codex, folio 152r.

As the ceremony at the palace ends, Huey Tlatoani Moctezuma II rises and calls to his entourage to follow him. He walks solemnly to the Huey Teocalli and the crowd follows. He climbs the steep steps, priests, generals and nobles in tow, to the very summit of the great pyramid of Tenochtitlán. There he enters the temple of Huitzilopochtli with the high priest. Next, they pass into the temple of Tlaloc.

Huey Tlatoani Moctezuma emerges facing the multitude, and raises his arms as though reaching for the sun. He steps forward and speaks:

People of the Mexica, children of the sun and stone – I have climbed the sacred steps, entered the breath of the gods, and offered my blood to the fire and the rain. I return not as priest, not as warrior, not as noble – but as Huey Tlatoani, chosen by the gods, crowned by your voices, and bound to the sacred burden of command.

From this day, I speak not for myself, but for Huitzilopochtli, whose fire guides our blades, and for Tlaloc, whose rains nourish our maize.

Let all know: the empire shall be as the eagle's flight – disciplined, fierce and unbroken. Tribute shall rise like smoke from every province. Nobility shall serve with honor, not excess. The macehualtin[171] shall be protected, for they are the roots of our tree.

I see imbalance. I see hunger. I see pride without labor. This shall end.

Let the temples be filled with song. Let the warriors sharpen their obsidian. Let the scribes record this day in gold and jade.

I am Moctezuma Xocoyotzin. I am the shield and the mirror. I am the breath of the gods made flesh.

Walk with me, and we shall rise.

In the weeks that follow, I feel a shift in the air. Tribute demands rise. Provincial divisions are redrawn. Advisors are replaced with loyalists.

Moctezuma speaks of imbalance – too many nobles, too few commoners to sustain them. Moctezuma seeks to limit the expansion of the noble class, aware that each new royal adds weight to the shoulders of the macehualtin, the common people who sustain the empire. He insists that nobles fulfill their duties independently, without leaning on the labor of those beneath them. Whether driven by a desire to preserve social order or by a quiet disdain for upward mobility among

---

171 commoners

commoners, his policy draws a clear line: the path to nobility is no longer open to those born outside it.

I listen. I watch. I wonder what this means for men like me – those who rose through valor, not birth. The gods remain, but the hands that serve them grow heavier with control.

⌇⌇⌇⌇⌇

For the next ten years, my brother and I make semiannual trips to Zaachila-Yoo. As the imperial ambassador, I visit with the queen, deliver items she requests from Tenochtitlán, and ensure her safety and happiness. I meet with Coquitao Cosijoeza to hear his concerns, resolve issues and disputes and offer assistance. On several occasions, I intervene in conflicts and negotiate with the Mixtecs and other nearby city-states. This period is marked by stability and peace between Mexica and Zapotecs.

THE EMPEROR'S CHIEF ADVISOR

In the year 1512, when I reach my sixty-second year, the long road to and from Tzapotlan begins to weigh on my bones. Upon my return to Tenochtitlán, I am summoned to the palace. The chambers are quiet, the air heavy with copal and the soft rustle of attendants moving like shadows.

Moctezuma receives me in a small audience room, not the great hall. He dismisses the attendants with a gesture, leaving only the two of us. His face softens when he sees me.

"Huitzilin," he says, "you have traveled far for many years. Sit with me."

I bow and take my place across from him.

"Huey Tlatoani," I begin, "I come to request release from my duties as ambassador. My strength is not what it was. The road grows longer each year."

Moctezuma studies me for a moment, his eyes thoughtful, almost nostalgic.

"I knew you would ask this," he says quietly. "And I will grant it. But before you lay down your burden, there is something I must tell you."

He leans back slightly, as though reaching into memory.

"I was a boy," he says, "no more than eight or nine, when I stood in Texcoco at the funeral of Nezahualcoyotl. I remember the drums, the banners, the weeping of the nobles. But what I remember most is you."

I blink, surprised. "Me, Huey Tlatoani?"

"Yes." His voice is steady, warm. "You stepped forward and spoke for the old king. Your words were not loud, but they carried farther than the drums. You spoke of wisdom, of humility, of the fleeting nature of life. I was only a child, but your voice stayed with me. I have never forgotten it."

He pauses, letting the memory settle between us.

"Since that day," he continues, "I have admired your thoughtfulness. Your judgment. Your ability to see beyond the moment."

I bow my head, humbled.

"You honor me, Huey Tlatoani."

"No," he replies, "I speak only the truth."

He straightens, returning to the present.

"You may retire from your travels," he says, "but I will not allow your wisdom to leave the palace. I ask–no, I require–that you accept appointment to the Tlatocan."

The words strike me like a bell.

"The Council of Advisors?"

"Yes," he says. "Twelve to twenty of the highest lords. They are my eyes and ears. They bring me the needs of the people, the state of the treasury, the tribute accounts, the omens, the messages from every corner of the empire. I want your voice among them."

I feel the weight of the honor, the trust, the responsibility.

"Huey Tlatoani," I say softly, "I accept."

Moctezuma nods once, satisfied.

"Good. Then your service continues–here, at home, where your counsel will strengthen the throne."

రరరరరర

On the day of my first meeting with the Tlatocan, we receive mystifying information from the Maya territories about two bearded *huecachane*,[172] strangers who arrived on the island of Tantun Cuzamil.[173] They were captured and are being held at Xman Há.[174] We remain on alert for further information, but none arrives.

రరరరరర

I have been on the Tlatocan for just two years, when Huey Tlatoani Moctezuma II calls me to his chamber. He tells me,

> Huitzilin, I have heard omens. We are entering unknown times. You are an elder and I value your wisdom and skill above all others. I need you in the Teuctlatoque, the Supreme Council, cabinet ministers who help me manage the affairs of state.
>
> There are four cabinet ministers: the Supreme Military Commander, Tlacochcalcatl; the supreme religious leader, Tlamacazqui of Huitzilopochtli; the Treasury and Tribute Minister who oversees economic flow and resource management; and the Principal Diplomatic Envoy who manages relations with all allied and tributary altepetls, which is the role I ask you to take.

Over the next seven years, I advise the emperor regarding the best course for expansion of the empire and the tributes to be gained. Tenochtitlán's population, power and wealth grow. Tenochtitlán, is a city at its zenith, perhaps the most beautiful that ever existed.

---

172 Strangers, foreigners
173 The island of Cozumel.
174 Modern-day Playa del Carmen.

X

1519, Arrival of Hernando Cortés

COZUMEL, MARCH 2, 1519

Late in the evening on March 3, 1519, I stand in the council chamber beside Huey Tlatoani Moctezuma Xocoyotzin, surrounded by his Teuctlatoque and priests, when guards announce the arrival of two *paynani*[175] bearing a message of great urgency.

Moctezuma raises his hand – a silent signal of permission. A court herald leads the messengers into the inner sanctum, where the emperor sits in state, cloaked in silence and power.

The two messengers, one carrying a feathered banner, enter the inner sanctum surrounded by the emperor's armed guards. With their heads bowed, they kneel, press their foreheads to the palace floor and repeat, "Our revered lord, most revered lord, we supplicate – our heartfelt thanks in your presence." Tlamacazqui Quetzalcoatl Totec instructs, "You may rise and speak your urgent message."

The lead paynani stands with his gaze to the floor and speaks with agitation, breathing hard,

> Revered Great Speaker, Moctezuma Xocoyotzin, our lord and ruler, we bring word from the sacred isle of Cozumel, land of the Maya and sanctuary of Ixchel, goddess of fertility, medicine, and childbirth. It is a place of peace, of pilgrimage, of prayer.

---

175 A military runner, messenger, or scout.

But peace has been broken. *Teules*,[176] white-skinned gods with bearded faces have arrived. They ride the sea on great floating houses, wings set to the sky; not one but many.

They accept offerings, but do not bow. They speak a tongue we do not know. They bring gifts, but also weapons. They move with the bearing of lords.

They ride beasts like deer, monstrous in size, thundering across the earth. Their weapons spit fire and smoke; strike like lightning. And beside them walk war dogs,[177] ten, perhaps twelve in number, creatures with eyes like burning coals and teeth, sharp as the obsidian edge. These beasts obey only their masters.

Their macuahuitl (swords) gleam with unnatural light. Their *ichcahuipilli*[178] shine like moonlit water. The Maya of Cozumel tremble. Confusion reigns. Fear spreads like smoke.

I stand as the lead paynani finishes his presentation. He quivers, his breath ragged, then collapses to the ground in a reverent bow.

I watch. The Great Speaker, Moctezuma Xocoyotzin, our lord and ruler, his eyes dark and searching, flicker with awe . . . and dread. He rises slowly and paces back and forth. The weight of prophecy – the unknown destiny these teules portend – presses upon his brow.

Everyone present falls silent. We wait. At last the Great Speaker speaks:

> We are reminded of Shaman Ocelotl's prophecy . . . bearded men arriving from the east. The signs . . . the omens . . . speak of a return, of change, of upheaval. Could these be the ones foretold? Quetzalcoatl returning from the east disguised as a bearded man . . . or something else entirely?

He stops pacing and turns to the messengers.

---

176 Divine beings, gods.

177 Mastiffs, some weighing up to 250 pounds and standing three feet tall at the shoulder, were used for brute-force attacks; trained to maul enemies.

178 Mexica quilted cotton protective vests. Here referring to the Spaniard's steel armor.

These divine beings are not like any men we have seen before. Houses that float upon the water...weapons that spit fire and death...beasts that carry men as one creature...

His brow furrowed, he continues,

The *itzcuintli*[179]...Fierce you say? Unlike our own? And these...deer-like creatures...what is their purpose? Do they fight? Do they carry burdens? Tell me everything you saw of them!

He listens intently, absorbing every word and his expression grows increasingly troubled.

These weapons...they defy all understanding. And these creatures...they must possess great power...to instill such fear.

He turns away, gazing out over the city.

These strangers, are they gods? Are they men? Or are they something in between...something the world has never seen?

He turns back to the them; his voice now edged with uncertainty.

Bring the wisest priests. Consult the codices. I must know everything about these...foreigners. Their origins, their purpose, their strengths, their weaknesses. We must understand them...before they understand us.

A shadow crosses his face and he pauses.

And send spies. Disguise them as traders, as pilgrims...anything. I want to know their numbers, their movements, their intentions. And find out if they are truly led by Quetzalcoatl himself or by some other, darker power.

He sits heavily, the throne no longer a seat of comfort but of burden, of fate.

The fate of our empire...perhaps the fate of the world...may rest upon what we learn of these strangers.

---

179 Dogs

Route of Cortés expedition from Cozumel to Centla, Veracruz and Cempoala.

CENTLA, MARCH 25, 1519

Early in the morning of March 25, 1519, Huey Tlatoani Moctezuma is deep in deliberation with the Teuctlatoque, supreme council, when a messenger is escorted into the chamber with a message of grave urgency. After performing obeisance, still breathless, he speaks in rushed bursts, his voice cracking with awe and fear:

I bear news of extraordinary events unfolding in the Tabascan lands of the Maya.

Divine strangers have come by sea to the Chontal Maya city-state of Centla. They demand submission to their distant king and conversion to a strange religion. The Maya chiefs refused: they would not allow the foreigners to set foot on their shores.

Just two days past, battle erupted when the teules began to disembark. Tabscoob, the Chontal Maya leader, rallied some eight thousand warriors who loosed volleys of arrows upon the invaders.

But the four-hundred divine foreigners proved too strong. They wore cloaks that carry the sun's rays, hard as stone that turned aside Maya blades and spears. The teules' weapons – firesticks of sorcery – struck down warriors with invisible force. They wielded giant tubes that burst like volcanoes, spewing fire and smoke, casting warriors down with one thunder-burst; their limbs broken, bodies shattered, scattered like broken reeds, blood flowing like water.

Some rode upon massive, supernatural deer-like beasts, charging and trampling all in their path like a river of molten rock.

After his defeat, Tabscoob offered the divine strangers twenty women. Among them is a Nahua noblewoman named Malinalli, who speaks both the Nahuatl and Mayan tongue.

Upon hearing this news our Teuctlatoque is in shock. One member shouts, "They are *teules*,[180] come to destroy us."

I counsel the emperor,

> We must be wary. These men may not divine teules, but powerful men. Their strength lies in their weapons and beasts, not in divinity. We must watch them — closely. Learn their movements, their intentions, their weaknesses.

Over the next moon cycle, our spies and messengers shadow the strangers, reporting every step, every word, every gesture. The empire listens. The gods, perhaps, do too.

CEMPOALA, APRIL 9, 1519

In early April I sit in the council chamber of the palace when a messenger is ushered in from Cempoala with an urgent dispatch for the emperor. He bows, breathless, and announces in hurried tones,

> An army of divine beings from the sea has entered the Totonac city of Cempoala, our vassal state. They are light-skinned with long, yellow beards. They are wrapped in gleaming skins, hard as stone. Their helmets glisten in the sun. Their swords and all their gear, all born of that bright, stone-hard substance unknown to us — nothing we carry can cut it. They carry weapons that roar like thunder and strike like lightning. Their deer carry them wherever they wish to go. They do not resemble any people we know.

---

180 Divine beings, in this case implying powerful foreigners.

We have met their *Yaotequihua*,[181] (military commander). A Mexica noblewoman is with him; interprets for him. Her name is Malinalli.[182]

Huey Tlatoani Moctezuma II grows pensive, his gaze drifting beyond the chamber. Then he speaks:

> We know our history. Quetzalcoatl, the feathered serpent, god of wind, culture, and learning, once ruled among our Toltec ancestors.
>
> Tezcatlipoca,[183] betrayed him, forcing his departure from our people. He retreated to a cave in the east and transformed into a celestial being, vowing to return in year One Reed as a light-skinned bearded man to reclaim his throne and restore order.
>
> Recently, I dreamed of a bearded man arriving from the sea. It unsettled me deeply.
>
> We all witnessed the fiery comet that streaked across the eastern sky – an omen of doom, heralding momentous change. Then, we witnessed the destruction of a temple by fire and the appearance of strange visions in water.
>
> Now it is year One Reed and light skinned men with bearded faces have arrived at our shores. Dare we challenge destiny?

We contemplate the emperor's words in silence. I ask for permission to speak, and say,

> We do not challenge destiny, yet who are these men from the sea, truly? They come as an aggressive army bearing terrible weapons. They bleed from their wounds. They crave gold and treasure, not like gods, but like greedy, unruly men.
>
> Quetzalcoatl is a god of wisdom, culture and the arts. He is not a warrior god. He does not need an army to reclaim his throne. When he returns, he will bring renewal and order, not conquest and bloodshed.

---

181 A war leader or commander who leads a military campaign.

182 Malinalli, meaning grass or twisted vines, is the day name for the date of her birth. She becomes known by the honorific, Malintzin to the Aztecs; "La Malinche" or "Doña Marina" to the Spaniards. Later, Aztecs refer to Cortés as Malinche.

183 "Smoking Mirror," god of fate, sorcery and transformation, often acting as a trickster and rival to Quetzalcoatl.

What are the true intentions of these men with bearded faces, these *tentzontin*,[184] bearded men? We must prepare ourselves. We must be cautious – and wait for destiny to reveal itself.

Nodding, the emperor thinks aloud,

We once called them teules, gods cloaked in thunder. But gods do not bleed. Gods do not hunger for gold. Now, we shall call them tentzontin, men with bearded faces. Men, not gods.

Moctezuma dispatches more messengers to shadow these men's movements, and commissions artists to record their likeness. Days later a messenger arrives from the Totonac city with an urgent dispatch.

Great Speaker, I must inform you: five of our tax-collectors have been arrested in Cempoala, and the Totonacs now refuse to pay tribute.

Enraged, Moctezuma, shouts,

Refusing tribute is cause for war! Instruct the supreme commander of the army[185] to prepare for battle. I will lead a vast army, commanded by many generals, to vanquish these men from the sea!

But days later, as war preparations begin, two tax collectors return and report:

The men with bearded faces have freed our tax collectors from the Cempoalans. They ask us to inform Huey Tlatoani that they wish to be the emperor's sincerest friends and most devoted servants.

Intrigued, yet wary, Moctezuma dispatches two young nephews and four senior ambassadors to meet the bearded ones to learn their true intentions. He instructs them to present lavish gifts – gold and

---

184 The Mexica referred to the Spaniards as "Tentzontin," the Nahuatl term for "bearded ones," or men with bearded faces Its literal meaning is lip hair, or chin/ face hair.

185 The war leader responsible for military action. *Tlacochcalcatl*

fine embroidered textiles – to demonstrate our wealth and power, and to dissuade the strangers from advancing toward Tenochtitlán.

I caution the great speaker,

> Beware of false friends. We do not yet know their true intentions.

When the entourage returns, their spokesman reports,

> Huey Tlatoani, we met with the leader of the men with bearded faces. He asked us to deliver these blue and green beads as a token of friendship. He declares that the Totonacs are now vassals of his emperor, and for that reason, they will no longer pay tribute to Tenochtitlán.

Moctezuma is stunned,

> The men from the east have made the Totonacs a vassal of their emperor and offer us beads? Beads – when we have offered them gold and our finest embroidered textiles? Cast those beads into the dung heap! This is an affront and a challenge to the Mexica Empire!

Tensions mount. The emperor sends a pantli of twenty warriors to Cempoala – not to engage, but to observe. We must learn more about these men with bearded faces. Their weapons, their words, their ambitions. Only then can we decide how to meet them – as gods, as men, or as enemies.

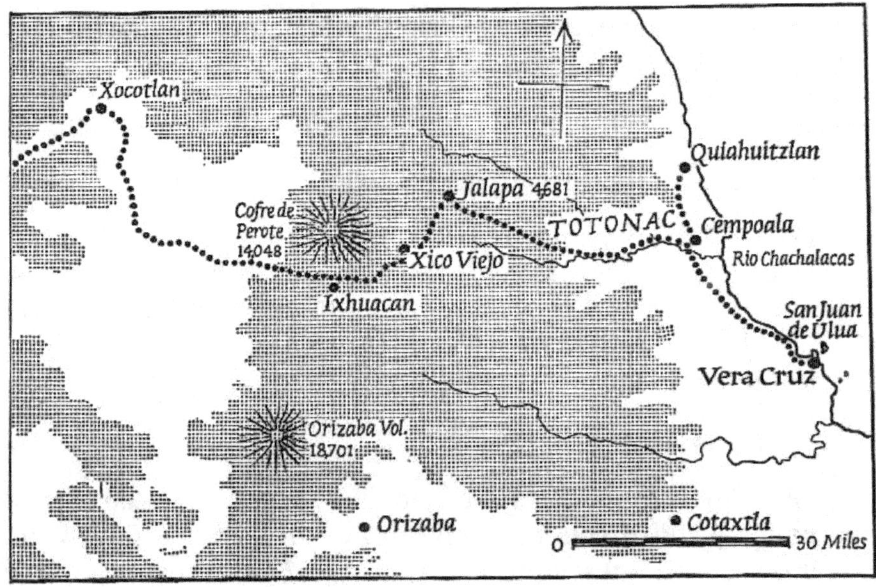

The March from Vera Cruz to the City of Mexico.

TLAXCALA, SEPTEMBER 1519

The Mexica maintain watch posts and relay systems throughout the empire, especially along sacred roads leading into the Valley of Mexico. Our scouts track the movements of the strangers and relay their findings to the capital with urgency and precision.

In September, the scouts report,

> The men from the east advance from Cempoala, joined by Totonac warriors. With each city-state, their ranks swell.
>
> On the first day of September, they reached the lands of the powerful Tlaxcaltec Confederation. There, near the village of Tehuacacinco, General Xicotencatl commands twenty divisions, above 40,000 warriors...but, the bearded ones, the ones they say are teules, resisted for two days and could not be pushed back. Their metal cloaks turn aside the warrior's blades and spears. Their great tubes thunder, shake the earth; dozens fall. Their mounts – towering creatures like deer – charge and trample warriors.

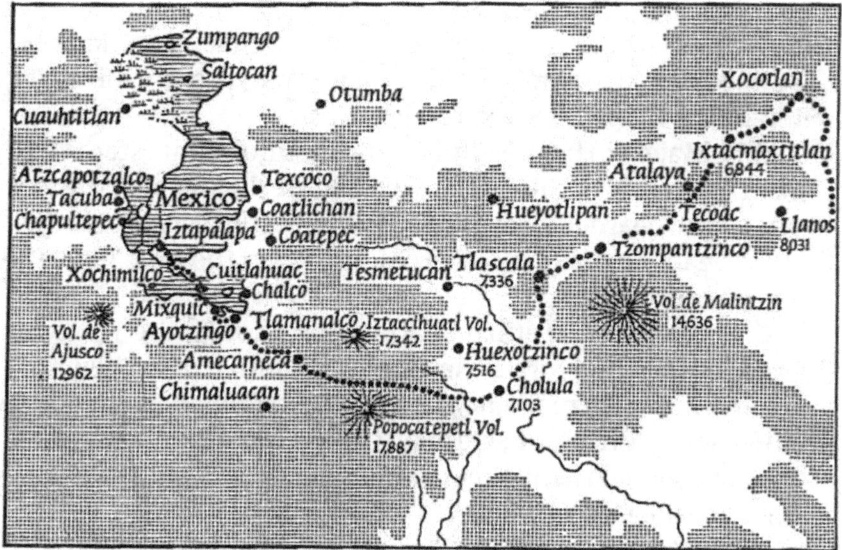

Five days later, another messenger reports,

> On September 5, 1519, Xicotencatl brought five chiefs each commanding 10,000 men. On an open field, six miles in breadth, covered with warriors, they battled the small army of 400 teules, they say. Attacking from the four corners, with spears, arrows and stones falling on them like a hard rain, the bearded ones held fast, repelling the Tlaxcaltec forces.

After two more days, a paynani arrives with more information,

> The day after the failure on the open field, soothsayers gathered in Tlaxcala and told that the teules could not fight after the sun set. So that night, Xicotencatl mustered 10,000 of his bravest men and attacked the strangers under the moon and stars, but were repulsed again.
>
> The elders spoke in hushed voices: "Thrice we attacked with all our mighty forces... by day and by night, yet we prevailed not." The nobles and elders were downcast on account of the unfavorable issue of the battles. They lament, "The teules have killed too many of our subjects, numbers of our sons, relations and chiefs in these battles."

The bearded ones seized seventeen Tlaxcalan spies and sent them back – thumbs severed, hands missing, blood marking their path. When Xicotencatl beheld their broken bodies, his will faltered. The fire in his chest turned to ash.

Your Majesty, the dreadful truth: our informants state that in each fight the Tlaxcalan forces were powerless against the weapons of the bearded ones. The fields of battle were strewn with their dead: on one day three chiefs fell, on the next four, then eight sons of chiefs.

Great Speaker, I return bearing this: though the Tlaxcalans brought their full force, they withdrew into truce. Their chiefs tell us they have made peace with the strangers from the sea. Whether by dread, or strategy, I know not – but they say they cannot conquer them, they cannot hold them back. The bearded ones advance.

Now, Tlaxcalans have allied with the bearded men and thousands of their warriors have joined the march on Tenochtitlán.

I now leave this for your wise deliberation.

Moctezuma's face darkens with dread. He speaks slowly, his voice heavy with history:

We have fought the Tlaxcalans since the time of our ancestors. Our empire of city-states surrounds them completely, yet we have never achieved what these bearded ones have done in seven days. They are no ordinary force.

Huey Tlatoani orders a message to be delivered to the strangers: a warning that the journey to Tenochtitlán is perilous, and the city is not prepared to receive them.

But days later, another report arrives. The men with bearded faces continue their march toward Tenochtitlán, undeterred.

Fearing the consequences of their aggression, Moctezuma sends a third message to Cortés, urging him to turn back. Still, our messengers return with the same answer: the strangers will not stop.

CHOLULA, OCTOBER 1519

In October, our scouts return with heavy hearts. Their faces are pale, their voices low. One speaks with tears,

The men from the east arrived in our city-state of Cholula, accompanied by their Tlaxcalans allies. They were welcomed with ceremony and goodwill. But without warning, while the Cholulans were worshiping at their temples, the strangers launched a surprise attack. Thousands were slain – priests, nobles, commoners – temples desecrated, the city set ablaze – sacred treasures stolen. They killed without mercy. These men do not honor life.

I am in the council chamber when the message is delivered. I rise, unbidden, my voice trembling with grief,

Cholula is the sacred heart of Anahuac.[186] It is the essence of our Toltec heritage. Our priests, nobles, merchants – even our humble macehualli – make pilgrimages there to seek guidance, to interpret omens. It is a place of learning, revered by all Nahua peoples.

Pilgrims from across Anahuac – Maya, Zapotec, Mixtec – journey to the Great Pyramid of Cholula, dedicated to Quetzalcoatl, god of wisdom, creation, and humanity. He is the patron of arts, crafts, trade, and peace.

The Cholulans are peaceful. They do not make war. They did not deserve this fate.

I pause, then ask aloud:

Could this be the moment of the great earthquake – the omen that foretells the end of the Fifth Sun?

Then, Huey Tlatoani Moctezuma speaks, his voice heavy with sorrow and resolve,

Could this be the moment of the great earthquake--the omen that foretells the end of the Fifth Sun?

It is my duty to protect our people from the fate of the Cholulans. We must avoid direct conflict. We must seek peace with these powerful strangers. Resistance may be futile against their weapons and alliances."

---

186 "Land Between the Waters," which encompassed the Valley of Mexico and the broader region they considered the Mexica cultural and political domain.

Three times we have warned the men with bearded faces not to come to Tenochtitlán, yet they persist. They have dominated every city – Cozumel, Centla, Cempoala, Tlaxcala – and now they have destroyed Cholula, our beloved altepetl.

They have defeated every army, even the mighty Tlaxcalans. They have shown their cruelty by massacring our venerated friends. With their magic fire tubes and wild beasts,[187] they are a force of terror. They have instilled fear in the hearts of our people.

It is my duty to go to them, to welcome them, to find a way to avert war, which I fear would bring ruin.

Therefore, with the blessings of the gods, I have resolved to go to the men from the East and peaceably invite them to our city. All members of the Council of Advisors will join me.

The chamber stirs with unease. Many lords are agitated. I return home Itzel – our children and grandchildren gathered. When she asks what troubles me, I recount the horrors of Cholula. I tell her I will stand beside the emperor when he meets the men with bearded faces.

As the men with bearded faces advance toward Tenochtitlán, Moctezuma sends diplomats bearing gifts, reaffirming our desire for peace. He instructs his emissaries to arrange a meeting with their leader – while quietly ordering his generals to fortify the city and prepare for war.

The diplomats return with word: the meeting will take place at Xoloco, near the entrance to Tenochtitlán, as Moctezuma requested – ensuring our forces maintain control over the encounter.

---

187 *Miquiztli* meant "wild beasts" referring to horses.

XI
Cortés Enters Tenotchtitlán

The sun rises over Lake Texcoco, casting golden light across the causeways. I stand among the nobility of Tenochtitlán, shoulder to shoulder with generals, priests, and warriors of the Eagle and Jaguar orders. We gather in solemn silence to honor our divine ruler, Huey Tlatoani Moctezuma Xocoyotzin, as he prepares to meet the armed force from the east.

Moctezuma is radiant in imperial regalia. His *tilmatli* (cloak), woven in sacred colors, glows with embroidered glyphs of power. Gold and turquoise shimmer across his chest, and his towering quetzal-feathered headdress sways gently with each breath of wind. His shoes gleam – soles of gold, uppers adorned with jade and turquoise. He is not merely a man today. He is the embodiment of divine authority.

Four tlatoanis from neighboring city-states lift him upon a golden litter draped in fine textiles. Above him, a canopy of green feathers, threaded with gold and silver, casts a sacred shadow. Pearl and jade tassels sway like prayers in motion.

I stand with the three other members of the Teuctlatoque, at the front of the emperor's entourage, flanked by high priests in feathered robes and generals bearing obsidian blades. The air is thick with incense and anticipation, and though we maintain strict protocol, I feel the weight of uncertainty – of unanswered questions, of what is about to unfold, of the destiny awaiting us – pressing against my chest.

As we approach the road beyond the causeway, Moctezuma sends emissaries ahead to greet the foreigners, offering words of peace. When they return with assurances, we proceed.

And then—we see them.

The men with bearded faces, stand waiting. Their leader, whom they call "El Capitán," steps forward, flanked by armored soldiers. At his side is Malinalli, whom we call Malintzin, the noblewoman who speaks for them. Moctezuma, in a gesture of diplomacy, refers to the leader, Cortés, as Malinche.

The two leaders exchange words of friendship. I watch Moctezuma extend an invitation to enter our city. My breath catches.

When the bearded ones arrive in our city, Moctezuma leads them not to a ceremonial hall, but to the palace of his father, Axayacatl. I am stunned. Around me, the Tlatoque murmur in disbelief. Is this is a gesture of trust—or surrender? This is no ordinary welcome.

Over the following days, Moctezuma lavishes Malinche with gifts. I see the heavy gold necklace he presents, its weight matched only by the tension in our hearts. He even offers his own daughter in marriage.

I do not speak of my doubts aloud. But in quiet moments I wonder: is this diplomacy, or desperation? Is this the wisdom of a ruler, or the fear of a man who sees the Fifth Sun trembling?

FRAY BARTOLOMÉ DE OLMEDO[188]

During my daily walk through the main square, I observe the bearded ones building a small altar to their gods. At its top stands a strange symbol—two crossed beams. Every morning, they kneel before it while their priest offers each a morsel and a sip of a red wine.

Today, I walk with Tlamacazqui Quetzalcoatl Totec and several members of the Tlatocan.[189] In the plaza we encounter Malinche and the priest of the bearded ones, whom they call Padre Olmedo. He is eager to speak of his gods. He begins,

---

188 Olmedo, Fray Bartolomé de, aka Padre Olmedo chief priest who accompanied Cortés to Tenochtitlán.

189 Council of advisors

Jesus Christ is the son of god – and he is god. He was executed by mortals, nailed to a wooden cross like this one [pointing to the small altar]. He died, but three days later, he rose from the dead. On the fortieth day, he ascended to heaven, where he lives with the father god.

He explains that during their ceremony, he becomes the voice of Christ, saying,

Take this, all of you, and eat of it, for this is my body, which will be given up for you . . . Take this, all of you, and drink from it, for this is the chalice of my blood.

With these words, the bread and wine become the true body and blood of Christ. The faithful consume them to be united with their god – he becomes part of them, and they part of him.

The third part of our Divine Trinity is the Holy Ghost, who is also god. He dwells within believers, guiding and comforting them.

We have divine winged angels who serve god and carry messages between heaven and earth.

We pray to saints – once men, miracle-workers – who reside in heaven with the lord god.

Then his tone shifts.

Now that we are here, we can help you. You must abandon your gods and cease human sacrifice – it is an abomination. You must convert to Christianity to save your souls. If you live a life of faith, you will go to heaven and be united with god.

Malinche interrupts, his voice haughty, sharp and confident:

Our army has defeated every city-state we have faced because our god is stronger than yours. We beseech you – abandon your gods. Pray to the cross, the symbol of our religion.

TLAMACAZQUI QUETZALCOATL TOTEC AT THE TLATOCAN

At the next meeting of the Tlatocan, I ask Tlamacazqui Quetzalcoatl Totec for his thoughts on the religion of the bearded ones and their desire to convert us to their religion.

Tlamacazqui Quetzalcoatl Totec rises, his gaze sweeping across the Tlatocan. His voice is strong, resonant with conviction.

Tlatoque, noble lords, hear me! I have pondered deeply on these bearded ones who have come to our land. I have watched them closely, and what I have seen casts a shadow over my heart and stirs the winds of sorrow.

They wield weapons that slay twenty warriors with a single blast – instruments of death, unlike anything we have ever known. They bring beasts of war and dogs with eyes like fire, creatures that terrify our people.

They speak of virtue, yet their actions betray them. They come seeking gold; they kill without hesitation. They defile our women and mock our traditions.

He pauses, his brow furrowed in thought.

I have listened to their prayers. I have asked myself: is this not a distorted reflection of what we already know?

They speak of a god who was killed – hung upon wood, pierced, and buried. Three days later, he rose from the dead and ascended to heaven.

But do we not honor those who sacrifice themselves for the greater good? When a warrior is offered to Huitzilopochtli, he is pierced upon the sacrificial stone, and his teyolia – his vital force – ascends to Tonatiuh-Ilhuicac, the Heaven of the Sun.

He gestures with a hand, emphasizing the parallel.

Padre Olmedo speaks of transubstantiation – a prayer uttered over bread and red wine, transforming them into the body and blood of their god.

But during our Teocualo ceremony, where we consume the flesh of the sacrificed, do I not say the prayer:

> *Your body now becomes teotl – divine force.*
> *With each bite, we take your courage.*
> *May your strength enter our bones.*
> *May your memory pass into our blood.*

A portion of the warrior's flesh is consumed in sacred communion. We absorb his strength, his honor, his divine spirit, whose soul resides with the gods.

He shakes his head, a look of concern on his face.

Padre Olmedo tells us of the holy ghost, a god who dwells within the believers, guiding, comforting, and strengthening them. He intercedes for believers in accordance with the will of god.

Is this not a mirror of our nagual, the divine, shape-shifting animal spirit within us, that guides us and provides inner strength and insight, enabling us to realize abilities that lie beyond our earthly bodies, and when necessary intercedes to give us the sudden inspiration needed to overcome a challenge?

His voice rises with passion.

And yet, these bearded ones demand that we cease our sacrifices, claiming it is against their god. This is a request we cannot, we must not abide.

They preach of virtue and purity of spirit, yet they do not act as civilized humans! They maim and kill without concern for the souls of the dead. They have no appreciation for beauty. They seize our divinely crafted gold jewelry and melt it down into crude bricks, driven only by their insatiable greed. Their murderous rampage in Cholula demonstrates that their only gods are gold and slaughter!

He pauses; his gaze fixed on Moctezuma II.

Are these the men we should follow, oh great Tlatoani? Should we emulate their ways? Should we abandon the traditions of our ancestors for these violent, avaricious strangers? These savages?

His voice thunders with conviction.

I say NO! We must remain true to our gods, to our traditions, to our way of life. Let us not be deceived by their words or intimidated by their weapons. We are the Mexica, the people of the sun. Let us stand strong and defend our heritage!

NOVEMBER 14, CORTÉS ARRESTS MOCTEZUMA

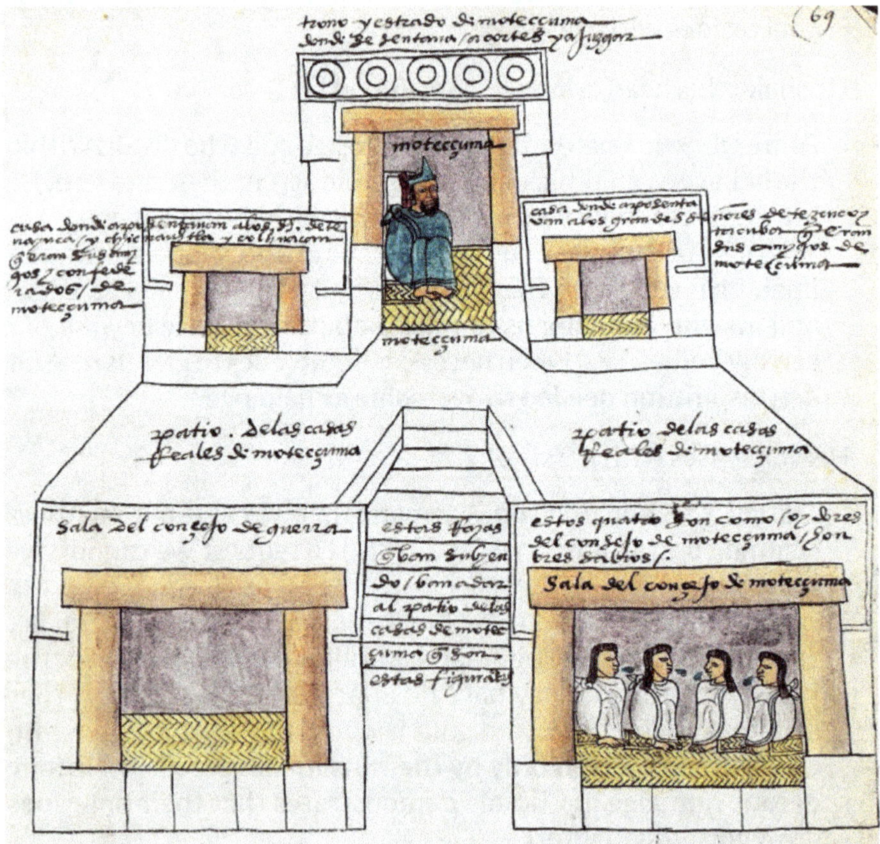

Moctezuma II's Palace. Moctezuma seated in his apartment (top), War council (lower left, empty), Council of Advisors with the four Teuctlatoque present speaking (lower right). The palace, known as the Casas Nuevas de Moctezuma, is a vast complex with multiple interconnected buildings, courtyard and chambers. Codex Mendoza

I am with the Teuctlatoque in the council chamber when Malinche arrives with five senior lieutenants – fully armed – and two interpreters. Their presence is unsettling, but we remain composed. Moments later, shouts and commotion erupt from the emperor's residence atop the palace. Tlamacazqui Quetzalcoatl Totec urges us to go together.

We ascend quickly. What we find chills us: five armed bearded ones surround our emperor, weapons drawn. Malinche shouts orders.

Without ceremony, they summon the imperial sedan and whisk Moctezuma away to their quarters in Axayacatl's palace.

When we return to our council chambers, we find the plaza in turmoil. Malinche has ordered the execution of two of our generals.

Armed men drag them to the plaza center. Without ceremony, without dignity, without the prayers that guide a warrior's teyolia to the Sun, they set the pyre alight. The fire roars. The flames leap upward devouring everything it touches. Flesh sizzles.

The crowd surges forward, then recoils as one.

A gasp ripples through our people. Voices rise around me – one cries, "This is a death without order." Another adds, "Without meaning!" A woman shouts, "They do not know the gods. They do not know the order of the world." Someone near the front shouts, "They burn warriors like refuse." And from behind me, a trembling whisper: "No prayers... no drums... their heart spirits wander alone."

I have seen death in battle, but never a death without meaning. I call out, "This is not sacrifice – this is madness. This is not death. This is desecration." The world feels tilted, as if the Fifth Sun itself has shuddered.

A messenger from the men with bearded faces informs us that Moctezuma will continue to hold court from Axayacatl's palace and rule the empire "as usual." But this is not usual. This is captivity masked as diplomacy.

The next day when we meet with our emperor, we are stunned to see him in chains. We offer to free him – our warriors are ready. But Moctezuma pleads for restraint. He asks us to return to our people and counsel calm, hoping to negotiate the peaceful withdrawal of the bearded ones.

We leave in silence, disbelief heavy in our hearts.

The next morning, I meet with Huey Tlatoani in private. His voice is low, his eyes distant.

> Huitzilin, my able and thoughtful advisor, I do not believe we can defeat these men with bearded faces. Their weapons are powerful. Their gods are strong. My only hope is to save our people

> from ruin – by living in harmony with these men and learning from them.
>
> Go to our people. Counsel patience. Let no harm come to them.
>
> Huitzilin, the gods have created the world four times before. Each era ended in cataclysm. We now live under the Fifth Sun. It too, will end. It is foretold: earthquakes, fire and rain.
>
> I fear that time is near. … I fear that time is near.

I leave the emperor's chambers filled with dread. His final words echo in my mind like distant thunder. I fear we are witnessing the end of our world.

That evening, the men with bearded faces seize two more of our finest generals and burn them alive before the Huey Teocalli. The flames rise into the night sky, and the people cry out in anguish.The high priest of Huitzilopochtli is present, standing next to me. Bowing his head and speaking in a somber tone, he says,

> This fire is not our lord Xiuhtecuhtli's flame.[190] His flame purifies and guides. This flame only devours. It gives the teyolia no road to walk and casts it into darkness. Without rite, the teyolia cannot rise. The fire of these strangers gives no passage. It leaves the spirit wandering, unseen by the Sun.

I convene the Teuctlatoque and the Tlatocan to relay the emperor's plea for peace. But no one is ready to accept it. Rage simmers. Voices rise. Some demand war. Others call for caution. There is no consensus. The meeting ends in bitter silence and indecision. The members turn away.

MASSACRE IN THE GREAT TEMPLE, MAY 22, 1520

The Feast of Toxcatl, honoring the god Tezcatlipoca, is held each year with solemn reverence and joyous celebration. This year, while Malinche tends to affairs near Xallapan, his deputy, Pedro de Alvarado, remains in charge. He agrees to permit our peaceful religious ceremony in the main plaza before the Huey Teocalli.

---

190 Xiuhtecuhtli: "Turquoise Lord," deity of fire, day, heat, and time; patron of emperors, hearths, and pochteca, honored as a source of renewal, vitality, and cosmic order.

It is a beloved event, attended by our most revered priests, nobles, and prominent families. Most of my kin are there – two of my children, their spouses, nieces, nephews, and grandchildren. I remain in the council chambers of Moctezuma's palace, overlooking the plaza. My knees ache, and I have learned to listen with my eyes.

From my seat in the chamber, I see dancers in brilliant regalia, priests offering prayers, and drummers summoning the gods with rhythm. The plaza pulses with sacred energy.

Then, without warning, the mood shifts.

Alvarado's men move swiftly, sealing the exits. I rise from my seat, heart pounding, as the bearded ones draw their swords and shields. I see them rush the drummers – slicing off their arms, silencing the sacred beat. Then they begin to decapitate. The celebration becomes a slaughter.

I pound the stone balustrade, shouting for help, for reason, for mercy – but no one can enter or leave the plaza. The massacre unfolds before my eyes and I am powerless.

I watch my own children fall. My grandchildren. My nieces. My blood. My soul.

With the massacre complete, Alvarado and his men retreat, leaving a lake of blood in the plaza, littered with limbs and lifeless bodies. I try to rise, but my knees buckle. The horror is unbearable. Yet, I must find a way.

"Matanza, Templo 22" Spanish soldiers block the plaza's four exits, drummers have their arms chopped off, nobles are beheaded. Códice Durán

Slowly, people enter the plaza searching for their lost brothers and sisters, parents and children. Finally, I climb down from my perch in the council chamber and walk through the plaza, blood squirting between my toes. Feathers, broken drums and shattered offerings lie scattered like remnants of a nightmare. I move slowly through the carnage, searching for familiar faces. I find my daughter's turquoise necklace still clutched in her hand. My grandson's embroidered cloak, torn and soaked through. I fall to my knees beside them, calling their names.

With the help of neighbors and surviving kin, we gather the bodies of our loved ones. We wrap them in woven mantles, and carry them to the sacred grounds near the lake. There, we build a pyre – not for spectacle, but for release. We place offerings of maize and obsidian beside them.

I collapse beside the pyre, my knees buckling under the weight of sorrow. I weep like a child – loud, broken, inconsolable. My hands tremble as I touch the blood soaked mantles wrapped around my children, my grandchildren. I cry out their names, over and over, as if the gods might hear and undo what has been done.

The fire is lit. The logs crackle, the scent of burning copal caresses the rising smoke of our dead. We stand in silence as the flames take hold, then lift our voices – not in defiance, but in invocation.

> O Mictlantecuhtli, Lord of death and ruler of the underworld, receive these souls with open jaws and gentle silence. Let them pass through the nine shadows without fear, guided by the breath of memory.
>
> O Tezcatlipoca, Lord of the Smoking Mirror, reveal the truth of this bloodshed. If this is the unraveling of the Fifth Sun, let our children rise as light within your obsidian gaze. Let their names be etched in smoke, not forgotten. Let their spirits walk with honor, even as we remain behind.

I hang my head, unable to watch the flames consume what I love. My legs refuse to carry me, but I force myself to stand. I wander the edge of the sacred ground, lost in smoke and memory. The scent of burning copal mingles with ash and grief. I am hollowed out, yet I remain – because I must. Because someone must witness. Because someone must remember.

As the smoke of burning bodies rises, I feel a part of me ascend with them.

That night, Itzel and I sit together in silence, the weight of grief pressing against us like stone. Her face is streaked with ash and tears, her breath ragged, her body trembling as if the earth itself mourned through her. She leans into me, and I into her, two broken branches clinging to the same root. The pyre has burned low, but the pain burns on within us. We speak – not to each other, but to the gods. I pray,

> Tezcatlipoca . . . I cannot carry this. I cannot breathe beneath it. My children are gone. My blood is ash. My spirit is torn. If you see me, if you still know my name, help me for I cannot stand. I cannot walk. I cannot live with this hole inside me. Help me!

Itzel offers her prayer,

O Mictlantecuhtli, receive my children gently. Let Xoloitzcuintli[191] guide them and care for their sweet souls. And if you see me … if you hear this voice that breaks …

How can I go on? I do not know how to live in a world without them. Where are my babies? Let the wind remember their names.

Together we sing,

> *Let the fire cleanse what the sword defiled.*
> *Let memory be stronger than silence.*
> *Let us remain –*
> *not whole, but worthy of remembrance.*

⌖⌖⌖⌖⌖

The morning after the massacre, the plaza is still. Not with peace, but with the weight of death. In the silence, screams of the dead can still be heard. Blood has dried in dark pools across the stone. The sacred ground is desecrated.

At that moment, I know: Tenochtitlán will never be the same. No Mexica will.

The people of every calpulli rise in fury. Farmers abandon their fields. Merchants leave their stalls. The canals overflow with rage. Armed crowds swarm every precinct of the city. I too am overcome with anger. But I am old. I am broken. I cannot change the course of time. I feel something inside me break again and again and again …

A priest is heard,

These men speak of a god who forbids sacrifice, yet they butcher women and children, priests and nobles, without reverence or remorse. They preach piety, yet they lie, steal, and kill for gold. They melt our finest works into bricks. They do not see beauty. They do not see spirit. They are savages.

---

191 Sacred dog who guides the dead in the underworld.

Tension builds. The city erupts. The siege begins – not just of stone and blade, but of spirit. The bearded ones barricade themselves in Axayacatl's Palace, trapped without food or water.

MALINCHE RETURNS, JUNE 24, 1520

On June 24, 1520, Malinche and his men, together with Tlaxcalan warriors, approach the main causeway into the city. A call to arms fills the air, and hundreds of Mexica warriors rush to meet them. But the bearded ones unleash their thunderous weapons – metal tubes that blast great balls of fire, killing our warriors and shattering our fortifications. After a brutal battle, they break through and enter Tenochtitlán. Still surrounded by angry Mexica warriors, they seal themselves inside Axayacatl's palace with Alvarado and his men.

For the next five days, I return to the work that once defined me. Though no title is spoken, I am again the Chief Builder of Tenochtitlán, but with a different plan. The knowledge flows through me – not from memory, but from instinct, as if the gods themselves etched it into my bones. I organize teams of workers, directing the construction of new barricades and ordering the causeways broken apart, stone by stone, to trap the bearded ones within the city.

We work without rest. The city pulses with urgency. My voice carries across the canals and plazas, guiding masons, laborers, and warriors alike. Every trench, every collapsed bridge, every fortified wall is a weapon forged from earth and will. The siege tightens.

Malinche and the bearded ones attempt to break free, but our forces are unrelenting. We shower them day and night with lances, stones and arrows. The bearded ones build two great towers – like wooden beasts that hold twenty-five men each, bristling with cannons and muskets. But they are no match for our fury. We set them ablaze and the towers crumble under the weight of our attack.

Our warriors train not to fear their war dogs, but to kill them with our weapons. Their horsemen, so fearsome in open terrain, flounder in our city. The wet stone streets betray them. Their mounts slip and fall. Our weapons pierce their armor. Dozens of bearded ones lie dead in the streets, their blood mingling with the rain. The survivors are battered, bloodied, and trapped.

I walk the causeways, feeling the stones beneath my feet. Stones I once laid with pride, I now help dismantle, tearing them apart to defend the city I love. The work is painful, but necessary. This is no longer the city of my youth. It is a battlefield. And I, once a builder of temples, am now a builder of war.

JUNE 29, 1520, MOCTEZUMA IS KILLED

After five days of relentless warfare, the enemy is cornered. Their desperation hangs in the air like smoke. Two lifeless bodies are found outside the palace where the bearded ones are barricaded. I rush to the scene, heart pounding.

I recognize them instantly: Huey Tlatoani Moctezuma II, our emperor, and his cousin Itzquauhtzin, Tlatoani of Tlatelolco. They lie crumpled on the stone. Their faces are bruised, their robes torn. I kneel beside Moctezuma's body. The man who once stood as the divine voice of our people now lies silent, cast aside like a crumpled page from the codex of our history.

We carry his body to Copulco, the sacred cremation site. The procession is quiet, but not reverent. Some onlookers mutter curses. Others avert their eyes. One man examines the emperor's wounds and shouts, "They placed a blade between his ribs and choked him!"

I too see where his body bears the mark. His assassination is not just the death of a man – it is the collapse of a world. The Fifth Sun trembles. Its light flickers. And in that flicker, I see the shadow of what is to come. As the flames consume his body, I feel no peace. Only dread.

JULY 1, 1520, "LA NOCHE TRISTE"

The men with bearded faces remain cloistered in Axayacatl's Palace, surrounded on all sides. We continue our relentless assault – spears hurled, stones slung, arrows loosed through windows and doorways. Our warriors hold their battle stations through the night, unwavering.

A corps of Jaguar Warriors, their leader fallen in battle, approaches me. One steps forward and says:

Dear revered Tezcatl Huitzilin, you are known throughout the empire for your hummingbird scar and your legendary valor as a Tequihua Warrior. We would be honored to fight under your command.

Though I have been absent from the battlefield for nearly forty years, I accept. The fire of duty still burns in my chest. With our forces gaining the upper hand, I anticipate the bearded ones will attempt an escape. We have sabotaged the causeways — broken, booby-trapped, made impassable. Their only hope lies in the short causeway to the west, toward Tlacopan.

My father once showed me a hidden alcove near his family's chinampas, facing that very causeway. I lead my warriors there, positioning them in silence. I instruct four to target the horses, four to strike the men with cannons. We have recovered many of the enemy's weapons and lashed their swords to our spears, forging new tools of death from their own metal.

At midnight, the city holds its breath. A harsh rain falls, slicking the stone streets. The bearded ones, battered and desperate, emerge from the palace carrying a wooden bridge which they place in the very spot I had selected. Once their force is on the bridge, I give the signal and the ambush is set in motion.

My men shower them with all our weapons. My corps strikes the horses, sending them sliding off the planks into the lake. The bridge collapses. Men, beasts and cannon tumble into the water. I watch. I can see in the eyes of these greedy men, their dreams of stolen wealth, of gold and jewels that weigh against the rushing waters as they fall. They sink into the deep water still grasping gold in fingers that will not release. There they are, their cuirasses, their brigandines, that they once so proudly bore against us, now bulging with stolen loot delivering them to their miserable end. My beautiful, sacred Lake Texcoco that I adore is now a graveyard — bloated with bodies, choked with iron and blood. Seeing this, the men with bearded faces break rank, fleeing in chaos. Most are slain. A few, including Malinche and his lieutenants, escape — leaving behind eight hundred fallen comrades.

With the bearded ones finally gone, we feel relief and some part of our honor restored. The city erupts in celebration. It is a day of joy for us – "La Noche Triste," a night of sorrows for the foreigners. May they never forget this night.

When the fighting ends, we gather our dead – Mexica heroes and martyrs – and give them proper funerals. Their names are spoken. Their spirits lifted to the heavens. We cleanse our homes, our temples, our wounded bodies. We long to return to life as it was before their arrival.

But the world has changed. The Fifth Sun trembles.

SMALLPOX, SEPTEMBER 1520

In September 1520, the *cocoliztli*[192] – the pestilence – sweeps through the empire. I am home with Itzel when one of our grandchildren falls ill. Her fever is high, her stomach and head ache. Soon, her mouth and face turn red. Our priests and ticitin – healers trained in the sacred arts – are unable to help her. Large red welts bloom across her skin like cursed flowers. Two other children become ill. Then more. Before long, everyone in our home is sickened – including me.

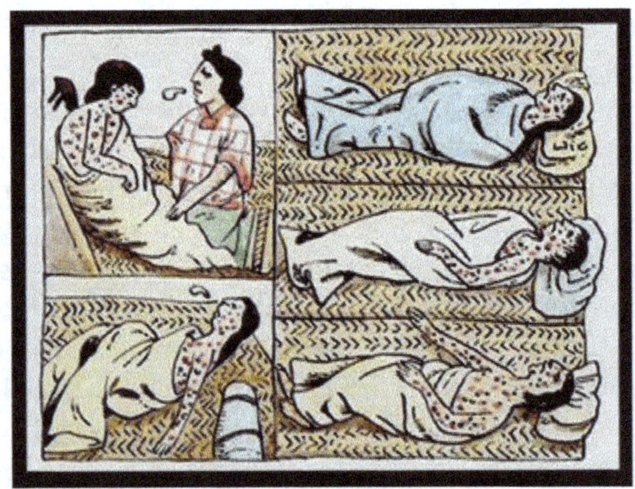

Cocoliztli, the smallpox epidemic, kills half of the population.in the Valley of Mexico. Florentine Codex Book XII folio 54. Colorized by anon.

---

192 The Nahuatl term for pestilence, used to describe the smallpox epidemic.

Death arrives swiftly. Itzel passes first, her breath shallow and eyes dim. Then the children. Then the spouses. The house grows quiet, except for the sound of coughing and weeping. Only two of our adult sons, one daughter, and I survive. But sadness follows us like a shadow.

Five to eight million Mexica, nearly half our people, die. The empire collapses under its weight. Schools close. Farms go untended. The government falters. The streets fill with waste and silence. No one comes to sweep. No one comes to bury. People wander, searching for food. Many starve. Many vanish.

I am now seventy years old, and I carry a sorrow too vast for words. With Moctezuma gone, I have no patron who values my counsel. The Teuctlatoque, once proud and wise, is disbanded. The new Huey Tlatoani, Cuitláhuac II, does not know me. I decide to leave the city with my three surviving noble children – two sons and one daughter. We set out for Zaachila-Yoo, the Zapotec city I have long considered my second home.

On the road, we are silent. We do not speak of the dead. We feel the doom pressing behind us, the weight of Tenochtitlán's unraveling. I recite a poem to the wind, a prayer to the Life Giver:

Here, let the drum appear!
Here, let the singer appear!
He's scattering a multitude of flowers.
There's richness, there's joy
in the presence of Life Giver's flowers.
But now you are hiding your riches, Life Giver.
What does your heart intend?
Near and in this Presence I weep:
I am despised; I want to die.
Let me yield to the comrades.
Near you and in your presence, Life Giver,
I weep, saying:
Let your heart be merciful.
What do you intend on earth?

We arrive in Zapotec country, tired and hungry. As we approach the capital, we learn that while Tenochtitlán was consumed by war and plague, the Mixtecs have seized control of Zaachila-Yoo, leaving Coquitao Cosijoeza on the throne. The Zapotec people are weary – frustrated by the heavy tribute demanded by their new overlords.

But we are lovingly received by Queen Xiloxochitl and King Cosijoeza. They welcome us into the royal palace, offer food, and show us to our rooms. In the days that follow, we speak of the bearded ones, the battles, the losses, and the fading glory of our city. We reminisce about old times and wonder what future awaits our people.

Cosijoeza and I become close like brothers. He listens. He asks questions. And then, with solemn grace, he invites me to serve as one of his senior advisors.

THE END OF TENOCHTITLÁN, MAY 22–AUGUST 13, 1521

In May 1521, a Zapotec messenger arrives bearing urgent news for Coquitao Cosijoeza, and I am summoned to attend. He speaks solemnly:

> The bearded ones have assembled a formidable army – 900 bearded ones, 80 crossbowmen, 80 arquebusiers, 100 horsemen, and 13 cannon. They wear metal helmets, shields, and breastplates. They have built 13 brigantines that dominate the waters of Lake Texcoco. Marching with them are 100,000 Indigenous warriors. They are coming for Tenochtitlán.

Over the next ninety days, we receive grim reports.

On May 22, the siege begins. The men with bearded faces surround the city, blocking the causeways and trapping our people. Days later, they destroy the aqueducts that bring fresh water and burn the farmlands, cutting off food. Starvation and disease spread like smoke.

Then comes word that Malinche has launched fourteen brigantines upon Lake Texcoco. Our canoes are no match. The waterways, once lifelines, become corridors of death.

Finally, on August 13, the last report arrives: the Mexica forces collapse. Disheartened and disorganized, they fall as the invaders continue their slaughter. Rivers of blood run through the streets. One hundred thousand bodies lie lifeless, scattered like broken offerings to gods who no longer answer.

Tenochtitlán has fallen. Fires burn every structure. Nothing is left as a harsh rain washes everything away.

The once-great Aztec Empire is no more. It is finished. Its temples and palaces are ash and rubble. Our books and libraries – burned. Our gardens, aviaries, and marketplaces – gone. All its beauty and grandeur, ruined. In its place: blood, silence, and the stench of death.

༄༄༄༄༄

In 1526, Spanish soldiers under Nuño de Guzmán arrive in Zaachila-Yoo. I counsel cooperation, hoping to spare the people further suffering. But during the takeover, Queen Xiloxochitl is struck and succumbs to her wounds. My sons rush to her defense and are slain. My daughter is taken away.

The invaders seize the lands and impose the encomienda system, enslaving the Zapotec people who survive.

XII
A Fitting End

My heart still beats in this, my seventy-seventh cycle beneath the Fifth Sun. I spend my time wiping away tears as I remember my long, fortunate life I have lived. After three days fasting, I sit alone in an empty room and say,

> The gods gave us Tenochtitlán and made it plentiful. Now it is dust.
> The gods gave me wives and children, now I am alone.
> The gods gave me riches, now have nothing.

Barefoot, wearing only a tattered maxlatl–as the ancients did when seeking truth in solitude – I leave my chamber. Alone, I wander deep into the pine forest, through ragged gullies and hillsides to speak with my ancestors whose breath moves in the wind, and with the gods who know. Searching for answers, I say,

> O Cuauhtli, Father, Eagle who watches over us from the heights, you spread your wings of counsel over me, you set my feet upon the straight and shining path. You taught me to speak truth, to labor without complaint, to polish my deeds until they gleamed like turquoise, until they flashed like obsidian. *Nezayotl.*[193]
>
> O Chicomecoatl, Mother, Seven Serpent, divine mother of sustenance, you sheltered us like the serpent who coils around her young. You nourished our bodies and completed our spirits. You were our wise teacher who revealed the mysteries of life: to know our shadow spirit, nagual, to know teotl, the celestial realm, and

---

193 An expression of deep gratitude, a gesture of humility not just spoken, but embodied by fasting, self-denial and spiritual focus.

to walk rightly in tlalticpac, the earthly realm. You wove my days as you wove the cotton, you set down the reed and the mat on which my life would rest. You gave me a childhood bright as maize tassels in the sun, filled with swift games and fearless laughter. Nezayotl.

O Tezcacoatl, Brother, Mirror Serpent, pochteca of long roads, we were companions in the marketplace of the world, in the journeys, in the burdens, and in the joys along the way. Side by side we walked, partners in the heart, partners in the song of life. Nezayotl.

O Xochitl, Sister, flower of our family, amanteca, mistress of feathers, your hand made the quetzal sing, you adorned the world with your plumage, you lifted our family's name high in the house of the sky. Nezayotl.

O Teoxochitl, divine flower, precious jade of our house, mother of our two children. You passed bravely into the place of mist and flowers. You gave life even as your own life went to join the sun on its journey, carrying the weight of cosmic mystery. Your seat and mat remain empty, yet your breath still warms our hearth. Nezayotl.

O Itzel, of noble heart, my goddess of love and divine femininity, you were the one my heart chose above all others. You gave me children; you filled our days with joy. Your presence was like shimmering water in the desert. Nezayotl.

Huey Tlatoani Axayacatl, under your command I served the empire in the military for ten glorious years. You honored me with medals and accolades in Tlatelolco and the Toluca Valley, where you bestowed upon me the titles of Tequihua Warrior and Jaguar Warrior. Nezayotl.

Huey Tlatoani Tizoc, you saw me, you valued my work, you made me Keeper of the Roads. Nezayotl.

Huey Tlatoani Ahuitzotl, you were my schoolmate and friend when I needed one. When you ascended the throne, you appointed me to lead the renovation of the Huey Teocalli, the Great Temple of Tenochtitlán. You ennobled me and sent me as ambassador to Tzapotlan. Nezayotl.

Huey Tlatoani Moctezuma Xocoyotzin, you appointed me to the Tlatocan and then to the Teuctlatoque. You listened to my counsel in perilous times. Nezayotl.

I cast these words like flower offerings to the wind and to the earth, that they may reach the place of our ancestors, where flowers never wither and the song never ceases.

I speak to the gods.

We only came to sleep.
We only came to dream.
It is not true!
No, it is not true that we came to live on the earth.
We are changed into the grass of springtime.
Our hearts will grow green again,
And they will open their petals,
But our body is like a rose tree,
It puts forth flowers and then withers.

Let the gods remember us not for our fall, but for our flowering.

⊡⊡⊡⊡⊡⊡

The forest darkens and I feel my end approaching. I have grown weary – not only from the years but from the lingering ache of a broken world. This weariness, not just of body but of spirit, embraces me like a heavy cloak.

Beside a gnarled ceiba tree I find a small cave and pause, searching for an answer to my sorrow. I contemplate my fate.

My hummingbird nagual appears, hovering above me. Her wings hum softly in the warm night air. She touches me with the gentleness of a mother's arms and gently signals, it's time to rest; it's time to be still. My eyes follow the flight of the hummingbird as it rises into the ether and disappears.

In my torpor, the image of the god Tezcatlipoca emerges – his jaguar nagual watching from the shadows. I speak into the rustling leaves, into the encroaching darkness. I hear my hollow voice echo my years and the grief of fate:

> Tezcatlipoca, Smoking Mirror, Lord of the Night.
> You, whose will carves the very fabric of existence,
> come, bring peace to my waning spirit.
> My kin are dust, swept away by sickness and the sharp metal of foreign swords.
> My home, Tenochtitlán, a shattered memory.
> My Zapotec protectors now bent under the conqueror's yoke.
> Much has been seen.
> Too much has been endured.
> Show me the way, Lord of the Night, my spirit aches.

As I slumber, the air is heavy and silence reigns except for the low growls echoing from unseen corners. My heart senses the jaguar's presence. It is there, watching from a low branch, eyes gleaming with celestial fire. I am calm. I do not resist.

The jaguar descends. Not with fury, but with the certainty of fate. I sense his shadow come over me, but it is not a shadow, it is darkness. I expire a final breath and my life in tlalticpac, the earthly realm, ends.

In an instant, the jaguar consumes my flesh and entrails and , with its final gulp, he takes my heart and disappears into the night, leaving only bones in the mud.

ㄹㄹㄹㄹㄹㄹ

My Ihiyotl, the vital energy of my breath, the force of courage and passion, leaves my body, joining the winds and wandering spirits.

My Tonalli, the vital energy that resides in the head, the fire of will and consciousness, fragments and scatters.

But, my Teyolia, the vital energy of my heart, the fire of my will and consciousness, loosens and rises in the darkness.

Xoloitzcuintli, the ancient hairless dog, emerges, sleek, silent and radiant with ancestral fire to guide and protect my teyolia, my heart-soul.

He takes me to the place where we must cross the river Apanohuacalhuia, the gateway to Mictlan. The river is deep and raging. Its treacherous currents strip away my earthly identity, washing away the burdens of the physical world, leaving my soul in its most essential form, unclothed and exposed.

Xoloitzcuintli carries my teyolia on his back to the far shore.

Over the next four years, he guides me through eight more levels.

My spirit passes between two mountains that are in constant motion, crashing together and separating. It climbs a mountain of obsidian knives. It endures icy winds, obsidian winds, and the scorching winds of the desert. Unseen hands hurl arrows.

My spirit plunges into black waters, surrendering all remaining attachments.

With each level, another tie to the mortal realm is severed. Each trial purifies and transforms my spirit, preparing it for eternity.

After passing through nine layers of the underworld and meeting every challenge, my spirit encounters Mictlantecuhtli and Mictecacihuatl the lord and lady of the underworld, who accept me into Chicunamictlan, the deepest level of Mictlan.

There, in the darkness, in the silence, I find cosmic stillness — and vanish.

XIII
Appendices

a. Rulers of Tenochtitlán

Mexitli – A war leader and priest during the Mexica's wandering years, thought to be as early as 1150. He helped shape Mexica identity while they were still a nomadic people, gathering them and guiding them out of Aztlán.

Huehue Huitzilihuitl (1272-1299) – "Ancient hummingbird feather," legendary Mexica leader during the migration period.

Tenoch (1325-1370) – Last Mexica leader during the migration from Aztlán. Witnessed the prophesied sign of the eagle perched on a cactus. Founded Tenochtitlán in 1325.

Tlatoani Acamapichtli (1369-1391) – "Handful of reeds," first Tlatoani of Tenochtitlán.

Tlatoani Huitzilihuitl (1391-1415) – Second Tlatoani of Tenochtitlán.

Tlatoani Chimalpopoca (1415-1426) – "Smoking shield," third Tlatoani. Assassinated by Mixtla of Azcapotzalco.

Xihuitl Temoc (1427) – "One who descended," ruled briefly, possibly uncrowned, before being killed by Maxtla.

Huey Tlatoani Itzcoatl (1427-1440) – "Obsidian serpent," fourth Tlatoani, formed the Triple Alliance with Nezahualcoyotl of Texcoco and Tlacopan, to defeat Azcapotzalco. First to hold the title Huey Tlatoani of the Mexica Empire.

Huey Tlatoani Motecuhzoma Ilhuicamina (Moctezuma I) (1440-1469) – "Stern like a lord; Sky-shooter," fifth Tlatoani. Led major expansion beyond the Basin of Mexico.

Huey Tlatoani Axayacatl (1469–1481) – "Face of water," sixth Tlatoani. Achieved victories against Tlatelolco and in the Toluca Valley, but was defeated by the Purépecha (Tarascans).

Huey Tlatoani Tizoc (1481–1486) – "He who does penance," seventh Tlatoani. Considered an ineffective war leader.

Huey Tlatoani Ahuitzotl (1486–1502) – "Spiny one of the water," eighth Tlatoani. Effective war leader. Oversaw major renovations to the Huey Teocalli and the Chapultepec aqueduct. Huitzilin's classmate and friend.

Huey Tlatoani Moctezuma Xocoyotzin (Moctezuma II) (1502–1520) – "The younger," ninth Tlatoani. Expanded the empire. Imprisoned by Cortés.

Huey Tlatoani Cuitláhuac (1520) – "Of the watery residue, algae," Ruled for 80 days. Died during the smallpox epidemic.

Huey Tlatoani Cuauhtémoc (1521–1525) – "Diving eagle," final Tlatoani. Captured by Cortés, who ordered him hanged.

b. Historical and Legendary Characters

Achitometl: In the legend of the flayed princess, he is the Tlatoani of Culhuacan.

Alvarado, Pedro de: Senior officer under Cortés. Ordered the infamous massacre in the temple square. Known for his brutality and ambition. Later became governor of Guatemala.

Chimalxochitl: Mexica princess whose name means "shield flower," prophesied the rise of the Mexica. Represented steadfastness, strength and courage.

Coquitao Cosijoeza (King Cosijoeza): Zapotec ruler of Zaachila-Yoo. Known for his diplomacy and resistance to foreign domination.

Cortés, Hernando: Spanish conquistador who led the expedition that resulted in the fall of the Mexica Empire.

Coxcoxtli : (Coxcox) Tlatoani of Colhuacan. Allowed the Mexica to settle in Tizaapan.

Cuauhtémoc, Tlacateccatl: Commanding general of the Mexica army, lead the convoy to Tzapotlan, later became Huey Tlatoani Cuauhtémoc, hung by Cortés.

Guzmán, Nuño de: Spanish commander who led campaigns against the Zapotecs and imposed brutal colonial rule.

Malinalli (Honorific, Malintzin): Mexica noblewoman who served as translator and cultural mediator for Cortés. Revered by some, reviled by others. She remains a pivotal figure in the conquest narrative.

Maxtla: Tepanec ruler defeated by the Triple Alliance.

Moquihuix: Tlatoani of Tlatelolco, defeated by the Triple Alliance.

Nezahualcoyotl: Tlatoani of Texcoco. Renowned philosopher, poet, and Master Builder. Built the dike that separated the saltwater of Lake Texcoco from its freshwater basin.

Olmedo, Fray Bartolomé de (Padre Olmedo): Chief priest who accompanied Cortés to Tenochtitlán. Played a key role in religious conversion efforts.

Tabscoob: Chontal Maya leader.

Tezozomoc: Tepanec ruler of Azcapotzalco, whose reign spanned 59 years. Died in 1426 at age one hundred.

Tlamacazqui Quetzalcoatl Totec: Honorific title held by the high priest of Huitzilopochtli, the highest-ranking priest in the Mexica religious hierarchy, responsible for overseeing sacred rites and temple ceremonies.

Tlilcuetzpalin: Otomi war chief known as 'Black Lizard.' Wounded Ahuitzotl in battle near Matlatzinco. Captured by Huitzilin in a pivotal scene.

Totoquihuaztli: Tlatoani of Tlacopan, one of the three cities of the Triple Alliance.

Xicotencatl: Commanding general of the Tlaxcalan armies.

Xiloxochitl: Daughter of Huey Tlatoani Ahuitzotl and wife of King Cosijoeza. A noblewoman who bridged Mexica and Zapotec dynasties.

c. Fictional Characters

Chalchihuitl: "Precious green stone," the old jeweler who befriends young Cuauhtli.

Chalchiuhtototl: "Jade bird," Tlamacazqui of the Royal Aviary, father of Itzel, Huitzilin's second wife.

Chicomecoatl: "Seven serpents," Huitzilin's mother, the family matriarch, weaver.

Cuauhtli: "Eagle," Huitzilin's father, rises from farmer to jeweler to the royal family.

Cuetlachtzin: "Honored wolf," name of person who served as steward of the tzompantli, keeper of the skull racks and ritual memory.

Huitzilin: "Hummingbird," main character, famed warrior, engineer, nobleman, ambassador, advisor to the emperor.

Itzel: "Radiance of dawn, morning star, beauty," from the Mayan language. Huitzilin's second wife, a noblewoman.

Nonantzin: "My dear precious mother," here used by Huitzilin affectionately, to refer to his grandmother.

Olintecuhtli: "He who guides through uncertainty," senior pochteca, friend of Cuauhtli.

Teoxochitl: "Divine flower," Huitzilin's first wife who dies in childbirth.

Teyacanqui: "He who is at the forefront, leader of people," the leader of Cuahutli's calli, neighborhood district.

Tezcacoatl: "Mirror serpent," Huitzilin's older brother, becomes a wealthy long-distance trader, businessman.

Tezcatl: "Mirror," father of Teoxochitl, Huitzilin's first wife.

Tlacaelel: "Man of strong heart, inner vigor," priest and head of the calmecac school, Cuauhtli's patron.

Tlaltequani: "Earth Eater," mentor and captain of Huitzilin's unit in the military.

Xochitl: "Flower," Huitzilin's sister, feather artisan.

Xolotl: "Dog deity," Hutizlin's first capture.

d. Aztec Gods

Cipactli: Crocodile water monster

Coatlicue: Earth goddess associated with life, death, and rebirth. Mother of Huitzilopochtli.

Coyolxauhqui: Sister of Huitzilopochtli, defeated by him to become the moon.

Ehecatl: God of wind. Blows the breath that moves the clouds and animates life.

Huehuecóyotl: A trickster deity associated with chaos, music, and mischief. Patron of dancers and storytellers. His name means 'Ancient Coyote,' and he embodies both wisdom and folly.

Huitzilopochtli: God of the sun, war and sacrifice. Patron deity of the Mexica people and Tenochtitlán, associated with fire and conquest.

Mictlantecuhtli: Lord of the underworld, ruler of the dead. Presides over Mictlan, the land of the afterlife.

Mictecacihuatl: Goddess of the underworld. Consort of Mictlantecuhtli, guardian of the bones of the dead.

Ometeotl: The original deity, a dual god embodying both male and female aspects. Creator of all other deities and the cosmic balance. Did not have temples or iconography.

Quetzalcoatl: "Feathered serpent," god of culture, wisdom, learning, wind and creation, symbolizes civilization – embodying the ideals of knowledge, artistry and moral order that define a refined society.

Tlaloc: God of rain, water and fertility. Essential for agriculture and sustenance. Feared for his power over storms and drought.

Tlaltecuhtli: "Earth lady." In one myth, her dismembered body was transformed by the gods into the earth. Her body parts became mountains, valleys, rivers, and trees, the source of life and all living things.

Tlazolteotl: Deity of lust, impurity, purification, fertility, and absolution. Her Nahuatl name means "Goddess of Filth."

Tezcatlipoca: God of night, fate, sorcery, and conflict. Often depicted as a trickster and rival to Quetzalcoatl. Known as the Smoking Mirror.

Tonatiuh: Sun god, associated with warriors and cosmic cycles. Demands sacrifice to sustain his journey across the sky.

Tozoztli: God of fertility.

Xipe Totec: "Our Lord the Flayed One," Deity who embodies agriculture, renewal, and rebirth. The ritual flaying of sacrificial victims symbolized the shedding of old skin to reveal new life.

Xochiquetzal: "Precious flower," goddess of beauty, love, fertility, and crafts. Patron of artists, lovers, and childbirth.

Xoloitzcuintli: The Sacred Dog, bred by the Mexica to accompany souls through Mictlan. Earthly emissary of Xolotl, symbol of loyalty and passage.

Xolotl: Dog-headed god, guides souls through the underworld.

Yacatecuhtli: Patron god of pochteca and travelers.

Yaocihuatl: Goddess of warriors.

e. The Three Vital Energies

Tonalli   *Vital force of the head:* Manifests as consciousness, governs fate and vigor. It is linked to the sun and warmth, influencing a person's willpower and destiny.

Teyolia   *Vital force of the heart:* Manifests as the soul. Represents wisdom, memory, and divine connection. It is the spiritual essence that persists after death, traveling to the afterlife or joining the gods.

Ihiyotl   *Vital force of breath:* Manifests as the rhythm of life, luminous energy and spiritual radiance. Governs vitality, emotions and personal magnetism. It influences charisma, instincts, passions and desires. Resides in the liver.

f. Glossary of Náhuatl Words

Acatl: Reed plant, also a day on the calendar.

Ahuacatl: Avocado (ahuacate in Spanish).

Ahuehuetl tree: The Ahuehuete, Mexico's national tree, has the largest trunk of any tree in the world.

Altepetl: A city-state.

Amanteca: Feather artisan who creates sacred regalia, shields, and headdresses; highly revered in Mexica society.

Atlatl: Long distance spear throwing device.

Amatl paper: Paper made from fig tree bark used for codices.

Axolotls: A distinctive amphibian from Xochimilco.

Azcamolli: Ant larvae, escamoles.

Azcapotzalcah: People residing in Azcapotzalco, capital of the Tepanec empire.

Cacaxtli: A wooden frame tied with a strap over the forehead, used by porters (tlamemeh) to carry tribute goods across long distances.

Cactli: Shoes, sandals.

Calli: Home or house.

Calmecac: School for the aristocracy.

Calpolli: Neighborhood, a political subdivision. (Cal = house, polli = group) Alt. spelling Calpulli. Also, a community or group.

Calpullec: Leader and administrator of a calpulli.

Canella: Cinnamon (canela in Spanish).

Chapulines: Grasshoppers.

Chapultepec: "Grasshopper hill," mountain on the western shore of Lake Texcoco.

Chichimecatl: Term used by Mexica to describe northern nomadic peoples; often connoted wildness or lack of refinement.

Chichimecs: A group of semi-nomadic, indigenous peoples of northern and central Mexico.

Chicomoztoc: Place of the seven caves, ancestral womb, birthplace of the seven tribes.

Chimalli: A round metal-reinforced wooden shield covered with leather.

Chinamcatl: A person of the chinampas, a farmer, Huitzilin's grandfather.

Chinampas: Raised beds floating on water for agricultural purposes.

Cihuateteo: "Divine Woman," one who dies in childbirth.

Cihuatlampa: Where Cihuateteo reside.

Comalli: Griddle (comal in Spanish).

Coquitao: King in the Zapotec language.

Cozcatlani: Honorable jeweler, craftsman.

Cuauhchicqueh: "The Shorn Ones," elite warriors with shaved heads.

Cuauhicpalli/oceloicpalli: Throne named for the eagle and jaguar occupied by the Huey Tlatoani.

Cuauhololli: Round-headed club embedded with stone or hardened resin, designed to crush armor and bone.

Cuauhteca: Royal guards.

Cuauhtin: The Eagle Warriors.

Cuauhxicalco: The circular ceremonial platform located at the foot of the Huey Teocalli.

Cuauhxicalli: "Eagle vessel," bowl for capturing blood of a sacrificial victim, receptacle for hearts or blood.

Cueitl: Skirt.

Encomienda: Colonial Spanish system granting land and labor rights over indigenous peoples.

Escamoles: Ant larvae.

Huehuecóyotl: "Ancient coyote," a trickster god.

Huehuetqueh: A respected elder known for his wisdom, character, and influence.

Huey: Great or greatest.

Huey Tlatoani: Great speaker, ruler of the Aztec Empire

Huey Tozoztli: Festival honoring great Tlaloc, god of rain, water, and fertility.

Huehuetl: Tall drum.

Huey Teocalli: Great Temple of God, Templo Mayor.

Huipil: Blouse.

Huitzilopochtli: God of the sun, war and human sacrifice.

Huizachtecatl: Sacred mountain near Tenochtitlán.

Ichcahuipilli: Warrior's protective vest.

Ilhuicatl: Refers both to the visible sky and, in a spiritual or cosmological context, to the heavens – especially the celestial realms inhabited by gods and virtuous souls.

In xochitl in cuicatl: "Flower and song," metaphor for poetry, truth, and divine expression.

Itzcua: Naming ceremony.

Itzcuintli: Dogs.

Itzel: "mirror," symbol of clarity, truth, and divine reflection – often associated with Tezcatlipoca.

Iztac: White.

Iztac-Mixcoatl: "White cloud serpent," the milky way.

Macehualli: Commoners.

Macuahuitl: A wooden club embedded with sharp obsidian blades.

Maxtlatl: Loincloth.

Mexica: Náhuatl-speaking ethnic group now known as Aztecs.

Mecatl: String or cord (mecate in Spanish).

Miccailhuitl: "Feast of the Dead" or "Festival of the Deceased." A ritual period dedicated to honoring the spirits of the dead.

Mictecacihuatl: Lady of the dead

Mictlan: The underworld.

Mictlantecuhtli: Lord of the dead.

Nagual: Animal spirit for each person, twinned at birth.

Neltiliztli: The state of being well-rooted – truth, virtue, and authentic goodness, a life of meaning, balance, and coherence, where existence is deeply anchored and actions resonate in harmony with the world and one's community.

Nezayotl: A gesture of deep humility and expression of gratitude not just spoken, but embodied by fasting, self-denial and spiritual focus.

Ocelomeh: Jaguars, jaguar warriors

Oceloicpalli-Cuauhicpalli: the Jaguar-and-Eagle Throne of Huey Tlatoani

Ollamaliztli: Ball game played throughout Mesoamerica.

Pantli: Military unit of 20 warriors

Paynani: Long-distance messengers.

Petates (pl. petlatl): Mats.

Peyotl: Peyote, mescaline.

Piochtli: A lock of hair of a youth or novice.

Pipiltin: Nobleman.

Pochteca: a long distance merchant, member of the hereditary merchant guild. Pochtecatl is singular form but only "pochteca" is used in this text.

Pulque: An alcoholic drink made from the fermented sap of the maguey plant.

Qualli tlacualiztli: Precious food, human flesh meant to be tasted with reverence.

Quauhtepetlthem: Eagle Mountain, known today as Sierra de las Cruces.

Quauhteputztli: Toothpaste.

Quiquiztli: Conch shell blower.

Techcatl: The slightly rounded, chest-arching sacrificial stone on which the victim was laid supine for heart extraction.

Tecpan: Tecpan is a government office building, the palace-complex of a ruler; an administrative and ceremonial center where governance, tribute, and judicial affairs are conducted.

Tecpatl: Obsidian blade sharpened on both sides carried by warriors, used for a coup de grace, and used in human sacrifice, a symbol for severed breath and release of the spirit.

Telpochtli: A young warrior, novice.

Tematlatl: (pl. tematlatlin) A sling for hurling stones.

Temazcalli: Temazcal (temezcal in Spanish) stone hut sweat lodge.

Tenochca: People of Tenochtitlán.

Tenochtitlán: Home of the Mexica (Aztec) Empire, located where Mexico City is today.

Teocalli: "House of god," temple.

Teocualo: Ceremonial banquet where flesh of a sacrificed warrior is consumed.

Teocuitlatl: Gold.

Teotl: (pl. Teteo) Sacred force or divinity. Foundational concept in Nahua metaphysics.

Teotlan: The celestial realm.

Teonanácatl: Divine mushrooms, psilocybin.

Teponaztli: Wooden horizontal drum.

Tepoztopilli: Obsidian bladed spear.

Tequihua: Elite warrior with four captures of enemy in battle, a rank signifying prowess and ability to contribute to Mexica war effort.

Teuctlatoque: The high council of four lords who meet directly with the emperor, similar to a president's cabinet.

Teyollotl: The essence of the heart, distinct from teyolia, the heart soul, vital energy of the heart. Teyollotl is its echo, its divine voice, associated with Tezcatlipoca.

Tezcatl: Polished obsidian mirror, a divinatory tool associated with god Tezcatlipoca. It implies a powerful and insightful person.

Tianquiztli: Sacred market day.

Ticitl: A healer, skilled in medicine, herbal knowledge, and divination.

Tilmatli: A cloak or tunic.

Tilxochitl: Vanilla.

Tizaapan: Tizapán, a city located south/southwest of Colhuacan.

Tlacateccatl: One of the two top battlefield commanders directly beneath the tlatoani (paired with the tlacateccatl), "chief of men."

Tlacochtli: Dart or javelin.

Tlacohtin: Slave .

Tlacatl: (pl. tlacah) Person or human being.

Tlacatlaolli: Sacred stew of maize, chili, and human flesh.

Tlacayotl: Mankind.

Tlacaxipehualiztli: The festival of sacrifice and renewal.

Tlachiani: Architect/engineer, master builder.

Tlacochcalcatl: Senior field general responsible for operations and the main armories. Could command the army in the field in the absence of the tlatoani. Also, a steppingstone to the throne.

Tlacualli: Feast or banquet.

Tlalcualiztli gesture: "kissing the earth," expression of humility, submission, and deep respect, performed when meeting the tlatoani.

Tlacuilo: Scribe.

Tlaloc: God of rain, water, and fertility.

Tlalocan: Paradise of the rain god Tlaloc.

Tlaltecuhtli: "Earth Lady," monstrous, toad-like entity whose body forms the very earth; her mouth (with flint knife teeth and a protruding tongue) symbolizes both a womb and a tomb – creation and dissolution.

Tlalticpac: "On earth" or "upon the land." The physical realm where humans live.

Tlamacazqui: Priest.

Tlamanih: Warrior who captures enemy for sacrifice, a capturer.

Tlamatini: A shaman, sage, a wise person, "someone who knows things" a "knower."

Tlamatlquiticitl: Midwife.

Tlamemeh: Porters.

Tlapatl and Toloache: Two varieties of jimsonweed.

Tlaqualli: Prepared food or a meal, may be a heart offered as food to the gods.

Tlatlauhcapatli: Toothbrush.

Tlatoani: "Speaker," ruler of a city-state.

Tlatocan: The council of lords, advisors who serve as the eyes and ears of the tlatoani.

Tlatocaxtiliztli: Coronation ceremony.

Tlazolteotl: Deity of disorder, purification, and moral renewal, governs lust, vice, impurity, but also confession, cleansing and renewal.

Toltecatl: (pl. Tolteca) Philosopher-artisan, reflecting the Toltec ideal, the highest form of divine artistry.

Tonalli: The soul of consciousness, resides in the head.

Tonalpohualli: "Count of the days," referring to the 260-day sacred calendar.

Tonalpouhqui: A diviner responsible for interpreting the *tonalpohualli,* the sacred 260-day calendar that determines fate and destiny.

Tonaltoca: Evening, the hour of fading light.

Tonatiuh: The sun.

Topilli: a judicial assistant, marshall, bailiff

Totocalli: the royal aviary

Teules: Divine beings.

Tzapotlan: Land of the Zapotecs.

Tzoalli: Energy food made from amaranth grain mixed with honey.

Tzompantli: Skull rack.

Xalli: Sand.

Xaltocan: City-state on the north shore of Lake Texcoco.

Xicales: Pitchers.

Xiquipilli: A military unit of 8,000 warriors.

Xiuhcoatl: A serpent of fire and lightning.

Xiuhmolpilli : 52-year Aztec calendar cycle, the binding of the years.

Xiuhuitzolli: Royal turquoise crown of a tlatoani.

Xochimiel: Honey (miel in Spanish).

Xochitl: Flower.

Xocolatl: Chocolate.

Yaotequihua: A war leader or commander who leads a military campaign.

Yollotl: The physical heart that beats and serves as the place for the teyolia.

g. Maps & Aztec Imperial Family Tree

Map of the Valley of Mexico ca. 1519. Wikimedia Commons, CC-SA 4.0.

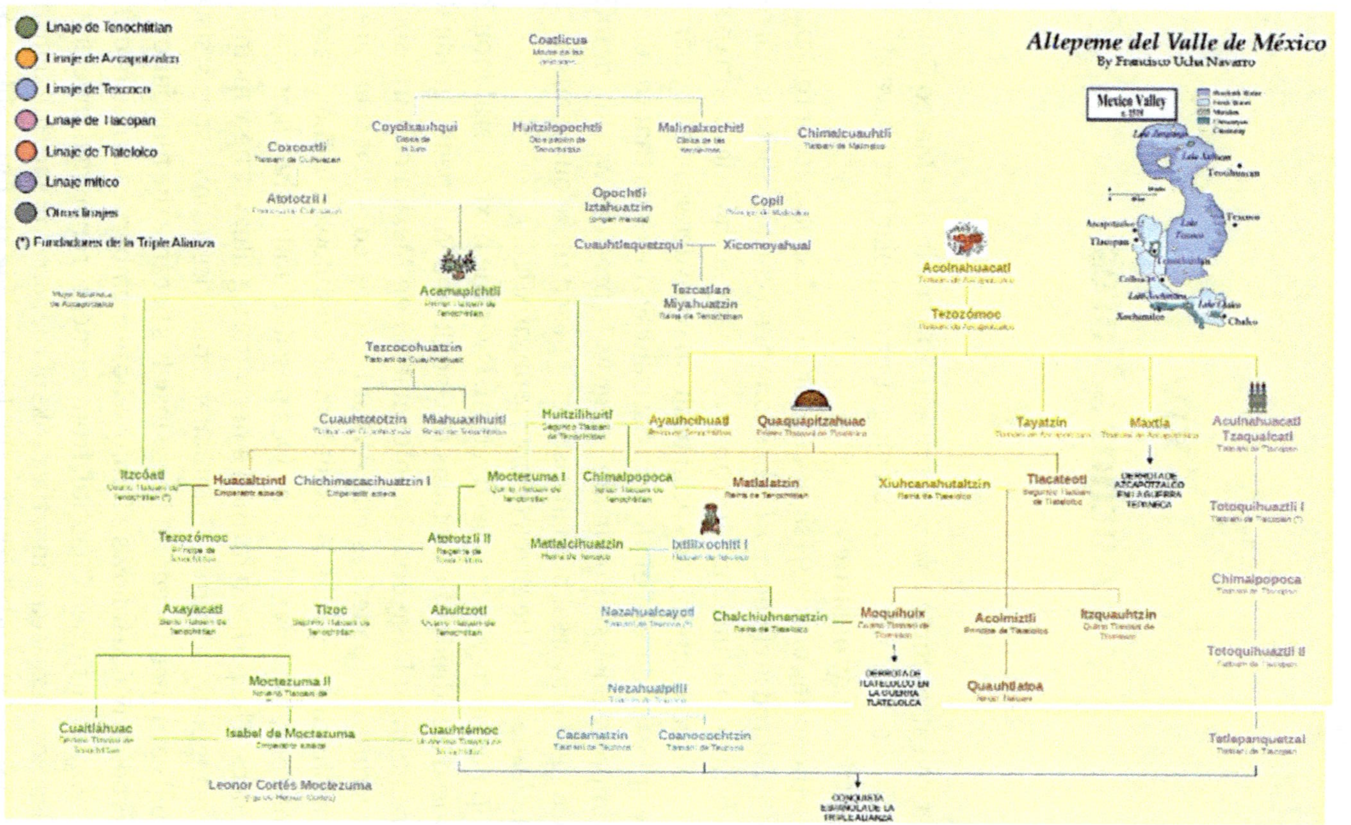

Aztec Imperial Family Tree (reddit r/UsefulCharts Fran_UN09)

XIV
Author's Notes

I retired after forty-five years practicing law in San Mateo County, California. I am not an archaeologist or a scholar, but I have always loved the study of history.

In the spring of 2024, I signed up for an archaeology tour to Oaxaca with a noted archaeologist. I had long been curious about social mobility in pre-Columbian Mesoamerica. Many authorities claim that a person's occupation and social position were determined by parentage or by the date of birth. Yet I have always believed that the desire to improve one's station in life – to grow in prestige, wealth, or influence – is a universal human instinct. I posed these questions to the tour leader, but the answers left me unsatisfied.

So I began my own investigation. Over the next several months, I posed hundreds of questions to Google and Wikipedia, gradually assembling a large body of information on Mexica culture, social structure, and belief systems. What I discovered is that there are exceptions to every rule. Yes, children often followed in their parents' footsteps, but advancement was possible under the right circumstances. The *pochteca* formed a hereditary guild, yet new members were regularly admitted. Commoners could rise to noble status; slaves could earn their freedom. These insights became the foundation for this book, which follows a family whose members each rise in different ways: the father, Cuauhtli, from farmer to renowned jeweler; the eldest son, Tezcacoatl, into the ranks of the *pochteca*; and Huitzilin into the noble class and ultimately the *Teuctlatoque*, the four cabinet ministers who served directly under the *Huey Tlatoani*.

I began developing the story in October 2024. By early 2025, I noticed that Google had begun incorporating AI into its search responses, and Microsoft had added Copilot to its Edge browser. Soon I found myself immersed in the rapidly expanding world of AI models and platforms. It was during this period that I became fascinated with Aztec poetry. I acquired John Bierhorst's *Nahuatl-English Dictionary* and his *Cantares Mexicanos Songs of the Aztecs,* a collection of ninety-one Mexica poems in the original Nahuatl and Bierhorst's English language interpretations. I found three different published interpretations of Nezahualcoyotl's poem *The Origin of Songs.* Over the course of a month, I created my own interpretation by comparing the published versions and consulting AI programs for their analysis of individual words and phrases. The result was a version entirely my own. That experience taught me to approach Mexica research with a combination of traditional scholarship and careful, comparative use of AI tools such as Microsoft Copilot, ChatGPT, Chatbot, Perplexity AI, and Gemini, but importantly, never relying on a single AI source.

I learned that AI can be an excellent teacher. It taught me much about the Nahuatl language, phrasing, imagery, metaphor and cadence. This style, known as *difrasismo,* pairs words to express a single idea, for example, "a path of thorns and rivers" to describe a difficult journey, or, "the fragrance of honey and light," to describe the scent of a flower. Metaphor is another recurring device, "His voice is soft, like wind through feathers," or "We were strewn like reeds on the wind." AI can also help polish wordy or awkward passages.

But I also learned that AI is capable of "hallucinating" – confidently providing incorrect or speculative information – and that caution is essential when dealing with historical topics where the record is incomplete. Not every detail I sought had a definitive answer. Where the historical record is thin, AI responses can differ dramatically. Some models rely on questionable sources; others extrapolate beyond the evidence.

My research into the Mexica battle of Malinalco is a good example. Between 1474 and 1476, the Mexica fought a series of campaigns in the Toluca Valley. AI models disagree about Malinalco's role. One asserts that there is no evidence that any battle took place there at all and that the town was incorporated peacefully after the fall of Matlatzinco. Another claims that Malinalco resisted and was defeated in the battle there. A third maintains that Malinalco was under Matlatzinca control at the time and did not participate directly in the fighting that occurred there. I adopted the third view because 1) nearly all sources report that a battle did in fact occur at Malinalco; 2) historical records show that Axayacatl visited Malinalco on friendly terms prior to the Battle of Too Many Ambushes, and 3) because Malinalco's later tribute obligations were minimal compared to those imposed on polities that actively resisted Mexica expansion.

Finally, I wish to acknowledge the Wikimedia Foundation for promoting the American legal principle that faithful reproductions of public-domain works – such as sixteenth-century codices, paintings, and manuscripts – remain in the public domain.